THE DEATH OF JANE LAWRENCE

CAITLIN STARLING

ST. MARTIN'S GRIFFIN
NEW YORK

For the observer

Published in the United States by St. Martin's Griffin,
an imprint of St. Martin's Publishing Group

THE DEATH OF JANE LAWRENCE. Copyright © 2021 by Caitlin Starling. All rights reserved. Printed in the United States of America. For information, address St. Martin's Publishing Group, 120 Broadway, New York, NY 10271.

www.stmartins.com

The Library of Congress has cataloged the hardcover edition as follows:

Names: Starling, Caitlin, author.
Title: The death of Jane Lawrence / Caitlin Starling.
Description: First Edition. | New York : St. Martin's Press, 2021.
Identifiers: LCCN 2021026475 | ISBN 9781250272584 (hardcover) |
    ISBN 9781250272591 (ebook)
Subjects: GSAFD: Horror fiction.
Classification: LCC PS3619.T3747 D43 2021 | DDC 813/.6—dc23
LC record available at https://lccn.loc.gov/2021026475

ISBN 978-1-250-76958-9 (trade paperback)

Our books may be purchased in bulk for promotional, educational, or business use. Please contact your local bookseller or the Macmillan Corporate and Premium Sales Department at 1-800-221-7945, extension 5442, or by email at MacmillanSpecialMarkets@macmillan.com.

First St. Martin's Griffin Edition: 2022

10 9 8 7 6 5 4 3 2 1

CHAPTER ONE

D<small>R.</small> A<small>UGUSTINE</small> L<small>AWRENCE'S</small> cuffs were stained with blood and his mackintosh had failed against the persistent drizzle. He looked damp, miserable, and scared.

Of her.

Jane Shoringfield couldn't take her eyes off him, even though her attention was clearly overwhelming. *This* was the man she intended to marry, if he'd have her. If she could convince him.

He was frozen in the doorway to her guardian's study, and she was similarly still just behind the desk. Even from here, she could see that she had several inches on him in height, that his dark hair was full, slightly waved, and going silver already at his left temple, and that his wide eyes were a murky green, and gentle, but almost sad in the wrong light.

She hadn't expected him to be handsome.

"Doctor!"

Her guardian's voice boomed down the hallway, and the man startled, turning to face it. "Mr. Cunningham," he greeted in turn. "I'm sorry, I'm afraid I lost track of your maid, and—"

"No matter, no matter. How good of you to join us! I was afraid you might change your mind."

Jane couldn't see Mr. Cunningham, but she could picture him perfectly: white hair carefully combed back, a fine but comfortable suit, bright brown eyes. Short and narrow, almost too narrow for his orator's voice and charisma.

"I'm afraid I may not be the best or most decorous company," the doctor said, hazarding a furtive glance back at her that lasted only one appraising second. "One too many house calls. I wasn't able to stop back at the surgery."

That explained the state of his cuffs, at least; but that meant he wasn't early. Jane looked at the clock and winced. An hour had passed while she wasn't looking. She wasn't ready. She was still wearing her reading glasses, and she could feel a smudge of ink on her temple. Mr. Cunningham's account books lay spread out before her.

She was not making the best first impression to aid her suit.

"Don't worry," Mr. Cunningham said, closer now but still out of sight. "You will find that this isn't a peacocking courtship."

The doctor's cheeks pinked. "I understand, but I have given it some thought, and I must—"

"Before you continue," her guardian said, cutting him off, "I want to remind you that you have not heard her logic yet. I think you should."

It had been Mr. Cunningham who had presented the match to Dr. Lawrence last week on her behalf, when the doctor had come round to evaluate his lungs in preparation for the Cunninghams' great move to Camhurst, capital of Great Breltain and a full day's ride away from Larrenton. However her guardian had framed the proposition, it had been enough to get the doctor here, now, today.

Looking very pale and very nervous. Looking like he was about to flee.

"Please do let me explain," Jane said, grateful that her voice came out more than a whisper. The doctor turned to her again, lips slightly parted in surprise, whatever protest he'd been about to voice—whatever demurring—silenced.

Mr. Cunningham laughed and appeared in the doorway at last. "Ah, that explains what waylaid you."

"I apologize, I hadn't meant to . . . spy," Dr. Lawrence said, weakly. "Miss Shoringfield."

"Dr. Lawrence," she said, inclining her head in greeting. "Will you allow me at least to make my argument in full?"

The doctor looked between her and Mr. Cunningham and recoiled, the reflex of a cornered animal.

She was coming at this all wrong; she should have paid better mind to the time, met him in the sitting room as Mrs. Cunningham had planned out the night before. But they were here, now.

Save me, she thought at Mr. Cunningham.

"The brandy," he said, not hearing her desperate thought, "is in the sideboard."

And then, chuckling, he was gone.

Jane and the doctor regarded each other again across the space between door and desk, and Jane gestured, as gently as she could, to a chair. The doctor hesitated, but at last took a few tentative steps into the study. He didn't sit. Jane turned from him and busied herself pouring two glasses.

As her hands moved, she summoned up the steps of her argument, and selected, for her opening, the strongest and least specific to her situation. "Marriage is, at heart, a business arrangement, not one of hearts or souls," she said, without turning. "It is best to discuss it plainly from the first."

She could hear his startled exhale.

Still too much. And yet she didn't know how else to approach this. She had already botched whatever chance at a gentle introduction they might have had.

Keeping her back to him as she stoppered the decanter, she continued: "I have evaluated our options thoroughly, Dr. Lawrence. Leaving aside dances, which I suspect you have no time for, and childhood acquaintances, whom I haven't seen in many years, there are few opportunities for courtship for us.

"So I start from a premise of shared goals."

She listened for his fleeing footsteps.

They didn't come.

"Shared goals," he said instead. "And what shared goals do we have? We have never met."

There was no derision in his tone, no mockery. He sounded wary, but curious. She seized on it and turned back to him. She came around the desk, holding out his glass from a respectable distance. He did not retreat; instead, he took it from her, careful to avoid brushing fingers.

"We are both unmarried, and at an age where that is beginning to raise questions," she said. "A man of your standing and appearance could choose whichever woman he wanted. You haven't. For whatever reason, you do not wish for a normal marriage. I'm not asking for one."

She watched him, trying to measure his response. At first, there was something very much like want in his eyes, but then it was replaced by the fear again.

Why?

She took a small sip of her brandy to keep herself from fidgeting.

"I cannot marry you," he said.

The brandy burned in her throat.

"I don't mean it as a slight against you, Miss Shoringfield," he added. "But while your logic is—impressive, it is not appropriate for me to take a wife. Any wife."

"You are unmarried," Jane repeated, confused.

"I am not married," he agreed. His jaw tensed as he considered his next words. The fear in his eyes had been replaced with something else. Something more distant, more pained. "Please, Miss Shoringfield. I understand that you have thought through your proposal at length, but I do not wish to cause you more pointless effort. I cannot accept."

The polite, proper thing to do was to apologize, accept his refusal, and subside. Approach the next man on the list she had drafted, another who met her criteria, who might be more amenable. She needed to sit, and to smile, and yet she found she could do neither.

"Dr. Lawrence," she said, gripping her glass tightly, "*please.*"

He ducked his head.

"My parents died when I was very young, when Ruzka began gassing

Camhurst during the war," she started, then stopped, hands shaking. She hadn't meant to say it; she never spoke of her parents. But her honesty worked a change in him; he lifted his chin, brows drawing together in concern. She pushed forward. "They left me in Mr. Cunningham's care, along with an annuity to support me. Here in Larrenton, it has been more than enough to cover my costs, even as I've grown into marriageable age. There is, however, no dowry, and now the Cunninghams leave for Camhurst within the month."

She fought to keep her voice even as she spoke.

"Were I to accompany them—and they have requested that I do just that—my expenses would outstrip my annuity even if I were to largely avoid society, which would be impossible given Mr. Cunningham's new judgeship." And she would be surrounded by shell-scarred buildings and new construction that tried to replace what had been destroyed, none of which she could stomach even the thought of. But that was too personal to share, by far. "They are willing to pay the difference, but I am not willing to let them."

The doctor's mind worked. "But as you can't remain here unmarried . . ."

"Exactly. If I'm to stay, I have to find a husband, or things will be quite a bit more difficult than even the capital would be."

He shook his head, finally looking at her again. "I understand your plight, and I feel for you, Miss Shoringfield, but you do have other options. Surely there are other options. You are . . ." His cheeks colored, and she remembered again how he'd looked at her from the doorway. Fear, fear that had been caused by her proposal hanging above his head like a sword, knowing he would have to decline. But perhaps it wasn't *just* fear—or if it had been fear, it had been fear of a different sort than she'd first thought.

His throat bobbed as he swallowed. "I can't imagine you will have much difficulty finding a more suitable husband."

"You are a perfectly suitable husband," she said, steeling herself and stepping forward again. She could hear his breathing, they were so close. The wariness in his eyes was entirely gone now, replaced by fascination. "And I am not asking you for charity, Dr. Lawrence. I have skills that would be useful to you."

"Skills?"

"I attended Sharpton School for Girls until I was fifteen," she said. "And I have kept Mr. Cunningham's books for the last six years. I maintain the ledger, I work with the banks, I help him set his fees and collect on them. I can only imagine work of the same sort must be done at a surgery."

He sucked in a surprised breath. "You weren't speaking in metaphors when you said this was a business arrangement."

"My remaining annuity funds are not so large as to directly benefit you, I suspect," she said. "But I do bring mathematical skill, and a methodical nature. I can run the business of being a doctor, and you can focus on the medicine."

"You know nothing about a doctor's life, about the business *or* the medicine."

"I can learn. I want to learn."

He hesitated, stunned, then fumbled out, "There is blood, and great sadness, and terror. Being part of it—it won't be easy." But it sounded less like a warning and more like a test. An invitation. "It is a calling, not a skill."

"Ledgers and sums are *my* calling, just as medicine is yours. The rest I can learn, when the most important element is fulfilled."

"It is thankless, and I often won't be home. Night calls, and—"

"But if this is a business arrangement," she interrupted, "then it is more employment than marriage. I won't mind your absence. You are suitable."

She had brought him to social concerns, down from professional; she was making progress. She held her breath.

He took a hasty swallow of brandy. He glanced toward the ceiling. Then he looked back at her, and said, "You would be alone. I spend my nights at my family home, several miles out of town. It would be an inviolable condition, that you never join me there."

She nearly fell to her knees in relief. He had begun to consider. He hadn't rejected her, not outright, not this time. She remained standing, but only barely, and managed to smile. "As I said—you are *perfectly* suitable."

From the way his brow creased, she'd surprised him again. "You knew?"

"I have heard rumors," she said. He had only been in practice in Larrenton for a little over two months, and Jane was no gossipmonger, but the Cunninghams always knew something about everybody in town. "Everybody knows you employ a runner at the surgery to fetch you, though most still think it's because you're often out on house calls at night. Only a few have noticed the extent of the waiting time, and how it's consistently necessary to wait."

"You *are* observant," he said.

She laughed.

The sound prompted a final transformation in him. The fear left him entirely, and he regarded her, shoulders straight.

"I should not marry you," he protested once more, but it was perfunctory.

"A chance," she said. "Give me a chance. Let me prove to you my worth. I will meet your conditions, if you will meet mine."

He thought a moment, then nodded. "Very well. Come by the surgery. See what it is like in the particulars, instead of the abstract, before we make any binding decisions. There will likely be blood, and certainly hard work."

"When shall I come by?"

"Tomorrow, midmorning. Wear clothing you don't mind getting soiled. I'll have you take a look at it all, the patient files, the finances, and you can sit in on any calls that come in. While sums may be your calling, you will still need to become something of a nurse, in case anybody arrives at the surgery in my absence."

"Of course," she said. "Tomorrow, then, Dr. Lawrence. I shall attempt to prove myself. And you can do your best to scare me off."

CHAPTER TWO

J ANE MADE HER way quickly across the center of town toward Dr. Lawrence's surgery with the Cunninghams' maid, Ekaterina, at her heels. Ekaterina was valiantly keeping up one side of a conversation: she had lived in Camhurst before coming to Larrenton, and was delighted to be returning, and with an improved position. Jane couldn't blame her— not everybody in town was ready to trust a Ruzkan girl, not here, not even so many years after the war—but she could not summon up the slightest interest.

She was entirely fixated on thoughts of Dr. Lawrence and his surgery.

She'd told him the truth, the night before, about her reasons for marrying him. She was fairly certain he'd believed her. That was nice. Most men would have looked for an alternate cause, if Mrs. Cunningham was to be believed. And most men would not have accepted her eagerness to keep the marriage as a business arrangement, eschewing all the expected intimacies.

And yet it had been that premise that had won him. Miracle of miracles!

She'd told herself, when she realized that marrying was soon going to be the best option for her, that she could only marry if that distance was maintained. She wanted courteous indifference, not unwanted touches and a passel of children. She was not built for intimacy; she was built for numbers. For work.

Her guardians, the Cunninghams, were not built as she was. They had always been entirely proper in front of her, but Jane saw the way Mr. Cunningham looked at his wife, saw the shared easy touches as they passed in the hall. When they'd taken her in at her parents' request, at the height of the war with their youngest child nearly full grown, they were still obviously in love. Jane admired them for it, but she was fully aware that the odds of her finding anything like they had were very low. She was not skilled at forming the sorts of emotional connections that affection seemed to require. No, a normal marriage was not for her. It would leave her harried and uncomfortable and resentful.

But some kind of marriage was a necessity, and so she had contrived to find a husband who would allow her to remain much as she had always been. And Dr. Lawrence, who lived well out of town and had to keep somebody in his place at his surgery, was impossible perfection. A man who wasn't married, despite being in his early thirties, despite being a doctor, despite being, in his own way, quite handsome—a man like that had a reason as good as hers. It put them on equal footing, poised to make a mutually beneficial bargain.

"Miss Shoringfield!" Ekaterina called from behind her. Jane looked over her shoulder. She'd somehow managed to put a great deal of distance between herself and the girl over the last few streets. Jane readied an apology.

Ekaterina reached her side, smiling up at her. "You certainly are excited, ma'am."

Her cheeks heated. Ekaterina had come to work for the Cunninghams only six months ago, but she had settled in quickly. To another woman, Ekaterina might have felt almost like a sister instead of a maid. She was certainly amiable enough.

The only problem was that Jane didn't know how to be *friendly*. She could be polite, and kind, and could engage over work, but small talk had always been a struggle. Friendship had always been a struggle.

"I think," Jane said, resuming her walk at a much more reasonable pace, "you will find the surgery very boring."

"Oh, I had not planned to go in with you," Ekaterina said cheerfully. "I'll get the shopping in, then perhaps walk you home after?"

"That sounds appropriate," Jane said. A younger, richer woman might have needed a chaperone, but the rest of the world had changed greatly over the last few decades. And besides—this was a business arrangement, not a courtship.

They walked the last few streets together. Between the Cunninghams' home and the surgery were mainly private residences with a few shops on the ground floor. Almost all had been built at least a century before, though a few were newer, made of smooth concrete instead of old brick or stone, and lacking the worn sculptures on their lintels that people had once carved to protect their homes. The Cunninghams had one such figure, a face surrounded by wings that roosted just above the front door, and as a child, Jane had been fascinated with it. It was so similar to the carved downspouts that had loomed above her in Camhurst, but the ones she'd grown up with had been painted. Theirs was varnished wood.

She and Ekaterina turned the last corner toward the surgery, which put them once more on one of Larrenton's main thoroughfares, alive with business in the clear weather. The street bustled with a mix of farmworkers, shoppers and shopkeeps, and visitors from farther afield. Larrenton was small enough to have only one doctor, but it was still a thriving town. Across the way, a small cluster of black-clad undertakers alighted from a retrofitted convent carriage and filed into a boardinghouse foyer.

Jane watched them a moment, their confident movements and swinging skirts. If the Cunninghams hadn't taken her in, she might well have been one of their number. They were no longer dedicated to faith and ritual, but such women had always taken care of the dead, and many orphans had found sanctuary in their order.

She might have enjoyed that life.

But Ekaterina had not stopped to watch, and Jane had to hurry to catch up. They passed only a few more buildings before they reached the surgery. She slowed to a bare crawl as she approached the door, then turned and looked at Ekaterina. "Come by in a few hours? The work will be done by then, I suspect." Her untrained part, at least.

"Yes, ma'am." Ekaterina inclined her head and strolled off back to the main streets. Jane watched her go, then turned back to the surgery.

There were no steps up to the front door, the better to allow the injured and infirm to reach the doctor. The door itself was wide and a deep red, set into two stories of brick wall. The lintel here was similarly carved to the Cunninghams', though this winged face was wreathed in incised laurels, and worn, nearly unreadable script down the sides of the doorframe. The building was old, built to house a previous physician of a previous era, with all the attendant faith behind it.

But Dr. Lawrence was a young, Camhurst-educated doctor; he likely held no truck with such superstitions. She wondered if he would have it all planed down or painted over.

She checked to make sure that her hair was still carefully pinned up beneath her black, broad-brimmed hat, then reached out and knocked.

The porter opened the door a moment later. He was an older man, perhaps once a laborer or even a prizefighter. He was stocky and muscular, and there was a faded scar across one side of his face, distorting the lay of his faint growth of stubble. He smiled at her, his cheeks a bit rosy from the day's chill. Jane suspected her own nose was bright red.

"Miss Shoringfield?" he asked.

"Yes," she said, surprised and pleased at being awaited by name. "The doctor asked me to assist today."

He stepped back, motioning her in. "He's just finishing up something upstairs. He said to tell you to feel free to explore, though not to touch anything in the operating theater. I've got some tea on, if you don't want to get into the nasty business right away. The butcher's boy brought over some sausages, too. Can I take your hat and coat?"

Jane felt herself smiling back, infected by his good cheer. Dr. Lawrence was widely known to be quiet, reserved, hard to read and unsociable, but generally kind and likable. His porter appeared much the same, which spoke to good judgment on the doctor's part.

"Oh, thank you, but I think I shouldn't give my stomach any ammunition for the day," Jane replied, stepping into the house. She looked around as she unbuttoned her burgundy coat and handed it to the man along with her hat. The hallway was filled with a stale, acrid stench that she tried to ignore, but her stomach flinched in warning. Books. She was best with books, not blood. At least chances seemed good that once she was working here properly, most coming to the surgery would be here from indigestion, or something else that could be solved by a small sit-down and a check of their files. The most ill would be bound to their homes.

She assumed.

"What's your name?" she asked, turning back to the porter.

"Mr. Lowell," he said, inclining his head.

"And you fetch him when he's out of town, yes?"

"That, and help him move heavier patients, keep the kitchen stocked, that sort of thing. Though I suppose you'll be helping with the kitchen more in the future, eh?"

Jane flushed. "He said that?"

Mr. Lowell chuckled. "In a fashion. Never expected him to take a shine to somebody, to tell the truth."

A shine? Oh, no. Her stomach leapt in an altogether different manner at that, and she absently curled her hands over her belly to still it.

Mr. Lowell's glance dropped down.

She lowered her hands, flushing. She was going to give him cause to spread rumors of *alternate causes,* and she couldn't have that. "To tell the truth, last night was the first time we met."

"Truly?"

How much to tell? He didn't know about the marriage arrangement, and now he knew she wasn't with child—at least, not the doctor's—so she concluded he knew about as much as he needed to. "Yes, strange, isn't it? I never thought to be a nurse," she said, then took a few steps down the hall. Best to change the subject. "Does he keep an office on this floor?"

"Aye, first door on the right."

"Am I allowed in?"

"He made a point of it, said you might look at his books."

She quashed a small, pleased smile. His cooperation was a good sign, and beyond that, it made her feel welcome. Hopeful. Perhaps Mr. Lowell was only reading too much into that cooperation; in any other case a man being so amenable to a young woman would likely be read as affection.

"Thank you, Mr. Lowell. I think I'll be fine from here, and I've kept you awhile now."

"Not a problem, miss," Mr. Lowell said, then inclined his head and went to a set of doors that she guessed led to the operating theater. The acrid smell increased for a moment as he opened one and slipped through it.

Jane looked at the hallway a moment longer. There were no portraits in the whole hall, and only one or two landscapes, right near the door and front sitting area. But there were some framed photographic prints of nebulous things. The daguerreotype closest to her appeared to be of a gnarled piece of wood. She frowned at it, puzzled, then made her way to his office.

The door stood open, and inside was a perfectly ordinary and clean room. Dr. Lawrence had a sizable desk that was in a much worse state than Mr. Cunningham's, but beyond that, the room was spotless. There were two chairs across from the desk, as well as a large armchair by the far window, with a raised cushion to put one's feet up onto. The walls were bare save for several bookshelves and cabinets behind the doctor's desk.

Settling her reading glasses on her nose, Jane peered at the various drifts of paper, finding hastily scribbled notes with names in large script at the top right of each page. The cabinets, when opened, revealed row upon row of small folders, also all labeled with names, as well as a pad of preprinted paper. *Ah.* A look back at the desk showed a few leaves of that paper, with carefully written notes all in order, and the same name on top as a few of the closest note pages. He was transcribing the important notes into a neater system, she realized.

Quite clever, and helpful for her.

Before she could begin reading, however, some organization was called for. She set about tidying the piles and retrieving sheets that had fallen to the floor. She was reconsidering Mr. Lowell's offer of tea when Dr. Lawrence cleared his throat from the office doorway.

"Dr. Lawrence." She stood up from his desk, guilty as if she'd been caught peeping in his washroom. He didn't look annoyed, however, as he entered the office and surveyed the stacks she'd made. He didn't even look embarrassed.

"As you can see," he said, "your skills would be much appreciated. Hypothetically speaking. If you are not too frightened by what you've found?"

"Hardly." She squared her shoulders. "Where is your logbook? Of patient transactions?"

"I don't have one," he said.

She frowned at him.

He lifted his hands in defense. "I intend to have one. But as I only bill at the end of the year, I intend to reconstruct based on my notes."

"That's a great way to miss out on money that may already be difficult to collect," she said. "Not only that, but you must need to replenish your supplies regularly—Mr. Cunningham has far fewer expenses, and he bills once every two months. I require that he keep a daily log of his work to make it simpler and more accurate. He balked at doing it by the minute, but a list of documents he creates, or procedures, in your case, is easy enough."

He looked at her a moment, stunned into silence, then shook his head in wonder. "You really are skilled at this, aren't you?"

"I have a lot of practice. I'm sure you understand that they're different things."

"Different, but often related."

She flushed with pride, and began to pace to disguise it. "Do you at least keep a list of what medications you've prescribed?"

"In patient notes."

"No, I mean an ordering list. How do you track inventory?"

He tapped his brow. "The age-old skill of eyeballing."

"That won't do at all."

"Without somebody like you assisting, while all that work would be very helpful, it's not particularly time-effective for me. I aim to survive and help others survive, Miss Shoringfield. That's the extent of it."

"Well, and now you have me."

The words were out of her mouth before she could think better of them, and she firmed up her lips and straightened her shoulders to mask the sudden frisson of embarrassment that went through her. *Too much.*

Dr. Lawrence turned away, briefly tugging at his collar. "You've certainly convinced me to employ you," he said. "But marrying—"

"Is essentially the same thing."

"It certainly is not," he said. "I'm not sure what kind of man you take me for, but I wouldn't—a nurse in my employ—such intimacy—it's insulting, Miss Shoringfield." But he didn't sound insulted. He sounded—

Flustered.

Frustrated.

He'd clearly been thinking about the implications of a marriage since last night's talk. She should have been relieved that he'd come to the same conclusion—that intimacy was not appropriate or desirous—but instead she felt her own cheeks burning. Best to get this out of the way formally, though. She removed her glasses, rubbing them clean on her dress. "I suppose a marriage would need to be consummated, legally," she conceded.

Dr. Lawrence choked, then turned back to stare at her incredulously. "You suppose," he echoed.

"I am sure, though, that we can find a way to balance the statutory requirements with how we wish to conduct the marriage. But if you feel I misrepresented anything last night—"

She was interrupted by a sharp, loud banging on the front door, followed by the harried ringing of the bell and Mr. Lowell's footsteps, fast and heavy, in the hallway. A muffled cry of pain from outside. The doctor's troubled expression disappeared, his features blank and still save for the focused light in his eyes. He rolled up his sleeves.

"Miss Shoringfield," he said, voice wholly transformed. "Please go into the operating room; leave both doors wide open. There are aprons and gowns in there. Have one ready for me."

"I—"

The front door opened, and Jane could hear screaming.

"Now, Miss Shoringfield."

CHAPTER THREE

JANE SPRANG INTO action, dashing across the hall to the operating theater. Mr. Lowell had left one door open, and she pulled the other one out of the way. She could hear a woman talking, fast, voice high-pitched in panic, as Jane looked around for the aprons. She found them on a coat stand out of the way, and pulled down one of them, then turned as the cacophony reached the doorway.

Mr. Lowell and another man were carrying the screaming patient, a heavy-boned, broad-shouldered laborer who was clutching his belly. "Get it out!" he cried. "Get it out, I didn't mean it!" Blood pulsed from between his fingers, through the soaked fabric of his shirt, spattering on the floor.

Jane swayed on her feet, then clenched her jaw, determined to stay upright.

Behind the man an older woman clasped bloody hands around Dr. Lawrence's forearm. "I heard him screaming from the woodshop," she said. "He had the knife, he was *cutting*, I don't know—"

"*Get it out!*" the man bellowed again, thrashing. Mr. Lowell nearly lost his grip.

Dr. Lawrence turned to the woman and murmured something with a nod of his head toward the door. He pried her fingers up so slowly Jane wanted to scream along with the patient, but when he was free, the woman disappeared back into the hallway.

He crossed the floor to where she stood, as behind him Mr. Lowell and the volunteer assistant hoisted the bleeding man onto the table.

Trembling, Jane draped the apron over Dr. Lawrence's head, and he turned so she could fasten it down the sides. Then he took her by the hand and pulled her over to a filled basin.

"Antiseptic. Wash your hands, Miss Shoringfield. Thoroughly. Rub under your nails, too."

She did as she was told, then tuned back to the table. Mr. Lowell had strapped the patient down at the chest, wrists, and legs. The volunteer who'd helped carry the patient stared as the man thrashed and howled. Mr. Lowell pulled a protective cover off an array of tools.

"Mr. Rivers," the doctor said, and the volunteer dragged his gaze away from the patient. "Please step outside. Miss Shoringfield, with me." Dimly, she realized she hadn't thought to grab an apron for herself, but one look at the patient told her why the doctor hadn't reminded her.

They didn't have time.

Through the sodden, gaping fabric of the man's shirt, Jane could see that his belly was split open. A makeshift bandage had been wrapped around it, but he had torn at it, pressing the ragged edges inside the flesh. Dr. Lawrence surveyed it in barely two seconds.

"Miss Shoringfield, I need your hands," he said. Before she could question him, he took one of her hands in his, clamping it over one side of the slit in the patient's belly, fingers around the separated flesh. She held on even as the man gave another bellow and the slippery skin heaved in her grip. Dr. Lawrence guided her other hand to the other side. "Hold the wound open. Mr. Lowell, wash your hands, then get me a flushing bulb."

He grabbed up a pair of shears and made quick work of the patient's shirt, then cleared the rest of the bandage away from the wound. Jane's fingers trembled. Blood covered her hands, seeping beneath her nails, and it stank. Spirits take her, but it stank. She'd never seen this much blood in her life, and it was slippery, and hot, and more of it forced against her hands and pooled in the too-large gap in the patient's skin with every rapid, desperate pulse of his heart. He was still conscious beneath her hands, still screaming, still *moving,* and every heaving breath he took made the inside of his wound rise and fall with it.

Mr. Lowell returned to the table and passed Dr. Lawrence a glass tube with a rubber balloon set above it. Dr. Lawrence squeezed the balloon and water surged into the wound, diluting the blood and forcing it from its pool.

Beneath it, she saw gleaming multihued ropes. Ropes, like sausage casings. Bile rose in her throat.

She hadn't known what a man looked like on the inside, before. He looked like meat. Brutal, horrible meat.

"He's cut all the way through." Dr. Lawrence did not curse, and did not stop with horror. He spoke with what could have been cold detachment in another man, but in him it was an attentive declaration, a statement of truth that helped orient and ground Jane in the moment.

He could fix this.

He had to fix this.

The doctor left her side, moving to the patient's head and pressing a cloth soaked with ether to his nose and mouth, the fumes burning her nostrils even where she stood. The thrashing lessened, and the howls that had become an unending, unchanging background noise turned to low, vague moans. Dr. Lawrence lifted the cloth and looked directly at her.

He is going to ask if I can handle this, Jane thought. *Please, do not ask that of me.* If he did, the answer would be no. As long as he kept silent, as long as he presumed she was capable, she would follow where he led.

He gave her a little nod, then returned to her side.

"Mr. Lowell, retractors," Dr. Lawrence said, his voice quiet, but the room was quiet now, too, all their breaths held. Mr. Lowell passed him two gleaming pieces of metal bent back upon themselves at one end. The doctor slid them each under the skin Jane clung to, then eased her fingers over them instead. Her hands slipped at first, and the metal was shockingly cold after the burning heat of the patient's flesh, but not feeling fresh blood on her hands was a relief. She held them firm and at the doctor's direction, spread the wound open a little further.

"What in the world—?" he murmured.

Jane, despite herself, leaned in.

His way cleared, Dr. Lawrence reached inside the man's belly, gently pushing the pearlescent ropes of the man's bowels aside. He eased forward a thicker section, tangled up in much same way as everything else around it. No—no, she was mistaken. It looked as convoluted, but where it folded back onto itself, it seemed to go *inside* itself, though there was no perforation she could see. The flesh simply melded together, and a faint shape moved beneath the surface, a form beneath a shroud. She could not keep it oriented in her mind's eye; it seemed to slide and twist.

"What did you do to yourself?" Dr. Lawrence whispered.

For the first time, she heard uncertainty.

But his hands did not falter as he grimly set about cutting the mess of twisted flesh away from the surrounding tissues, exposing more of the larger organ until it ran even and smooth. "It's a miracle, perhaps, that he was driven to cut himself open—had this gone unnoticed, he would have died of septicemia within the week." He lifted the tangled mass from the patient and set it aside carefully, almost tenderly. Jane stared at it as Dr. Lawrence took up needle and thread. It still looked vital. Alive. Blood coated it, and she thought she saw it move.

"Miss Shoringfield, please keep tension on the retractors," Dr. Lawrence said.

She forced herself to look down again, to watch as he stitched up a lower reach of disrupted gut, then fed the freshly cut section of bowel through the gash the patient had carved in himself. She removed the retractors when he indicated and watched, transfixed, as Dr. Lawrence miraculously closed membranes up, and then the man's skin, his stitches precise. He worked like a master craftsman, like an artist, and the confidence in every line of him bewitched her.

The patient moaned and the spell was broken. Her body threatened revolt.

"Grab a cloth and soak it in antiseptic, then wipe down his skin. Get him as clean as you can. It will speed recovery," the doctor said, calmly redirecting her.

Tasks. Tasks helped. She got her cloth and began with the bottom of the man's rib cage, then gently blotted the margins of the wound. When it was clean, she moved to the man's hands, pulling the scraps of fiber from under his blunted nails. He was sleeping now, face drawn from pain and exhaustion, but otherwise peaceful.

Wiping a bit of grime from his brow, she looked up at the doctor. He was bent over the man's torso, quickly cleaning and stitching up other small lacerations. He spared one glance up at her, as if he could feel her eyes on him.

"We have done good work here," he said, smiling. "You have helped save his life."

Golden warmth bloomed in her chest, and she realized she'd begun to shake, for the first time since he'd placed her hands on the man's bleeding gut. "Oh," she said.

Dr. Lawrence soaked a sponge in fresh antiseptic, then set it over the opening still left in the man's stomach, where the hole of the bowel protruded. A few more minutes, and he was done, stepping away from the table and going to the sink. She trailed after him, unsure of what else to do.

"You did well," he said, turning on the faucet with an elbow and rinsing blood from his hands in the sputter of water. "Come here, clean yourself up. I should have told you to don a gown, but I suppose I didn't think you'd— well. Many wouldn't have been able to stay standing the whole time. It's a grisly business, as I warned you."

Jane glanced back at the table. The patient looked whole and slumbering, as if Dr. Lawrence's surgery had been some form of magic.

"That was incredible," she said, then looked at him, at the lines of his face, his steady hands. "I didn't know such surgery was possible."

"It isn't, in most cases. I was taught by the greatest instructors in Great Breltain." He said it without pride or boasting.

"What happened to him? That thing you removed, what was it?"

"The large bowel, malformed from . . . something. I will send for a specialist."

"But he'll live? Now that it's removed, now that you've . . ." She trailed off, left without the right words or understanding, but she nodded back to the man's abdomen, the covered hole.

"The sponge will catch the output of the digestive tract, and as long as the site is kept clean and he is lucky, the tissue will callous and he may live many more years. But this is no amputation, where we understand everything that we do, and our patients survive more often than they do not. I hope he will live." His gaze dropped, his hands tightening on the edge of the sink.

Jane approached him and resisted the strong, surprising urge she had to lay a hand upon his shoulder. "We have done good work here," she echoed back to him instead.

He glanced up at her with a small, thankful smile.

Her heart sprang into an erratic, unfamiliar rhythm.

They were alone in the room. Mr. Lowell had left, unnoticed, some time before. She tried to focus on the stink of blood and bowel, the astringency of the antiseptic, the faint whiff of ether on the air. Anything besides him, because his smile felt intimate and intoxicating in the wake of that horror.

"How are you feeling? If you feel at all faint, I'll get you to a chair." He searched her face, no doubt seeing her confusion, reading it as weakness. Waiting for her to say she'd changed her mind about being a doctor's wife.

"I feel . . ." *Inappropriate.* It was inappropriate to fixate on him like this, now. But there were other emotions below that. She felt elated, as though she were soaring, but also bone-tired and worn out, and she knew, somewhere below it all, she was still horrified. Her skin still burned where it was coated in blood.

"You feel alive," the doctor supplied. "And it's sometimes a very overwhelming feeling. You should wash up, then sit for a while in my office. I'll send Mr. Lowell out for a change of clothing as soon as the patient is settled in the recovery room."

She looked down at herself, at the blood soaking through her gown in dark, spreading stains. Her nails were caked black, the lines of her palms filled with drying gore. She shook her head, then joined him at the faucet, mechanically rubbing the blood away in the ice-cold water.

"Here," he said, taking one of her hands. His fingers were lightly calloused, and he worked quickly, methodically, getting soap up under her nails and leaving her skin more or less what it had been when she arrived. Her breath caught in her chest, and she wanted, desperately, confusingly, for him to cradle her hands in his, to stroke his thumb along her knuckles.

But he didn't. He simply took her other hand and repeated the work, then shut the tap off and handed her a clean towel. And then he left her, shedding his apron and tossing it onto a pile of stinking laundry, ready for Mr. Lowell to pick up as soon as his other tasks were done.

CHAPTER FOUR

J ANE LOOKED AFTER him, unmoving. His office seemed miles away, her world contracted to the four walls of the operating theater and the rasping breath of the patient. His chest rose and fell, the rhythm gently off-kilter. Slowly, she walked around the table.

She froze when the tangled length of bowel came into view.

She'd half expected it to be gone, swept away into a bucket of bloody rags and torn clothing to be discarded, but it sat, the blood on it congealing but otherwise just the same as when Dr. Lawrence had removed it. It had not deflated in any way, and even now it gave no sign of death. She leaned forward, frowning, refusing to blink. If she didn't blink, she was certain she would see it pulse with the same slow beating of his heart.

"Miss Shoringfield," Mr. Lowell said from the doorway.

She tore her gaze away. "Yes?"

"I'm about to move Mr. Renton here to the recovery room," he said.

"Can I help?"

"No, no. But before I move him, do you need anything? Tea? Brandy?"

"Oh, no," she said, clasping her trembling hands together and lacing her fingers to still the shaking. "I, ah, I'll just move to the office, then. Oh—our maid, Ekaterina, she might be by soon. You can send her for my clothing. I expect you're more needed here than running errands."

"It's no trouble, but I'll look for her. Maybe take an apron to sit on, though," he said, and with a nod of his head, stepped past her and over to the table. She colored, took one of the aprons she should have donned earlier, and hurried out, down the hall and into the office. Dr. Lawrence was nowhere to be seen, though she could hear his voice, far off, too far to make out the words. Closing the door behind her, she looked around.

Could she really live here? Work here? Could she handle another Mr. Renton, whether she was in the bloody theater with him, or across the hall, listening to his screams and speaking with his relatives?

And the way she had felt when Dr. Lawrence had taken her hand—thinking of it now left her adrift. Confused.

She laid the apron out on the chair by the window, but stopped just short of sitting when she heard footsteps. Sound traveled in the surgery, including voices, even those hushed so that she had to strain to hear them.

It was Mr. Lowell and Dr. Lawrence.

"She said she found him in a circle of chalk and salt," Mr. Lowell said. "Should we call the magistrate?"

Chalk and salt? All thoughts of touches and blood were pushed away. She took a few steps toward the door, the better to hear. Surely chalk and salt weren't sufficient signs of a crime to send for the local judiciary.

But Dr. Lawrence did not immediately respond, and Jane's certainty wavered. It rocked entirely when he said, so quietly she could barely hear him, "Superstitions do not cause medical malformations, Mr. Lowell. But they do cause madness, occasionally. Accidental poisonings, certainly."

"And mutilations?" Mr. Lowell pressed. "Could it be some kind of—ritual?"

Jane frowned. Great Breltain had cast off its church over a decade ago, though of course not everybody had stopped believing. Some of Mr. Cunningham's clients even clung to practices older than religion, small offerings left to ensure a better harvest, love potions, and the like. But ritual mutilations? She had never heard of such a thing.

No. No, it had to be the fruit of madness only. If anybody were to know the reality of such dangers, it would be the magistrate.

"He cut his own stomach open, sir," Mr. Lowell pressed.

Dr. Lawrence's response came quicker this time, his voice firm and growing louder. "There is no way the larger insult to his descending colon was done by his hand. I may not be able to explain what caused it, but such a malformation would have been excruciating enough to drive any man into questionable decisions. I know that is uncomfortable, Mr. Lowell, but you must believe me. He was simply unlucky."

It was Mr. Lowell's turn to fall silent. Dr. Lawrence's words must have wrapped around him in much the same way they had around Jane, the certainty in them bolstering her and dispelling her unease. Superstitions could cut both ways, after all; they could cause people to do irrational things, or to assign irrational meaning where there was none.

"Aye, Doctor," Mr. Lowell said at last. "Hot or cold, for Mr. Renton?"

"Hot. Build up the fire until he sweats, then bank it."

Their voices receded, and she sat at last.

He was a good doctor. She had not known it for sure when she proposed to him, had never imagined him the luminary she had seen in the operating theater, but it soothed her soul to know it now.

No; that was a lie. It didn't soothe her, it sparked something in her that refused to die down or be contained.

If Mr. Renton had lived in any other town, or if Dr. Lawrence had never come to Larrenton, she suspected he would have died. But in Dr. Lawrence's care, he had survived. She couldn't forget his screaming, but she also couldn't forget how deftly Dr. Lawrence's hands had moved, how his directions had steadied her, how they had worked in concert to set the body to order. She had never before seen the appeal of a physician's task, but now it made sense to her. They shared the same goals, the same lens through which they viewed the world. She sorted numbers; he sorted humors.

And yet where she analyzed impartial numbers, he cared for the most human of concerns. He was likely with Mrs. Renton even now, and Jane pictured him holding the woman's hands lightly, telling her all that would need to be done to care for her suddenly incapacitated husband.

Husband.

She had thought of Mr. Renton as a body just now, so easily, and as *meat* in the heat of the surgery.

What sort of monstrous woman was she? Perhaps she was not as like Dr. Lawrence as she thought, or as she would need to be to remain here. That remove had kept her on her feet through the surgery, had helped save him, but guilt rocked her. He wasn't a body. He was a man. He was a living, breathing, thinking man.

She heard footsteps again, and the creak of the office door, but didn't look away from the window where she gazed unseeing onto the street. It was the clink of a saucer and cup that made her, at last, turn.

Dr. Lawrence had placed a cup of tea on the small side table by her elbow.

"When I said there might be blood, I didn't expect for today to be quite this exciting," he said, after a minute.

"But it is part of a doctor's life." She made herself pick up the cup. The porcelain rattled against the saucer.

"Sometimes. Not all the time. Is that too much?"

Too much? Yes, of course. And the match was hardly settled. All she had to do was say, *Yes, it was too much. I have reconsidered.* Or perhaps she should echo his words from the night before: *It would not be appropriate for me to marry you.*

But she found she couldn't say either. She didn't know what to say, but she didn't want him to stop talking.

"I just need time to think," she managed at last.

When he had looked upon her in fear the night before, yet still yielded to her demands, what had he felt? She had run roughshod over his logic and desires with her own. She should have accepted the first no, for both of their sakes.

He was still looking at her, though, and when she glanced up, she found his expression had gentled. There was no impatience there, no judgment at her weakness, no relief in finding her unable, perhaps, to meet his requirements.

"And what exactly are you thinking of?" he asked.

You. She turned away, searching for a better answer. She'd never been talented at talking past an issue. "The patient," she settled on. It was closest to the truth, not really a lie at all. "Who else?"

"Who else, indeed," he said, and crossed the remaining space between them, settling down on the footrest. The apron had spared the majority of his clothing, but there was drying blood spattered across his sleeves. It was nothing compared to what she must look like.

She was just about to beg off, to send him back to his patient where he belonged, when he said, "You were incredible in there." It stopped her cold. He flushed, rubbed at the back of his neck. "For somebody with no experience, no training, you were able to keep your wits about you. To do what had to be done."

What could she say to that? She fumbled for some matching compliment. "And you were a virtuoso with a needle," she said, thinking of how he had handled the flesh. And there it was again, the immediate jump to meat instead of man. She winced.

"Miss Shoringfield?"

"I . . . that is, I think I was only able to help because I stopped seeing him as a person."

She watched him for horror. It didn't come.

"Is that not monstrous?" she pressed.

He offered a gentle, almost patronizing smile. "Hardly. I was the same, in my first year of medical school. It made bearing their pain easier, made *inflicting* the pain that was needed to save them easier. Many doctors never get past that, but many more grow beyond it. It becomes a tool, rather than a retreat. You recognize what happened—that is a good first step."

He was being too kind to her. They were not made of the same stuff. She frowned down at her tea.

"I've sent for that specialist," he said. "She may be able to help Mr. Renton's recovery. No matter what, her work will benefit from our efforts. You should be proud of yourself, Miss Shoringfield."

His words touched her with a surgeon's precision, and she did feel pride. She shivered with momentary relief, and in that breath of weakness, she said, "I believe you can call me Jane, now. If you like."

"I would like to."

Her heartbeat syncopated. "His recovery," she said, hurriedly returning to sobering ground, away from the strange intimacy that the heat of the surgery seemed to have created between them. "What will it entail?"

"He will be out of work for several weeks. Months, perhaps."

Her mind went reflexively to the numbers. Months of not working, of not earning a wage. His house would founder. His bills would go unpaid. Dr. Lawrence's would be one of them.

"He will not be able to repay you."

Perhaps she could learn to be better in the surgery, but what of her numbers? They were her constants, her rules. Their logic flowed through her like blood, but they led now to horrible conclusions. Life was worth more than a sum on a page, and yet it was only worth a sum on a page.

"Mrs. Renton will pay as she can," Dr. Lawrence said, oblivious to the nausea rising up in her. "Currently, that is not much. I don't lose anything by not charging her more."

Her fingers tightened around her teacup. "But sums don't lie. I agree with you, I do, on moral grounds. But you will need to pay for equipment. Rent. Food and clothing. If you don't, you cannot remain a doctor, can't continue to save lives."

The numbers had no room for kindness and humanity.

"There will be donations. There always are, in these cases."

"Donations cannot be controlled," she protested. "Cannot be relied upon." She would see the disparity every day in the ledger. It would be her job to collect when she could.

"I'm sorry, Miss Shoringfield—Jane. I don't claim to have an answer."

She grimaced, ducked her head. "And neither do I. But I have a mind for sums. If I were your wife, I feel that it might lead to tension. Anger. Misunderstandings. I apologize, this isn't something I anticipated when I made my proposal. Work has always been straightforward, and yet this is . . . not."

It would not be appropriate for me to marry you. The words were so close, so ready to come out. This was foolishness. They were at odds with one another after only a day. Fondness was too much to hope for, but she needed them to agree with each other. Anything else was less than optimal.

"I will understand if you've reconsidered my suit," she said, too embarrassed and stubborn by half to break the arrangement herself.

"I have not."

Her heart sped.

"To be clear," he added, "I am still not sure I wish to marry at all. But if we were to proceed, is it not natural to expect that we would learn over time how to sort all of this?"

Her mouth was dry. Her head ached. She wanted too many things all at once, and couldn't see any of them clearly. "And what of your other misgivings?" she pressed instead. "The issue of—consummation?"

His gaze dropped, and he blushed. "I am sure that if we decided the marriage must be consummated, we could find a way for it to be consummated on mutually beneficial terms. There is room for me to see you as more than my employee, while still respecting your desire for distance. Don't you think?"

His patient logic stunned her once more into silence. She searched his face, looking for some explanation. What had changed, over the course of one blood-soaked surgery? How had they transformed from him arguing against the idea, and her for it, to her trying to poke holes in both of their defenses?

Perhaps they agreed on some deeper level than she had been focused on.

"You would still consider me, knowing I will never stop talking of bills and expenses?" she ventured. "That I may not always see our patients as people?"

"Knowing that you are, in fact, human, and not some fevered fantasy of a lonely mind?" he responded.

Human. He heard her monstrousness and thought instead that she was human. He had come up against the limits of her plan, a plan that had felt so thoroughly considered until she'd actually met him, and devised ways that they could still proceed.

"You have clearly given this some thought since yesterday. Beyond my initial arguments."

"More today—particularly since about halfway through my discussion of post-surgical care with Mrs. Renton," he confessed, still not looking at her. "It occurred to me that your starting premise had merit. Marriage is always a business arrangement, of a kind, and not only do you have the skills to recommend yourself to me, you are . . . quite nice to be around."

"Quite nice to be around," she echoed. She wasn't sure that she had ever been described in quite those terms.

"That is to say," he continued, "if I didn't enjoy speaking with you, your skills would have made it hard not to hire you, but marriage would have been out of the question. But as I do, even if the marriage would never be more than a strange employment arrangement between us, with a single legal obligation met, I don't necessarily object to it being called a marriage."

"I see," she said. And she did; she saw more murkiness, more blurring of the original boundaries. She could still demur, could still apologize and terminate the courtship. She could still walk away, try again with someone else, hope for something less awkward and convoluted.

But Dr. Lawrence *understood* her. Perhaps it had been the blood, or the fear, or simply the work, but he saw her now in a way she would not have chosen to be seen, and he did not turn away. He didn't think her a child in need of protection, the way the Cunninghams still did, and he did not think her a monster because her brain focused on logistics instead of emotion.

She hadn't realized such an outcome was possible. And if the original lines were blurred, what did it matter if the truth of the arrangement continued? Them, married, with polite kindness between them. Him, understanding her, respecting her.

"I'm glad you're still considering it," she said. "I . . . it did feel good, to help Mr. Renton."

"Yes," he said. "It did. How do you feel now?"

She took inventory of herself. There was still blood on her skirts. Her hands still ached from gripping the retractors. Before all this, there had been a man, and he was alive now. She had done that, in part. "Proud, I suppose," she ventured. "And before, almost ecstatic. But it's layered with my fear of failing a patient, with my worries about the accounts."

"Open up to the positive emotions. Focus on them," he said. "This is the best part. It's like having a sun inside you. Let it light you up."

"What did you call it? Feeling alive?"

He stood. "Alive, yes. It thrives off itself. You're alive, and they're alive, and so you feel them being alive as if it were yourself, and it doubles. It's intoxicating."

Jane stood up as well. The chair and footrest were close enough that standing put her just a few inches from him. The effect was disorienting.

"Intoxicating?" she asked.

"It can make you do very silly things," he said, his gaze dropping for a moment to her lips. Her heart fluttered in her chest, despite herself.

Then he shook himself and stepped back, one hand rubbing the nape of his neck. "That is, try to enjoy the feeling, but be careful on your walk home. I don't want you back in my surgery today."

"Are you sending me away?"

"Yes," he said. "Wouldn't you agree it's for the best? We both have much to think about, and I have my work to attend to. As do you, I'm sure."

"I—Yes. I do," she said. "When shall I return? Tomorrow?" He hesitated, and her heart sank. "That is, if you think working together would help you in your decision."

"I do," he said. "If you think it would help *you*, that is."

"I do," she said, perhaps too quickly.

He smiled, perhaps too widely.

"Then I will send for you as I can. Keep thinking on your fiscal dilemma."

"I will." It and all the rest.

CHAPTER FIVE

J ANE WORKED ALL that evening in an attempt to set her mind to order, and late into the morning the next day. She wrote out final bills for Mr. Cunningham's clients and prepared a clean account book to begin his judgeship with. Each itemized document brought with it the memory of Dr. Lawrence's ledgers and his challenge to her. As much time as she spent with her head bowed to her work, though, she also found herself looking out the window, measuring the gait of every man who passed, searching for Dr. Lawrence's dark hair and stained coat—just in case he happened to walk by.

He stubbornly refused to appear, and she could not logic away the fact that she missed Dr. Lawrence, no matter how hard she tried. Missed him, though they had left on good terms, even after they had laid bare the complexities of her proposal. She had only to wait.

She did not want to wait. She kept remembering the strange magnetism between them in those last few minutes in his study, when he had spoken of intoxication. If he had come another step closer, if he had touched her cheek with those skilled hands of his . . .

With a lurch, she realized that she had wanted him to kiss her.

They had made a mistake, clearly. They had strayed from arguing compatibility to discussing enjoying talking with each other, and rated that an optimistic sign. *Quite nice to be around*, indeed. And now here she was, desiring. She'd never considered the possibility, and so hadn't included it in her calculations. Now she was left embarrassed and confused.

It was one thing to reveal herself to be undone by thoughts of financial ethics, but this? This was so far beyond what she had offered him, what she had *promised* him, that there was no way he could rationalize it with her.

The thought shouldn't have hurt, but it did. Could there not be other options? She had never felt like this before, and though it had not passed in an evening, might it still not dissipate in time? She tried to think instead of her pride in saving Mr. Renton's life. She had dreamed of it, the night before, of blood on her hands, but also of his even breathing, after the worst was over and the ether had set in. Her hands had let Dr. Lawrence do his work; she had proven herself useful. She would only become more so with time, with practice, with dedication.

It was a stronger drive, her need to work and succeed, than any alien tenderness she felt for her potential husband. It would win out in the end. In fact, if she were to lean into these odd fancies of hers, she would only be left cold in time. Such a strange part of herself, unglimpsed until now, could not be long-lived.

Best to focus on the work. She could master her unruly, unfamiliar longings and be the business partner she had offered to be. She was sure of it. All that she needed was a task. Sitting here wondering was doing her no favors.

Jane was in the hallway before she could second-guess herself, pulling on her oiled wrap. He had not sent for her, perhaps would not even be in, and Ekaterina would be setting out lunch shortly; she should wait, should at least tell the house where she was going.

She donned her hat and slipped out into the late morning.

The sky was gray and Larrenton busier than it had been the previous day, everybody working double-time ahead of the threatening rain. She took a different path this time, a tangle of backstreets that would keep her out of the throng. There was little chance of being recognized, but she could not bear the thought of being seen.

Her feet took her past small houses with kitchen gardens out front, and from there through the half-deserted plaza before the old church, now the magistrate's offices. The courts were closed for the morning, the curtains drawn. When Jane had first come to Larrenton, when she had been officially signed into the Cunningham's care, the walls had still been covered in vibrant murals, though they were old, flaking, and only half cared for. Now, everything had been whitewashed. The change had been slow but steady, and when it was done, Mr. Cunningham had said he was glad the old leering figures had at last been covered.

From the plaza, she came out once again onto the main street. The crowds were thinning now, thunder rolling gently on the horizon. But as she approached the doorway, the rattling of wheels drew close behind her. Turning, she watched an elegant black carriage draw to a halt opposite the surgery. Its fineness was distinctly out of place in Larrenton, and it bore a crimson emblem on its side, only partially obscured by the mud of travel:

CROWN UNIVERSITY ROYAL TEACHING HOSPITAL

The driver hopped down from his box and opened the carriage door, and out stepped what could only be Dr. Lawrence's specialist, come all the way from Camhurst. She was short and spare, with sharp-edged cheekbones and dark hair drawn back severely from her brow. Her skirts spread out around her like an inky cloud. She wore a surgeon's coat, but it was trimmed incongruously with fur. She carried no doctor's bag, only a small case hardly larger than a book, and she regarded Jane with a chill focus.

Jane inclined her head in greeting. "Are you the specialist Dr. Lawrence sent for yesterday?"

"Yes," the woman said. "My name is Dr. Avdotya Semyonovna Nizamiev."

Ruzkan; her accent was stronger than Ekaterina's, and Jane was seized by the wild thought that the other woman was currently emphasizing it, perhaps to gauge Jane's reaction. But no; why would this Dr. Nizamiev test her?

"You must have ridden through the night to get here so quickly." Camhurst was nearly a full day's journey by carriage, and that didn't account for the letter's transit. The speed with which she had arrived was scarcely believable.

"I left as soon as I received Dr. Lawrence's summons. Health waits for few, and death for none."

"Are you a surgeon, then?"

"No. Neither surgeon nor generalist. I administer the asylum run by the Royal."

"The asylum," Jane repeated, doing her best not to frown. What need would Dr. Lawrence have of her services?

But then she remembered *chalk and salt*. Superstitious madness. Except he had decided on sending for Dr. Nizamiev while still in the operating theater, before he knew.

Ah. A man cutting himself open for no reason except, perhaps, pain—the much simpler explanation.

"I expect," Dr. Nizamiev said, voice cool and dry, "that I am needed inside. Not explaining myself to . . . a nurse?" The woman looked Jane up and down again, measuring. She couldn't be much older than Dr. Lawrence, but in her sharp appraisal, she seemed ageless. Unyielding.

"Not exactly," Jane said, straightening her shoulders. "I am an accountant, training to assist Dr. Lawrence."

"I see," Dr. Nizamiev said, and her tone was empty, empty of amusement or confusion or derision. She opened the door to the surgery and stepped inside, and Jane trailed after.

The door swung shut behind them, and a moment later, Dr. Lawrence appeared in the operating theater doorway. Jane felt a wayward surge of excitement, then stilled as she took in his expression: he was wearing his surgeon's focus.

"Come, come quickly," he said, voice harsh. Jane's stomach dropped. "It is Mr. Renton. Avdotya, you can wait in the office, it's just—"

"I will come as well," Dr. Nizamiev said, and though no surgeon, she strode into the operating theater with a confidence Jane could not conjure in herself. Mr. Renton. What could have happened? Why was he back for more of the knife?

Was there another impossible tangle?

She followed and donned a gown with trembling hands.

Their patient lay on the operating table. He was quiet, but not from ether, and though he was strapped down, there was no need for it, for he did not move at all. Dr. Lawrence had laid bare his belly and removed the sponge covering the gaping hole of his bowel. His skin was red and taut around it.

"Hands," he said, and Jane obediently scrubbed herself clean, then joined him at the operating table.

"What has happened?"

Dr. Lawrence looked up at her, grim-faced. "His pulse has grown very weak. I have attempted purgatives and bleeding, but there has been no improvement. He may have a hemorrhage in his gut, either that we missed or that I caused." He delivered the facts in a rush, controlled but too rapid for confidence. "I will need to open him up. Retractors, if I may impose upon you again, Miss Shoringfield?"

Jane found them laid out on a nearby counter. She was back at his side in seconds. He worked the stitches open, and a slow-moving gout of filth oozed forth, clotted into masses and stinking of death. It was impossible for Jane to make out any other details, but Dr. Lawrence swore, then demanded, "The bulb, the flushing bulb. Jane, take it, fill it with water, just water."

Her hands refused to still as she grabbed up the equipment, as she turned on the tap, as she manipulated the fine glass-and-rubber instrument. Where was the confidence that he could create in her? Dying on the table, curdling in her heart. Slipping away, too fast.

She handed the equipment to Dr. Lawrence.

Black filth ran from Mr. Renton's abdomen as Dr. Lawrence worked the bulb. She looked for any hint of red or healthy pink beneath the skin and found none. He plunged his hands into the wound and methodically slid his fingers along sick-slick organs, feeling where he could not see.

"If we can clean the rot, if I can find the perforation—"

Mr. Renton's chest rose and fell, shallowly, slowly. The doctor pushed his hands deeper.

His chest moved slower still, shallower still.

Dr. Lawrence swore.

Mr. Renton's chest moved not at all.

It was a small change, from shallow breaths to nothing, and yet without that last vital scrap, Mr. Renton was transfigured. Dr. Lawrence kept working a few desperate moments longer, and then he pulled his hands out entirely. They were black.

"He is gone," the doctor said.

Jane looked between the corpse and Dr. Lawrence, simultaneously numb and on the verge of tears, and then retreated to the sink, turning on the spigot and washing her spotless hands as if they were coated in blood.

When she was finished, she turned around to find Dr. Lawrence unmoved.

"This is my fault," he said.

Behind him, Dr. Nizamiev arched a brow but said nothing. She was watching Dr. Lawrence with predatory focus. For what, Jane couldn't say. If Dr. Nizamiev had been a surgeon, Jane might have seen competition, or judgment, but no. No, it was something unidentifiable that nevertheless left Jane uneasy.

"I moved too quickly during the initial surgery," Dr. Lawrence continued. "I flushed the wound at the start, but not at the end. The wound was befouled. I could have caught this."

"Dr. Lawrence," Jane murmured.

He did not respond, stalking past her to wash his own stinking hands. He scrubbed hard with lye soap.

"May I see the specimen?" Dr. Nizamiev asked.

"The patient is dead," Dr. Lawrence snapped, turning the tap off sharply and rounding on her, his fingers clutching tight to the sink rim behind him. "There can be no certainty. You might reach Camhurst before midnight if you set out now; I apologize for calling you out unnecessarily."

Dr. Nizamiev did not look frustrated, as a woman called away from the capital for nothing and sent back unceremoniously might. She also did not look sad for the corpse between her and Dr. Lawrence, or uncomfortable, or much of anything at all. "You sent for me for a reason, Augustine," she said after the silence had stretched far too long.

"I said that it was a small chance," Dr. Lawrence said, voice clipped. He shed his soiled apron and tossed it into the laundry hamper with startling ferocity.

Dr. Nizamiev glanced at Jane, though Jane had made no motion or sound. Uncomfortable, Jane, too, shed her apron.

"And your own research?" Dr. Nizamiev asked.

"Abandoned. You'll forgive me, but I am not one for company today," Dr. Lawrence gritted out.

"Next time," the woman said, approaching Dr. Lawrence in an almost inhuman glide, "wait to ensure your patient will survive before you send for me, then. I do not appreciate being called out on a maybe, when you are not willing to stand beside your instinct. You know that I have never cared for playing games."

Dr. Lawrence clenched his jaw, but nodded and gestured Dr. Nizamiev out of the room. He walked her to the door, Jane following them both.

Before he showed the specialist out, Jane thought she heard him mutter, "I called you here to set my fears at ease, not stoke them."

"I am not here for your comfort," Dr. Nizamiev returned. And then she was gone, sweeping out to her carriage.

Dr. Lawrence stared after her, his breathing harsh and shallow. Jane drew up beside him. She should have commented on Dr. Nizamiev's strangeness, or perhaps asked questions about what her specialty was, exactly, but she could not find the words.

The triumph of yesterday was sour. Everything had gone wrong. She wanted to roll back time.

"I must call upon the undertakers," he said softly. "And Mrs. Renton, too, I must send word to her."

"Of course. I—Should I return home, then?"

He turned to her at last, and seemed about to take her hands, but clenched his at his sides instead. "Jane, I am sorry that you had to witness death here today. I am sorry, so sorry, that I could not save him."

"It would have been magic, if you had."

He flinched. "I should not keep you."

No, of course not. She took a deep breath, turned to go.

And then he said, "But I am weak, and I would ask that you stay. You do not have to assist me today, or work, but I do not want to . . . I don't think you should be left to deal with this loss alone."

His voice bled with pain.

She didn't want to leave his side, not now, for a hundred selfish and virtuous reasons all twined together. And more than that, she couldn't imagine going home, returning to Mr. Cunningham's office, holding the death of Mr. Renton inside of her.

"Of course I'll stay," she said, turning back to him. "I can even come with you to visit the undertakers."

"No, the weather is beginning to turn once again. I will go to them when it passes." Outside, the gathered clouds had taken on the fullness of impending rain, blotting out the sun. "I'll clean up, prepare the surgery for other visitors. Mr. Lowell will be back within half an hour and can take over for a short while, and then we can sit together. Upstairs, to the right of the landing, is my personal study. There is whiskey there, and books. Please, make yourself comfortable. I will not be long."

Jane nodded, though she watched uneasily as he passed through the operating theater doorway once more. Saving Mr. Renton had given her such pride, and his death now perverted it, made her feel hollow and dirty. She was happy to flee the sensation, climbing the stairs to Dr. Lawrence's study.

The walls were crowded with shelves, and on all of them were books piled upon books. His desk here was a smaller thing, but more well-loved. Behind his desk, as he had promised, was a decanter and two glasses. Jane poured herself a draught despite the early hour.

She sipped at it, standing before a glass-fronted cabinet. Within were many strange things she did not recognize: several branches with thick blisters on their bark, a stone cracked open to reveal a lattice of brilliant crystal, a string of something white and creased like cauliflower. What first appeared like a strange red flower in full bloom resolved on closer inspection to be a wax model of a human head, the nose gone and the skin falling away from disease.

Strange and gruesome, all of it. Jane drew back and made to turn, then noticed a newer addition, free from dust. It was a large glass jar, filled with a lump of something floating in pale golden liquid, somewhat cloudy, sediment already accreting at the bottom.

It took her a moment, but then she recognized the mass. It was the warped tissue Dr. Lawrence had excised from Mr. Renton's abdomen yesterday morning.

The specimen. Was this what Dr. Nizamiev had wanted to see? She frowned but could not take her eyes away from it, even as she remembered it lying, inert, on the operating table, even as she remembered that Mr. Renton's lifeless body still lay below her.

Would he get rid of it now that his patient was dead? Why keep it in his study? But even as she questioned, she began to suspect the answer.

It was fascinating.

She traced the curves of it, and, this close to it now and with less panic clouding her mind, she could see that it *did* disappear into itself, the way she had perceived the day before. It twisted not in the way of rope or sausage, nor was it knotted like string. She could not make sense of its exterior and interior, its top or bottom. It made her head ache.

Footsteps on the stairs. She turned to face the door just as Dr. Lawrence entered, still looking worn, drawn. He regarded her silently, then looked behind her to the cabinet.

"What do you think of it all?" he asked. "I confess, I forgot you would see my collection when I recommended you come up here."

"What is it for?" Jane asked, caught between disgust and interest.

He came to her side and poured himself his own small glass of whiskey, then leaned back against his desk, regarding the shelves filled with stones and wood and jars. "My own education. I collect curiosities," he said. "I have for many years. Models or samples of medical oddities, strange natural phenomena, that sort of thing."

"Including that," she said, nodding to the jar. "Mr. Renton's . . ."

"His large bowel, yes," Dr. Lawrence said.

"Do you intend to keep it?" she asked. "After . . . ?"

"Yes. I've never seen anything like it. I may never again. Does that trouble you?"

After some consideration, she said, "No, I don't think so." She did still step away from it, and pressed a hand to her eyes. It smelled faintly of death, though she had not touched the foul seepage.

She shuddered and thought again of Renton's blood on her hands the day before. Her hands inside the wound.

The wound that had been fouled. She had scrubbed her hands before she'd touched it, but she might have done it wrong.

She quailed at the thought. Another mistake. Another misstep that rendered her unfit for . . . whatever this was.

"What is it, Jane?" Dr. Lawrence murmured, seeing her distress.

"You . . . blamed yourself down there, for Mr. Renton's death," she said, not looking at him. "Do I not share equally in it? I am inexperienced. I distracted you. I—"

"No," Dr. Lawrence said fervently, setting aside his glass and taking her free hand in his, drawing her farther away from the cabinet. "Don't think like that, Miss Shoringfield. Jane. Please promise me you won't think like that, not ever."

"Dr. Lawrence," she murmured, stunned by the warmth of his skin and the passion flashing in his eyes.

"Jane, if the fault lies in anybody, it lies in me. I am the one with training and, more than that, I was the one in charge of the operating room. You cannot blame yourself. That shame is a path you cannot come back from, once you start down it," he said firmly. "I am a doctor; I am built to carry that load. I have sworn to do so. You were simply there, willing to help. You did all you could, and that is all anybody could ask of you."

"And so did you."

That stopped him, his jaw working. "Perhaps," he said at last. "But I'm the one who can bear it, not you. I can't ask that of you, not even if we are engaged."

Jane stopped breathing. Her thoughts raced, unable to maintain her guilt, her fear, her confusion all at once. "Engaged," she repeated, voice barely more than a breath. Her head was full of buzzing, too many emotions in too short a time. She wanted to flee into the night, but also wanted to be here, only here, and for him to look at her again. Instead, he withdrew and straightened his cuffs.

"That is," he said, "even if you are my potential wife. Forgive me."

"Dr. Lawrence," she said.

"I find my thoughts are quite out of order today," he continued. He was blushing, she realized, beneath his worn pallor. "I should not have asked you to stay; we have hardly agreed to—"

"Augustine."

His given name stopped him cold.

"Yes?" he asked.

Take it back. He must take it back. She had been impulsive, foolish, wild to come here just to see him again. She could not let him do this, unknowing of how she'd betrayed his trust. She had demanded a business arrangement, and he had agreed to it. Anything else was against both their wishes.

And yet . . . and yet she wanted, more than anything, for him to say it again. She set her glass aside and clutched her hands together, so tightly that the skin looked bleached. She hoped wildly, in two antithetical directions.

"Engaged?" she asked.

Without a word, Augustine reached for her, then past her, to the cabinet. He drew out one of the lower drawers. Several small curios were arrayed on the velvet-lined interior, and right in the center were two rings.

"I meant to give these to you," he said. "Not today, of course. Even if— even if Mr. Renton had lived, it is still much too soon, but now it seems the most inauspicious start possible." He glanced at her at last. "As I said, please forgive me."

She joined him and looked more closely at the rings. They weren't simple bands of metal, or even gem-studded jewelry, but instead made of many interlocking pieces of something white and matte.

Carved bone.

She reached out and traced one porous curve. At her ear, Augustine murmured, "I had a patient once, a man whose entire body ossified over his lifetime. I removed a series of growths that locked his elbow in place, and he had them fashioned into these."

"The bones of a man," she repeated. A man with an uncommon illness, one she had until now never imagined—she was beginning to see a pattern.

He picked up one of the rings and turned it around in the palm of his hand. "His name was Julian Aethridge. He had a unique sense of humor and asked that he be allowed to keep whatever we removed. Said he'd made it himself, after all. So we gave him the pieces, and he had some of them made into these rings. He tried to give them to his son and his son's new wife, but they were disturbed. When he offered them to me, I accepted."

Really, what better gift for a blood-soaked surgeon to give to his bride than a ring made of the fruits of his labor? And perhaps it was best that she bore a reminder of the inevitability of death, to chill her fevered thoughts.

She plucked the other ring from its velvet nest. She turned it over, looking at how the white bone had been carved so finely, with such care. A gentle touch with the pad of her thumb pushed the pieces into a new configuration, the hoop they formed narrower but taller than before. Genius, to take such a one-of-a-kind material and design the rings in such a way that they could fit throughout the seasons of life, on any number of people. The geometric figuring to make such a thing would have been extensive. She wished she could see the plans.

But Augustine was watching her. She should say something. *Thank you,* perhaps. Or *no.*

Or *yes.*

When she had decided to marry, she'd had Mrs. Cunningham write down a list of all the unwed men in town between two years her junior and fourteen her senior. From there, she had narrowed it based on income, filtering out all who made more than her guardians, and anybody earning much less. She'd used statistics, mathematics, to purify her choice. Her intent had been to avoid the most heated competition for the wealthiest bachelors, to save the Cunninghams from embarrassment at a lower match—and to increase the chances that she would be spared from bearing nine children to mind the family farm or trade, instead of working herself.

In the end, Larrenton and the nearest towns had boasted thirteen men who matched those requirements.

She'd asked only Augustine. He'd been at the top of her list. Perfect in every way. And then she'd met him, and for the last two days, she'd hardly been able to think straight.

She wanted, so badly, to say yes. And that was the problem. Her heart, normally such a measured and predictable thing, had grown erratic. For him. He had been so hesitant to consider marriage at all, and it had only been her terms, her dedication to avoiding intimacy, that had persuaded him.

There was still a chance she would return to normal. That he might never notice. But if he did . . .

Her fingers played with the ring, spiraling it in and out. "People aren't static," she said at last. "People aren't perfect. An employee you can replace. And though this is a business arrangement, uppermost, a wife cannot be replaced so easily."

Something darkened in his eyes. Thinking, no doubt, of all the widowers he had known in his career. And then he said, "Jane, I would never replace you."

"You are sure," she asked, looking up at him, "that you want to marry me?"

"I can think of little else," he said, finally taking the ring from her and gently, so gently, slipping it onto her finger. "After a just a few days, I find I've completely lost my mind over you."

Oh.

It wasn't only her heart, then, that sped when they drew close.

"Doesn't that terrify you?" she asked, voice soft. She leaned in, her heart beating wildly in her chest.

He swallowed, nodded. "It terrifies me. But you don't, and I can't leave the thought of you alone."

"Me, neither," she said, and kissed him.

CHAPTER SIX

T HEY WERE MARRIED with little fanfare less than a week later. Neither had large numbers of guests to invite; in fact, Augustine invited none. Jane had Mr. and Mrs. Cunningham, Ekaterina, and a few friends of the family.

The ceremony itself was bare-bones and unremarkable. After the devastation and horror of the war with Ruzka, the government had officially abandoned its theism. The church had already become decrepit and half ignored as industrialization unsettled old ways of life; the terrible new engines of war and their attendant death toll had simply finished the erosion in a single, spectacular blow. Halfway through the war, three score people had sheltered in one of Camhurst's great cathedrals, certain it would not be targeted, that they would not come to harm. They had all been dead by morning, the building a burnt-out, poisoned husk. Faith had hobbled along after that, yes, but it had shed its adherents, its bones and flesh, with every step.

What little religion did remain in the civil ceremony mirrored what remained among the citizenry: a half-grudging, half-panicked belief in spirits and the movements of the heavens, and a deep, abiding fear of chaos and conflict. So Augustine and Jane had passed, independently, through a series of small "rooms" separated by draped fabric in order to shake off anything negative that might follow them into marriage, before meeting in front of the magistrate for the signing of the marriage contract, which was written in archaic, highly structured legal prose that left no loopholes or misunderstandings.

They removed their rings and placed them in a small bowl with an assortment of offerings, and it was taken up to the top of the courthouse spire to bathe in the midday sun while the contract was read out in full. When they put their names to it, the bowl was brought back down, they slipped the rings back on to each other's fingers, and that was that.

They were married.

Through it all, Jane could not stop thinking of their first—and only—kiss. She had kissed him, and he'd folded his arms around her hesitantly even as he returned the kiss with greater fervor. She'd never kissed anybody before, and had been fumbling and awkward. He had seemed unsure at first as well, but soon had grown bolder, guiding her with a touch of his fingers to her jaw, a pass of his tongue across her lips. Her rational mind had deserted her for a few beautiful, burning moments.

By the time they'd been interrupted by the sound of patients entering the surgery below and she pulled away, the damage had been done. He'd looked at her like she'd ripped his heart straight from his chest, before finding a smile and laughing awkwardly. They'd apologized to each other, he had spent fifteen minutes with his patient, and then he'd walked her home, the both of them careful not to touch. Augustine had told Mr. Cunningham his decision, she had affirmed it, and he had left to fetch the undertakers for Mr. Renton.

It had been the last sobering reminder she needed. Her growing attraction and their increasing intimacy still frightened her, felt uncertain and fragile. And unnecessary. They might have spoken of temporary madness, but not of changing the terms of their marriage.

And Augustine seemed to agree; they hadn't been alone together since.

She had spent the rest of the week setting up an account book for him and going through two months of patient records to start filling out who had received what treatment, and she had done as much of the work at home as was possible. She had come round only when he had several patients to see in the surgery, and he had insisted on her sitting in to observe. He'd kept a respectful distance, and there had been no more . . . indiscretions.

But she hadn't been able to keep her eyes off him. She'd watched how gentle he was with his patients, how firm when it was needed and how solicitous when compassion was called for instead. A few mornings, he'd arrived looking like he hadn't slept at all, though she knew from his notes that there hadn't been any house calls during the night. She hoped only that he had not been kept up by thoughts of her.

He looked the same now, as they emerged from the ceremony hall into the blinding sunlight of an unseasonably favorable day, surrounded by a bustle of activity that seemed too great for the scant number of guests they'd invited. Jane stopped in the doorway, staring, the size of the crowd far too much. Mr. and Mrs. Cunningham led the charge as it converged in on them, and she went rigid as they were both hoisted into the carriage that would take them to the surgery. The gathered crowd cheered, growing as people she did not know, drawn by the commotion, circled the carriage itself. The horse threw its head at the attention and the noise, and Jane retreated into the marginally quieter, very much darker interior of the cab, shutting the door firmly behind them.

"Well, Dr. Lawrence," she managed.

"Well, Mrs. Lawrence," he responded, voice a little huskier than usual. He stole a glance at her in her bright blue wedding dress. A boyish smile curled his lips, then fell as he looked out the window. "There are so many," he said.

She shrugged helplessly. The carriage lurched into motion, and Jane waited for the sound of the crowd to fade.

It didn't.

As they rattled through the streets, the wedding guests and the accumulated onlookers kept pace, shouting and laughing and hugging one another. Jane turned bright red as she stared out the small window in the cab door. She'd seen these parades before, friends and family escorting the newlywed couple to their home, some wearing masks, others playing loud music intended to celebrate, to confuse, to mark the transition from independence to marriage, but the thought that they could do the same for her seemed alien. Terrifying, the weight of their attention on her far too much. What was she meant to do, how was she meant to act?

"I truly didn't think anybody would care about the wedding," he said. "And yet we have an audience, and just this morning I received a letter from my colleagues in Camhurst, proposing that they come to celebrate the nuptials in person. I turned them down, of course," he added hastily, as she tensed still further. The crowd outside was bad enough—hosting house guests would have stressed her far more.

Across the small gap between them, Augustine seemed to feel much the same. He grew paler with every second the noise outside did not abate, and he clutched the edge of the seat, knuckles white.

"They mean us well," she said, trying to reassure them both.

But with the crowd around them, the carriage wasn't able to make the turn that would take them to the surgery. Instead, the crowd bore them faster and faster toward the edge of town.

Augustine made a pained sound, and finally lurched toward the door, opening it even as the cobbled road gave way to dirt beneath them. "Mr. Lowell!" he called.

The older man appeared, grinning and doffing his hat in congratulations. "Dr. Lawrence! Mrs. Lawrence!"

"We are meant for the surgery!" Augustine's cry barely surmounted the din of the crowd, which seemed to double, triple, with every passing minute. Jane couldn't recognize half the unmasked faces in the crowd. She trembled, unsure of how to process such a great parade. It wasn't for her; it wasn't for him. Was it only for a marriage?

Were they all relieved to see her gone?

Mr. Lowell had lost his words and was turning a brilliant vermillion. "I, ah—" he stammered. "I had thought you would both be headed to Lindridge Hall tonight, sir. It being your wedding night and all. Mrs. Lawrence's traveling case has already been sent on ahead."

Augustine went very still, even with the jolting of the wheels, and Jane thought for a moment he might throw himself from the carriage. As she watched, he closed his eyes, as if fighting for control over himself.

Jane leaned into the open doorway. "It's all right," she said. "I can send home for another set of clothing. We just need to turn the carriage around. Can you help us?"

Mr. Lowell worried at the brim of his hat. "So you mean to live at the surgery . . . regularly?"

"Yes. I will be living there full time. Dr. Lawrence will continue living at . . . what did you call it? Lindridge Hall?"

"Aye, Lindridge Hall." He struggled to keep pace with the carriage and stay close to the door, the crowd pushing on him from all sides. Frustrated, he hopped up onto the rail below the door, grabbing on to the top of the carriage to brace himself. Well-wishers cheered, grinning at Jane, waving and shouting and dancing. Somewhere behind them, a full band had begun to play, a cacophony of off-tempo brass and flutes. She was trapped in a nightmare.

Mr. Lowell turned his attention once more to Augustine, who was clutching tight to the door handle. "Sir, I apologize, I had thought when you asked for the spare bedroom to be fully appointed that, ah, that you meant it for later, when you'd both stay here on occasion. Not tonight. But I don't know—" He grimaced, looking over his shoulder. "I don't know that I can stop such a great crowd without causing a scene."

She didn't care about causing a scene, not really—but she could see her guardians out among the crowd, delighted and happy and *proud,* and she didn't want to hurt them.

She froze, unable to decide.

"Mr. Lowell," Augustine said at last, "have you also sent ahead the ingredients I had you purchase for dinner?"

"Yes, sir."

He sat back in his seat, letting go of the door. Mr. Lowell braced it instead. Grimacing, Augustine said, "Then I suppose we will be dining at Lindridge Hall tonight. But I will be sending Mrs. Lawrence back to the surgery at sunset. That way she can fetch her belongings and the crowd need not be disrupted."

He said it all in a strange, strained voice, but Mr. Lowell only nodded and said, "Yes, Doctor."

He dropped back to the ground and shut the door behind him.

Jane searched Augustine's face. He'd very eagerly agreed to the part of their arrangement where they would live separately, even more than the proposed lack of intimacy. He had never gone back on that element, even as they had discussed consummation and flirted around the edges of their business arrangement. It had struck her as odd, but it had aligned with what she'd needed, even as the rest of her plans fell apart, and so she hadn't questioned it. But now, even given how uncomfortable the wedding procession was making the both of them, she couldn't understand.

"I wouldn't mind staying the night at Lindridge Hall. It would no doubt be much easier," she said. "We can satisfy the legal requirements, then resume our arrangements tomorrow."

"No," he said, looking directly at her for the first time since the crowd had formed. He didn't blush, didn't flinch.

She frowned. "It *is* our wedding night. It seems appropriate that we—"

"You will never stay the night at Lindridge Hall." His expression took on a darkness that she'd never seen before, not even the day that Mr. Renton had died, but then he shook himself. "Please understand that," he said, voice softening. "Whatever else may or may not change about our . . . arrangement, *that* needs to remain true. You will never stay the night at Lindridge Hall, and I always will."

"Why?"

He ran an absent hand through his hair. His dark suit and shirt were rumpled from the ride already. He looked abstracted and beautiful. Jane once more found herself wanting to kiss him, damn everything else.

She pushed the impulse away.

"Why, Augustine?"

"Because," he said, "if a patient comes to the surgery when I am out—"

"Mr. Lowell can send for you tonight, if he has to, just as I would if that happened."

He didn't answer immediately, looking away from her and out at the crowd. His eyes grew unfocused. At last he said, "Because Lindridge Hall is not fit for you. It's been empty for many years, and while I employ a cook and a maid, they are not there full-time. It is a very dark place. You'll be far more comfortable in the surgery."

"Why must you stay there, then?"

He grimaced. The carriage rocked as the dirt track they were on grew rougher, but the noise from outside continued despite the less pleasant terrain. "It's my family home and there's nobody else to keep it."

"You can't rent it out? Or stay only a few nights a week?" When he'd first laid down this rule, she'd accepted it at face value; she had marked it as none of her business. But now that she had kissed him, had worked beside him, had learned the sort of man he was beyond her statistical analysis, none of this made sense. Augustine Lawrence should have wanted to stay close to his patients, if not to her.

"It—has a lot of history," he said at last. "It's complicated. Call it my pet irrationality. But we will hold to the terms of the arrangement. Won't we?"

Her unease refused to quiet, but she could rise above it for the sake of the pain she could see in his eyes. She nodded. "Of course. I'll leave before sunset."

CHAPTER SEVEN

THE CLOSER THE carriage came to Lindridge Hall, the stranger Augustine became. He shifted restlessly in his seat and worried at the cuffs of his jacket. His eyes fixed not on her, nor on the crowd still following them, but on the horizon beyond.

His agitation disturbed her—what could be so horrible about a neglected home? It couldn't be so bad, or else he couldn't live there. But if there was something she needed to know, something that threatened the happiness or safety of their marriage . . .

Well, isn't that what you get for agreeing to marry a man you've known for a week?

She looked out the window at Mr. and Mrs. Cunningham, the former having taken up a small drum, his cheeks high with color. *They* were happy for her. They trusted Augustine, approved of the match. They trusted her judgment.

"Are you all right?"

Jane turned back to Augustine in confusion. He was watching her closely now. "What?"

"You've gone a bit pale. Are you feeling nauseated? Carriage travel can—"

"I've ridden in carriages before, Augustine," she said, smiling despite herself. "I'm fine. But thank you for your concern."

He nodded, adjusted his high collar. He certainly still looked distracted, but his impulse to check on her health had broken through it.

She took the opportunity. "Your cook. What's her name?"

"Mrs. Luthbright," he said. "And the maid's name is Mrs. Purl. They both live on farms that pay rent to my family, and come in every day."

"But they don't stay at the house at night, either?"

"No," he said. "They have families to return to, and I hardly need their help to sleep." He offered a sheepish smile. "I'm sorry, this must be making you nervous. It really is just that the place is in a bit of disrepair, and I only stay there out of duty, not enjoyment. You'll be much happier in town, I promise. And I am loath to have our . . . our entourage see it, as well."

Oh, Augustine. She could sympathize with his embarrassment all too well. "I didn't know that they would do this. But you are much loved, even after only these past few months. Perhaps we should have realized."

The carriage drew to a halt again, and when she leaned over to look out the window, the mass of what had to be Lindridge Hall towered over her. It was made of green-gray stone and rose three stories, with an imposing entryway flanked by thick columns. It was the largest house Jane had ever seen, and was ornamented with intricately carved flanges demarcating seemingly random sections of stone. Many of the windows were shuttered, and the few that weren't had thick, waving glass panes, several dirty and fogged over.

The crowd around the carriage stilled and grew quieter. They, too, were fixed on the edifice and its front garden, dead and withered despite the good summer they'd had.

"Is this it?"

"It is," he said. He opened the carriage door and stepped out. The cry of celebration from their well-wishers was strained and weak. She waited for him to hand her down, but his attention was fixed on their audience. He had not touched her since they had exchanged rings at the ceremony, she realized with a selfish pang—but why should he have? To reassure her?

She pasted on a smile, following him out onto the dirt path that led to the front door, clasping hands with Mrs. Cunningham, with Ekaterina, with Mr. Lowell. Everybody wanted to touch her shoulder and give her advice, but they were also all distracted. The mood had soured.

The grounds around them were overgrown, the lawn covered in weeds and shrubs, the grass endlessly encroaching at the edges of the road. The shadow cast by the house felt like a solid thing, and the wedding party began to withdraw, waving, smiling, but pulling inexorably away. She should have felt relief. Instead, she felt . . . alone.

Mrs. Cunningham was the last to turn away and looked the least unsettled. She came to Jane one last time and kissed her cheek. "May you be happy, my dear," she said, squeezing Jane's hands in hers. "The house will be quieter without you."

And then she, too, joined the procession back down the hill.

The music resumed when they reached the main road again.

Behind her, she could hear Augustine talking quietly with the carriage driver, arranging for him to remain so that he could take her back to town. Relief flooded her, followed swiftly by guilt.

Their agreement had said nothing about accepting and loving every part of each other—far from it—but she couldn't sort out what *she* intended to do anymore. His gentle care and honesty had undone her, and this house threatened to scatter the pieces.

Augustine came to stand beside her. "I'm sorry," he murmured. "I didn't want you to see this."

"It's not so bad," she assured him, making herself turn to look at the house again. This time, she mastered her expression first, then took a more measured inventory. Lindridge Hall had a pitched roof, with peaked dormers studding its lower edge and short towers capping the corners. This close, and without the waiting crowd, Jane fancied she could see mathematical proportions in the windows and decorations. At the far end of the west wing of the house, the top floor was crowned with steel and murky glass.

Augustine gestured to parts of the roof that were covered in heavy moss, and a stretch of wall that was crumbling under the onslaught of a large ivy plant. "My parents haven't stayed in it for quite some time, and I was gone away at a government posting for the last two years. It's . . . embarrassing. I should have told you sooner."

"Have you never hired a groundskeeper?"

"My parents have other endeavors they prefer to spend their money on, including their residence on the sea." He shrugged as they started walking toward the front door. Again, he did not proffer so much as an elbow. "And I . . . well. You know very well now how little country doctors are paid."

Yes, she did. "It must have been beautiful in its prime."

"It was glorious. Now I keep to only a few rooms of it. The rest are either empty or have moldering furniture in them. Eventually I'll have the whole place cleared out, but it just hasn't been a priority."

They climbed the stone steps up to the main doors, which were pulled open hastily by a short, thin woman with a frilled cap and a simple brown dress. The woman was perhaps in her midforties, curls of thinning flaxen hair escaping her cap.

"Hello, Mrs. Purl," Augustine said. His tone was warm, with a faint hint of apology. "There was a misunderstanding with Mr. Lowell. He had Mrs. Lawrence's things sent here instead of keeping them at the surgery, as I'd intended."

Mrs. Purl glanced at Jane appraisingly, then smiled at Augustine. "I hardly mind, though your room—"

"She'll be returning to the surgery after dinner," he interjected, quickly. "Is the dining room fit for guests?"

"It certainly can be."

"I wouldn't want to keep you."

"It's a special occasion, Dr. Lawrence. I don't mind." She curtsied to Jane then, saying, "A pleasure to meet you, Mrs. Lawrence."

Jane had opened her mouth to respond to the greeting, but Mrs. Purl had already turned away and headed deeper into the building. "Well," she said after a moment. "She seems—"

"Nice and professional," Augustine suggested.

"Yes."

He turned toward her, and finally took both her hands in his, looking into her eyes. The contact was electrifying, lightning coursing through her bones and making her heart seize. She leaned in reflexively.

"Are you happy?" he asked.

"Happy?" Her thoughts were lagging behind, caught up in the sensation of his skin on hers.

"You're not regretting today, are you?"

"No. No, I'm not regretting it. And yes, I'm happy."

He smiled. "I'm glad. Well, I would give you a tour, but there's not much to see, and I think Mrs. Luthbright will want some input on dinner. I could show you to my study here, if you like?"

He let go, began to walk away.

She hurried after him, as if on a lead.

"What about the conservatory?"

"The conservatory?"

"The room on the third floor, with the glass roof."

Augustine laughed. "Oh, that. It's a library, not a conservatory. It's also entirely empty, I'm afraid. Books moved to the seaside house."

"Perhaps I'll just wander, then." At his pained look, she reached out a hand, then let it drop, unsure, to her side. "You don't have to be embarrassed by this, Augustine. If I'd had a requirement that my husband have a fine, well-kept house, I would have checked that," she said, hoping it would get a laugh out of him. It didn't. "Is it unsafe, to wander?"

"It . . ." He trailed off, thoughtful, then said, "No, Mrs. Purl hasn't told me of anything like that. But I would feel much better if you didn't."

She was pushing too much, she realized, on too many fronts. She schooled herself back to propriety. "I understand. Your study is . . . ?"

"Upstairs," he said. "Come with me."

He turned and led her up a staircase, its carpet worn but clean, its banister polished to a serviceable soft finish. The entry hall was two stories tall, with an arched dome of a ceiling. The stairs curled up along its sides, then out into the wings of the house. They turned down the eastern corridor, into a long, wide hallway with bay windows made of the same murky green glass of the library's roof. The windows let in little light, and Jane could see that the iron girding was in a different pattern in each window. She wanted to slow for a closer look, but Augustine kept moving.

They reached the first corner, where he indicated a door but did not move to open it. "My room, the same as when I was a boy. Extremely boring, I assure you. The study's just around here, though."

It was just a few more doors down the hall, and he let her in with a small smile. The room was large, larger than his study at the surgery, and every single wall was covered in bookshelves or cabinets. Many of the bookshelves held not books but more of his collected curiosities: jars of unknown substances, wax models of sores and growths, and more than a few skulls, glowering down at them with empty sockets. Some were human, some were not. The rest of the room was arranged around two long, low couches and a great armchair in front of a cold hearth. A gasolier hung on the opposite side of the room, providing the only illumination.

"It was piped for gas?"

"Yes, about ten years ago, while I was off at university. It's quite handy in such a large house." Augustine crossed to the hearth and reached for the wood stacked nearby.

"I can imagine." She stepped into the center of the room and turned slowly. There was one bank of windows, but they were covered in heavy curtains, the better not to let in a draft. A writing desk was tucked into the far corner and looked largely unused. "You have quite the collection. Have you traveled much?"

"Some," he said. "But many are either from Great Breltain originally, or I purchased them from travelers."

"The skulls?" she asked.

He straightened for a moment, looking around at them as if he'd forgotten they existed. "Do they bother you?"

"I'm not sure," she said. "I . . . I've never seen them. I mean, I've seen drawings, and I've seen our cook defleshing a few animal heads, but it's a little different, looking at a skull and knowing it was once inside a person."

And yet her own curiosity was stirred again, the way it had been when she looked at Mr. Renton's twisted bowel.

"Medical training attracts odd people, and makes us even odder." He offered a self-conscious smile, then crouched back down at the hearth.

Jane watched for a moment, reflecting that in a normal house, the fire would be lit from its own coals, or with coals from another fire—but Lindridge Hall wasn't a normal house. She hesitated to even call it a *home*. It was . . . a building. Only that.

No wonder he wanted her to leave before sundown. She only wished he would come with her.

"Should I call for Mrs. Purl?"

"I'm entirely capable of lighting my own fire," he said, and so saying began working steel against flint.

She found herself appreciating the flex of his coat across his shoulders, and returned her attention to the skulls. "Where *did* these skulls come from?"

"The animal skulls are largely from my friends who hunt for sport. The human skulls . . . several were specimens my primary instructor kept. They were from his own patients. They all have malformations or unusual injuries of some kind. The others are actually fakes, some made of plaster, but I find them amusing. Like the one on the shelf to the left of the windows, with the horns? Peddled as proof of demons walking among us. That's a child's skull, with two goat horns glued on with pitch. If you look closely, they tried to carve the skull itself in a few places, then abandoned it."

Satisfied that the fire was growing steadily, Augustine dusted off his hands and stood up. "They're bothering you," he said, coming to stand close to her, close enough that she could hear his breathing. Her thoughts grew muddy once more, and she fought to keep her wits.

"I enjoy learning the connections," she said, fighting the urge to move closer still. She kept her gaze fixed firmly on his eyes and away from his lips. "You have a brilliant mind, Augustine."

He laughed at that. "I have a suspicion you're the quicker-witted of us. You're certainly the more determined and adaptable."

"Am I?"

"I don't think, in your place, that I would be nearly so accepting, and yet also still curious," he said. "I wish . . ."

Jane waited, but he didn't finish the thought, staring off somewhere over her shoulder. He had gone somewhere else again, like he had in the carriage. It did not look like a happy place. Her resolve fractured, and she reached up and lightly touched his jaw, bringing him back to her. Her fingers trembled slightly. She did not know this dance, did not know what he would welcome, or what she could offer.

But she couldn't resist any longer.

Her touch brought him back to her. Augustine gazed into her eyes, then closed his, leaning his forehead against hers. His skin was warm.

"I should go see Mrs. Luthbright about the menu," he murmured.

He was right, but the thought of him leaving again conjured up anger in her breast. Just another few minutes, alone. Couldn't they have that? Long enough for them to sort out where they stood now that she wore his ring, long enough for her to untangle the snarl of emotions and desires that writhed inside her.

"Don't go," she whispered.

"Jane?" He pulled back, eyes open once more. He searched her face for some explanation.

She was too embarrassed to put it into words. "There *is* one last part to today's wedding," she blurted instead. "That is . . . if you're not going to come back with me to the surgery—"

"I can't," he said.

"If you're not," she continued, "then perhaps we should take the opportunity now to consummate the marriage."

Silence. She looked down, unable to meet his gaze.

"*Consummate the marriage,*" he repeated at last, and she expected frustration, perhaps even anger. And then he laughed, a breathy little thing. He folded his arms around her. His embrace was light, easy to escape from. Tentative.

She stepped closer, heart stuttering. Her hands settled against his chest. His next exhale ghosted over her lips. "So romantic, Mrs. Lawrence."

"I'm a businesswoman above all else, Dr. Lawrence," she countered, unsure if he was teasing or not. "What was it *you* said? *Consummated on mutually beneficial terms?*"

Augustine pulled back a fraction of an inch, a stunned but pleased expression on his face. "You memorized that?"

"It was hard not to." She cringed, fingers curling lightly into her waistcoat. "I've thought of it—often."

"As have I," he confessed, voice dropping to a husky note. His throat worked, and his thumb stroked her cheek.

Her toes curled in her shoes, unbidden, and the urge to kiss him returned, nearly overwhelming her. But she still resisted. She had pushed them too far ahead once more. They should discuss this properly, at a safe distance—if they both were comfortable, truly comfortable, with this change to their plans.

And yet she could only resist so much. She did not kiss him, no, but she whispered, "Will you have me?"

A knock cut off any response.

He pulled away, smoothing out the rumpled front of his waistcoat. "Yes?" His cheeks were stained as red as hers felt.

"Pardon the interruption, Doctor, but Mrs. Luthbright has asked for you downstairs."

Augustine shot Jane an apologetic look. She shrugged. What excuse could they offer?

None at all. Augustine touched her hand briefly, then went to the door.

CHAPTER EIGHT

JANE LINGERED IN the study for over half an hour, hoping Augustine would return to her, but it was the maid who came to fetch her.

She followed Mrs. Purl down to the dining room, where Augustine greeted her with a faint smile. He pulled her seat out for her, and she sat, gazing up at him. But shutters had closed across his features. The openness from before was gone, and she realized, when Mrs. Luthbright entered with the first course, that they had an audience. When he commented on the weather, and the likelihood of an autumn storm that night, she picked up the thread.

Mrs. Luthbright set out roasted river eels and fennel soup and a host of other dishes, made small for only the two of them but no less sumptuous for it. They spoke of nothing of substance as Mrs. Luthbright bustled in and out, and as they heard murmurs behind the door, Mrs. Purl commenting on their comportment.

"I hope dinner was to your liking?" Augustine said, when the dishes had been cleared. "I should have asked what you preferred."

"No, it was delicious," she said. She searched his face, waiting, hoping for an invitation to repair upstairs, or to another sitting room. An excuse for them to be alone again.

"It's been a long day," he said instead.

"It has," she agreed. She thought to say more, to be more forward, then caught sight of her reflection in the window. The sun sank low on the horizon, and the growing darkness outside, combined with the bright gas lighting, made the polished glass nearly impenetrable.

They'd run out of time.

Augustine rose and came around the table, offering his arm to her. She took it, reluctant and eager all at once, unsure of when she'd get to touch him again. Together, they went out into the main hall. The carriage was waiting outside, and Jane could see her traveling case safely loaded onto the back already.

He paused at the door, then looked at her, a myriad of emotions dancing over his face. What happened now? Did they shake hands? Did they kiss like amorous newlyweds? She wanted to reach out and touch him, wanted to beg him to let her remain just one night.

"I'll see you in the morning," she said instead.

Augustine nodded, summoning up a small smile. "I'm looking forward to it," he said. "You'd best get going."

As Jane watched Lindridge Hall recede behind her, its unkempt grounds and lowering gables fading into shadow, an acute loneliness settled around her. For the first time since her early childhood, she wouldn't be sleeping under the Cunninghams' roof, and though she liked Mr. Lowell well enough, she hardly knew him. She hardly knew Augustine, either—but he was her husband, and without him, and without her guardians, she was a woman under her own power, and at her own mercy.

She would have to get used to it. It was, after all, exactly what she'd asked for.

Jane rested her forehead against the window as her carriage rattled along, hoping its movements would jar the sentimental, almost fearful thoughts from her head. This was not the first time she had been left alone, she reminded herself. Her parents had joined the volunteer forces when the war had reached Camhurst, and then they had left her. They had sent her far away, to the home of one of her father's old friends, Mr. Cunningham. For those long hours in that crowded carriage into the heartland, still trembling from the shelling that had stopped only a few days before in a temporary cease-fire, she had been without a single person in the world.

She had survived then, and she could certainly survive a wedding night on her own.

They were only a half mile along the dirt road back to Larrenton when the rains started. At first, it was only a few scattered taps along the top of the carriage, but within minutes it was pouring, hammering on the roof and sheeting down the small glass windows. The water blotted out the hills they traveled through.

The carriage lurched, slowed abruptly, and listed to the left.

Jane reflexively pressed herself against the opposite wall of the carriage, but her weight wasn't enough to stop it from tipping, wavering on two of its wheels, and finally crashing over.

Outside, the horse screamed.

The impact threw her against the seat, and she curled up, trying to protect her head. Even on its side, the coach continued to move, sliding. Were they on a relatively flat portion of the road, or on one of the many ridges that wound their way through the hills?

Another inch. And another. She pulled herself to her feet, hunching almost double to stand in the much shorter width of the cab, and scrabbled for the door handle.

The carriage driver's shadow fell across the window and he hauled the door open from the outside. He leaned in, hat dripping and greatcoat-clad shoulders slick with rain, and grabbed her by the arms. With his help, she heaved herself from the cab and tumbled out onto the ground below. Rain swiftly plastered her hair to her face, destroying the careful coiffure Mrs. Cunningham had arranged for her that morning. And it was cold, so cold.

The driver left her side, and as she pulled herself to her feet in a tangle of wet silk, she saw him struggling to free the horse. The road had been washed out by a mudslide coming from the hill to her right, and the carriage was within a foot of the drop off to the dale below. The horse's every spasmodic lurch dragged it closer to the edge, the swift flow of water and crumbling earth promising disaster.

At last, the driver freed the horse. It shot to its feet and bolted. Jane watched it go, great hooves churning up the muddy soil.

Her driver swore viciously, then turned to her, feeling for his hat and righting it on his scalp. "Are you all right, ma'am?" he asked. "The mudslides, they come out of nowhere this time of year. I barely saw it before it hit us."

"Yes, just rattled," she said, looking back at the carriage. It had stopped its wild slide. "Your horse—"

"I'll find him." The driver came over to the carriage, reaching out and touching one of its wheels, then giving it a tug to see if he could right it. It didn't move. "Best that you wait here, ma'am."

At that, a great jag of lightning split the darkened sky, followed by a seemingly endless rolling boom. The rain came harder, and the wind with it. The carriage was useless for shelter, and the rain would only continue. She looked behind her, up the road toward Lindridge Hall.

Augustine would not be happy, but he would hate for her to be out here in the elements even more.

"No, we're not too far yet from my husband's house. I'll walk back," she said.

He frowned, looking past her. "Are you sure, ma'am? This isn't weather to be out in."

"I will be out either way," she said. "Find your horse and get yourself somewhere dry, sir. I'll be safe."

The driver hesitated, then tipped his hat and turned from her, taking off at a jog. He looked over his shoulder only twice, both times at his carriage.

Her case—where was her case? It was no longer on the back shelf. She peered over the edge of the road for it down below, but it wasn't there, either. Turning in a wide circle, she finally spotted it thrown some distance behind the carriage. There was nothing in it to combat the rain, except for a hat, and she didn't relish the thought of soaking the rest of her clothing just to get it out. So instead, she hefted it into her arms and began to walk.

The slip that had formed so disastrously on the surface of the road with the initial rains was quickly giving way to true mud, and as she walked, the weight of her gown and her case made her boots sink in deep. Each step was met with a great sucking pull at her soles, and she quickly moved to the shoulder of the road, so that the grass might provide her some protection from the earth's covetousness. Half a mile was nothing on a sunny day, or when she intended to be out in bad weather, but now, with the rain beating on her shoulders and thunder cracking the sky every few minutes, every yard was a small victory. The night chill was settling fast into her bones, rattling in her chest. She clawed her fingers more tightly around the case, hugging it to her.

At last, she rounded the bend and saw Lindridge Hall looming once more out of the darkness. Night had descended entirely, and only one light burned in the manor's many windows. But between the lightning flashes and a lingering, unearthly grayness from above, she could make out its form. She hurried for it, nearly tripping over her sodden skirts, and threw herself upon the doorstep.

Dropping her traveling case at her feet, she brought her fist down on the heavy wooden door, and waited, panting, for a response. The cold tore at her lungs. The portico shielded her from the rain, but not from the winds, and she was growing more frigid every minute that passed.

She banged on the door again, her hands stinging. Then, desperate, she retreated from beneath the portico and craned her head back. The light in the window was still there, unchanging. There were no shadows moving in front of it. No other sign of life.

But that made no sense; she hadn't been gone more than an hour, and even if Mrs. Purl and Mrs. Luthbright had gone home before the storm crashed upon them, Augustine must still be inside. Surely he wouldn't leave somebody to freeze on his doorstep. And yet the front door remained resolutely shut, and Jane realized she was afraid.

She was stranded. The cold felt colder, her hammering pulse heavier and more final. She had to get inside. But he would never hear her shouting through the stone walls.

She returned to the door and tried the latch.

It gave.

Jane stumbled inside, holding back a relieved sob, and dragged her case in behind her with a dull screech across the polished floor, into the thick darkness of the foyer. The door shut behind her. Small blue lights danced in the dark overhead.

The gasoliers. She felt her way to the wall, then along it, hands questing across the wallpapered plaster. There would be a switch. There would be a—

Her fingers found a dial, set in an ornate housing, and she twisted it. Light sprang into being, bathing the foyer in a soft glow.

She sagged against the wall, then pulled away, afraid of staining the paper.

"Augustine!" she called out, retreating back to her case, shivering as her soaked gown clung to her skin. "Augustine, it's me, Jane! Are you there?"

A dull noise echoed from above. She grabbed her case and hauled it with her up the stairs, to the second floor, down the hall to the study. She lit the gas sconces with the dials she passed, blessing Mrs. Purl for leaving them all lit with a pilot instead of extinguishing them for the night. It was the only path she was certain of, and she hoped, desperately, that that was where the light had been shining from.

That it was Augustine who had made the noise.

"Augustine!" she called again, and again there was no response. Her skin was gooseflesh. All she wanted was a hot bath, a change of clothing. If she doubled back, if she went to his room . . . she could do that herself, couldn't she?

But why hadn't he come to the door? For all he knew, she could have been a patient. She could have been Mr. Lowell. He was so dedicated a physician; why hadn't he come?

She at last reached the study door, the gap between it and the floor glowing warmly, invitingly.

And then it went dark.

She dropped her case with a heavy thud and pressed both hands to the door. "Augustine," she said, voice catching. "Are you there?"

What if it wasn't him?

Jane shuddered. This was ridiculous. She was still overwrought from the carriage crash, and she was cold, and if only Augustine would open the door, it would all be made right. It would all—

The door opened a half inch.

The light from the hall spilled in across him, revealing wide eyes, pale skin. His hair was wild, and his posture was of a man hunted. His fingers held tight to the doorframe in terror.

And then she blinked, and he was himself again.

"Jane?"

"The road washed out," she stammered, brushing at her sodden gown, self-conscious. "You didn't answer the door. Why didn't you answer the door?"

He said nothing. His mouth worked, and his face flushed with shame, but he made no sound.

A heavy shiver wracked her body.

"You'll catch your death," he said reflexively. "A hot bath. I'll go draw one." Mechanically, he walked past her. He trembled, though he clenched his fists tightly in an attempt to disguise it. What had happened? Where had her husband gone, the man who could leap into action when the worst horrors were brought through his surgery doors?

"What if I had been Mr. Lowell, come to fetch you to a patient?" she asked.

He stopped, silent, then at last turned back to her. "Is the driver all right?" he asked, and as she watched, Augustine covered the last of his weakness by drawing his doctor's duty around him like a mantle. "Is anybody injured?"

"No, not that I know of."

"Are *you* all right?" He searched her face, as if seeing her for the first time.

"Yes," she said. "Just cold, and tired, and scared. Augustine—"

"Good. A hot bath," Augustine said, more firmly this time. "And some tea and brandy, then . . ." He glanced at the window. "Then bed, if you really are to remain here."

He sounded so disturbed by the idea that she fell back a step. "You wouldn't really send me back to Larrenton in this storm, would you?" she asked. "It's only one night. I—"

"Of course I wouldn't," he said. But he kept a distance between them that felt different from his unease that first night at the Cunninghams', and different from their calculated dance after their kiss. "I'm sorry, Jane. I'm not myself just now. Lindridge Hall is not the best for my nerves. A howling storm isn't wonderful for them, either, when you're not sure if all the windows will hold through the night. But my room is safe, regardless; you'll stay here, and in the morning if my regular carriage doesn't come, I'll see if I can't borrow Mr. Purl's horse and ride out and see how bad the damage is."

"I called for you," she said. "You didn't answer."

He ducked his head. "I thought—I thought I was dreaming," he said.

Dreaming. She'd caught him half awake, confused. Of course. That made all the sense in the world. Relief loosened the tight knots of her shoulders a fraction of an inch. "You're not dreaming," she said. She reached out to touch him, but he evaded her smoothly. "Perhaps—perhaps my presence will make you feel a little safer tonight?"

He laughed, though it was weaker than he usually sounded. "Lindridge Hall cannot be fixed by company and good cheer alone, I'm afraid."

She stooped to grab her case, her fingers stiff and sluggish. She followed him down the hallway to his bedroom, and then, inside, to the small washroom. It housed a deep porcelain tub. He stepped around her to turn the taps and after a few rattling pops in the walls, water splashed down into the basin. A push of a button on the wall-mounted geyser set it steaming.

It looked like bliss.

She turned to him, unsure what to expect next.

"Where will you sleep?" she asked at last.

"In my study, I suppose. My bed is too small for the both of us."

"Is there no other? Your parents', perhaps?"

"Trust me, my room will be more comfortable, and warmer. I'll leave you to your bath."

She had half a thought to ask for his aid, but he wanted to flee every second he remained with her. *Embarrassed.* Of the house, and of his ill response to her appearance. "Of course," she said, giving him quarter. "I'm freezing."

Augustine turned to the door, then paused and came back to her. "A part of me is still afraid I'm dreaming you," he confessed.

Her heart ached. "You're not," she said, and touched his face, as lightly as she dared.

He clasped her fingers for just a moment, his skin hot against hers. And then he left the room and shut the door behind him.

CHAPTER NINE

S HE WOKE SEVERAL hours after first light to the sound of voices far
off in the hall. They weren't the voices of the Cunninghams, or of Mr.
Lowell and a patient, but after a disoriented moment, she remembered
where she was. The mudslide. Augustine's nerves.

That wasn't how she'd planned her wedding night.

She wasn't sure exactly what she'd imagined, but it hadn't been a storm,
hadn't been her husband's strange confusion and fear. Was he all right?
Could a man truly believe his wife wasn't real?

Augustine was too young to have served in the war, but that didn't mean
he couldn't have memories clinging to him like a shroud. After all, hadn't
she herself balked at just the idea of returning to Camhurst? She had spent
years tucking away those terrible memories of the shelling and the gas attacks where she would not think of them, and yet she still had nightmares
occasionally. Maybe that was what she had roused him from, and why he
was too afraid to stay at his surgery, where anybody could hear his weakness, or see him wandering his halls, disoriented and fearful.

Or maybe he stayed out of sentiment, despite whatever nightmares plagued him here. People were irrational. So was she, wanting to be close to him, hoping he still felt the same feelings she did despite their awkward courtship, the rules they had both begun from that they now seemed destined to break one by one.

Was it so strange that he might stay here for similarly strong emotions, illogical but impossible to resist?

Just at the edge of her hearing, she could make out Augustine's voice. With the sun so high already, he would surely be on his way back to Larrenton. She was amazed he hadn't already gone. She pulled herself from his bed and dragged on her housecoat, slipped on a pair of shoes, and made her way out of the bedroom and toward the foyer.

Down by the door, Augustine clutched his bag, talking with Mrs. Purl. It was Mrs. Purl who caught sight of Jane first, and Augustine followed the line of her gaze, turning and smiling up at her. Daylight illuminated his face, and he looked healthy. Well rested.

"Good morning, Mrs. Lawrence," he said. "Did you sleep well?"

"Yes," she said, descending the stairway, marveling at how *Mrs. Lawrence* curled her toes. At her approach, Mrs. Purl quietly excused herself and disappeared down the hallway that led back to the kitchen. "Has the road cleared?"

"Not yet," he said. "I'll be taking Mr. Purl's horse into town. If it's safe enough by midday for carriages to be out, I'll send somebody to retrieve you. Otherwise, you may have to stay another night."

"That wouldn't be so bad."

He hesitated only briefly, then asked, "Can I send you anything from town?"

She had two clean gowns in her valise, and bringing more would be troublesome without a carriage. She would manage. But there was one thing. "A parcel may have arrived for me from Camhurst," Jane said. "A mathematical treatise. If Mrs. Cunningham drops it off, I would very much like to see it."

"Of course," he said. "And you may have the whole use of my study."

She couldn't stop herself from smiling.

"Mrs. Luthbright will have breakfast set out for you in the dining room in a little bit," he added. "I will miss you today. At the surgery."

He looked very much as if he wished to reach out and touch her. She stepped closer, the hem of her skirt brushing over his shoes.

"Forgive me, Mrs. Lawrence," he murmured. "I treated you horribly last night. It's been . . . a long time, since I've had guests. Since I've had to remember *how* to have guests."

"I'm not a guest. I would never judge you," she assured him. In fact, she was perversely grateful that the storm had wiped out the road and thereby brought her this far into his confidence.

"I wanted you to be here so badly," he said, "that when I heard your voice, I feared I had conjured you from nothing."

"But I am here, now. Truly." She thought, for a moment, to tell him about her own fears, memories of the shelling, the gas attacks, all her childhood pains. She stopped short, unsure of how it would help—but what a strange feeling, to want to share them.

At last he reached for her. He cupped her cheek, his thumb stroking her skin as he gazed into her eyes. "I must apologize for how foolish I was, thinking that you staying the night here would pose any problem at all. In fact, having you here made everything that much easier."

She felt a surge of pride at that. "If the roads are clear, I would very much like to stay the night again. With you. Will you consider it?"

He hesitated. Barely a breath, but she caught it and the slight tensing of his jaw. "I would still ask you to return to the surgery," he said, though he kept his tone light. "Mr. Lowell will need the night off."

She *had* agreed to those terms, and she would live up to them until they both agreed she need not. "He will," she said. "I understand."

"I do have something for you, though." He pulled a thin book from his bag. "My monograph, on Mr. Aethridge. I thought you might like to read it."

"Of course," she said. She took it from him and opened it to the frontispiece, where Augustine's name was printed in large, bold letters. "How horrid is it, though? The illness, I mean, not the writing."

"Well, I wouldn't recommend it for bedtime reading," he said. "Even with all of the medical theory laid on top of it, it is a terrifying tale. He was always in good cheer, but sometimes, when I think of what he went through, his body turning to bone around him until he could no longer move—it's not the best for the nerves even on a good day."

"I shall take that into consideration," she said. "But you may be surprised to learn that I have nerves forged of steel."

"I'm not surprised at all," he said, tucking an errant strand of hair behind her ear. That single touch made her feel half drunk. "I'll see you this evening."

"I look forward to it," she said.

He looked at her for another long moment, drinking in the sight of her in his foyer like a patient tasting rich broth for the first time in weeks, and then he turned from her, took up his oiled coat, and left the hall.

DRAPED IN DAYLIGHT, Lindridge Hall was still undeniably strange. Hallways did not run in sensible lines, and the house sprawled more than it needed to, given the rooms it contained. She found several fake doors that only confused her more. On the third floor, the pressed-tin ceilings were embossed with intricate geometric patterns, eschewing the more common botanical inspirations. More than once, as Jane wandered the halls that morning, clutching the chatelaine she had borrowed from Mrs. Purl, she would catch a glimpse of a room or the angle of a hallway and think that she saw some grander design to it, some shape that was only visible from a certain perspective. And then the illusion would disperse.

The things that made Augustine feel ashamed—the undusted gasoliers, the wainscoting with its chipped paint, the worn, mildewing runners in the hall—all barely registered in the face of such undefinable oddities.

She drew back dusty curtains to let the watery sunlight spill inside the house, and wondered at the small things she found abandoned. An iron candlestick with a half taper of melted wax here, a sheaf of pianoforte music there . . . all of them fragments of a life that had once been lived here. Beyond those shards of history, the rooms were empty, suppurating with an omnipresent damp. The west wing of the third floor smelled of must and rot, and it only grew stronger as she opened the last door onto the library.

Ceiling-high, empty bookshelves surrounded dusty chairs and tables. A great arching bowl of green glass, condensation running down its metal girding, crowned the room and trapped moisture within. Some of the panes no longer fit well in their frames, and rain entered along the seams, flowing down to where it had begun to rot away at the floorboards. The stench of mildew was relentless.

It had been abandoned, just like all the rest. This entire grand house, abandoned. How did that happen?

And yet how beautiful it must have been when the glass was polished and the sun shone in undisturbed, when the room smelled of wood smoke and paper and ink! She could have spent days lost in stories there. But now, here, she left it with a saddened heart.

At the stairs, she met Mrs. Purl, who was carrying something dark in her arms. It was sooty, the surface cracked like a half-burnt log, but the shape was all wrong. "Strangest thing, ma'am," Mrs. Purl said when she noticed Jane looking. "I found it in the old master bedroom. But I am sure I cleaned the whole room last week, and there have been no fires there since I came here. It must be new, though the ashes seemed very old."

"What is it?"

"A doctor's bag, I think. But I can't imagine why it would have been burned." She shifted it in her grip and the contents rattled—metal and glass. She looked uneasy, holding it, and Jane held out her hands.

"I can take it," Jane said. "I'll get it cleaned up."

"It's no trouble, ma'am."

"I have little else to do," Jane said, and Mrs. Purl passed the bag to her. It was heavy and cold.

Mrs. Luthbright was not in the kitchen when she arrived, so she took the bag straight over to the basin sink. She eased it open, wiggling free the stubborn catch. Its structure held, revealing pockets filled with broken glass, several scalpels, and other tools she was not as familiar with.

Mrs. Purl was right. Why burn such a thing? The tools were of fine make, and aside from the fire damage she could see no other defect.

Jane fished out each shard of glass, piling them off to the side. The bag was likely unsalvageable, but it was an easy place to start. From there, she freed the larger tools, pieces of metal and horn she didn't know the names for, and several clamps, delicate when compared with those used by carpenters but horrible when she thought of them applied to flesh. She washed them all under the tap with slivers of castile soap, then set them out to dry much as if they were silverware.

She'd learned a thing or two about instrument preparation from Mr. Lowell over the past week, most notably when she had assisted Augustine in what he'd called a pupillary incision surgery. She'd watched as he had taken a scalpel to an old woman's eye, clouded over from an old injury and exposed by a metal spreader, and cut a slit that, he said, would become her new pupil, restoring some measure of sight.

The woman had thrashed when her eyelids had been opened, and had moaned from the ether, but when the surgery was done, she had thanked Augustine over and over again. The paradox of medicine: pain and relief, life and death.

She was cleaning the second scalpel when she slipped and cut the tip of her finger.

The metal clattered into the sink, and she hissed, closing her eyes against the pain. When she opened them again, crimson blood was spattered along the sides of the basin, tainting the water as it spiraled down the drain. Grimacing, she shoved her hand beneath the tap and squeezed at her finger until the blood finally slowed.

She eyed the rest of the implements warily. There were only a few left, and she made short but careful work of them, ever mindful of another prick.

CHAPTER TEN

BACK IN THE foyer, Jane gazed up at the staircases and the gallery walkway, considering resuming her explorations where she'd left off. Aside from Augustine's room and study, she'd seen very little of the second floor. But to her left stretched another hallway, and even with her knowledge of the rest of the house, she couldn't picture where it might lead. She followed it.

There were only a few rooms branching from that hall: servants' quarters or storage closets, only one of which was in active use by Mrs. Purl. Jane almost turned back. But then she saw a glint of metal in the dim light at the far end of the hall. There were no windows, and the gaslights did not extend all the way to where a door stood, shut tight. And yet the light caught, glittering, and drew her closer.

The door was sealed with a line of three old keyholes, and one newer padlock; that was what had glinted in the dark. It was attached to the door and frame by brackets that looked much weaker than the lock itself, out of place and hastily applied.

Frowning, she tried each of the keys on her chatelaine. The keyhole locks gave way, but the padlock remained steadfast.

She ran her thumb across the metal. It was bitingly cold, and she pulled away with a wince and a flash of reflexive, alien dread. The chatelaine fell from her hand. It swung from where it was attached to her dress, rattling in the silence of the hall.

What could be so wrong with a room that it would be locked up so tightly?

That the servants could not access it?

She stared at the padlock for a long time, waiting for her mind to present a solution, waiting to laugh, to be ready to move on. But instead, she only imagined breaking the brackets, smashing the door open, and looking inside.

Air. She needed air, to clear her head of these strange thoughts. She forced herself away from the door and upstairs to Augustine's room, where she determinedly switched out her house shoes for her mud-caked boots from the night before.

The grounds outside of Lindridge Hall were ill-kept, rambling hillocks of dead shrubberies, all of it overgrown with vines now bare from the season. The rains had held off so far this morning, but the soil was still damp and spongy, and the sky was gray from horizon to horizon. No birds sang, not even as she climbed a low, sloping hill to the house's left, the top of which was covered in the outmost edges of a young forest.

Everything was still.

When she'd come to Larrenton, not even ten years old, soon to be an orphan and shell-shocked by the violence that had descended upon Camhurst, she hadn't known how to feel about such wide open spaces. She'd lived all her life in an apartment in the center of Great Breltain's capital. She'd been torn between the terrible fear of being exposed and alone beneath a menacing sky, and the stranger feeling of peace. Now she could see over a mile in every direction.

She was alone, and wasn't that a good thing?

Down below, on the road, a dark figure moved fast astride a horse. *Augustine.* Her heart leapt in her chest, and she found the last of her nerves fading away. She'd tell him about the tools, and about the locked door, and he'd have a sensible explanation for everything. He would tease her for fearing padlocks while accepting his medical curiosities, his skulls, and they would turn to more substantial topics, patients and plans and fascinations. They would return to Larrenton. Together.

She picked her way back down the hill. A few times the ground gave way beneath her foot, compressing into a slick slide, but she managed not to twist her ankle. Finally on level with the house, she quickened her pace.

But the rider, who now stood in front of the door, wasn't Augustine.

It was Mr. Lowell.

Jane slowed to a walk, then stopped entirely at the foot of the small set of stairs leading up to the door. "Mr. Lowell," she said, causing him to start, then twist to face her. "Is everything all right? Dr. Lawrence should have arrived in town by now."

"Aye, he did," Mr. Lowell said. "Sent me with his apologies, ma'am."

She frowned. "Apologies?"

"He won't be able to make it back tonight. The road is still washed out this far, and he wants to be on call for night emergencies. I'm actually here to return Mr. Purl's horse, and give this package to you."

"And how will you get back? Surely he's not expecting you to walk."

"There's a carriage waiting by the farms. The road is still intact between there and Larrenton, heavens be praised." He considered a moment, then said, "Pardon my asking, ma'am, but I could likely get you to it, if you wanted. There was only so much I could bring with me. If you'd rather be at home . . ."

She almost agreed. But the clouds seemed darker now, heavier with rain than they had been just a few minutes ago. She was not eager to chance another carriage wreck.

And Lindridge Hall was just a house; she had seen its roof rotting from her vantage on the hill. There would be no danger here, except of nervous fancies.

"No, it makes more sense to stay. What did the doctor send?"

Mr. Lowell smiled and went over to the horse, which was tethered to the bare-branched husk of a young, dead tree. He opened one of the panniers and pulled out a bundle wrapped in oilcloth. She took it from him, feeling the familiar weight of books. By the size, she suspected at least one of them was the surgery ledger.

"He said you'd be inclined to work," Mr. Lowell said. "So I gathered up some of the accounts from around the surgery."

"Thank you," Jane said, smiling. Augustine already knew her well. Idle wandering wasn't fit for her spirit. Work would set her back to rights.

"There's also a package Mrs. Cunningham came by to drop off."

"The treatise I've been waiting on! Thank you again, Mr. Lowell."

He grinned and tipped his hat. "Glad to be of help. And you're sure you don't want to go back?"

"Not just yet." She hugged the package to her chest. "Send my regards?"

"Of course, ma'am. And with any luck, they'll have that bit of the road shored up by tomorrow."

THE RAINS BEGAN again less than an hour after Mr. Lowell's departure. She settled herself in a front sitting room, where she could hear the comforting sounds of Mrs. Luthbright going about her day. Mrs. Purl came and went, leaving tea and a stoked fire in the hearth.

Mr. Lowell had packed her the large ledger book she had begun for Augustine, as well as haphazard records of occasional payments from patients who feared later debt, and orders he had sent away to Camhurst for. Behind it was her mathematical treatise and a slim volume she hadn't seen before. But she ignored all of those in favor of a letter, for it bore Mrs. Cunningham's familiar handwriting.

Sipping her tea, Jane opened the seal and spread the paper out on the desk. She donned her glasses (also thoughtfully packed), and read:

To our dearest Jane,
You looked so lovely on your wedding day, full of a life we haven't seen in you in many years. I do apologize for the parade, which, knowing your temperament, might have been overwhelming, but we could not let our final child leave our home uncelebrated, and

we knew that if we told you our plans, you would reject them. I hope you can forgive us our exuberance.

Mr. Cunningham and I are both very proud of you, you know. You are one of the few young people of our acquaintance who will directly identify and act on what you want with a detailed plan, and while Mr. Cunningham likes to take much of the responsibility for that, I think it rests entirely on you. You have always been very special.

And how is your doctor husband? Mr. Cunningham and I watched the two of you together, during the ceremony and throughout the parade. We suspect that it's perhaps less of a business match than you had originally planned. Though your situation is unique, it is not so far removed from the commonplace. Most marriages, arranged or not, are begun knowing next to nothing about your spouse. Mr. Cunningham and I were such a couple, as were your parents. Most who marry under their own desires do not see that. They believe they know the other person, even if they met them only a month past, even if they have never seen their beloved in all seasons. You simply have no illusions. And trust, from my experience, that knowing your partner from the start has little bearing on happiness. The things we didn't know were pleasant surprises, generally. I have faith you'll find the same.

I implore you to move forward with an open heart and open eyes. Your plan to serve as little more than his employee is understandable. Numbers have always made things easier for you. But if you will take the advice of an old lady, be patient. And listen to him. You'll learn a lot by listening.

With all my love,
Deborah Cunningham

Jane traced Mrs. Cunningham's signature with her thumb, smiling at the page. They hadn't always understood each other, but Mrs. Cunningham had always been an earnest, loving woman, not quite a mother but close enough to count. She was also perceptive in a way that had Jane blushing. No, this was not just a business match. Not anymore.

Jane was just about to set aside the letter when she saw on the back of the page a small postscript:

> P.S. In the aftermath of your wedding parade, I spoke with several well-wishers, schoolmates from your time in Sharpton. It seems Dr. Lawrence acted as relief to Dr. Morton there, while Dr. Morton was dealing with his illness. Lindridge Hall is much closer to Sharpton than it is to Larrenton, and they expressed surprise that he had not returned after his government posting, as they were all quite fond of him. I know not what we have to thank for our good fortune, but I am grateful he chose our town, if only for your own happiness.

Sharpton—she had not thought much about her school days in recent years. Strange, to think they might have seen each other in passing back then. There was much about Augustine she did not know, Jane reflected. Not just his nature and desires, but his history as well. She found herself looking forward to hearing more of it, as much as she desired to share her own past with him.

She let herself drift with idle fancy a while longer, then turned to the ledgers.

As always, work was a relief. It quieted her other thoughts, helped melt away the hours. The rains, though gentler than they had been the night before, grew relentless, and the chances of the road being opened tomorrow were dwindling. The clouds also blotted out the afternoon sun far sooner than it would have set, and even after Mrs. Purl came by to turn up the gaslights, Jane soon stopped and capped her ink, rubbing her eyes.

Mrs. Luthbright and Mrs. Purl were once again in earshot, speaking in the dining room as they set out her supper. Jane rose and went to the sideboard, pouring herself a small measure of drink. She did not mean to eavesdrop, but their voices were soothing, and she drew close enough to make out the words.

"Mr. Purl ought to stop coming 'round to bring me home, when I can walk just as well," Mrs. Purl was saying. "He's going to get himself lost or thrown some night, with these rains. And you know, just last week, I was already in bed when he rides in over the hill between here and there, smelling like whiskey, and asks me about the 'red-eyed woman.' I kept telling him there is no woman, or if there is he'd better not tell me about her."

"It's a spirit," Mrs. Luthbright said, all solemn sobriety. "He should wear his shirt inside out when he comes by, so as not to be bewitched by it."

"It's a spirit, all right." Mrs. Purl snorted. "A spirit made of barley. He says he went to knock at the front door here, but the lights were all out, so he turned to go. And then there she was, looking at him. But, I ask you, if there was a spirit living in the house, wouldn't we have seen it? In these past three months, I can honestly tell you I haven't seen a single thing, here or on the path back home."

Jane did not believe in spirits, and yet she had to suppress a shiver at the thought.

"Truly, it must be a ghost," Mrs. Luthbright said. "Don't you remember that nice carriage that came by here two years ago, a few months before they closed up the hall?"

"There were always nice carriages back then," Mrs. Purl responded, slowly. "So no, not as such."

"A young woman moved into the house. From Camhurst."

Jane frowned. A young woman from Camhurst. A sister, perhaps? Or a cousin? Perhaps even one of his schoolmates, a fellow surgeon.

"And how do you claim to know this?"

"Mrs. Young reminded me of it, just last night." Mrs. Luthbright's voice dropped low, and Jane crept closer to the doorway, drawn as a moth to fire. "A few months after the woman moved in, the undertakers came up the lane, but there was never any funeral. And then the doctor's family up and left, and boarded up the hall."

A young woman, undertakers, no funeral.

The pit of her stomach filled with ash. It meant nothing at all, and yet the dread was back, sevenfold, all the relief of her work dashed.

"I've never heard of any of this," Mrs. Purl said. "I think Mrs. Young is just trying to scare you."

Mrs. Luthbright said nothing for a long stretch, the only sound the soft tap of silverware being set out. "I did see something, once," Mrs. Luthbright finally confessed.

"When?" Mrs. Purl demanded, sounding eager.

"But it wasn't a woman."

"Of course it wasn't a woman," Mrs. Purl scoffed, but Jane could picture her leaning in, thrilled by this old-world, superstitious talk.

"It was more like a shadow," Mrs. Luthbright said. "That time I stayed a bit past sundown, because the doctor wasn't home yet and I didn't want to leave the soup cold on the stove. I was in the dining room for just a minute, putting out the candlesticks I'd polished. There was something there, in the hallway."

"No!"

"Truth, Genevieve. Absolute truth. I saw it with my own eyes. It walked past the door, and I thought maybe the doctor had come in quietly, but then he rode up a few minutes later."

"Did you tell him?"

"And be discharged? Don't be silly."

"He wouldn't do that!"

"Can never be sure."

"True enough."

Their voices faded and she heard the kitchen door swing shut. Jane tried to remember how to breathe. The stories—they were haphazard. Half-truths, rumors, ramblings of drunken men. None of the pieces fit together, and the environment did tend to influence one's thoughts. A crumbling house, alone on the hill, was enough to make isolated women given to wild imaginings, herself included.

But then she thought of Augustine, afraid she wasn't real, frightened by the storms.

All that meant was that it affected them all in similar ways. She had slept well last night, but how many times, in the past, had she woken up disoriented and anxious, with her thoughts tumbling with numbers, sums that made no sense and ledgers that rearranged themselves? There was nothing for it but to wait for the unsteadiness to pass, as he had.

Dinner was quiet and simple, baked eggs with gravy. As she ate, she heard the rattle of Mrs. Purl closing the house up for the night. Strange, that the night before it had been left unlocked, but she assumed the two women must have been in a hurry to get home.

By the time she was finished, the dining room had grown dark, with long shadows stretching across the table, the gasolier suspended above not turned up bright enough to illuminate the whole room. Jane rubbed her brow as she stood.

She was halfway to the door when something moved in the corner of her eye. Jane turned to find nothing, save for her reflection in the darkened window. But for just a moment, her reflection looked short, hunched perhaps, and Jane frowned, stepping closer.

Her reflection had red eyes.

CHAPTER ELEVEN

WHEN JANE BLINKED, her reflection was her own again.

She took a deep breath. The servants' ghost stories had clearly frayed her nerves. She was not normally so given to jumping at shadows, and she would do well to stop it now, before it could worsen. Work; work was still the antidote to her girlish frights. Numbers, sums, and organization would set her right.

She took her emptied dishes to the kitchen, then retrieved her books and repaired upstairs, forcing herself to turn down every light on the way. In the study, she added logs to the banked coals and tended the hearth until between it and the gasolier above, the room was warm and bright. She ignored the strange shadows cast by the skulls on the shelves and settled down at the desk.

Working through the remainder of the ledger should have taken at most an hour, but her mind fought the yoke of focus every step of the way. She glanced over her shoulder at the slightest sound, and found herself flinching each time she looked up at the window and saw herself reflected there.

"Just ghost stories," she admonished herself. "And you've never believed in ghosts."

Never ghosts, never spirits, never monsters; her parents and the Cunninghams had raised a practical girl who knew better than to fear the unknown when she could fear bombs and armies. She had always been the logical one, the child obsessed with rules and procedure and schedule. A practical girl was frustrated and annoyed when her plans were disrupted; she didn't feel this sort of distracting fear.

What was she becoming?

The last page of the old ledger had only three lines filled in, and once they were copied, she stared at them, willing them to create more. She didn't have the focus for her mathematical text, with its philosophical discussions on the implications of the number zero and its uses in novel arithmetics, and she was in no state to read Augustine's monograph on Mr. Aethridge, but her brain needed to be occupied.

What of the thin volume that had come tucked between the ledger books?

A quick glance inside revealed it to be Augustine's personal accounts, kept meticulously since he had begun his medical studies. The entries were written in the tight, messy script Augustine used when he wasn't taking his time, just like his first-draft patient notes, but after a week of going through his records, she could make out the majority of the words. There were notes for trips to clubs with friends, as well as entry after entry of university gowns, new equipment, daily meals.

She could learn a lot about Augustine from his ledger. She'd known Mr. and Mrs. Cunningham very well by the time she began keeping their books, and so she'd never realized it before, but here she could make out the edges of a man she'd only just begun to know. Where and how he ate, if he cared enough about food to mark it (and he did, at least in his younger years, eating out frequently and recording specific dishes), where he traveled, what sort of apartment he kept . . . it all spread out at her fingertips.

She dawdled in his young life, luxuriating in now-meaningless indulgences. She found his time in Sharpton, two years prior. Her thoughts went to Mrs. Luthbright's story, and the arrival of the undertakers, and so she skimmed ahead, through his return to the capital, and then a town on the far southern border—the government posting Mrs. Cunningham had mentioned.

Finally, she reached his arrival in Larrenton.

Jane turned to the back half of the accounting book, then pressed a ribbon into the gutter to mark the point of change. From there, she began copying out the relevant expenses line by line, making a small mark of her initials beside each original. She didn't go so far as to cross them out; she wasn't sure if he'd want to keep his funds somewhat commingled as they were now, or if he'd want to separate them out as she was doing. The record she was making might only serve as a quick reference, rather than as an active tool.

Food purchases, tea for the patients' families, restock of bandages—she copied the last two over—and . . .

A payment to a Mr. and Mrs. Pinkcombe for a large portion of his recorded balance, described only as *Elodie*. It was still marked as pending, though it had been entered nearly a month ago. Paging back to before he'd moved to Larrenton, Jane found similar entries every few months. None had actually been subtracted from the ledger balance, as if the Pinkcombes had rejected the cheques.

Elodie.

She shifted uneasily in her seat as she kept paging through the ledger. The *Elodie* entries persisted back to just shy of two years ago. Two years ago, when he had left Sharpton. Two years ago, when a woman had come to live at Lindridge Hall. Two years ago, when the undertakers had been called and all the Lawrences had left the area.

A red-eyed woman looked out from the windows when Mr. Purl came by in the evenings.

You will never stay the night at Lindridge Hall.

She sat back in her seat, limbs leaden, skin crawling. The timing might have been a coincidence, but Jane couldn't convince herself of it, even as a possibility. Something had happened to a young woman, perhaps named Elodie, and it had happened in this house.

Mrs. Cunningham had proclaimed Jane had married Augustine under no illusions, but no, she'd had them, basic ones she hadn't questioned the logic of. She'd assumed he was a good man, and that his reasons for keeping apart from the rest of the town were as harmless as her own requirements.

Could she have been that much of a fool, so deceived by her desires and his apparent kindness?

Elodie. She touched the entry in Augustine's ledger. It didn't matter. These cheques were never cashed. It wasn't a present threat to the stability of his practice. There could be other explanations, ones that weren't half so dark, but perhaps more lurid still. Perhaps there had been an affair with Mrs. Pinkcombe, perhaps a daughter named Elodie. Maybe a payment to a brothel. Neither was her business, and ghost stories even less so.

And yet she felt betrayed.

JANE DID NOT sleep that night. When the sun rose, she dressed and made her way down to the dining room for breakfast. But though dawn drenched the room in gold, it did not pierce the numbness she wore like a shield to guard against the uncertain pain inside her.

It was well-worn armor, crafted first in Camhurst, against the panic in the streets and the fetid gasses that had filled her lungs when the Ruzkans had begun their shelling. She had tempered it in Larrenton while she sat with strangers and waited to learn if she was an orphan. Now it stilled everything within and without her.

She passed the day walking the grounds, then inspecting the curiosities in the study. Malformations and disease. What did it mean, that Augustine kept them? She had assumed, before, that they were only the fascinations of an eccentric mind, but they were dark things, sometimes violent, often linked to death. Perhaps they should have been her first reason not to trust him. She traced the brittle wings of pinned insects and breathed away dust that crowded on fine metal objects, the purposes of which she could not guess.

She took her meals and twice attempted to shake off her bitterness. *It is not your business,* she told herself. *All men have such secrets. If you had followed his directives, if you had gone back to Larrenton before the storm or despite the storm, you might never have known to wonder.* But the pain remained, and so, too, did her shell.

A few hours before sunset, Augustine returned to Lindridge Hall.

As he alighted from his carriage, Jane left behind his ledgers on the study's desk, open to the first mention of Elodie in case she should require evidence. The house was silent around her, the very runner along the floor taut as if with a held breath, waiting for an answer.

She reached the landing overlooking the foyer just as Augustine asked Mrs. Purl, "Where is Mrs. Lawrence? Is she about? Is she well?" He hadn't seen her yet, and she took the moment to study him. Could a man's secrets be divined by the angles of his cheekbones, the curve of his shoulders?

"I've hardly seen her today," said Mrs. Purl. "Shall I fetch her?"

It was then that Augustine raised his eyes and spotted her. A bright smile blossomed over those features she'd been inspecting, and now, with his face tilted up to her, she could see no falsehood written in his skull. She gripped the banister and fought back the answering smile that wanted to erupt from her.

His expression fell.

Did he look guilty? Or merely worried? The shame of a man who had done her wrong, or the concern of a husband who fretted over her health? Her stomach somersaulted. The shell flexed, but did not crack. "Hello, Augustine," Jane said.

Mrs. Purl quietly took her leave.

"Jane," Augustine responded. He stepped forward and held out a hand. She hesitated; she did not want to touch him, and simultaneously she wished to fall into his arms, lose herself in the overwhelming certainty she'd felt just a day before. Balanced between the two, she descended the stairs, taking his hand at the final step.

"I'm sorry I left you here for so long," he said.

"I kept myself entertained."

"I hope you haven't been staring at sums this whole time."

Sums. Was he testing her? Or did he somehow not realize what his books had revealed? Her fingers tightened against his reflexively. "Oh, yesterday I explored the house," she said. *The house with a woman in the windows. The house with a locked door.*

Augustine tensed, as if he could hear her thoughts. "And did you find anything of interest?"

"Mrs. Purl found a bag of yours," she said, instead of all the rest.

He frowned. "A bag?"

"In the third-floor bedroom." She led him to the dining room. "It was in a fireplace, badly burned. Some of the scalpels were still fine, though, and I've cleaned them for you. Was it a very sick patient, then?"

In your parents' bedroom? She hadn't thought to question it, then, but suddenly it seemed all of a piece. How could it not be?

"Yes," he replied after a moment's thought. "Yes, several years ago. How strange, though, I can't imagine how we didn't have the hearth cleaned." He shoved his free hand into his pocket, but not before she noticed a tremor in it.

He hadn't known about the bag? Or he hadn't imagined she would find it?

"Augustine?"

"Sorry, it was a particularly unpleasant case," he murmured. "Difficult to think about." He stopped at the entrance to the dining room, turning and smiling up at her. "I did miss you," he said. "Greatly."

"And I, you," she said, half by reflex, half by desire. She hated herself immediately for it.

He must have seen the frustration in her. "There's a carriage," he said. "Down at the end of the drive. Are your things packed?"

"No," she said. "I had intended to stay tonight."

"The roads are clear now," he said, glancing not to the front door but to the stairs. "Jane—"

"Let us go in for dinner," Jane said. "I will pour us claret."

And she left him there without listening for argument. He followed faithfully.

The dining room was cleaner than it had been on their wedding night, the windows polished, the curtains drawn back to admit the gentle afternoon sun. There were no cobwebs, no dust hanging in the corners, and even the upholstery had been scrubbed. The wine glasses were newly cleaned, and she tried to feel pride in it as she poured the wine at the sideboard. The feeling didn't come.

They sat down at the table in silence, and a few minutes later Mrs. Luthbright emerged from the kitchen and laid out several steaming dishes for them. Augustine murmured a few words to her about sending the carriage away. Jane hid behind her meal, eating without taste. Each bite went down hard, scoring her throat.

How to begin?

When the cook had left, Jane decided to come at it from the side, the way it had struck her. "You know, Mrs. Luthbright believes the house is haunted."

His fork scraped against the ceramic of his plate as he gathered up more morsels of stewed venison. Sitting back in his chair, he chewed, swallowed, without expression, without hurry.

Jane's heart beat harder.

"I didn't know she was the superstitious type," he said, once he'd washed down his food with wine. "Do you agree with her?"

She resisted the urge to glance at the nearest window, searching for a woman with red eyes. "I don't really know," she said. "I haven't given it much thought."

"And does Mrs. Purl share Mrs. Luthbright's fears?"

"No, she doesn't," Jane said slowly. "Though she did say her husband has asked several times if you entertain guests."

"Mr. Purl is a notorious drunk," he said.

"So I've heard." Now. She must ask him now. Steeling her spine, she leaned in slightly. "Who is Elodie?"

His face went still and ashen, the way it had when Mr. Renton's life had slipped away beneath his scalpel.

When he gave no answer, she pressed the attack with dispassionate logic. "I finished going through your ledger books. Mr. Lowell included your personal expenses, I suspect not at your explicit request. The payments to the Pinkcombes—what are those for, Augustine?"

She expected him to beg out of answering, to tell her it wasn't appropriate dinner talk or that it was personal. Not suited to their potential lurking audience. But Jane didn't care; better to keep on, to corner him. She reached for one of her earliest hypotheses, ridiculous though it felt.

"Is she your child?" Jane asked.

His eyes shot open, and he . . . laughed.

"Lord, no," he said, shaking his head.

She flushed, embarrassed. He was keeping *something* from her; what did it matter if an explanation seemed out of character? What did she know of his character at all, really? "Well," she said, struggling to keep her composure, "who is she, then?"

"Was," he corrected, laugh failing in an instant, his expression turning to a grimace. "She was a patient I wasn't able to help."

"A patient," Jane repeated.

The way his face fell. Like when Mr. Renton died.

"I feel uniquely responsible for what happened to her. I've been trying to make amends with her family ever since, but they always turn it down. I suspect they hate me for trying, but I can't leave it."

"Was she the woman who lived here for a time? Who died?" Jane asked, desperate to prove to herself that *something* here was amiss.

His brow furrowed. "Where did you hear about that?"

"The servants," Jane said.

"Yes, she was," he said, running a nervous hand through his hair. "She's also the cause of that burned doctor's bag. She died of a terrible fever."

"A patient, here?"

He hesitated a moment, then shook his head. "She was the daughter of a close family friend. They didn't feel they could care for her at home, and they didn't trust her to the local physicians. I told them it was foolish, that I was ill-suited to care for her, but they insisted."

"And she died here."

"Yes. To my great shame."

Shame. Well, they had that in common.

She sat back in her chair, body softening. She was ill-suited to such isolation, it seemed, and returning to the surgery in the morning sounded more and more appealing. A little distance, and she'd stop jumping at shadows.

"A patient," Jane repeated, and she rubbed at her temples, willing her blood to leave her enflamed cheeks. "And here I thought you had some grand, dark secret."

"Really, a *child*?"

"A child, or—some standing arrangement with a mistress, who stopped accepting your payments years ago?"

That drew another laugh out of him. Leaning across the table, he reached out and took her hand. She gave it over to him gratefully, sheepishly, needing the warmth of his touch, the solid connection of it. "I promise, I have no such sordid history for you to discover."

"Truly?"

"Truly." He came around the table to her side, never letting go of her, and she rose to meet him. Gently, he cupped her face with his free hand. "I know our start these last few days hasn't been the most auspicious, but I swear to you, I am yours. Every inch save what this house demands of me."

Their lips were almost touching. He looked at her with longing, as if her suspicion had not disrupted anything between them. Jane's breath caught. Her heart quickened.

"I think I have been very foolish," she murmured.

He smiled. "No. Not foolish—cautious. Cautious but bold. Traits I admire greatly."

His thumb traced the line of her jaw. She was melting at his touch, in happiness and relief. Relief that, perhaps, she had not been foolish after all, that she had not let herself be misled.

That he was as good as she knew him to be.

"I was afraid that I would have to hate you," she confessed, intoxicated by his breath against her mouth, by the intensity of his gaze. "And angry that I had to."

He did not answer, but closed the bare distance between them and kissed her fervently, heedless of who might be listening, watching. She was momentarily stunned; he had touched her fondly the morning after their wedding, but that had been all, and she realized she'd thought, perhaps, he might not ever touch her so again, let alone with desire, with passion.

But no, it had only been the house between them. Bad nerves.

His kissed her slowly but with such intensity that her knees weakened, and she wrapped her arms around him as if to keep herself upright. His hand slid along her waist, down and around her hip, and nudged her closer to him.

What had she been afraid of? Nothing; there was nothing to fear, especially not as she drank him in, learning how to kiss by each touch of his lips. She followed him as he pulled away, as he took her hands again and led her after him.

On the second-floor landing, Augustine pulled her close once more, stealing another kiss, as if the distance between the top of the stairs and his bedroom was an unfathomable, unmanageable distance, as if he would die without another drink from her lips.

Then the bedroom, where he fumbled with the fasteners of her dress, and she with his waistcoat. She forgot to be ashamed of her nakedness as soon as she could see his shoulders, his collarbones, every inch revealed to her becoming a marvelous whole. She kissed him again, let him lead her to the narrow bed, tumbled to the mattress wrapped around him.

After, they lay quiet together among the pillows, tangled together. She studied him, how his dark hair clung to his skin from sweat, how his brow no longer held its near-constant furrow. He looked at ease, as at ease as she felt, and she stretched out along the sheets, breathing in that freedom.

What had she been afraid of?

Isolation was the culprit, not this house. The burned doctor's bag, Mr. Purl's drunken stories . . . why should she fear them?

She had only one question left, one last worry, inexplicable and whispering.

"What of the door?" she asked as she nestled beside him. "There are so many locks."

He was silent only a moment. Then he murmured, "It leads to the old cel-lar, but it's dangerous," pressing a kiss to her temple as he drew the coverlet over them. "The tunnels could collapse."

"What's down there?" she asked, eyelids heavy, voice thick.

"Nothing," he said. "Nothing at all."

CHAPTER TWELVE

SLEEP CAME, BUT did not remain for long. Sometime after midnight, rain drumming on the windows of Augustine's room, Jane rose and pulled on her nightgown. She'd woken up, overheated by her husband's body in the narrow confines of the bed. He had been right; it was not built for two.

And yet she could not help but feel pleased at the stiffness of her limbs. She looked down at him, wondering, a moment longer. He had wanted her, and she had wanted him in return, and it had been miraculously simple, past a certain point.

Buttoning her housecoat by touch, she shuffled across the bedroom floor until she reached the door to the hallway. With one last glance at the bed, she slipped out of the room, then felt for the knob mounted on the wall that would bring up the gas lighting. The study couch had been good enough for him, and so it would serve for her.

But though the couch proved comfortable, the hearth was cold, and the shadows cast by the skulls and other oddities unsettled her too much to sleep. She left the study behind and climbed up to the third floor instead, her mathematical treatise and Augustine's monograph on Mr. Aethridge clutched to her chest. The library hadn't been piped for gas lighting, likely due to the arching glass ceiling, but a candelabra was set on a small table by the door. She took it, lighting it from one of the sconces in the hall. Inside the library, the air was still thick and musty, but no longer unpleasant, and the room was warm despite the ceaseless drum of the rain on the glass above, courtesy of a fire Mrs. Purl had built that morning to help dry the room out.

The sitting room would have been a more comfortable spot, perhaps, but she did not intend to sleep now—only to read long enough to exhaust her mind, so that she could return to bed, worn out enough to slumber once more.

Mrs. Purl had freshly polished the long table in the center of the room, and chairs now sat around it, clean and handsome. Jane set the candelabra down. The library's green, liquid light folded around her, bathing her like water.

After a moment's thought, she set aside Mr. Aethridge for the daylight. Instead, she opened to the first page of her mathematical philosophies. The writing was dense, the type small, and deciphering the logic took up the whole of her attention within minutes. Her only regret was that she hadn't brought her pen to make notes in the margins, but sliding her finger along the text worked almost as well. As she read, the rain came down harder, the sound echoing across the high-ceilinged room.

The book sketched out the possibilities of seemingly impossible mathematics, derived from division by zero. Zero did not function the same as one, or two, or twenty; it erased or expanded beyond the bounds of reality. And so, this text argued, one could use zero to take the volume of a rounded barrel without needing to fill it and measure the contents in a more standard container after. One could find the area below a theoretical curve, calculating smaller and smaller regular areas below it into infinite nothingness. One could find the answers that must exist, but that no Breltainian scholar had ever been able to reach with exactitude.

Magic. It sounded like magic.

Reaching the end of the second chapter, Jane paused to rub her eyes.

Tendrils of sleep were beginning to tug at her shoulders, but she knew herself; if she went back down now, she'd just be wide awake again after a few minutes. Still, the words were starting to dance before her eyes. Sighing, she looked up and gazed out the darkened windows.

Something was there.

Her breath caught, and she stared, willing the shadow to resolve. "Augustine?" she called, but her voice was barely above a whisper. Her pulse racing, she rose from her chair and picked up the candelabra.

Whatever it was moved. As it turned its head, she made out a fall of golden hair—not her own, for she was perfectly still. And then she saw the terrible red eyes. She fell back a step, a cry beginning to build in her throat. The empty shelves surrounding her seemed to grow in size, to loom and pen her in.

Elodie.

No. No, it wasn't Elodie, couldn't be Elodie. And yet who else could it be? She pinched at her fingertips, as if that would dispel the illusion, but Elodie remained. Her features were indistinct, her face seeming to warp and blur around those red eyes, but her gaze stayed fixed on Jane.

She had to get to Augustine. Had to get somewhere safe, where she could realize what an anxious fool she was being. It took all her willpower, but at last she tore her eyes from the ghostly figure to look toward the well-lit hallway. She took one step, then stopped, a half-formed cry leaking from her mouth.

Shapes moved against the far wall.

There were three of them, and they were tall, taller than any man. They had elongated heads, downturned, shallow crescents. In the gas lighting, those crescents looked like some kind of headdress, with the wearers veiled and robed beneath them, almost hiding their strange proportions.

But she could see. She could see how their shoulders sloped unnaturally, how long their limbs were as one lifted what might have been a hand. From the headdress, there was an unbroken line curving out to the shoulders, masking any hint of face or throat.

All three turned toward her.

She staggered back into one of the shelves, breath coming in sharp, shallow gasps. Her hands were shaking, the wax from the candelabra splattering and stinging her bare feet. The flames guttered as she sank to the floor, wrapping her arms around her knees as if that would offer any protection.

One of the figures in the doorway turned toward the windows, and Jane helplessly followed its gaze back to Elodie. But Elodie was gone, and the three figures were static only a moment more before proceeding down the hall.

Toward the stairs.

Toward Augustine.

Outside, distant thrums of thunder shivered through the night. The beat of raindrops on glass was cacophonous, out of sync with her pulse, out of sync with everything.

They're headed toward Augustine.

She had to move. She had to go to him. But fear had locked her joints up tight, and her shoulders shook with reflexive, silent sobs. She'd never believed in spirits, not even as a child, but what else could Elodie be? The monstrous statues? And if they were spirits, they were beyond her understanding. They were beyond her power. She was helpless.

Augustine was helpless.

And then she realized: he had known. He *knew* about these things. *This* was why he'd tried to keep her away, why he sent the servants home at night. It wasn't baseless superstition. It wasn't war-bred nerves. It was real danger.

She had to get to him, and she had to get him *out*.

When she reached the doorway, she watched as, one by one, the gaslights leading down the hall were snuffed out by an unseen hand.

She felt her way to the stairs. Ahead of her, the figures descended in single file, barely visible in the gloom. They didn't walk as she did, but seemed to flow downward. Heaving for breath, she grabbed the doorframe she stood in with both hands, knuckles white and nails straining. Her bravado faltered, then rebounded as they reached the second-floor landing and turned into the darkened mouth of the hallway leading to the bedroom.

If she shouted Augustine's name, would he wake up? Would they disappear? But her voice still refused to work, refused to come out as more than a hitching, whimpering sob, and she was too far away. She stumbled down and into the second-floor hallway, the lights ahead of her guttering out as the creatures passed by. Moving slower now, terrified to catch up to them and see them turn once more to her, she crept along the carpeted floor in their wake.

They passed the bedroom without a moment's hesitation. Jane stopped, not daring to breathe. Had she been wrong? Did the things not care about him, either?

But then she saw the barest shadow of them turning the corner, and she knew. *He's not asleep. He's in the study.*

Desperate, she opened the bedroom door and peered into the darkness. The bed was empty.

She raced down the hallway and around the corner, the way ahead pitch-dark save for the faint light below the study door. She stumbled to a halt before it, the hallway empty; she had not seen the door open for the creatures. But it gave under her barest touch.

Augustine stared at her from across the room.

His hair was mussed from sleep, but he didn't look any different from usual. And then, as he took in her wild expression, his own turned grave. "Jane," he said, and crossed the room to her, taking her still-trembling hands. "Jane, what is it?"

She couldn't find the words. Her throat was closed as though a fist were tight around it. But they were alone. They were safe. Those creatures, whatever they were, hadn't come to him.

Then the window behind him rippled slightly, as if it were the surface of a lake, and the shadows resolved themselves into the faint outline of a dead woman.

Elodie held a finger to her lips.

Augustine's arms closing around her were the last thing Jane knew before she collapsed into oblivion.

CHAPTER THIRTEEN

J ANE WOKE UP in Augustine's bed, the coverlet rumpled and tugged half off. Daylight streamed in through the windows. She wasn't wearing her nightgown; it sat, carefully folded, where she'd put it the previous morning. Her dress remained in a crumpled heap by the side of the bed where she'd discarded it. Her housecoat hung neatly where it had hung the night before.

The night before.

Cold panic washed through her, and she looked around, frantic, for any sign of Augustine. The last she remembered, she'd been in his study, had seen the red-eyed woman in the window. And then there was nothing, no memory, not even the sense of lost time. Augustine's side of the bed was empty, but the pillow still had a deep depression in it, as if he'd only just left.

She rose from the bed cautiously, flinching away from the bedframe and the gathered shadows beneath it. She couldn't bring herself to dress fully, too afraid even in the light of day. Instead, she drew her housecoat around her. She paused just long enough to pull her slippers on, then went to the door.

Jane hesitated, biting down the urge to call Augustine's name like a fright-ened child. It was day. The rain had stopped. The halls would be brightly lit by the gas sconces, and below she'd find Augustine sitting down to break-fast. Mrs. Luthbright would be there, and Mrs. Purl.

She had nothing to fear.

Easing the door open, she peeked out into the hall. Everything was as it should be. She slipped out and padded down the runner, down the front stairs. The house revealed nothing, and her heart had begun to slow by the time she stepped into the dining room.

Nobody was there, but she could hear sounds coming from the kitchen. She started toward it, only to be interrupted by the creak of a door. Her entire body went rigid.

"Good morning, Mrs. Lawrence," Mrs. Purl said. "I didn't know you would be wanting help getting into your clothing this morning. If I had—"

Jane turned, pasting on a gentle smile, or her closest approximation of one. "Oh, no. No, don't worry. I'm quite used to dressing myself. I just . . . wasn't sure where Dr. Lawrence was. Is he out on call?"

"No, ma'am. He's walking the grounds, but breakfast will be set out shortly." She turned to go, then paused. "Pardon my manners, Mrs. Lawrence, but Mrs. Luthbright and I were both happy to hear that you remained in resi-dence another night, with the doctor."

"Is that so?" Jane asked, then flushed as she remembered how wild with abandon they had been.

"It's a large house to be alone in at night," was Mrs. Purl's response, before she dipped a curtsy. "I'll go out and fetch the doctor, tell him you'll be down to breakfast shortly."

"I'll be down to breakfast now," she said.

Mrs. Purl looked pointedly at her quilted wrap, but Jane just took her seat at the table, once more fixed upon the thought of lurking shadows.

It was only a few minutes before Augustine appeared in the door. He was fully dressed, his jaw freshly shaven and his hair carefully set. Just as com-posed as he'd been on their wedding day. There was no trace of concern in his eyes, and confusion rocked her.

He had to know. He had to be worried for her, for what had driven her into his arms.

"Good morning, Jane," he said, smiling. "How did you sleep?"

Her brow furrowed. What an odd way of putting it. He was acting like she hadn't collapsed in an overwhelmed faint. She looked to the doorways. Was he concerned about an audience again?

"I . . ." She couldn't find the words. Instead, she watched him closely as he sat down across from her, willing him to give her any sign that he remembered last night.

His smile faded to a concerned frown.

"Bad dreams?" he asked.

Her heart sank. "No," she said. "I had trouble sleeping last night. As did you."

"I slept like a child. For the first time in quite a while, to be honest."

Something is wrong. "You were awake," she said. "I saw you. In your study."

His brows drew down farther, and he reached across the table, offering her his hands. She gave him one of hers, and he clasped it loosely, thumbs stroking at her knuckles. "The house—it tends to provoke bad dreams. Nightmares, even. I was in bed all night, with you. It must have been a dream."

"It wasn't," she said, shaking her head.

"What was it about?"

"I . . . I came to the library to read. I saw people, but they weren't people, and they ignored me and headed for your rooms. I followed them, and . . ."

The more she spoke, the less real it all seemed, but the panic was there, thick in her chest. It *felt* real, even if it sounded like a nightmare. "I left books there," she added, voice barely above a whisper. "My treatise. Your monograph on Mr. Aethridge."

"Mrs. Purl didn't tell me about any books she found," Augustine said. "But I will look, if you want me to."

Yes. Yes, look. But if he was right, if there were no books there . . .

She shook her head. "I was so scared," she whispered. "I've never had a nightmare like that before." Why didn't he remember? It couldn't have been a dream. It felt real, far too real.

But her housecoat had been where she'd put it the evening before. If she checked his study, would his monograph still be there? Would her book still be in the stack of texts on his desk? She tried to think back to what she'd read, but her memories were too fuzzy. Her exhaustion had made it impossible to take everything in. She'd thought she woke up in bed because Augustine had moved her there after she collapsed, but if she'd fainted, surely she would have come to again far before morning.

Maybe he was right.

Three nights ago, she'd woken him from a dream and he had feared she wasn't real. Wasn't this the same thing? What she'd seen was impossible, but it was so beyond any nightmare she'd ever had, and—

"Let's get you back into town today," he said. "I'll arrange to stay the night at the surgery with you. Would that help?"

Yes. She shut her eyes, exhaling raggedly. If, somehow, it hadn't been a dream, she would have wanted him to come away from this place at all costs. And if she really was just being ridiculous, it would be nice to be somewhere else, and not alone. "Yes, that would help."

She thought of going to him, of settling into his arms for just a moment's comfort, but stopped half out of her chair when she heard footsteps.

"That will be Mrs. Luthbright with breakfast, I wager," Augustine said, smiling.

But it was Mrs. Purl, who entered at a quick trot.

"Mr. Lowell is here," she said breathlessly. "He says it's the Maerbeck farm, the eldest son is, ah—"

"He's vomiting uncontrollably," Mr. Lowell said from the doorway. "The middle child rode into town to fetch you, says it's been going on since last night."

Augustine swore. "I'll be right out," he said, then looked back at Jane. "I'll have to go straight there, and it's a fair way from Larrenton."

"I'll come with you."

"There's no time for you to dress, and whatever has happened with the Maerbeck boy, it might be catching."

"I could help," she said, pitching her voice quieter so that Mrs. Purl, who was lingering, couldn't hear. Mr. Lowell had already taken off, no doubt to see to the horses so that they would be ready to move again soon.

"If it were an injury, I might take you up on the offer, but this is different." He fixed her with a serious gaze. "Mr. Lowell will need to stay with me in case we need to rush the boy to the surgery, so it may be some time before we can fetch you back to town. Will that be all right?"

She nodded, numb in the face of his determined, rushing pace.

Without so much as a glance at Mrs. Purl, he drew Jane close and pressed a fervent kiss to her lips. "I wish I had more time," he murmured. "That nightmare seems to have distressed you so much."

"It's fine," she said, voice weak. "I'm possessed of a rational mind. I'll re-cover." She managed a faint, wry smile.

He gave her shoulders one last squeeze, and then he was gone.

Ten minutes later, Mrs. Luthbright did bring breakfast. It was toast, salted fish, and porridge. Jane barely tasted any of it and didn't speak more than a few words to either Mrs. Luthbright or Mrs. Purl except to send Mrs. Purl for her treatise. Mrs. Purl returned within a few minutes, having had no trouble finding it in the study. She'd never moved it, then.

It really had been a nightmare.

Several hours later, with her senses steadied by the sunlight and pro-longed quiet, Jane set aside the book. The logic was so unfamiliar that she couldn't say if she'd ever read it before. Rubbing at her temples and wishing for her spectacles, she stood up. The sun was already past its peak; she'd lost half the day in her work. Would that she could lose more.

She needed to forget all traces of Elodie, of her red eyes and her finger held to her lips. No wonder that Jane would dream of her, in the burst of chaotic relief at learning the tragic details of her story. But she needed to be practical, hard of spirit. Augustine needed her so; he needed a wife who could help his patients and who could stay by his side in this house with him if need be, a partner in every sense. She wanted to be that, for herself as much as for him.

And then, as she climbed the stairs to the bedroom, she saw it. There, bright pink against the pale skin of the top of her left foot, were the faint dotted burns of candle wax.

It hadn't been a nightmare at all.

Augustine had lied.

CHAPTER FOURTEEN

J ANE STOOD IN the doorway to Augustine's bedroom, looking at the rumpled sheets, her heart so in tumult that it seemed to be numb with the constant turning. They had lain together last night, and it had been sweet, and gentle, and passionate; she had been so glad to trust him, so glad to learn there were missing details, details that made it all make sense.

She wanted it all to make sense.

Why would he lie about Jane collapsing in his study? She knew he had lied, and yet the lie itself vexed her. He hadn't known what she had seen. Even now, though she could still conjure up the image, she couldn't name what had happened. Ghosts? Spirits? They did not fit into her orderly world, and surely they could not fit into his.

And yet he had not wanted her to stay at Lindridge Hall at first. He had been transfigured when she found him hiding in his study on their wedding night. He had been afraid, as afraid as she had been to see the woman in the window behind him. And now he had lied to her, elaborately and emphatically.

When she'd come up with her marriage plan, she'd somehow thought it would be simple. That there would be no drama, no uncertainty. And perhaps, if she'd chosen a different man . . .

Her heart ached. She didn't *want* to choose a different man.

She wanted Augustine to be who she'd thought he was. That man would not have lied. That man would have confided in her. The day Mr. Renton had died, they had bared their souls to each other. They had worked together through blood and loss, and when she had looked into his eyes she had felt safe. She had felt *seen*.

Had that been a lie, too?

No. No, there was something she was missing, some variable that, once solved for, would put all of this into alignment. They would laugh, as they had last night.

But she could not stand the sight of their bed.

She dressed quickly, movements sharp enough to nearly tear the delicate lace neckline of her plum gown. She did not look at the bed, and as soon as she was suitably put together, she took up her valise and left the bedroom, shutting the door tight behind her.

The house seemed to grab at her as she descended toward the foyer, splinters in the floorboards catching at her skirt hem. Shadows reared up into unearthly, half-remembered forms.

This was not a place for her. She no longer wanted to be at Lindridge Hall, this desiccated funereal husk. Yesterday, her shield had been built up high and firm, ready for the assault of what the name *Elodie* might mean. Now it lay in ruins around her, dismantled by her desire and trust, leaving her vulnerable. Her time in this house had brought her nothing but fright and grief.

The roads were once more open. Sending for a carriage from town would take too long, but though she was too poor a rider to ask for Mr. Purl's horse, perhaps she could beg one of the nearby tenant farmers to take her back to Larrenton by cart. Perhaps, once away, once back in the rhythms of town, the ache of betrayal would fade. Augustine could explain what had happened. She could understand. They could balance the two sides of their equation, confusing lies against honest passion.

She reached the foyer and had taken a few steps toward the kitchen when she paused, the flesh between her shoulder blades tensing. Jane turned toward what felt like a thousand eyes upon her and saw only the empty hallway that led back to the locked cellar door. The world went still around her, and she could hear Augustine's voice whispering in her ear, feel his breath hot upon her throat.

Nothing at all. It's dangerous. The tunnels could collapse.

Her feet moved without her willing them, her hands remembering the unnaturally cold bite of the padlock. If he could lie to her so completely that he erased her from the previous night, then what of his reassurances? His promises?

She could not trust them. She could not trust *him,* not now, not in this house.

The hallway settled around her, its lights dim, all sound from the rest of the house muffled. The padlock gleamed as she drew closer. The chatelaine rested heavy against her skirts, useless, and she stared at the gnarled wood of the door. The answers to her questions were beyond it. She knew without knowing how, a sharp hunger rising in her.

But just as she reached out to touch the lock once more, the door shuddered with a deep, insistent boom. She jumped back, staring, as another came, and another. The door did not move, though surely something inside was striking it, striking it, striking—

And then the world came crashing back, and she heard the front door open. Laughter spilled in from beyond, of ten men, a hundred. And a woman, saying:

"We were invited."

CHAPTER FIFTEEN

THE WOMAN WAS Dr. Georgiana Hunt, and she had brought with her seven of Breltain's great surgeons and physicians.

Jane dug her nails into her palms, lurking in the hallway. The doctors filled the foyer with their valises and their laughter, running roughshod over Mrs. Purl. Jane tried not to cry with the confusion of it all, the disaster. She was in no state to remain in this house, let alone entertain guests, but she could think of no way to turn them out without humiliation.

As if hearing her thoughts, Mrs. Purl grew defensive. "I beg your pardon, Doctor, doctors, but Dr. Lawrence made no mention of house guests."

"Just like him!" a man proclaimed, then laughed heartily. The sound was unnatural, bouncing off the arcing ceiling of the foyer. Jane recoiled, then bore up in reflexive defense of her husband. He had written to them, dissuaded them from coming—he had said as much to her!

And yet here they were. The thought sobered her. Had he lied about that as well? But to what end? No, she had grown too sensitive, too quick to blame, and these visitors were haughty, proud, and just the sort to ignore Augustine's protestations.

Just as she had.

"Surely you do not want to stay in an empty country house for the day, doctors," Mrs. Purl said, still desperately attempting to turn them away, and Jane was thankful for it even knowing it arose from shame at the state of the house. "We have no gamekeeper, no stables even. Larrenton is far more entertaining." And a better place for them, where they would be Augustine's problem, not hers.

The suggestion went unheeded. Dr. Hunt's contralto boomed through the vaulted foyer as she said, "But what of Mrs. Lawrence? We would like to see her just as well!"

Jane went cold, cringing farther into the cellar hallway, where she had no excuse to be.

"I—Yes, she is in," Mrs. Purl answered. Jane pictured the bobbing of her head as she curtsied, though she could hear the strain in the woman's voice. "If you'll come to the sitting room, Doctor, doctors, I'll go and fetch her."

More chatter, more indistinct words, moving away. Jane crept closer to the foyer, and caught the edges of their shadows as they entered the other room.

Pulling her skirts up around her knees and trying to move as swiftly and as silently as possible, Jane raced up the staircase. She stopped only when she reached the bedroom door. She quailed at the thought of stepping back inside, but she could not be found clutching her valise. Too many questions if she were, questions she could not answer in front of an audience. She forced herself to open the door once more, and, averting her eyes from the bed, she placed her bag back down.

She all but ran to the study, then, because it made far more sense for Mrs. Purl to find her there. But stepping inside was a new blow. She remembered Augustine finally taking her in his arms on their wedding day, his eager, bashful smile—but also the shock of a woman's name in his ledger, her own uncertainty, the anger that she could not summon now. And there, in the window, was her reflection, so much like what she had seen the night before. But it was hers, through and through.

Her eyes were sunken, her hair limp, her lips pursed tight. Evidence of her distress. Jane had never cared much for her appearance, except when it would draw attention. This, among doctors, would.

She pinched furiously at her cheeks, trying to draw color up into her pallor. She stared at her reflection and willed herself to be placid and pleasant. She sought out the Jane that had been and wrenched her into the form of a mask.

In the window, a happier woman looked back at her. Jane smiled, and though it felt thin, it looked easy.

Mrs. Purl mounted the stairs below her, her footsteps echoing up as Jane threw herself into the desk chair and cracked open the ledger.

The tidy columns sickened her.

"Ma'am?"

Jane turned in her seat to look at Mrs. Purl, her face as pinched and drawn and clearly unhappy as Jane's own had been. She wanted to throw herself down at Mrs. Purl's feet and to beg the woman for a way out, for a way home. But instead, Jane said, "I heard a carriage. Is it Dr. Lawrence?" The lie sat ashen on her tongue but sounded smooth and calm enough. Was this how Augustine had felt when he had lied to her that morning?

"No, ma'am. It appears," Mrs. Purl said, wringing her apron in her worn hands, "that Dr. Lawrence invited several of his colleagues over. Did he mention anything of the sort to you, Mrs. Lawrence? They intend to stay the week, but we don't have the stores, or the beds, and . . ." She trailed off, helpless.

Jane wanted to blame Augustine in that moment, wanted desperately to have Mrs. Purl on her side, aligned against a master who kept the truth from them. But that would not solve their dilemma. "I'm sure it's a misunderstanding," Jane said instead. "I'll go attend to them." She approached the door, and Mrs. Purl stepped out of the way. But as Jane made her way down the hall, Mrs. Purl cleared her throat.

"Pardon, ma'am," Mrs. Purl said. "It's just, you didn't ask where to find them."

Jane froze. She ducked her head. *A poor liar, I.* "Oh, I—I had assumed you'd put them in"—*the sitting room*—"the dining room, seeing as it is quite clean."

"The sitting room, ma'am. I cleaned the curtains just this morning, thank everything."

Jane looked over her shoulder with a sheepish smile that was not hard to fake. "Of course. What good timing," she said.

Mrs. Purl smiled back, but it was not happy.

Jane descended the stairs.

THEY WERE WAITING for her; a cry went up as she reached the doorway.

"Mrs. Lawrence!" a small woman with brilliant copper hair declared, leaping up from her armchair (faded, embarrassingly understuffed, but clean). She crossed the room to Jane, holding out her hands. "We are so glad to finally meet you. I am Dr. Georgiana Hunt." Her cheeks were ruddy with drink already, courtesy of a snifter she'd left behind on the end table by her chair, and her eyes sparkled as she took hold of Jane, drawing her fully into the room. She wore fitted men's trousers, a high-necked blouse and vest, and a long coat, tailored precisely. The coat wasn't a surgeon's apron, but it had certain similarities. It was still rumpled from a day's journey in a carriage.

Come all the way from Camhurst, against Augustine's direct request, and so soon upon the news of the marriage. Why? It could not be just to meet her.

"Augustine's new bride, doctors!" Dr. Hunt announced. Another cheer went up from all assembled. There were five men scattered about the room, as well as two other ladies in the company. One wore a dress closely modeled on traditional undertakers' garb, with a black high-collared vest and narrow skirt. Her brown hair was trimmed in a startlingly masculine style.

The other was Dr. Nizamiev, the specialist from the asylum in Camhurst.

Jane's world contracted, tilting ever so slightly off-kilter. But of course Dr. Nizamiev was here; if these other schoolmates of Augustine's had come, why not her, whom he had seen much more recently?

Dr. Nizamiev barely marked her now, all her attention on the notebook she wrote in. It was the others who watched her, and Dr. Hunt who was waiting for her to speak.

"I'm glad to meet you all," she managed after a moment. "I hope you will forgive me for the state of the house, however; we were not expecting you."

"Well, if we had waited for a formal invitation from Augustine, it would never have come. We are quite familiar with his nature. We had, however, hoped to find him here, as his surgery was empty."

"He's with a case. A child," Jane said, flushing as she realized she had forgotten all about the Maerbeck boy, concerned with her own distress. "Violent vomiting, throughout the night."

"Hyperemesis," one of the men said gravely, and it took her a moment's awe before she realized he was not offering a diagnosis, but simply restating what she'd just said with more erudite words. He rose from his chair and joined her and Dr. Hunt, inclining his head. He was quite handsome, with jet hair and umber skin, and finely crafted features of the aristocratic sort. He was broad-shouldered, too, and the fingers that clasped hers were long and finely made.

"Mrs. Lawrence, it is a pleasure," the man said with a controlled smile. "My name is Andrew Vingh. I'm head surgeon at a private hospital in Camhurst—your husband and I trained together in medical school. I must admit, I'm saddened to not find him at home. Are you certain he is with a patient?"

Jane went very still. "Excuse me?"

"I fear he's avoiding us," Dr. Vingh said.

They know he lies.

But no, he could not have been lying about his patient. He had no reason to, and no way to have brought Mr. Lowell in on the deception. And yet that patient had left her in this house, a house he had before claimed he did not want her anywhere near, and . . .

And she had company. She had to comport herself appropriately, not spiral out in paranoia. "I am sure he is with a patient," Jane said. "He left here in great haste this morning. Hopefully he will return tonight."

Vingh sighed. "He's going to get himself killed, attending virulent cases. He's too good with his blade to be wasting his life out here." He paused, then inclined his head. "No offense, ma'am."

"None taken," she said, despite her bristling. "I've seen his skill firsthand."

"Have you?" He sounded surprised.

"The second day I knew him, I assisted with an emergency surgery." The scent of blood filled her nose as if she still wore her soiled gown. With it came the memory of their charged, quick touches, and the full-force bloom of her intoxication with him. A mess. It was all a mess, right from the first.

Vingh leaned in. "Really? What sort?"

"Ah—abdominal. A man came in with a malformation of the bowel." She tripped over the words, though she remembered them issuing smoothly from Augustine's lips.

"You're trained, then? Where at? Almonth? Edonbridge?"

"No," she said, smile tightening. "No, I was merely there. He needed another set of hands."

Vingh regarded her curiously. Jane looked among the highly educated faces of surgeons and physicians crowding around her, and realized that she was not what they had expected to find.

"I see," Vingh said, pulling her back. He offered her a patient smile. "Well, what I wouldn't give to have seen that! Augustine is a wonder with a knife. Some concentrated practice, instead of this generalist nonsense, would quickly bring him to my level. Maybe higher."

She could almost feel Renton's blood under her nails again, and this man only cared about skill. "The patient died the next day."

Vingh shrugged. "It happens," he said, without embarrassment or empathy. "Abdominal surgery carries risks."

"Yes, I suppose it does." But his nonchalance sat ill with her. A man like him—she could see his dismissal. By comparison, Augustine seemed almost too good. Too generous of spirit. *He* had never quizzed her on her education. Should that have its own clue?

"You said that was the second day you met?" Vingh asked, gaze fixed on her as if she were a curiosity, vivisected. Her skin crawled. "With no nursing training at all?"

"No. I'm actually an accountant. I keep Dr. Lawrence's books."

That got a laugh out of him. "An accountant! He did find an *interesting* wife. Did he hire you first, or . . . ?"

"In a manner of speaking," Jane said, then inwardly relaxed as Hunt brought over two glasses of brandy, one of which she pressed into Jane's hand. Jane took a quick but determined sip.

"Are you boring Mrs. Lawrence out of her mind, Andrew?"

Vingh shrugged. "I was just getting around to making my case for Mrs. Lawrence to draw her husband back to Camhurst. If you had been a nurse, Mrs. Lawrence, I would have described to you the wonders of the Royal. They're always in need of skilled nurses. I wonder if they'd be in want of an accountant."

A *self-taught accountant,* she did not add. After all, grammar schools hardly trained tradeswomen.

Instead, she tried to picture Camhurst, tried to picture Augustine in a grand operating theater, sought after, with the easy arrogance of his class-mates. If only he had been *that* man instead, a man without time for spirits, a man whose secrets might have been more prosaic. Though perhaps that man would not have wanted her.

"I can't imagine him going so far afield," Jane said, taking refuge in bit-terness.

"A pity. We have missed him, these last two years."

Two years. Two years ago, a patient had died in this house. Jane paused halfway to another swallow of brandy. It seemed the eyes of all gathered had turned on them in that moment, as if sensing the sudden quiet that had come over her thoughts.

"He's been a hard man to track down since then," Hunt confided, sitting on the arm of the nearest chair, crossing her legs and leaning one elbow on her knee. "He was under consideration for a lead surgical post, and then he was gone. Off to the southern counties, treating chronic injuries left over where the gassing was worst. It was all very sudden."

Just the government posting. That was all. She was still jumping at shadows.

"I still can't believe he accepted the job," Vingh sighed. "Giving up his future . . . and for what? Of course, it was a hard thing, Elodie's death."

Jane went very still.

Elodie.

Vingh continued, heedless. "But surely he—"

"Did you *know* her?" Jane blurted, before they could devolve to sniping about achievements and the lack thereof.

Vingh bared his teeth in an unconvincing smile, as if he was very rarely cut off. He adjusted his cuffs, shot a look at Hunt. "Who, Elodie? Of course, we all did. Georgiana stood up at the wedding."

The wedding.

The wedding.

Jane could not breathe. She choked down another mouthful of liquor to hide her pain, her panic.

"She was in residence with her family while we were attending university," Hunt offered, "and was a frequent guest at the parties we attended. She was a wonderful woman. It was a terrible shame, what happened. And," she said, with a glare in Vingh's direction, "no surprise at all that it hurt Augustine so deeply."

Those payments weren't to a patient's survivors. They were to his in-laws. The parents of his *wife*. She felt a scream building in her chest, and it took all her willpower to wrestle it down, to only wince and look away.

Her hands trembled, and she clasped them both around the base of her snifter to hide their shaking. "And what did happen?" she asked, fighting every inch of her that wanted to strain forward, to grab Vingh and shake the truth from him. She had no idea how she sounded as she croaked out, "All my husband has told me is that she was sick." *And that she wasn't his wife, that she was only a patient, that everything was safe in this house.*

Her guests did not seem to mark her distress. "Sick, yes," Vingh said. "She died of yellow fever. She and Augustine had moved into this house, I believe, while he covered some physician's posting in Sharpton, and when he was no longer needed, Augustine joined us on holiday. She'd been under the weather recently, so she stayed behind. A week into the trip, he received word that Elodie had taken ill, and by the time he reached home, she was dead. Even if he had received the message three days sooner, he wouldn't have been able to return in time to do anything."

Jane rocked back on her heels, the picture of polite, sympathetic grief, while inside she burned. Lies building upon lies—she could not support it all. He had lied about his dead wife, a wife she now saw haunting the windows at night, a wife with bloody eyes who looked at her from behind Augustine and held a finger to her lips.

It was all impossible, and yet it seemed more and more real with each new revelation. Had Augustine told the truth, that he hadn't been able to save her?

Jane chanced a glance at the window. The sun was still solidly above the horizon, but sunset could only be an hour out, two at most. And suddenly, she wanted to stay. She wanted her guests to remain, to bear witness to what she had seen the night before. They could tell her the truth of it.

She so desperately needed the truth.

"It *was* a tragedy," Vingh continued, and a scrap of real emotion crept into his voice. Elodie, it seemed, had been one of them—unlike Jane. "It's a wretched, horrific illness—destroys the organs, great gouts of blood every-where, and nothing that can be stitched up—but I'll never understand why he would blame himself so much for it that he would take himself off to the hinterlands to atone."

That shame, that flight, meant something. Jane sank into a chair, sure of it, unmanned by it, gaze firmly fixed on the road back to Larrenton.

"That's because you are far too cold," Hunt answered, as if Jane were not present. "Even *ignoring* the fact that she was his wife, he became a doctor to save lives. As, I would hope, did all of us."

"A man's skills have limits. And if he can't handle losing a few patients, he certainly shouldn't have pursued surgery, or doctoring at all, no matter his natural talent."

"He told me," Jane said woodenly, "when our patient died that I should never blame myself. That *he* would take the blame."

Vingh snorted. "Martyr of a man. Bring him back to Camhurst and we'll quickly cure him of his weakness."

"I do not think I could entice him to go," Jane said. Her head had begun to ache. One night ago, this had all been so much simpler, so much easier, and for a moment she once more wished she had never found out the lie.

But if it had not been last night, or this morning, then it would have happened now. Despite his best efforts to keep his old companions away from her, they had come, and they had broken his illusions with their idle chatter.

She wondered what Augustine would say if he returned to Lindridge Hall and found them all here. How would he act, how would he dissemble, how would he excuse himself? Could he even handle the pressure of it, or would he simply collapse?

And as if it had been summoned by her thoughts, she caught sight of his carriage upon the road. Jane started, and Hunt asked after her, only to look and see the carriage herself.

"Our good doctor?" she asked, and Jane nodded.

Hunt capered away with a delighted shout, and Jane tried to draw on her good humor, rising from her seat with a thin smile. "Let us go to welcome my husband," she said, and led the assembly back into the foyer.

CHAPTER SIXTEEN

Augustine's carriage pulled to the top of the drive despite the crowd of other carriages that his houseguests had abandoned. Augustine alighted from it in a rush, his face pale, his hair more disordered than its normal gentle curl.

Jane had not expected the sharp pang of desire that came with seeing him again, the heady rush of wishing that he would take her hand in the crowd of his colleagues and make her feel less adrift. She had steeled herself for the rising of her rage, but it lay stunned, still nascent, still uncertain. Its lassitude left her vulnerable.

A wife, she repeated to herself. *A dead wife.*

Looking at Augustine, she was certain he knew what she had learned. It was subtle, but Augustine was wild in front of her—afraid of the coming night, afraid of his lies being overturned, afraid of Jane left alone with these men and women who did not have the common decency to heed a rejection. He hid it well, through some great practice or effort of will. Behind her, Hunt was indifferent to it, and Vingh, too, and all the rest. They cried out greetings happily, and only Jane saw his panic.

He came straight to her and took her hands, pulling her close. "How long have they been here?" he whispered. "I swear I did not know they would come. Are you all right?"

Jane was silent, because the only words that wanted to come from her lips were, *And why should you be so afraid of their presence here?*

"They cannot stay the night," he said. "We don't have the beds, and—" He faltered, hesitated.

Say it, say it, she willed, but he did not.

Instead, he leaned in to kiss her cheek. "I will take care of this."

She jerked away, as if his touch burned, and twisted to look at their guests. Insolent perversion made her say, "And here is our good doctor, here to join us for the dinner that Mrs. Luthbright must no doubt be conjuring for us even now."

Augustine's hand tightened on hers, a question and a plea, but then he stepped away and bowed to his guests. "My dear friends," he said, once more the confident, kind man she had known, tempered by just the barest edge of the haughty pride that all assembled seemed to wear as a second skin. "I bid you welcome, though I would beg you to read my letters more closely next time. Lindridge Hall does not have rooms grand enough for you."

Hunt laughed and closed the small distance between them, looping her arm with his and urging him into the house. "You don't need to stand on ceremony; we are well aware that Larrenton cannot offer the amenities of Camhurst. We have come prepared to rough it, if your gracious servant— Mrs. Purl?—can locate blankets."

Jane feared they did not have even that, and, following the group back inside, watched Augustine, trying to guess how direct he would be.

"The inns in Larrenton are much better, and your drivers would prefer it, I'm sure. Lindridge Hall has no stables of its own, not anymore." The horses were presumably tethered around the side of the manor and grazing on the unkempt fields, their grooms watching the darkening sky and wondering if they were to return to town before nightfall.

"Then I will send the drivers to the inn," Vingh said, peeling off from the group. "They can come back in the morning."

"Doctors," he said, and though he must have been afraid, she could not hear it in his voice. "I wish to be a good host. Please allow it."

"Augustine, your company is all we require. And when have you known us to sleep a whole night away when games await?" Hunt said.

Augustine's thumb worked at the ring on his finger, and Jane saw the bone pull tight.

What games?

"You should leave," Augustine said, patience wearing thin.

Vingh, by the door, broke out into laughter. "Augustine! You would not send us away! And your surgery is no place to host company; I hardly wish to drink amid drained boils and whatever chickens you've operated on today."

"We will not judge you in the slightest," Hunt added.

Jane opened her mouth to add to their protest, only to find Dr. Nizamiev regarding her. She watched Jane—*Jane,* not Augustine, not them together—as a hawk watched difficult prey, and Jane recoiled instinctively. She stood, frozen, as Hunt clapped Augustine on the shoulder and led him firmly into the sitting room, as Vingh slipped out the door and the rest of the doctors once more took up posts by the fire or the window.

"Careful," Dr. Nizamiev said, bringing up the rear of the procession, just far enough behind to murmur so quietly only Jane could hear her. "You wouldn't want to appear unsociable." Her skirts whispered past.

Jane's cheeks burned and her hands trembled. She had not been subtle with her shock or displeasure; she had forgotten she had any need to be, in front of such an oblivious audience as these doctors. But she was watched by at least one, and she did not want Dr. Nizamiev to read into the symptoms of their discord. She watched as Augustine poured new rounds of brandy, as he pressed Mrs. Purl to encourage Mrs. Luthbright to produce small finger foods, ahead of the dinner that must surely be straining her and Lindridge Hall's pantries to the breaking point already. *He* had pulled himself back together quickly and gave no further sign of unease. He laughed off his earlier stridency.

Shaking herself, she donned her practiced smile as she was cornered by one of the other men, who probed about her family and education. She was recounting her introduction to sums and records when Vingh returned to the room and came straight to her side.

"The drivers have all been sent back to town," he proclaimed. "And I begin to see why you are so pessimistic about your ability to change our Augustine's mind. He is quite different from how I knew him."

"Is he?" Jane said, moving with him to the sideboard. Her previous glass had been abandoned, but Vingh found a fresh one for her and filled it, pressing it into her hands. He was careful not to touch her. "I have only known him thus. Dedicated to his work." *And dissembling.*

"He is transformed. Prickly and recalcitrant," Vingh said.

"I didn't know about Elodie," she confided, desperate for some reaction, hoping that he would perceive the wrong that had been done to her and present a solution.

But Vingh only shrugged. "I'm not surprised. I hear it drove his family from him, as well. They cared for Elodie like a daughter and were happy to accept his responsibility for the death." He snorted. "They should have blamed the marshlands, and their mosquitos and agues, and the doctor they called to aid her in Augustine's absence. They should have blamed *themselves,* for leaving Camhurst for this—pardon the aspersion—damp manor. Foolish, to blame *him.* He's a surgeon by nature and by training, not an internist."

Jane looked to Augustine, then stiffened as Augustine caught her gaze and came to her, drawn as if by magnetism.

"Andrew," he said.

"Augustine. Your wife is lovelier than I could have pictured."

He inclined his head, lifted his glass, and smiled at her. "She is a wonder." Jane felt bile rise in her throat.

Augustine turned to her, taking her hand. "Can I beg you to ask after Mrs. Luthbright?"

He was trying to get her away from Vingh, of that she was certain. But she could not read if his countenance was fearful or jealous. Vingh laughed and grasped Augustine's shoulder. "Surely you can rely on your staff."

"They are not accustomed to such guests," Augustine returned, never looking away from Jane.

Jane considered asking him about Elodie in front of witnesses, then thought better of it. Vingh had already excused Augustine once; she could not stand to have it waved off again, as if the lie meant nothing. She smiled and fled to the kitchen.

The pageantry continued. Every time she returned to the sitting room, Augustine was there to ask another favor of her. Ask Mrs. Purl to fetch the linens from the third-floor closet, make sure Mrs. Luthbright had found the remaining good silver. He interrupted every time she began to speak with one of his guests, and her suspicion grew with each deflection. On her third trip to the kitchen, she asked Mrs. Purl to draw Augustine into the hallway, so that she could speak with her husband about sleeping arrangements. The sun was nearly set, and Mrs. Purl was all too eager to oblige.

Augustine stood, frowning, as Mrs. Purl left him without much in the way of explanation in the hallway by the kitchen door, but before he could retreat, Jane was on him. She crossed the gaslit hall between them, and saw his eyes widen as she trapped him in the corner.

When she was close enough that she was sure nobody else might overhear, she whispered, "I know you lied to me, Augustine." She was so close she could feel his breath upon her chin, stuttered out, a crack in his façade. She drove her fingers into it, pried it apart a little farther. "I remember what I saw last night."

"Jane—"

"I know about Elodie, about who she really was. A patient, Augustine? A patient, not your wife?"

His flesh went white, his expression shuttering. Triumph flared in her breast.

But then his jaw firmed. He met her gaze.

"This was never supposed to be a true marriage, Jane," he said.

She stepped back as if struck.

"You asked me to marry you as a business arrangement only," he continued, voice lowering. "I agreed, for that reason only. I told you that you could not come here, and you were more than happy to agree as well." His brow furrowed, and he reached out as if to clasp her shoulders. But his hands fell short, tensing in the air, then falling back to his sides.

"And yet I am here," she said. "And you have betrayed me."

He grimaced. "Is it betrayal? Or is it jealousy, this fury over Elodie? Because you do not own this part of me. I did not offer it in the bargain."

He was right.

Curse her heart, traitorous organ, for hating that fact. She wanted to scream, to argue, but their terms had been clear, and she had never demanded honesty. She had only assumed he would give it to her, that she deserved to know everything, that his life was now hers as well.

She hadn't *known* to ask for honesty. She hadn't realized all that she had wanted.

A miscalculation. An error of judgment.

His hand settled at last upon her shoulder, and it was gentle, not angry. "You should never have had to know any of it," he murmured. "It should never have touched you."

"And this morning?" she said, clinging to the sharp edge of betrayal that still remained, aching and blood-soaked in her chest. "You made me think I was going mad. You erased me from reality."

He flinched, and when he answered, his voice was low and soft, a caress. "I thought only of your happiness."

"I saw things. I saw Elodie, Augustine."

The intake of breath through his teeth was sharp. "If you had known it to be only a nightmare, you would have been free."

Her heart thundered in her ears. "Free from what?"

But before he could respond, Jane heard footsteps fast approaching. Augustine stepped away, smoothing down his waistcoat, as Hunt came around the corner.

"I'm afraid we have exhausted the decanter," the doctor said, then, "Oh, did I interrupt?"

"Strategizing only," Augustine said, and he sounded embarrassed but composed. There was no hint of fear in his voice, and Jane drew strength from his playacting. They would offer no hint of weakness to their un-wanted guests.

Jane turned to Hunt, the demure smile she had learned to wear for Mr. Cunningham's clients settled on her features. "I'll send for Mrs. Purl to re-plenish it," she said. Hunt nodded and disappeared.

Jane buried her face in her hands, taking refuge for just a moment. This was too much, all of it. She needed answers. She needed some kind of plan to move forward.

But when she looked up once more, her husband was already ducking back into the sitting room.

CHAPTER SEVENTEEN

Mrs. Luthbright conjured a feast from nothing. The table groaned under the seemingly endless parade of small courses. Half a dozen root vegetables, cooked in just as many ways, their staggered arrival buying time for the stews of dried meats, rehydrated in a desperate rush with wine, off flavors masked with young herbs sown only months ago. Liquor drenched every item to communicate luxury and wipe away any criticism. Jane clasped Mrs. Luthbright's shoulder and whispered a fervent thanks, but what put a smile on the cook's face was Jane's promise to wash the dishes herself. Relieved, Mrs. Luthbright had gone out under the darkening sky, followed less eagerly by Mrs. Purl, whom Jane had promised was not expected to find beds for the raucous crowd inside.

Jane sat beside her husband at the head of the table. Hunt produced from her valise more wine from abroad, sparkling and sour. Conversation ranged widely, tides shifting, words forming changing webs across the long table. At one moment, Vingh was describing a heroic surgery where the patient had writhed despite the ether but his bowels, perforated by industrial equipment, had been stitched whole again after the labor of five surgeons over three hours. (Whether the patient survived the night went unaddressed.) At another, Hunt was discussing the newest advances in the theory of disease transmission. And then the conversation would turn to gossip, to absent friends and hated rivals, to who was receiving funding for what, and what the Crown might ask of its physicians next.

Despite herself, she was entranced.

These were great and brilliant doctors, finely educated in a way she could not match but found herself desiring. In another life, she might have been one of them, able to discuss mathematical theory with the authority of a university graduate. Philosophical debate sprang up and consumed the whole table, and Augustine dove in as well. It was impossible to resist as her intellect thrilled. She found herself sparring with him over points of logic. It was glorious. Delirious.

In the service of their guests' comfort, she cast aside her memories of the night before, of strange, statuesque figures and red-eyed wives lurking in windows. She gave herself over to the fantasy instead, and for two hours, her guests *saw* her and did not laugh, and it seemed as if the impossible could become real. It seemed that if she could only contrive to divide the world by zero, she could have everything she'd never thought to wish for.

And then the dinner finished, and her guests rose and retreated back to the sitting room. She could smell tobacco smoke curling in the air as she gathered up the dishes and carried them off to the kitchen. The darkened windows of Lindridge Hall held no figures. The lights remained lit. She had passed through the fire, and on the other side was a better reality.

On her fourth trip to gather dishes, Jane realized the dining room was no longer empty. Dr. Nizamiev sat in Augustine's seat and caught Jane's gaze as she inexpertly stacked greasy platters. She rose and approached Jane with such precise steps that she almost seemed to glide across the floor, as she had in the surgery. The image of the figures outside the library returned to Jane, and her stomach turned to lead.

"Dr. Nizamiev," she said, in proper greeting at last.

"The new Mrs. Lawrence," Dr. Nizamiev returned, inclining her head slightly. Her eyes never left Jane's face. It had been barely a week since

Mr. Renton's death, but it felt like half a lifetime away, with everything that had changed. And Jane's unease with Dr. Nizamiev had only grown.

Given the strange mysteries of Lindridge Hall and her husband's lies, precisely what kind of specialist had he called forth from Camhurst to see a patient with an impossible ailment?

"How do you find married life, then?"

For all she knew, the question was a trap. "New," Jane said, hoping to end the conversation.

Dr. Nizamiev laughed. It was sharp and short and, to Jane's ear, calculated. "So it is. May we speak of your husband, given your better vantage point?"

"I—Yes, though I don't know what I could tell you that you don't already know."

"It is what I can tell *you*," Dr. Nizamiev said.

And Jane was caught.

She had no solid ground to stand upon anymore; all her assumptions had been torn apart. She would take all the data she could get to measure out this new reality. Make sure she missed nothing, figured everything correctly this time.

She could see her guests silhouetted in the warm lamplight of the other room, and heard Augustine's laughter among the voices, but she sat in the chair the doctor pulled out for her.

Dr. Nizamiev remained standing, studying Jane's face. "I had never thought he would marry again, not after Elodie."

That unwelcome pang in her chest again; was it growing gentler yet?

"I do not believe he intended to," Jane replied. "But he did."

"I take it that your arrangement is . . . uncommon, given our first meeting." Her words were clipped and controlled. Cold. Analytical. She sounded like Jane did when Jane was deep in her work, and though Jane had never felt ashamed of it before, now it made her skin crawl.

Dr. Nizamiev saw something. She was at work, even here. Doing what?

"Yes," Jane said, warily. "Yes, it is *uncommon*."

"And do you stay often at Lindridge Hall? Had you visited it before the marriage?"

Jane's hands fisted in the fabric of her skirts. Her gaze drifted to the window behind Dr. Nizamiev, half expecting to see Elodie there, watching.

Only her reflection looked back.

Dr. Nizamiev canted her head, a falcon judging the distance of its next strike. "You know," she said after a moment. "You've seen things."

Seen things. An unwise admission to an asylum's specialist, and yet Jane could not stop her forward lurch, her desperate query of, "*You* know?" Her pulse began to pound. "He told you?"

"Yes. He's told me."

Jane could no more leave the conversation now than she could follow the Cunninghams to Camhurst.

"There are some things you should be aware of," Dr. Nizamiev said, pulling over another chair and settling into it.

"But why?" she asked. "Why tell me?"

"Don't you want to understand?" Dr. Nizamiev asked. "I marked you for a creature of curiosity, not a coward."

Jane bristled. "Of course I want to."

Dr. Nizamiev sat back with a self-satisfied smile. Her voice dropped low, so as not to carry. "When Elodie fell ill, your husband was a guest at a retreat organized by the others in this house. The purpose of the retreat was to practice magic."

Jane stared.

"I certainly have—*seen* things here, but—"

But what?

If spirits were real, if she could see the imprint of Augustine's dead wife in a darkened window . . .

No. Blanching wedding rings in sunlight, wearing a shirt inside out— those were not spells, they were hope. The world was governed by logic and emotion, not esoteric power. Magic was not real. It was a fantasy, an impossibility, something from old superstitions.

But then she thought of Mr. Renton, of Mr. Lowell's whispering, of *chalk and salt.*

"Magic is very real, Mrs. Lawrence," Dr. Nizamiev said. "But what they were doing that week wasn't. They were schoolmates reunited after several years of being separated by their residencies, and they were playing. At university, we were all part of a particular eating club, a covert gathering that performed rituals and had shared secrets. There are many of them in many universities across the country—and outside of it, too—and most are playacting at best. Ours was no different. We had gathered that week just to relive our younger days.

"And then the news came that Elodie Lawrence was deathly ill."

Jane found herself leaning in, desperate to hear more. "And he left, but not in time to save her."

"Correct. What happened next I wasn't present for, but he told me some of the details when he came to me for help three months ago."

Just before he came to Larrenton. At the end of the long disappearance that Vingh had wondered over. Jane felt the pressure increasing inside her skull.

"What did he tell you?"

"He was distraught after Elodie's death, and both his family and hers blamed him for it. He was desperate. So he worked a spell. He tried to fix what he felt he had broken."

Her skin crawled, and she hunched forward, shivering. "He tried to . . . bring her back?"

"Yes."

Impossible. But she had seen Elodie, holding her finger to her lips. And so had Mr. Purl, and others, too, no doubt. "It didn't work, though." She breathed, desperate to maintain the foundations of her world, the logical constructs that had bounded her decisions, led her here to this moment, married to a man who believed in the ridiculous. "It couldn't have worked. Elodie is not here. He—he is married to me."

"You're right, it didn't work," Dr. Nizamiev said, and Jane's eyes watered with relief. But the doctor was not finished. She said, "It didn't work, because transmutation of that sort is impossible. I don't know where he found the spell, but at most it should have let him speak to her spirit, not make her body so much as twitch. Except nothing happened at all. The families found out and were disgusted. They felt he had profaned their home. And so they left him."

Jane scrambled to slide all these new fragments into the expanding portrait of her husband. They fit easily.

"Why tell me this?" she asked again. Dr. Nizamiev had some less altruistic aim, but what it could be, Jane did not know. It yawned, black and indistinct behind the glittering sharp edges of the truth of Augustine.

"You are clever, Mrs. Lawrence; let me set the puzzle pieces out for you, and you can tell me what you see."

Jane's throat bobbed. And then she nodded, wordlessly. *Go on.*

"His spell was unsuccessful," Dr. Nizamiev said, "but that does not mean it had no consequences."

"The hauntings," Jane said.

Dr. Nizamiev nodded. "He fled, trying to avoid them. But he sickened. When he came to me three months ago, he was barely able to stand, but no doctor had been able to diagnose him. He came to me first, instead of seeing Georgiana Hunt or the others, because he was afraid they would discover what he had done. He knew I was circumspect, and that I was . . . experienced."

"Experienced how? Are you a—a sorceress?"

Dr. Nizamiev smiled then, animating her face, which Jane realized had been oddly blank while she related her story. "I study those who perform magic, and those who think they perform magic. It's a personal curiosity of mine, after being a part of that eating club."

"Mr. Renton," she said, eyes widening as the logic clicked into place. "He called for you to attend Mr. Renton because he may have worked magic."

"And then he turned me away, because he did not want to *know* what had happened, only to have me remove a problem from his hands. And because, I suspect, he resents that I could not help him when he first came to me. But I have been doing research on his behalf and have tracked down some texts that may be of help."

Jane looked at the sitting room doorway, mouth gone dry. "Let me get him," she said. "You should be telling this to him, not me."

"I have already spoken to him," Dr. Nizamiev said. "He refused my aid."

Jane frowned. "Refused?"

"Something has convinced him that he deserves whatever punishment finds him inside these walls." Dr. Nizamiev shrugged. "If that is his choice, so be it. But if you have also seen things, you deserve the choice to arm yourself."

"To work magic, you mean." *Impossible. Impossible.*

"Yes, or to convince him to do it himself."

Was that it? Genuine concern for her safety? Jane scanned the other woman's face and found only that unsettling stillness. No; there was more here than wanting to rescue Jane and Augustine. There was more that she was not saying.

Jane would be a fool to believe Dr. Nizamiev, when her explanations were so thoroughly tempting and wrapped with approval that had not been there the day Mr. Renton died.

"You'll forgive me," she said, gathering up her skirts and standing, "if all of this sounds ridiculous. How am I to believe you? To believe *this*?"

"My colleagues are skilled at diagnosing abscesses and fractured bones, but I am skilled at locating fear. You're terrified, Mrs. Lawrence."

Jane could not argue that.

But it didn't matter. "I am returning to the surgery tonight. I will never come to this house again. I was never meant to come here—this is not meant to concern me."

"Is that so?" Dr. Nizamiev said. But before she could press her argument, Augustine's raised voice broke through the seductive murmur of the next room. She heard the scraping of furniture against wood, and saw again the blackened windows of full night.

The spirits had arrived.

Jane rushed into the sitting room, sure that she would see red-eyed Elodie in the window. But instead, she found Augustine red-faced, unable to find his words, and Hunt at his side, grinning.

"It's only a little spell," Hunt said. "Can't we go back to the way things used to be?"

CHAPTER EIGHTEEN

"THIS HAS GONE on more than long enough," Augustine snapped, jerking away from Hunt as if her touch at his shoulder burned. He was panicking. "I—*we*—have enjoyed your company, but it is time to be reasonable, Georgiana."

Hunt's delighted expression fractured, and she raised her chin a hair. "Do not treat me like a child, Augustine."

"You come to my home despite my objections, you impose upon my wife and my staff, you refuse to listen to our polite suggestions that you return to Larrenton—"

Jane stepped fully into the room, and Augustine stopped, looking at her, eyes wide.

"I must," he said, mastering himself with visible effort, "return to the surgery, at any rate. My patients may have need of me."

He was running away.

From her? From his guests? It hardly mattered. He was a man beset, a man who rejected aid. If Dr. Nizamiev was telling the truth, he had chosen to suffer and so leave them both vulnerable, when he could have fixed this all. Could have acted so she would never have encountered the spirits of the previous night.

Selfish, foolish man.

"My husband tells the truth," she said, and watched his shoulders fall in limp relief. "One of us must always be in attendance at the surgery, if possible." Soft murmurings rose from the back of the room, wagers of if she'd go and leave the doctor to them. Flight called to her, the simplest answer she had. But she did not want to leave. She felt as if she stood balanced upon a precipice. Answers on one side, ignorant bliss on the other.

And her heart burned too hot for bliss.

She stepped closer to Hunt and held out both her hands, palms up. They did not tremble, because she clenched her calves and pressed her feet into her shoes to root herself to the ground.

"If Augustine will not take part, may I join in his stead?"

"Jane! Jane, you can't."

"Why not?" she asked, looking to Augustine with as much need, as much honesty as she could summon in front of an audience. *Tell me I can trust you. Tell me this can be fixed.* "Dr. Nizamiev has told me of your games."

Behind her, Dr. Nizamiev's skirts brushed over the flooring. Hunt tore her gaze from Jane and looked to the Ruzkan woman, brow arched. "You preempted me."

Augustine struggled to pick his words. To her left, she heard one of the men murmur, "She has not been initiated." But Vingh patted the man's shoulder and came to stand beside Hunt.

"You would be most welcome," he said. Smoke curled from the cigarette he clasped between his fingers.

She tried not to look surprised. But she recognized the smile on his face: he was needling Augustine. This wasn't about her.

"She can't," Augustine repeated weakly. "Jane, please—"

"She's here," Vingh said. "It's that simple. And Augustine, as much as we would be honored by your own attendance, I'm sure we all understand the demands of your profession. You do not have a locum installed, and there must be nobody else about for miles. Go, go to your patients. Only give us the use of your cellar."

Jane's mind went immediately to the padlocked door. He had said the cellar was crumbling. Dangerous.

A muscle in Augustine's throat jumped, and he turned away, going to refill his glass with a shaking hand. "There is no cellar," he said.

Jane's heart sank at his boldness.

"That is not what Elodie told us," Vingh said.

Augustine was silent for a long moment, shoulders bowed. He was considering something. At last, he spoke: "You must be mistaken. Elodie was initiated in the library. My parents could hardly have excavated entire new rooms beneath the house to play at magic."

Her head spun. Too many new details unspooled themselves around her: His parents, playing at magic before him. His parents, disgusted with Augustine for trying to work magic himself. Elodie, playing at magic by their side, dying somewhere in this house.

He was lying about the cellar. She knew it with a horrible certainty.

"Then Augustine, we will just use the library," Hunt said in placating tones. "There's no need to be so distraught. It's only a bit of fun."

"A bit of fun," he spat.

"A bit of fun, and a nudge to the universe to preserve our patients in our absence."

"Then go back to Camhurst! Tend to them there! Jane," he said, rounding on her, "these games are childish folly; there's no need for you to stay. All of you, please—I will send the carriages back to you, I can find space for you all somewhere in town. But do not drag this madness back into my home."

"Augustine," Jane murmured, and he clung to his name, leaning ever so slightly toward her, a desperate light beneath his features. Hope that she would side with him. Hope that she would believe him.

She trembled with the effort of resisting the easier option, of going to him, taking his hands, choosing to accept the version of reality he was so desperate to maintain. "Go back to Larrenton. We'll follow in the morning."

THE SITTING ROOM gave over to uneasy conversation when Augustine had gone, his carriage retreating down the road. Hunt stood by the hearth, scowling, glaring out the far window. Jane came to her side, mulling over her new array of facts.

"What is initiation?" she asked.

The doctor shrugged. "In university, there was a—process for joining the club. A series of tasks, a hierarchy of knowledge."

"And Elodie was initiated?"

"Yes, as was I, and Augustine, and all the rest. It's usually required before you participate in ritual workings." Jane braced herself for a rejection, now that Augustine was gone. But it didn't come. "We can work around it," Hunt said. "After all, you're here."

Vingh had said the same thing. "I don't follow. It can't be that simple."

"It's not," Hunt said, "and it is. That you're here at all means that it will be of value to you. Like seeks like, like resonates with like." If she sounded less than convinced, could Jane blame her? They weren't alike at all. "There have always been groups like our little club, and they always grow by synchronicity. Those who would benefit from learning the great secrets will find themselves placed in the path to learn those secrets. Initiation only provides an imposed structure, to help make sense of strange new truths. But regardless of preparation, when the time comes to awaken to the truth of the spirit, the world finds a way to midwife."

"I see." She didn't. It sounded preposterous, the logic of a group determined to feel special, unique. She was here because Hunt had invited herself, because Vingh wanted to drag Augustine back to the city, not because Jane wanted to play at magic.

But she was also here because she had seen spirits in the hallway, and because Augustine had lied to her. And if Elodie had been initiated, if what transpired then had led to whatever Augustine was now avoiding, she would learn more by following in their footsteps.

"I suppose I must, then," Jane said.

"Exactly. You begin to understand."

She turned from Jane then and clapped her hands. The physicians came to attention, to a one. Even Dr. Nizamiev fixed on her. "To the library with us. Avdotya, will you be joining?"

The woman shook her head. "No, I'll wait down here for you all to finish."

"Of course," Hunt said. Her attention had already slid away from Dr. Nizamiev, and back to Jane. "Lead on, Mrs. Lawrence."

Jane did not relish the thought of going up to the library with the sun set and Augustine gone. What would happen if she took them to the cellar door instead? She might convince them to help her break the lock, based on their memories of Elodie. And what would they find behind it? But she was not sure she could explain herself, and so she led them up, turning on the lights as she went.

None of them guttered. No shadows moved. The rug remained smooth and even beneath her feet—no doubt Mrs. Purl's doing, a quick tidy for their guests.

"Now, before we begin," Vingh said, falling in next to her as they reached the second-floor landing, "what has Avdotya been filling your head with?" He held in one hand a valise. Several of the other guests carried cases with them as well.

"Just that you have done this before," Jane replied. "I confess, I'm not convinced of it."

"That is the adult, rational mind speaking," Hunt said behind her. "It veils what we know to be true as children. Children, you know, often see spirits, often feel things. But they don't have the context. It is the marriage of sight and context that leads to understanding. Do you follow?"

No. She had never seen anything of the sort; her childhood visions had been of bombs. Spirits were a monster of a different age. They should have been left behind along with all these superstitious practices.

"As much as I can." They reached the third-floor hallway, and she led the way to the closed library door. She hesitated only briefly before turning the latch. The room was chill, but empty, blessedly empty. She scanned every window, every pane of glass that arched above her head, but found nothing but their own reflections.

The rest of the guests filtered in, talking to one another in low voices. She watched as they set out their cases and pulled out loose, pale robes, pulling them on over their traveling clothes. All wore pale colors, except for Hunt and the other woman, Dr. Reese. Theirs were dark, embroidered with something akin to star charts.

She took a deep breath.

"If you're afraid," Vingh said softly, by her ear, "you should know that none of this ever works. We haven't figured it out."

She twisted to look at him. What an oddly vulnerable admission from such a proud man. "Do you believe it could? Work, I mean."

"Oh, yes. With all my soul. I have . . . seen things," he said, quick to justify himself. "And read things, too many things to doubt that there is *something* else to this world that we can only barely touch. We have centuries of stories of ghosts, of monsters, of beasts beyond understanding. They fall off as the march of progress continues on, but they must have had their root in something. Tonight, though, nothing will happen here besides chemistry and theater."

"So it's fake."

"Not at all." He pursed his lips, then shrugged. "The best explanation I can give is that we are following a path laid out before us by a lineage that goes back many generations. To before those magical stories stopped. By following the path, we learn things each time, and we move closer to the truth of it."

She thought of following proofs that greater minds had devised for mathematical conundrums, and how, though she followed the steps, she did not always understand the whole of the progression until she'd tried it many times.

It was . . . reasonable.

The whole room took on a peculiar scent as her guests lit curling incense, at once pungent and faded, acrid and sweet. From the empty shelves, the doctors hung painted cloths, covered in brilliant pigments, laying out intricate paths of symbols that Jane vaguely remembered from church services as a child and decorations in the magistrate's office. They were combined with what she imagined were the iconographies of other peoples, married to some form of map. Geometric designs wove in and out of the depictions of fanciful figures, and the whole array created a sensation of deep uneasiness in her, of being lost in another world where different laws held sway.

The other woman, Reese, inscribed a circle of chalk upon the floorboards. *Chalk,* Jane thought, her breath catching as Hunt took her hand and led her to the edge of the circle, then across it, all the way to the center, where the table she had read at the night before still sat. "Kneel here," the doctor said, and Jane swallowed, lowering herself to her knees. Hunt let go of her hand and unfolded a square of fabric, a silver veil. She draped it over Jane's face.

"As you are in the role of a new initiate," Hunt said, "and as this is not an initiatory night, you will not be privy to any of the secrets. You will watch through a veil, and you will see the shape of things, but not the detail. Follow the guidance of my voice, though, and you will still be able to lend your aid to our Work."

Jane shivered. Vingh might have claimed that this was only pageantry, but she was growing less certain by the second. The whole thing was too elaborate, too *real*-looking.

"And what is the purpose of the circle?" she asked.

"Many things," Hunt replied. "Containment, protection, focus."

And Jane was at the center of it. She chanced a glance at the nearest window.

Through her veil, it remained blank.

She watched as they all arranged themselves about the circle, inside the chalk line, all their murmuring, intoxicated conversations ceasing. Nobody held a lit cigarette, nobody held a glass. They moved solemnly and with great focus, as if it were a dance upon a stage. Then Hunt took up a ceramic bowl with a spout at one end. Standing at the inside edge of the circle and facing outward, she began to move her lips in a soft whisper. Slowly, she poured a stream of *something* from the bowl, walking sideways as she marked the perimeter.

Salt.

When she reached where she had begun, she handed the ceramic bowl to the man who stood closest to her. She and Reese left the perimeter and approached the center of the circle, taking up positions across the table Jane knelt before. She could barely see them, between the angle and the veil. Instead, her eyes focused on the two candles sitting on the table. One was small and already burning, the other tall and in an elaborate setting, unlit and fresh. The room filled with an expectant silence, one that almost thrummed upon the air. It felt real. It felt alive.

"Let this candle be the light that guides us in our Work," Reese said, her voice clear and deep, ringing across the space. She held something to the burning flame, and once it caught, used it to light the taller candle. "Let the power in its incandescence enchant the circle that circumscribes the realm that we inhabit, so that we may do the Work safely and in total focus."

Jane should stop them. Mr. Renton had played these games of chalk and salt, and ended up dead on the operating table. This was dangerous. This was not *right*.

"By the senses, we align ourselves this night to the Work before us. By the burning of these offerings, we place ourselves upon the path to the Work."

Hunt set fire to the contents of a bowl. As Jane watched, the smoke that rose from it turned dark before bursting into a dance of colors, sparking and leaping, that she could see even through the veil. There was a sharp crack. Several of the participants jumped at the sound as the bowl fell to pieces, smoldering.

Jane smelled blood.

She tried to stand and found herself immobile. The iron stench grew, grinding against the empty spaces of her skull. She wavered on her knees. Somebody was hurt. Somebody had to be hurt, perhaps from the breaking of the bowl. She straightened her spine, trying to see over the table, trying to see Hunt's hands, the other woman's, but the world was growing dim.

Distantly, she heard Reese intone, "We guide ourselves to the imbalance, to the missing member of our ranks. His mind has been clouded by grief and his hands turned clumsy by doubt. By the flowing of this water, we align ourselves to the forces at work and begin to see their origin, their path, their conclusion."

They had come for Augustine, to call him home. This was all for Augustine. They had put her in the circle as—what? An offering? A sacrifice?

The stench of blood grew. Her head spun. She tried to scream and could not.

Instead, she saw Elodie.

Elodie laid stretched across a shining white plinth of stone before her. There was blood in her eyes, on her lips, obscuring her features. Crimson oozed from beneath her. But she was alive. Her chest rose and fell, her breath rattled. Jane gasped but could not move, could not turn her head. Could they see this?

Dr. Nizamiev. She needed Dr. Nizamiev.

But instead of Dr. Nizamiev, she saw Augustine, dressed in traveling clothes. He rushed into the room, the library blended with an unfamiliar chamber of hewn stone walls. She tried to reach out for him, to beg him to stop this. And he turned to her, her and Elodie. He ignored the dim shapes of the men and women around them. He ran to the table—the plinth—and for a moment she was overjoyed, because Elodie might still be saved. She could not speak, could not explain, but there he was, rucking up his sleeves, pulling out a blade—

No. This was wrong. This was no operating room, and this was no way to treat his dying wife. Where was the grief, the tenderness? Where, even, was his doctor's manner, his steady reassurances that he would help?

Absent. All absent, replaced with a fevered look as he slit Elodie's nightgown open down the front.

And then he split her chest in two.

Elodie was weak but alive. She was fighting, thrashing, screaming, and Jane felt tears upon her cheeks as she stared up at the plinth in horror, so close that she could feel the chill radiating from the stone, feel blood spattering across her brow. Her hands spasmed and she jerked forward, but she could not rise from her knees. *Stop! Stop! You'll kill her!* she tried to scream, but the words would not leave her throat. She could hear nothing but her own heartbeat, the crack of bone, and Elodie's convulsing limbs sliding weakly over the stone.

Augustine plunged his hands into the wound. Blood coated him, coated Elodie and the white stone below her, and it was all Jane could smell. His hands were inside her chest, and he was sobbing. He was laughing. There was none of his calm control during surgery, none of his procedure, his confidence, his solemnity. He looked wild.

Jane screamed. She had to stop him. She had to stop him!

What has he done?

Hands gripped her, and Jane wailed, thrashing. The veil slid from her face, and then the cool, musty air of the library flooded her nose.

She couldn't smell blood anymore, and when she blinked, the vision was gone. She was being held fast by Hunt and Vingh, and all around her the doctors murmured to one another in their playacting robes. Tremors rocked her as she looked between the gathered faces.

"Mrs. Lawrence?" Hunt asked. "Are you back with us?"

"I saw—" She gasped, then fell to shaking once more, confused, in pain. Augustine had lied to her, had hidden Elodie from her, had left her unable to trust her own memory, but she had not thought him a monster. Had never feared him to be a brute. The Augustine of her vision refused to co-alesce, not only with the man she wished him to be, but with the man she had observed. His outline did not match the wretched horror she had seen.

And Hunt, Vingh, Nizamiev—they'd all been clear. Elodie had been dead when Augustine arrived. Whatever ritual Dr. Nizamiev claimed he had worked, it had been after her death. Not—not whatever it was that she'd just conjured, on the scaffolding of Hunt's pageant.

And yet it had felt so real. And yet she could not explain it. She remembered the words of Reese's incantation: *By the flowing of this water, we align ourselves to the forces at work and begin to see their origin, their path, their conclusion.* They had tried to summon up Augustine's affections and draw him back, and instead, they had revealed to her . . .

What?

She was helped to her feet, then down the stairs. Hunt settled her in the sitting room and pressed more brandy into her hand. Behind her, Jane could hear muttering, make out only isolated words: *sensitive, perceptive, a true medium.*

"I am sorry," Hunt said, touching her shoulder.

"Leave me," she mumbled.

"Drink your brandy."

Jane took an obedient sip, the liquid sloshing from the shaking of her hands. She stared at it, and then beyond it, to the darkened window. Her reflection stared back at her. She willed her features to be transformed, for her gray eyes to weep red. She willed Elodie to appear before her, to offer some explanation, some condemnation, *anything.*

She could hear, distantly, Hunt's voice. Discussing diagnoses and treatments with one of the other doctors. They would take her apart to find what was wrong with her. The thought filled her with revulsion.

"Give Mrs. Lawrence some space," Dr. Nizamiev said, moving in front of her, the fabric of her skirt obscuring the window. Jane looked up. Dr. Nizamiev looked back, impassive. Hunt left without argument.

Dr. Nizamiev was, after all, an expert in madness.

All the other voices faded, retreating out to the hall. The foyer. Perhaps they would leave, and at that thought, Jane started forward. *No, no, I cannot be left here alone for the night.* But Dr. Nizamiev caught her shoulder and eased her back, then sat down beside her on the small couch, not looking away. Jane turned to face her mechanically.

"You saw something," Dr. Nizamiev said.

I saw horror.

"I don't understand," Jane mumbled, gripping her glass tightly. "I don't understand what I saw."

"The ritual can be affecting," Dr. Nizamiev said. "The power of suggestion, a type of hypnosis."

"No." Jane seized Dr. Nizamiev's hands with one of her own. "I need you to tell me what Augustine did. I need you to tell me about magic."

CHAPTER NINETEEN

Y OU MUST PROMISE me one thing, before I continue."

Dr. Nizamiev's notebook was open on her lap, and Jane watched as she penned a quick observation. Whatever it said, she could not read, but Dr. Nizamiev looked pleased.

Jane's skin crawled. "Of course," she said. "What is it?"

"That you will accept as true everything I am about to tell you. It will not be easy, but it must become a part of your understanding of the world, or else I will have wasted my time."

"I promise," she said hastily, desperately.

Dr. Nizamiev set the pen down in the gutter of the book but did not close it. "Good. Now. I do not know precisely what Augustine did to try to bring Elodie back from death," she said. The admission kindled quick anger in Jane, but before she could argue, Dr. Nizamiev held up a hand, stilling her. "He only told me of the results. But I can tell you the logic of it."

Lindridge Hall was silent around them. The lamps beyond the sitting room had dimmed, and they sat alone in a small pool of light. "Please."

"You are an accountant."

"Yes."

"Perhaps you can think of magic, then, at its most basic as changing numbers," she said. "Shifting the reality of a thing. Making it into something else. Alchemists strived to change lead into gold, water into wine. But it's not simply replacing a two with a three in a column of sums. It is changing what two represents."

"I don't follow," Jane said, though she could feel herself leaning forward, the mathematical logic seductively familiar. "You could say that the *word* two means three things, but two items would still always be two items."

"It's a strange sort of logic," Dr. Nizamiev said as if conceding a point.

Jane frowned. "It doesn't work."

"Remember your promise, Jane. Here, another option: change the meaning of an operator. Summing goes from one thing being added to another, to one being added to another and another."

"This is all semantics," Jane said. The nascent headache from earlier that evening had turned to pounding. She could still hear Elodie's screams if she was not careful to keep her focus. Semantics could not stop that. Semantics could not save her. She could not accept semantics as a new truth. "It's impossible."

"And that is why you and I cannot work magic. Because we know it is impossible."

Jane's head jerked up. "Because it *is*."

"The premise of the working of magic," Dr. Nizamiev said, "is first and foremost that the practitioner believes—that she *knows*—that it *is* possible."

"But it isn't!"

"If the practitioner knows that magic is possible, then the practitioner can change the rules by which the world functions. But that knowing extends beyond belief, extends beyond mere acceptance. Magic must be a part of the practitioner's every waking moment. It is an altered state of being."

There was an odd light in Dr. Nizamiev's eyes, a hunger, an alteration of her predatory gaze. She was not just watching Jane now, she was watching *for* something. Some response. Some slip.

"It's madness," Jane said.

But Jane's mind was working, turning over the problem, faster and faster. The properties of the number zero were, in and of themselves, impossible. To divide by zero produced irrationality. But if her text was to be believed, that irrationality then produced real, true answers. The area under a curve, the volume of an irregular object, all *real* things. Her treatise even contained a proof that if division by zero was allowed, one number could be proven to equal another—just what Dr. Nizamiev was now describing.

Except the properties of zero could be tested by reality. Magic could not.

"It's madness," she repeated again, quietly, to herself.

Dr. Nizamiev arched her brow. "Madness," she mused, sitting back. "Yes. It is."

Jane shivered. "*You* lock the mad up." This was it. The trap that Dr. Nizamiev had laid. Jane, mad, removed from this house and her husband's life—

But Augustine had shown no signs of wanting her gone, and Dr. Nizamiev had no reason to claim her as a patient. And Dr. Nizamiev had made her promise to believe so as not to waste her time; hardly the behavior of a doctor set to commit her.

"I study madness," Dr. Nizamiev said, lips faintly curved. "And I study the practice of magic. As I said, magic is my personal curiosity. Madness is my professional one." She paused in thought for a moment, then shrugged. "Have you ever had the experience of somebody telling you a new fact, and it changes how you perceive the world?"

"Of course." She searched Dr. Nizamiev's face for a flicker of a joke. There was none. She thought of the proof that had demonstrated to her, as a young girl, that the area of any triangle, of any arrangement, could be found using the measure of its component parts. The unmeasurable calculated from the measurable.

And she thought of Elodie.

"For the moment, let us grant that changing the rules of the universe is impossible."

"Granted."

"Then a magician—one with *proven ability* to do things beyond what their fellow humans can—is somebody who has a particularly focused kind of madness. Does that sit better with you? Their belief in an impossible thing is so strong that if they turn their will on a question, they can change the answer for other people without ever telling those other people what they did. It changes how those around them perceive the world, even if the underlying fabric of the world remains the same."

"The ghosts I've seen," Jane said, hand tightening on her glass. "You contend that Augustine's force of will did that."

"Yes."

"But the logic is circular. Because the ghosts exist, you've proven Augustine can work magic. Because he can work magic, he is the reason for the ghosts. What if it's something else?"

What else is there? Augustine's hands in Elodie's chest—

"Simplified concepts for the introduction of ideas aren't ever accurate," Dr. Nizamiev said. "The ghosts exist. That is our constant point in this puzzle. The rest is supposition. Likely supposition, but supposition all the same."

The throbbing in Jane's head was so insistent now that she wondered if she'd cracked it open on the library floor, and she rubbed at her temple with her free hand. "If it's a matter of simply believing in the impossible, why couldn't he have brought her back from the dead? Why isn't she here, right now, at his side?"

Because he did something worse than what he confessed to Dr. Nizamiev, her mind proffered. *Because what you saw was not the action of a man desperate to save his dying wife.*

But her throat closed up and she could not voice the thought aloud. If willing something could make it true, voicing her suspicions could surely do the same.

"Magic," Dr. Nizamiev said, her accented vowels focusing Jane's attention, "is, at its basest nature, knowing the reality of something to be different from what it is. But it is not a matter of *wishing* for an end result, or we would all be capable of it. The magician must understand every element that must change in order to produce the desired result. Every equation must balance and proceed from one to the next. The changes to the world that would be necessary to truly bring somebody back from death would require knowledge too complex for the mind of man to comprehend."

"So instead he . . . what, trapped her spirit?"

"If the ritual he found was incorrectly structured, it's possible. The ritual guides the magician's force of will. It cements the magician's knowledge of the working of the world and thereby lets her choose exactly which thread to pull on, which number to change the meaning of."

With a sickening pop, something clicked into place inside her brain. "A proof. Rituals are like mathematical proofs," Jane said wonderingly. "Dr. Vingh said rituals function by reproducing the steps over and over again, thereby learning the logic of it by the practice. Like studying trigonometry. But couldn't you just as easily practice nonsense? Just because a thing is written out, step by step, doesn't mean it leads anywhere."

Dr. Nizamiev inclined her head in approval. "Just so. A poorly designed ritual can lead a magician astray. A magician gets what she asks for, whether she meant to ask for it or not."

And what had Augustine asked for? What plea had he been making, up to his arms in gore? Jane shuddered, bowing her head and curling in upon herself.

"Tell me," Dr. Nizamiev said, voice quieting but not softening, "what happened up there."

"They were asking to be shown what had led Augustine away from his old life," Jane said. "And I saw her. I saw Elodie." She swallowed.

"As you have before?"

"No. Before, I saw her in the windows. She was silent. This time—this time, it was as if she was in the room, and she was screaming. Augustine was—Augustine had—I don't understand."

"Tell me." It was a command, and Jane flinched, drawing back reflexively. She did not want this cold, strange woman to see into the house's darkness, but who else could she turn to?

How could she return to the surgery in the morning? How could she greet her husband?

"What ritual," she asked, voice weak, "would lead a man to cut open his wife's chest and reach in to take her still-beating heart?"

Dr. Nizamiev inhaled sharply, the first scrap of surprise Jane had seen in her all night, the first crack in her control.

"What you saw," the woman said, "may not be literal reality. You must remember that."

"But what if it was?"

"I have no answers."

"It doesn't make *sense*," Jane whispered. "I have seen him with his patients, and he is caring, and kind, and skilled. I have never seen him be cruel. I have seen him lie, I have seen him manipulate, but never *harm*."

"Neither have I," Dr. Nizamiev agreed. "Which is why I wonder if it might not be, instead of the truth, a filtered perception."

"What do you mean?"

"If Elodie is here, in these walls," Dr. Nizamiev said, rising from her chair and gesturing around the room, "then does it not follow that she may still retain some measure of coherence? Of thought? Of feeling? Stories tell us that ghosts are fixed in time by strong emotion. Fear, or grief, or confusion. What if you saw not what was, but what the ghost of Elodie remembers? Fractured interpretations, reassembled into something that goes against truth."

"I cannot take that chance," Jane said. Her hands fisted in her skirt.

"Then what will you do?" Dr. Nizamiev asked. "A nightmare is not evidence for a magistrate."

Jane plucked at the cloth, picking at threads. She stared straight ahead. What options did she have?

"Why ask about magic," Dr. Nizamiev said, "if you have no plan to use it?"

"I just want things to make sense," Jane whispered. "I just—"

She was interrupted by Vingh appearing in the doorway. "Pardon," he said, ignoring Jane entirely. "Nizamiev, have you seen my instrument case?"

Jane frowned and rose from her seat. "Is something wrong? Is somebody hurt?"

"A little accident," he said, gaze flicking to her and away again. "Georgiana went to pick up her glass and it shattered. But I can't find my blasted bag."

Dr. Nizamiev said nothing, looking at Jane instead.

"I haven't seen it, but there are tools here," Jane said. "A-an old bag of Augustine's, I just had the contents cleaned up the other day. It's in the kitchen, if I'm not mistaken."

"That will have to do," he said grudgingly, but he did not move. Instead, his skin grew pale.

"Dr. Vingh?"

He was looking at the darkened window.

Jane turned to look as well, but found only their reflections looking back.

"I've never known you to be skittish, Andrew," Dr. Nizamiev said.

"I had not expected screaming tonight. No offense, Mrs. Lawrence."

"I would have preferred to be spared it myself. The glass shattered?" Jane asked. She motioned for them to follow her into the kitchen. Vingh and Dr. Nizamiev followed at her heels. There, on the counter, were the cleaned scalpels and other tools. Vingh went to them immediately, fingers hovering just above, until he found a sharp, curved needle.

"It was the strangest thing," he murmured. "Never seen it in my life. Like the offering bowl, it just—split. Reese is convinced that she closed the ritual wrong in all the chaos of your fit. She's up in the library again, trying to fix things." He scoffed. "What a load of nonsense, if you ask me. Mrs. Lawrence, do you have sewing thread?"

"Somewhere, I'm sure," Jane said, and began checking drawers, hoping that Mrs. Purl kept her belongings close to Mrs. Luthbright's, instead of in some unknown closet.

"Where's Augustine's? His bag must have had some in it."

"It had burned away," Jane said.

"Burned?" Vingh's voice grew more strained.

"It was found in a hearth upstairs."

Vingh swore and dropped the needle. It clattered against the ceramic of the kitchen basin. "Burned! Has Augustine seen these?"

"No, but he said he burned the bag after a particularly virulent case."

"Yes, *Elodie's*," he snapped. "These aren't fit for anything. No telling if they still carry the pestilence."

"Surely, not after years—"

"It's not worth the risk." He seized up a graying dishrag and stalked out of the kitchen. Dr. Nizamiev followed behind.

Jane lingered in the kitchen, looking at the gleaming metal, barely blackened anymore from the flames. She thought of the scalpel that had bit into her finger. Creeping closer, she looked for any trace of blood on the cloth they rested on and found nothing.

Of course there was nothing. They'd been cleaned. They were identical to the instruments at the surgery that had seen a hundred patients. The past did not cling to them, any more than it should have clung to the house.

When she emerged from the kitchen, she found the doctors all gathered in the foyer, checking their bags. Hunt's hand was bound tight, and she was swaying slightly where she stood. There were many hours still until dawn. Jane frowned.

"What has happened?"

"The spell," Reese said as she cinched her valise shut. She had shed her robes—they all had—but she still looked slightly abstracted as she had inside the circle. She eyed Jane warily. "I haven't been able to right it."

"Leave off it!" one of the men snapped. "You're just riling everybody up with your spiritualist talk. The carriages are hours off still, and if any of us is going to get to sleep, we need to drop the act for the night. It's not fun anymore, Reese."

Reese scowled, and Hunt laughed shrilly. "It's not *fun* because you know it's real now."

"See, look what you've done!" the man shouted.

"Doctors," Jane said, stepping into the fray though she quaked in her shoes. "This house is not the most comforting place to spend the night, as Dr. Lawrence and I attempted to warn you." *You are not safe; we should all leave immediately.* But she could hear rain beginning to drum on the roof far above, and she felt again the carriage turning, sliding toward the ridge.

It was a risk to remain, but it was plainly dangerous to leave. "Let us all settle in to the sitting room; I will fetch blankets. Though I understand your unease, I assure you that you are in no danger."

The spirits had yet to attack her.

She had to believe that would hold.

CHAPTER TWENTY

THERE WAS LITTLE sleep in the sitting room, though Jane saw no more visions or ghostly specters, statuesque or otherwise. There were no more disappearing bags, though one of the doctors—an ophthalmologist named Dr. Guernsey—thought for five minutes that his cravat had been stolen from his very neck, only to admit, sheepishly, that perhaps he had loosened it earlier and it had slipped off on its own.

Murmurations swept through the room in cycles, Reese still wide-eyed and convinced that she had put them all in danger, Hunt on the edge of hysterics, and all the rest vacillating by the hour as to whether they thought everything a game that had overstayed its welcome, or a real threat. Dr. Nizamiev sat quietly by the doorway out to the hall, contributing nothing, entertaining no theories and offering no guidance, merely writing in her notebook. Jane watched her nervously.

Nobody spoke to her after she provided the blankets and Reese had checked her eyes and balance for any sign of lingering disruption. Once she was proven sound, in body if not in mind, they all avoided her. She was grateful; all the safety of not being alone, all the privacy of being ignored. It was only quietly that she wondered if they were afraid of her.

When the sun finally broke over the mist-draped hills surrounding Lindridge Hall, and Mrs. Purl and Mrs. Luthbright arrived, bearing apologies that there would not be much breakfast beyond bread and tea, the tension in the house lessened—but did not leave entirely. Vingh immediately imposed on Mrs. Purl to have her husband go to town and summon back their carriages, despite her protests that he would already be working in the fields. Jane saw a small amount of money change hands, and then Mrs. Purl was out the door.

Jane left the group as they sat down to breakfast, retreating up to the bedroom to splash water on her face and change her clothing. The bed galled her now to her very core, and for a moment she considered telling Mrs. Purl to ready the upstairs bedroom for her alone. But no; she had no plans to remain. Not in this house, and not in this madness.

The carriages seemingly arrived as soon as she had buttoned up her fresh dress, and Jane realized she must have drifted off where she was standing.

She shook herself and went back out into the hallway, watching from the landing as her guests gathered up all their belongings. She descended the stairs, smoothing out her skirts, and came to Hunt's side. The woman was bleary-eyed, her hair frizzing wildly.

"Where will you be staying in town?" Jane asked.

"Nowhere."

Relief warred with embarrassment in her heart. "Are you sure?"

"Where else in your wretched town could put us up outside a hayloft?" Hunt snapped.

Jane went very still.

Hunt immediately looked contrite, but she squared her shoulders and shoved both of her hands into her trouser pockets. "You're a rational woman," she said, not quite meeting Jane's eyes. "You understand logistics."

"I do. But what of Augustine?"

"What of him?" Hunt asked, a muscle in her jaw twitching. "He was very clear last night. He wanted us out."

"He wanted warning."

"He's right," she said, abruptly moving again, scooping up her bag. "About the magic, about everything. It's time we moved on; he clearly has already made his choice. He can keep his rotting mansion and his provincial practice."

Jane should have responded, but she was frozen with anger. She was furious on Augustine's behalf, then disgusted with herself in the next heartbeat.

"Come," Hunt said without looking back, "we'll drop you at the surgery. You shouldn't remain in this place."

No.

The vehemence of the thought surprised her. She wanted to leave this place, wanted to rest, wanted to feel *safe*. But she was not prepared to see Augustine, not prepared to ask questions she did not want to hear the answers to. Her disgust would overwhelm her. Her fear would overrun all reasonable thought.

And she did not think she could manage the carriage ride back to town without strangling Hunt.

"I'll remain," Jane said stiffly. "As you said, I understand logistics. I need to help my household recover from your invasion."

The words were more bitter than she had intended, but Hunt seemed to shoulder them without a flinch. Already written off, already relegated to a box that read, *unpleasant host, unpleasant locale.*

The other doctors left with tipped hats, or brief, polite commentary, or nothing at all. Finally, as the carriages began to roll away one by one, she made her way back to the sitting room and began righting the furniture. It was Mrs. Purl's job, and she was far too violent with the carved wood, but the movement helped vent her frustration.

It was two minutes later when she realized Dr. Nizamiev sat at the desk.

"Do you plan to stay, then?" Jane asked, voice rough.

"No."

Jane felt nothing, and so much at once that it could only be perceived as nothing. "Then please, leave me."

Dr. Nizamiev rose and held out a small package, wrapped in crisp, thin paper. It contained several thick photographic printings.

"Take these," Dr. Nizamiev said.

Jane hesitated, then took the package, sliding the first out.

In the photo was a young man lying on a cot, staring at the ceiling. He looked like any other patient, or any other fresh corpse. Jane looked up at Dr. Nizamiev, confused.

"A magician," Dr. Nizamiev explained. "He was delivered to me in the dead of night with a note pinned to his shirt. It was brief, but it said he had participated in a ritual intended to summon what he called a demon. It went wrong, whatever happened, and he hasn't moved once in the three years he has been in my care."

"Dr. Nizamiev—"

"There exists a whole floor of my hospital that is for those patients with unique ailments."

Jane turned to the next photo, this one of a woman who wept bitterly as she clawed at her face, her skin protected by the thick leather mitts strapped over her hands.

"Magicians or suspected magicians," Dr. Nizamiev continued. "I fund their care, and in turn, I observe them. From what I have seen, Mrs. Lawrence, all magic eventually leads to ruin. Every magician will reach a point where they harm themselves or others. And when they do, they can rarely be rehabilitated."

"Monstrous," Jane whispered, thinking of Mr. Renton, of his twisted bowel. "It is monstrous, to lock them away."

Dr. Nizamiev made no response, clearly unbothered.

"Our patient. If he had lived, would he have . . . ?"

"Perhaps," Dr. Nizamiev said.

"He clawed his belly open," Jane said. "His flesh had distorted."

"Then you have seen firsthand the risks. Very few magicians know about this. All who do think they're different, special."

"Dr. Hunt? Dr. Vingh?"

"Have both seen my patients in person. They fall into the arrogant category, instead of the ignorant. Your Dr. Lawrence, as well, up until recently."

"I have no intention of ever attempting magic, if that is your concern."

She half expected anger, but Dr. Nizamiev's tone was unchanged as she said, "You promised me to accept it all as true, and I can see that you have done so. I cannot tell you what you need to do to unravel the mess of this house, but you have a mind for magic."

Jane flinched. "You said that we were the same—that we knew it was impossible."

Dr. Nizamiev smiled. "Logic can be brought to bear in powerful ways. But at the very least, Dr. Lawrence will certainly have to return to the practice, if he is to be rid of his affliction."

Jane shook her head. "If you're so certain, why show me this? Why frighten me?"

Dr. Nizamiev tapped the photographs, and Jane turned to the final print. It looked for all the world like a body hanging from a noose.

But there was no noose. The body was a woman's, and her toes hovered limp an inch above the floor, the rest of her body floating above. Her head had fallen to one side. She stared at the wall.

She was impossible.

"This world is real, Mrs. Lawrence," Dr. Nizamiev said. Her voice, chill and emotionless, made Jane's skin crawl. "There are ghosts in this house, and they will not go away merely by wishing it to be so. They will not go away if you ignore them. And now that you've seen them, you can't go back to the understanding of the world you had before."

Jane swallowed, lifting her chin to look at Dr. Nizamiev. The other woman was watching her closely, as if taking note of every minute detail of her. Studying her. Measuring her for a cell.

As if one day, Jane might end up in her care after all, and Dr. Nizamiev was eager for it.

"I have penned my address on the back of the first photograph. I have a wealth of research available to you, should you want it."

Jane frowned. "Strange, that you brought these with you for a house party. Were they for Augustine?"

"No," Dr. Nizamiev said. "He has also seen these patients in person."

"Then how could you have known to bring them?"

Dr. Nizamiev picked up her bag, and at first Jane feared she would not answer, so calmly was she moving toward the foyer. But then she looked back, lifting one elegant shoulder in a shrug. "Georgiana explained the concept of synchronicity, did she not? Call it that, if you like."

CHAPTER TWENTY-ONE

J ANE STOOD IMMOBILE, clutching the photographic prints, until
long after the door had shut and the carriages had all driven away. Her
head swam with exhaustion. Tears pricked at her eyes. She closed them
and saw, faint and confusing, a blond woman on a red-soaked plinth. She
shuddered.

Dr. Nizamiev was right. There was no option for a simple life anymore.
Slowly, Jane peeled herself from the sitting room, leaving behind the stale
scent of old cologne, of spilled brandy, of what might have been a pleasant
night except in the particulars. Friends from afar; stories of her husband's
life; a brief dance with him where he proved to her that he could have played
his role far better, if only circumstances had been different. But the night
had been sour from the first.

The contorted figures in Dr. Nizamiev's photographs and memories of
the shadows in the hallway pressed in on her, leaving her barely able to
breathe. If the servants crossed her path, she didn't notice. She thought
of impossibilities, and mathematical proofs, and the steady cadence of

Dr. Reese's voice. The world falling away. Fear. Anger. Desperation. Hers, or Elodie's?

She reached the locked cellar door. The final padlock stood, unmoving, taunting her. The cold dread she'd felt the other day rose from the floor, curling around her calves, reaching for her heart. This time, she knew it for what it was: the promise of knowledge. Another hidden secret, one last place she could not go. Augustine had been quick to anger after Hunt had begged the use of his cellar; had it only been that he hoped to keep Jane from realizing that he had played at magic, or because the cellar itself was not what he had said? He had made it sound so sensible, so simple. *The tunnels could collapse.* She would have believed him, had it not been for the wax burns on her foot. For his agitation in front of his guests. For his hands, drenched red, inside a body where they should never have gone.

Her headache spiked as she stalked back through the halls, up the stairs, making her way to the library. Dr. Reese had taken away all her ritual implements, but the candelabra Jane had clung to so desperately in the face of the spirits that haunted Lindridge Hall was still there, off to the side of the faded chalk circle. It was made of good iron, kept rust-free by Mrs. Purl's attentions, and the weight of it felt powerful in her hand.

Minutes later, the padlock gave way after only three great swings against its upper arc. It clattered to the hall floor. There was no answering sound, no shout from the kitchen or running feet upon the stairs. Jane carefully replaced the candles, which had been knocked free of their holders, and lit them one by one in the gas sconce nearest to her. Her fear had made her as cold as the metal in her hand.

She hauled open the door.

Inside it was pitch-black, and there was no switch for gaslights on the inner walls. This part of the house had not been modernized with the rest. The candlelight was her only illumination as she made her way into the gloom. She followed a short hallway to a set of stairs that began as wood, but as she descended, they and the surrounding walls were replaced by old white stone. Familiar white stone. Cold, damp air rose up from the blackness beneath her, chasing away the last of the midmorning warmth that clung to her shoulders.

She welcomed it. She wanted the chill. It made her stronger.

Because the room she now stood in the middle of was no collapsing cellar.

It was a crypt.

Its ceilings were high and vaulted, and the sections her candles illuminated were made of more of the same carved stone. Niches lined the walls and several halls branched off into the darkness. This had been here first, she was sure of it, before the house, before the horror. It was old, and solid, and *wrong*.

Picking a passageway at random, she entered a room that was longer than it was wide. Jane's light fell on a stone chair, facing away from her. Another few steps and she could make out the bulk of a long banquet table, with chairs on either side, all made out of the same glimmering white rock. Her heart seized in her chest, and she clutched the candelabra with both hands, trying to offset her sudden shaking. There was no red stain upon the table, and her vision had not shown her chairs, but she knew. She recognized the plane of the stone, and saw where Elodie's nightgown had lain, spread out across it. One of the seats had words carved into it. She approached, fear weaving through her spine.

JEREMIAH LAWRENCE
1714–1769

She checked the others. Most had names inscribed upon them, all members of Augustine's lineage, and one, the one she stopped at, was carved with the name *Elodie Lawrence*. Two years dead now, at only twenty-four.

At the far edge of the room, she saw a faint movement in the shadows. She froze, eyes widening, free hand reaching out to steady herself on Elodie's chair. Augustine? The servants?

Or worse—the strange figures from the other night?

Her eyes darted around the room, frantic to find where the first figure would come from, looking for the elongated bodies, the unnaturally shaped heads. Instead, a human-sized shadow stepped out of the gloom. Jane's chest heaved in sputtering gasps, and she clutched the chair and candelabra more tightly. For one wild moment, she felt sure it was Augustine, scalpel in hand, but the silhouette was too curved.

Elodie.

She could see the waving outline of her floor-length nightgown, could smell the iron tang of blood. Jane staggered back, knuckles white on the candelabra, staring as Elodie emerged from the blackness, passing by the table that was now red and slick. It shone wetly in the candlelight, pocks of flesh distorting the shadows. It looked more like the operating table in the surgery than a monument now.

Crying out, Jane looked over her shoulder and moved the candelabra toward the doorway.

It wasn't there.

The wall was smooth and unmarked, but she was certain it was the way she had come through. She pressed her free hand to the stone, searching, searching. There was no indentation, no hint of a corner, no indication a door had ever stood there. She let out another wretched sob, running along the wall, feeling desperately for some mark, some symbol.

Nothing.

She reached the corner and pressed her burning forehead to it, too afraid to look behind her. There were no footsteps, no rustle of fabric, no wheezing, rattling breath of the etherized or dying. Impossible, that a dead woman was behind her. Impossible for the dead to walk at all. A hallucination, a vision; that was all it was.

But without sound, she couldn't tell how close the impossible dead woman might be. Jane's pulse pounded in her ears, counting down until she was certain Elodie was close enough to touch her. She jerked and turned, helpless against her panic.

Elodie was only inches away. Even this close, the lines of her face seemed to waver and shift, as if she were reflected in uneven glass; but her cheeks were hollow, her lips blue and cracked. Her eyes were red, red as the blood that soaked the front of her gown, that poured from the ragged edges of her skin and muscle and bone.

Slowly, Jane sank to her knees.

She needed to speak. She needed to understand. If Elodie truly stood before her, if Elodie was bleeding all over this cellar floor, then Jane had to save her. She had to rush to her, as surely as Augustine had rushed to Mr. Renton's side. She could not hesitate.

She could not be the monster.

"What do I do?" she whispered, reaching out to touch the hem of Elodie's stained gown with her free hand, the other still clutching tight to the candelabra. "What do you need from me? Tell me, please, what he did, and I will make it right."

Elodie looked down at her, face pained, opening and closing her mouth without sound. She was still. Her chest did not rise or fall, and Jane felt sickly grateful, because if it had, the ribs would have spread and blood would have drained faster still from the wound.

"Tell me," Jane begged. "They said you died before he ever returned, and that he only called your spirit forth, but what I saw—what I saw last night—is it true?"

Elodie grimaced, then reached down and seized Jane by the hair.

Jane swung the candelabra instinctively, its limbs striking the ghost's shoulder. It rebounded, Elodie as immovable as stone. The candles tumbled from their iron holders, guttering, going dark, all but one that glowed feebly by their feet.

Her hand stung from the impact. The candelabra slipped from her grasp as she reached up, hooking her fingers around Elodie's cold fist. Elodie moved, shifting her grip to cup Jane's chin, thumb against her cheek. She bowed low over Jane's prostrate form, and her eyes bored into Jane's, the fine lacework of vessels within burst in a hundred places.

Her fingers slipped lower. They pressed hard to Jane's pulse; there was no kindness in her touch.

Jane struggled but could gain no purchase. Her knees slid on the blood spreading beneath the both of them, her legs tangling in the fabric of her dress, tearing it. Her vision swam, and she remembered the burn of gas in her nose, the creeping darkness that had pressed in on her in the cellar of her mother's house. She was going to die down here. Heavens protect her, but she was going to die. Would she be put in one of those chairs? Had Elodie . . . ?

Her head pounded as her heart beat double-time. If Augustine found her down here, would he simply shrug? Or would he suffer? Would he miss her? Would he realize he had done this?

She felt a desperate kindling in her gut, a horrible certainty that she could not die, that she would not die. It was like a mass, pressing upon her stomach, her diaphragm. It forced a scream up out of her throat, and she surged upward, grabbing Elodie by the hips. She pulled herself along the spectral form, soft now, like rotten fruit beneath her fingers.

The pressure against her throat released. Jane shouted and threw Elodie from her, then scrabbled for the candle. It was almost dead, and she scooped it up, her frantic motions making the faint light flicker out for a moment before it blazed again. She brandished it before her with shaking hands.

Elodie was gone.

No blood coated the floor below her; the stone was no longer slick. Her other hand sought behind her. There—her fingers hooked around the doorframe. She backed through it, then felt along the wall toward the stairs, eyes darting around the darkness. She couldn't see more than a foot on any side of her, but she came across no bloody ghosts, no lurking creatures.

She found the stairs and climbed.

She didn't stop moving until she was in the foyer. Melted wax coated her fist, and her knees were bloodied, but she couldn't feel the sting anymore, and the ichor that had soaked her skirts had disappeared. She fumbled with the latch to the front door, glancing back at the hallways, at the decaying grandeur of the staircases. The latch gave way, and she stumbled out into the sticky, humid brightness of midday, nearly falling down the front steps.

The front gardens stretched out ahead of her, tangled and half dead. Staggering, she made her way down the drive past withered trees and the desiccated remnants of old blooming vines. She could feel the sickness rolling off the edifice at her back, the lies clinging to the shingles of the roof, the menace rising up from the cellars. She could still smell old blood. Augustine had killed Elodie; Elodie would have killed her; Elodie was telling the truth; Elodie was lying. She could not sort one thought from the other, and it was all she could do to start off down the dirt lane, headed back to town.

She had to get out.

She had to escape.

CHAPTER TWENTY-TWO

S HE REACHED LARRENTON hours later, her feet aching, her house
shoes in tatters. She held her skirts carefully, trying to disguise the tear
across the front. The noises of town immediately pressed in on her
from all sides and she flinched away from people who passed too close. She
would have turned and fled, except that she had nowhere else to go.

The long walk had given her overwrought mind time to parse out *some*
logical thoughts, the half-formed semblance of a plan. She could not go back
to the surgery; of that she was certain. The thought turned her stomach, and
she didn't know what she would do when she saw Augustine again. He had
promised her explanations, but could he explain what she had seen? Could
he explain why her throat was bruised?

No; she could not face him yet, if ever. She could not live inside those
surgery walls that stank of blood, not any more than she could live in Lindridge Hall.

When the Cunninghams had been young, the obvious choice would have
been a priest. But the passage of time and the changing of the world had
rendered such men useless and almost gone, replaced by magistrates who

were just as likely to send her to an asylum or hand her over to Augustine as they were to listen to her.

She still had one option left to her, however. She would go to back to Mr. and Mrs. Cunningham, and beg on their kindness. Impose on them for a night, or two, and then ask if they would take her to Camhurst with them after all. She could bear it, must bear it, in the face of all that had happened. The marriage could not be annulled, now that she had consummated it, but Mr. Cunningham would know some tactic she could use. They would want to help her.

Wouldn't they?

She threaded her way through the streets, keeping her head down, constructing the narrative that she would offer them. No ghosts, no magic— unkindness, then? Unspecified betrayals? Would it be enough? They had entreated her to move to Camhurst with them, and she had refused, had set herself on this path. With their support, yes, and yet . . .

Jane reached the familiar lane that she had lived on for so many years, and quickened her pace, lifting up her head at last. She was nearly running by the time she reached the doorstep, her plans cast aside in the face of simple, pure relief. *Home.*

Jane knocked.

There was no answer.

She stared up at the house's façade for several long minutes, willing herself to see motion in the upstairs window. Mrs. Cunningham bustling about, or Ekaterina stripping the beds. But there was nothing, and she became acutely aware of the traffic behind her, carts and footsteps, murmuring voices, jarring shouts. The carved face in the lintel above her leered down. She was near the center of town, the house convenient for a solicitor's clients, and suitable to a solicitor's standing. She hunched in on herself, imagining a hundred eyes on her, judging, weighing, evaluating. The Cunninghams' strange ward, falling to pieces now that she had left their oversight.

Jane knocked again. Again, no footsteps. Where could they have gone? It was not market day. Had they gone visiting? Ekaterina could be out doing the shopping, and the Cunninghams away to the next town over for tea and joyous conversation before they left for Camhurst. But she needed them *here*. Her heart was thundering in her chest, and she tested the latch.

The door opened.

The house was barren.

Jane stepped into the gloom, lifting one shaking hand to her mouth and letting the door fall closed behind her. The house's inhabitants were gone, and with them all the furniture Jane had grown up around, all the landmarks of her youth. What had once been Mr. Cunningham's office now stood empty, even the rug that would have borne the impression of the heavy desk's feet rolled up and carted away. She checked every room, wide-eyed and hoping, hoping that even if the first few carts had gone to Camhurst already, she would find at least the bedrooms untouched. A promise that they would be home by evening.

The bedrooms were empty boxes of wood and plaster.

Stifling a wordless cry, Jane sank to the floor of her old room. She stretched out along the floorboards, rough where the rug had kept padding feet from wearing them smooth over the years. She stared up at the ceiling, searching out the water-stain shapes the way she had when, as a girl, she'd woken up at night hearing phantom shelling in the distance. But the rabbit and the fifteen speckles all in a line were gone. They'd had the ceiling repaired before moving out.

How had they accomplished this all so quickly? It had been not even a week since she was married.

Had they been so glad to be rid of her?

No. The judgeship was important; it made sense that they had set off quickly to their new life. But couldn't they have left the house to pack up later? A week was not enough. A week should not have been enough. They should have been *here*.

They should have at least said goodbye.

Jane's eyes stung with tears, and she tilted her chin up, willing them away. But that last abandonment was the final crumbling of her walls, battered by the carriage nearly slipping over the embankment, by her houseguests'

petty needling, by Lindridge Hall and Augustine and Elodie. Sobbing overtook her, and she rolled onto her front, pressing her forehead against the
wood. This had been a mistake, all of it, set in motion when she had decided that marriage was her best option. If she had never made that list,
if she had only followed the Cunninghams to Camhurst as they'd wanted
her to, she would have been happy. Or, if not happy, at least content; Camhurst's courts would never have let her serve them, and she would have
been bound to socialize and curtsy and smile, and the scars of the war
would have resurrected her old terror, perhaps, but it would not have
been *this*.

It would have been predictable. It would have been manageable.

How did one manage a blood-soaked husband and a vicious ghost?

How did one manage *magic*?

She stayed there, on the floor of her childhood bedroom, weeping for
herself and her arrogance and her fears, until the light changed to a darkening golden glow. Only an hour at most remained until sunset, and for a
moment, she considered remaining right where she was. Augustine would
leave the surgery soon, if he hadn't already. And as soon as he was gone,
the surgery would be safe for her. She only needed a bed. In the morning,
before he arrived, she could buy a seat on the mail coach to Camhurst.

But no, she could not stay in this house past dark. Its empty walls held
as many memories as Lindridge Hall held ghosts, and she did not want to
be run out for trespassing. She looked wild, her hair tumbled down from
its chignon, her dress muddy and torn. Trembling, she sat up and pulled
her hair down, then plaited it. She did her best to disguise her ruined dress.

And then she went back out into the streets of Larrenton and walked the
familiar path to her husband's surgery.

CHAPTER TWENTY-THREE

I T WAS FAR too fast a walk. She remembered with consuming clarity how long it had felt to hurry through the streets to meet Augustine that second day, and the third, eager to test her skills against his needs and find herself well suited. She had been enamored from the start. She had been fixed upon him. A part of her still rose in welcome to see the familiar door of the surgery.

It was only three steps away that she seized up once more, staring at the building. What if he hadn't left yet? What would she say to him? What would she demand? Could she just bow her head and continue on, and allow the both of them to sidestep the anger that filled her? She had to manage only another day—surely that was not so difficult?

She could do that. She *would* do that. It was not so hard, to pretend for a fixed duration; it was only eternity that she could not bear.

She entered the surgery.

The hallway was empty. The door to Augustine's office was mostly closed, though she could hear within the low murmur of conversation. He was with a patient, then. Relieved, she hobbled to the kitchen. She would tell

Mr. Lowell that she was here, and ask after dinner, and hope that Augustine would leave without knowing to check on her.

Mr. Lowell, however, was not in the kitchen, and Jane eyed the kettle with longing before easing herself down into one of the chairs. A few minutes. She just needed a few minutes off her feet, and then she would get herself upstairs and washed. Dinner could wait.

She woke up to the sound of the front door closing.

Grimacing, she sat forward, rubbing her neck. She must have dozed off, exhausted after the previous sleepless night. But that would have been Augustine leaving, or Mr. Lowell arriving, and—

"Jane."

Augustine stood in the kitchen doorway. By his expression, he hadn't expected to find her there. Anger flooded her, and fear, and confusion, and she thought she must look like a cornered, hunted animal. She wasn't ready. She wasn't ready to see him, to speak to him.

Damn him. Why couldn't he be in his corrupted house, bedding down with his secrets and spirits?

"Hello, Augustine," she said. It was a struggle to keep her voice light and even. She did not want to. She wanted to scream. "Where is Mr. Lowell?"

"Off to bring you home," Augustine said.

Jane flushed with guilt. She said nothing.

"How did you get here, Jane?"

"I walked."

Augustine stared at her, then seemed at last to see how disheveled she was, how her skirts were muddy and her cheeks wind-chapped. "Stay there," he said, then filled the kettle and set it to heating. He disappeared into the supply room, emerging with bandages and compounded unguents.

"Augustine, don't."

"You must be blistered. That is not an easy walk." He knelt before her, reaching out for her ankle.

She jerked away, as if his hands were still drenched with gore.

"Jane?"

He did not know what she had seen, what had happened to her. She did not want to tell him, not yet, not ever if she could help it. And yet she had no other explanation for why she shied from his touch, though her feet throbbed, though he was a doctor.

She wanted to scream accusations, but instead Jane placed her foot into his hands.

He gently pried off the scraps of her house shoes and washed her swollen, blistered feet. She had not realized how badly they hurt until that moment, and she found herself choking down pained sobs. He did not falter and made no comment on her poor choice of footwear, her impulsive flight from Lindridge Hall. By and by, the wounds stopped bleeding and the dirt washed away.

Distantly, she heard the door open. She heard footsteps on the stairs, the sound of a door opening above, a soft thud. Footsteps, again. Augustine did not look up as Mr. Lowell appeared in the doorway.

"Doctor, I—oh, Mrs. Lawrence," he said, and his hands loosened on his cap, where he had been wringing it. "I have brought your things from Lindridge Hall."

"Thank you," Jane said, too embarrassed to meet his gaze above Augustine's bowed head.

"I would have come sooner," Mr. Lowell said. "It was just—"

"No harm done," she said, throat catching. "No harm done at all."

His cheeks were red; they must have made a strange tableau. "Will you be needing me to cook dinner, then?"

Her chest burned. "We will be fine," she said, meaning nothing of the sort.

Mr. Lowell ducked his head and left.

When the front door had shut once more, Augustine withdrew and went to the stove, adding fresh wood from the pile and tending it. "I shouldn't have left you there," he said at last. "It was cowardly of me."

And cowardly to lie, and cowardly to take me to bed to distract me from my questions, and cowardly to make me believe I dreamed a nightmare instead of witnessing your secrets. Through great force of will, Jane did not say any of it. Instead, she covered her cleaned and bandaged feet with her skirts, and said, "It was."

Augustine began to cook in silence, frying up fish that had been soaked in wine and herbs. Jane thought of fleeing, but just as she'd drifted to sleep as soon as she was seated, now her stomach was reawakened. The scent was heady, as was the wine that Augustine set down before her.

The meal was large enough for two—her and Mr. Lowell, she presumed—but he still gave her the better share, keeping only a little for himself.

She devoured the meal.

"Have Georgiana and the others remained at Lindridge Hall?" Augustine asked, when she was only a few bites from finishing. His own plate was barely touched.

Jane set her fork aside and sat back, swallowing down a mouthful of wine to clear her throat. "No. They left this morning."

Augustine glanced to the window.

Night was falling.

Go, Jane dared him. *Go. Go back to your spirit-infested house, your wretched magic, your horror show.* She had seen him covered in blood. She had seen him murdering Elodie.

But then Elodie had turned on *her.* Jane could still feel Elodie's fingers on her throat, and that cold pressure once again turned her anger to frustrated confusion. Her appetite turned to ash.

She pushed her remaining dinner around her plate. "The Cunninghams have gone," Jane said into the drawn silence between them. "Without a word. Did you know?"

He frowned. "No," he said, "though a letter arrived here for you, two days ago." The day she had refused to leave Lindridge Hall. If she had left, she would have been able to say goodbye. If she had left, she would never have known what lurked in that house.

She should have left. Damn her curiosity, damn her suspicions.

"You should rest," he said. "May I help you upstairs? There are two bedrooms."

"If you are going to Lindridge Hall tonight, you should leave now."

"I'm staying," he said.

Jane looked up at him wordlessly.

"May I help you upstairs?" he repeated.

In answer, she tried to stand up, but her feet, now that they had been tended to and rested, roared with pain. Wincing, she fell back into her seat, then nodded. "It appears to be necessary. Yes."

Augustine gathered her up in his arms and bore her from the kitchen. Through his shirt, he felt warm. More than warm—fevered. Sweat beaded his brow. "You are not well," she said.

He laughed bitterly, and mounted the stairs. "No, Jane, I'm not. I think that's very clear."

They reached the second floor, and he toed open the door to a small, clean bedroom, warm from a banked fire, and perfumed with dried flowers to counteract the smell of human suffering below. Her valise rested by the door. He eased her down onto the bed.

For one last breath, he was close enough for her to smell the sickness on him. His hands were tender as they withdrew from her, and that contrast of bleak honesty and gentle care unsettled her, more than anything else.

He pulled away and made as if to leave, then hesitated in the doorway. He looked back at her, at her bandaged feet.

"Jane," he murmured, "why did you walk, all the way from Lindridge Hall? What happened?"

And where before she had been able to resist, to wave away the question, now she crumbled. She wanted, so badly, for him to explain everything.

"Dr. Nizamiev told me about magic, about spells to bring back the dead," she said.

He paled but did not reject it. And he did not look at her with a liar's false pity, the way he had when she told him of her "nightmare." "What else?" he asked.

"I saw you," Jane said. "When they played at magic, I saw you, covered in blood. I saw Elodie, dying. You had your hands about her heart."

He closed his eyes tight, as if in pain, but did not deny it. He did not fight her, did not threaten or excuse or lie.

Jane pushed herself upright in her bed, emboldened.

"Augustine, I saw her, down in the cellar. She was there, soaked in blood, and she seized me. She would have killed me." Her voice cracked with anger and frustration, and she did not try to hide it. "We have gone so far beyond our arrangement. Please, tell me: What have you *done*?"

Silence. Outside, she could hear the sound of night insects and the murmurs of a living town, so different from Lindridge Hall's preternatural stillness. She held her breath and waited for him to run.

"I lied to you," he said at last. "I summoned the dead, and I held my wife Elodie's heart in my hand, and all of it, every single foul action, was because I was desperate and afraid." He related it all without emotion, eyes downcast. "That first night we met, I told you we could not marry. But I was weak, and I gave in when you pushed just the slightest bit. I am ashamed of many things that I can never forgive myself for, Jane, and that, as much as all the rest, pierces me to my soul. And last night, I compounded it by blaming it on you. That was not fair, and I am sorry."

Jane pressed her hands to her face. She heard Augustine leave, his steps heavy—and then his pace quickened, a door cracked against the wall as it was heaved open, and she heard him retch.

He was not well.

Everything she had learned was true. She should ignore him, sleep, and in the morning she would go to the magistrate. The marriage could be broken, now that he admitted that he was a murderer.

But he did not *feel* like a murderer. Her heart whispered, traitorously, that she knew him, and she could not shut it out.

Damn him.

Jane levered herself off the soft, new mattress, and hobbled out into the hall, each step a necessary agony. The door to his study was open, though none of the lights were on. The sound of his breath drew her inside. He was crouched behind his desk, bent over a ceramic dish, and she passed him without a word. She went, leadenly, to the couch where she had first kissed him and sealed her fate.

"Tell me everything," she said. "I want to understand. I thought I knew you."

He said nothing as he wiped his mouth on his sleeve. As if in pain, he eased himself back against the curiosities cabinet that contained Mr. Renton's bowel and closed his eyes.

Jane waited.

"I loved Elodie," Augustine said at last. "Our parents were close friends, and we always knew we would marry. By the time we were grown, I truly loved her. Shortly after we were wed, she took ill, then rallied. I had thought to cancel my travels with my colleagues to be by her side, but she encouraged me to go to them, only sad that she was not strong enough to travel with me. I left her at Lindridge Hall with my parents and hers, all gathered together because of her illness, and all but her displeased that I would abandon her while she was still recovering.

"And then I received the letter saying they had been right, that she was dying once more, and if I could have conjured flight, I would have flown back. As it was, the journey took three days. By the time I got to Lindridge Hall, she was almost dead. I did everything my training had taught me, and more besides. Her pulse was fading, her heart on the verge of stillness." He paused. His jaw tensed, his teeth grinding. "But a person does not die when their heart stops. They have a few moments more, borrowed from the universe, and I have seen it done, where the heart can be brought back."

Her world began to slow. Her eyes burned. "Augustine," she warned, but he did not stop.

"I split her chest open, and I held her heart in my hand, and I pumped it for her, to squeeze the blood through her veins. It could have worked. It could have worked, Jane.

"But she died, instead, and in the end, it was I who killed her."

Hot, filthy tears slid down her cheeks, and she wasn't sure who they were for. For Elodie, who had surely wished to die in peace, but had instead suffered the brutality of her husband's desperation? For Augustine, falling into such depths of self-hatred whenever he lost a patient, faced then with an even dearer loss? Or for herself, for having to know these things that she would have preferred never to touch on?

"If I had simply left it there," Augustine said, after a long pause, "I might one day have forgiven myself. But I was arrogant, and I was ashamed, and

I was grief-stricken, and so I turned to magic. You heard that Elodie was initiated; so was all my family, and all of hers. We had books upon books of magic ritual, and a thousand empty beliefs, a hodgepodge of old religions and practices cobbled together into an entertaining whole, and I believed. I believed in it, and I thought our families would understand. Down in that cellar, I worked a ritual that I thought would bring her back."

"But you cannot bring back the dead," Jane whispered.

"No," he replied. "No, you can't. But you can open the doors to something— some*where* else, and your house can fill with the ghosts of every patient you have failed, their ranks added to with everybody who dies under your knife. And your family can find you in that cellar, with their daughter-in-law's chest cracked open, the woman who is the child they always wished they'd had for their own, and they can blame you, and abandon you. I ran after that, unwilling to set foot in that house, unwilling to face the punishment that I had earned with every candle I lit and every incantation I said, but it made me sicken."

She looked at him, truly looked at him, and saw his heaving breath, his feverish brow, smelled the stink of his illness. "At night, you must return to Lindridge Hall," she said. She remembered how he had winced from his headache the night he had returned to her, and saw again his untouched dinner plate tonight. Remembered Dr. Nizamiev telling her about his mysterious illness.

How could he run, if staying away just two nights made him retch and burn with fever?

He nodded. "Each night I don't, I worsen. I am sorry, Jane; I tried to tell you all I could, when I knew I would be too weak to cast you aside. I thought if we obeyed your rules, perhaps I *could* be happy again, and perhaps you could get out of life everything you desired. I wanted it to be enough. I wanted all of it to be enough. I thought I could keep you safe."

Jane clenched her fists into her skirts. "But I didn't want to follow my rules. And then the carriage crashed."

"And you came to me, and saw nothing that first night, though I had heard Mr. Renton howling in the halls before you arrived," Augustine said.

"And nothing the next night, though I was not there to protect you. I began to hope. They stopped coming to me, Jane. I saw nothing, I've seen *nothing*, since you stepped foot in Lindridge Hall."

"But now I have," Jane said. "You lied to me, told me it was a nightmare, but I remember. And I have seen Elodie, in that crypt."

"That is the only thing I don't understand," Augustine said, leaning forward. "I have never seen her, not once. And all the ghosts that haunt me have never once laid a hand on me. They have terrified me, yes, and pursued me, and mired me in the knowledge of my own failures, but—to have *seized* you—"

Jane stood slowly, leaning heavily against the couch. She spread her hands so that he could see the great tears in her skirt. She lifted her chin and hoped that there were bruises there for him to mark. "I ran all the way back to Larrenton," Jane said. "You saw my feet. Do you think I would have done that for anything less?"

He bowed his head.

"That night," Jane said, "I did not see your patients. I did not see Mr. Renton. I saw inhuman figures headed for your study, and I went to save you. I thought you were in danger, and that, together, we could fight it."

"Jane," he whispered, pained.

"Fight it. Fight it now. You cannot live like this. The creatures of Lindridge Hall would kill me, Augustine. Fix this." *For both of us.*

He shook his head violently. "I am condemned," he snapped. "It is not something to be *fixed*. You will never go back to Lindridge Hall and I will suffer the way I am destined to. I am not like Andrew or Georgiana, who believe that because of our medical degrees, we can do no wrong. They think we are like *gods*. If we err, it is never our fault; it's the patient's choices, or the weather that day, or a hundred other things. They think magic is their birthright, a game they are entitled to play. But I know what I do. I know what I have done to deserve this."

Jane's lips pulled back into a snarl, anger cracking through her like a whip. "Augustine, listen to yourself. You may not be like them, but you are their exact inverse. You believe you are just as much a god, that every illness can be stopped, that every injury can be repaired, if only you do the right things, exert enough effort."

His face went scarlet, then pale once more.

"It is not just arrogance, Augustine, it is also cowardice. Because if everything is your fault, you don't have to face the truth that the world is a cruel, unpredictable place, and that you cannot ever control all of it. Death always wins, Augustine. You cannot stop it. You could not stop it."

"You don't understand," he said. "You can't understand."

"I know that my mother and father are dead, and I could not have prevented it, no matter how much I screamed and cried and begged them not to volunteer." Her heart blazed within her chest, and she stepped forward, desperate to make him hear, make him listen.

And Augustine refused to meet her. "Death always wins," he said, "except in a world where it doesn't. Once, I came so close to changing that. And then I failed. This is my punishment; it cannot be denied."

Death always wins, except in a world where it doesn't. What if he was right? What if she could have screamed and begged enough to make her parents stay? What if she could do the same here, help him, do anything, if only it would make him heed her? Change the boundaries of the world, change the truth of what rested, rotting, in his brain? If he had come as close as he thought to changing death itself, couldn't she do at least that much?

She wanted, so desperately, to be happy with him. To build a future by action instead of acceptance.

"Look at the ring on your finger," he said, interrupting her wild spiral of thoughts.

Jane clenched her hand, feeling the bone curves press into her palm. "What of it?"

"Mr. Aethridge," Augustine murmured. "Did you read the monograph?"

"No." A surge of guilt rose in her. She hadn't had time to.

"As a young man, the planes of his back began to distort. A few months after he noticed the first changes, he was thrown off his horse. He broke his leg, and though it was appropriately treated, bone grew up and around his knee, locking the joint for the rest of his life. From there, the illness crept into his very muscles, injuries that would have been little more than bruises on you causing great sheets of tissue in his arms to transform.

"I tried everything. I cut the bone away with a saw, burned the remaining fragments where they sat in the muscle, gave purgatives and had him fast for weeks, then ordered him to eat only rich foods. Nothing worked.

"He wasn't the first to suffer so, though it's rare, and usually afflicts young children. They die before reaching adulthood. Nobody knows what causes it, and nobody knew why he was different. Except me. I knew, because he told me that as a young man, he'd discovered certain books, and had played at spellcraft until he felt something quicken inside of him. It wasn't until a month later, when he found the first growths, that he realized he had made a mistake. Even still, until the day he died, he remained a magician, trying to fix what he had set wrong inside of him. He failed, Jane. He *failed.* He died a horrible death, starving, drowning with pneumonia as he was locked inside his own body, and it was because of magic."

Jane couldn't respond, overwhelmed with the horrible images Augustine had conjured for her. She thought, too, of Dr. Nizamiev's photographs: men and women locked in an asylum, heedless of the world outside, trapped in some unknowable suffering. And her parents, putting her in the carriage to Larrenton, turning back toward death.

"Do you see?" he asked, voice softening. "Do you see the danger now? I am lucky to have escaped with so *gentle* a punishment. It is a reminder not to reach beyond what we can understand."

His terrible logic made sense. It settled over her like a leaden pall. Why fight? Why reach for something better, greater? But she wanted him to. She remembered his confidence, his kindness, his humanity in the face of Mr. Renton's surgery, a surgery that had left her feeling half monstrous. She remembered his hands on her hips, his quick wit, his mastery of the scalpel. She remembered the happy piece of her that he had quickened, the way she felt her world expanding just from being near him. She had never realized, until him, that she might love and be loved.

She wanted him to risk it. Because if she could see only the best in him, if they could agree he could be what she had thought he was, he would be the best man in all the world.

She wanted him to try.

"Jane," he murmured, "I told you from the first that our marriage was inappropriate. If you want to leave, you may leave. If you want to stay, you may stay. But I will always be this man. I will always be tormented, and I will always fight to save my patients, even as it kills me. But now . . . now you can make your choice honestly. I can at least give you that much."

"You have given me nothing at all," Jane whispered, and left the study.

CHAPTER TWENTY-FOUR

ALONE IN HER bedroom, Jane couldn't sleep. When she closed her eyes, she smelled blood, or felt again Elodie's cold hands on her throat, or heard Augustine's retching echoing from the washroom. Her mind twisted and turned, fighting to reorder her newly disordered world. Magic and death, lies and desire, all of it upending everything she'd thought she knew as surely as zero destroyed the logic of mathematics.

He had killed Elodie. Yes, she would have died no matter what. Yes, he had been desperate to save her. But in her final moments, he had cut her open and gripped her heart, and all for nothing.

And yet, when Mr. Renton had been dying, Augustine had plunged his hands into his body in an attempt to save him, and she had seen him as a hero, not a butcher. And even though Mr. Renton had died, Jane did not feel the same disgust for the surgeon's actions that she felt now for what had been done to Elodie.

Had Elodie trusted him? Had Elodie believed that, no matter what Augustine did, he did for her benefit?

If he was not a murderer, then he was still a liar. Yet a liar was a far smaller thing than a murderer. And what did Jane's hurt matter, now that it was done? He couldn't do worse to her. It had been painful, to learn this lesson, but it was learned.

So she was left to go on, and build for herself a life that would satisfy her, a life she could comprehend. In time, she might forget ghosts. She might forget a dying woman she could never have saved. She might forget magic. None of them were her responsibility.

The worst of it, she decided, was that she did not hate Augustine. The more honest he became, the more tragic he grew and the less she knew how to be happy with him; but she did not hate him. It would have been far easier to hate him.

It would have been easier to fear him.

She looked for a long time at her mathematical treatise, brought back to her with her gowns. It was not so different from Augustine's magic. She could bury herself in figures and equations, follow footnotes and stray thoughts until she'd filled sheaves of paper with annotations and experiments, practice and exploration. The book held the impossible, as surely as Lindridge Hall did.

There was no need for her to learn such a thing. There was danger in it, and danger in her fascination, too.

She cast the book aside and turned off her light.

WHEN AT LAST she dozed, she dreamed of Augustine's arms around her. She dreamed of tearing out a rotted pit inside of him where his martyrdom resided, and of Lindridge Hall burning to the ground, and of Elodie, laid gently to rest, and made reparations to for the desperate horror Augustine had worked upon her.

She dreamed of Elodie, her hands gentle upon Jane's cheeks, her lips on Jane's brow, her blood-soaked gown clinging wet to Jane's flesh even as Jane tried to flee.

She dreamed of blood.

Blood.

Lurching from her bed in confused panic, Jane at first could not separate reality from her vision of Elodie, the stench of blood filling her nose and turning her stomach. She gripped her dresser, begging reason to reassert itself. A glance out the window showed that it was midmorning. She took deep breaths, fighting to drive away the nightmare.

But the stench remained. Fearful, she opened her bedroom door.

Mr. Lowell had just reached the head of the steps. "Ma'am, you're needed downstairs, in the surgery."

A patient.

She had the wild urge to refuse. Her hands trembled from exhaustion and her feet were still painfully swollen. She had no real training and no real experience. She had been married only to do the books.

But she could not abandon a patient. Augustine would not have sent for her unless he needed her, and the stench of blood would not be so strong if things were not dire.

"Of course," she said, and disappeared back into her room. She threw on her simplest gown, ignoring half the fasteners, ignoring her plaited hair that had grown wild and bulging from its confinement through the night. She stuffed her feet into shoes, ignoring the pain, and rushed down the stairs.

The surgery doors were shut, but not latched, and they opened at her touch. There, on the table, was the body of a woman. Younger than Jane. Pale, too pale. Her head lolled, her eyes heavy-lidded and unfocused. Her chemise was pushed up around her breasts, her bared flesh stained scarlet, and she was dying.

And all Jane could see was Elodie, Augustine's hands inside her chest. She felt the pulsing of hot blood across her arms as if she were already cradling the body on the slab. It took every ounce of strength within her not to fall upon her husband, black clad and bloodstained, and tear him away from the pale woman on the altar, the woman dying in her dreams.

This is not Elodie. This is not Elodie. This was a patient, teetering on the edge of death. A dying woman who needed help.

Jane donned an apron, rinsed her hands, and came to Augustine's side. "What can I do?"

"Retractors," Augustine said, and Jane shuddered with grim, hysterical humor. *Retractors.* Just like Mr. Renton. The retractors were discarded on the operating table itself, already bloody, and she slipped them into the wound Augustine had made in the woman's belly. The flesh was distended.

She was pregnant.

Augustine set his scalpel aside and slid his hands inside the incision, pushing and pulling. He muttered a curse, and Jane looked up at him, startled. There were dark circles below his eyes, and his skin was sallow. His forehead was still beaded with sweat.

He was not well. The dawn had not brought relief, not enough.

His hands trembled as he took a pre-threaded needle and began stitching something deep inside the wound, quickly but precisely. Skill and training won out over exhaustion, at least for the moment, and Jane made herself focus on keeping the surgical site clear for him. She used the flushing bulb when he demanded and shifted the angle of the retractor to open up more room to one side of her abdomen.

This was all too much like Mr. Renton. She could see him again, hear his moaning. But no; if this was not Elodie, this was also not him.

"Jane, look away," Augustine said, softly.

"I—"

"Look away, please."

She did so reluctantly. Augustine whispered what might have been a prayer. She felt the retractor shift as his hand went beneath it. Something wet squelched and thudded, and Jane's stomach flipped.

Perhaps he was right to have her look away.

"Why isn't she screaming?" Jane asked.

"Ether, exhaustion, blood loss," Augustine responded. By the vibrations in the retractors, he was stitching again. Another flush demanded; another curse. He closed the skin, set the body to rights, inch by painful inch.

At last, he pulled away from the patient, exhaling a long, shuddering breath. He reached up to mop his brow, leaving a slash of blood across his face. His whole front was soaked in it. He looked monstrous and tired as he staggered over to the sink. Jane remained behind to wash the woman's belly.

Her chest rose and fell in shallow rhythm. Jane cleaned up the woman's legs and hips, then found a cloth to drape over her bare skin. From there, she focused on her stomach, cleaning gently around the sutures.

She circled around to the woman's other side, then covered her mouth to contain the shriek that came from her lips without warning.

There, in a ceramic dish, lay the unmoving remains of a small, half-formed infant, alongside a mass of bloody flesh the color and texture of raw liver. The world seemed suddenly very far away, and she staggered to the wall, bracing herself against it and vomiting.

The tap turned off behind her. "She arrived several months pregnant and hemorrhaging extensively," Augustine said. "Her husband reported that she'd been bleeding on and off for her whole pregnancy, but without pain. When they went for a ride together this morning, the bleeding began again and wouldn't slow. I suspected a miscarriage, but when I attempted to induce labor, she only bled more and reported extreme pain. Palpation revealed that her pregnancy was taking place outside of the womb."

"Outside?" Jane whispered.

"The fetus had damaged her womb beyond repair. The placenta had grown into the outside of the uterine wall, and had been torn from it during the ride. The tearing and subsequent bleeding meant that the only course of action was to remove everything. I had hoped maybe to save the child, but—" He shook his head, and she thought again of the still form in the pan.

Bile rose in her throat again, but she pushed it down and turned back to the patient, and to Augustine. She met his gaze across the woman's body, then went to the operating table. She ignored the dish at her feet, and gently mopped the woman's stomach.

"She will probably die," Augustine said, more softly this time.

Jane shook her head, fighting down the urge to clap her hands over her ears. "Don't say such things. She can still hear you."

"Ether clouds the mind. She won't remember. Jane—"

"If any part of her believes she will die, especially in such a clouded state, it may become reality," Jane snapped.

Augustine stared back at her, confusion surfacing through his numb exhaustion. It took her a moment to realize she had echoed the basic concept of magic that Dr. Nizamiev had tried to explain to her. Before, it had been only impossible, insane thinking. Here, now, it made sense.

"Is it too dangerous to move her to my room?"

"Your room?"

"So that she can be comfortable."

Augustine shook his head. "The stairs are too narrow. We will take her to the recovery room."

The recovery room was a bare thing, built for practicality, not comfort. "She deserves better."

His jaw tightened, but he said, "I will see what can be done in my office, then."

"Good. Go."

He stared at her a moment longer, then left.

The woman's skin was white, not from lack of sun but lack of blood. When Jane touched the top of her belly, she could feel her pulse, thin and fluttering. The door to the operating room opened, and Mr. Lowell stepped inside, his own skin tinged green; he must have been too horrified to be of any help. "We should get her warm," she said to him. "Can you go up to my room? There's a heavy housecoat in the wardrobe."

"She's likely to bleed again," Mr. Lowell cautioned.

"I don't mind," Jane said.

He looked down at the patient, then nodded. Halfway to the door, he paused and turned to her. "Her name is Abigail Yew. I'm glad you're back, ma'am."

And then she was alone with the patient.

Abigail Yew.

She'd gone to school with her, Jane realized with a guilty start. Now that the chaos had slowed, Jane took the time to look at Abigail's face. Her curling russet hair was plastered to her forehead with sweat, her lips slack and chapped from the ether. They hadn't been close; Jane hadn't been close to any of her schoolmates. But they had shared a schoolhouse for several years, and Jane had even attended her wedding just over a year before. True, her invitation had been only a formality, but she *knew* this girl, and it hadn't even registered.

No wonder the Cunninghams had left so quickly; they had ample evidence to suggest she wouldn't have cared to see them off, so wrapped up in her own self, so abstracted from the town.

Jane pulled Abigail's chemise down, then smoothed the hair from her brow. Abigail moaned, eyes twitching beneath their lids. Her flesh was growing cold, and Jane clasped one of Abigail's hands in her own, hoping that some measure of warmth would pass between them.

The door creaked as Mr. Lowell returned. She motioned for him to hand over the housecoat and together they maneuvered the girl into the quilted cloth. They tried to keep the coat out of the blood, but there was too much on the table, too much in the room.

"Let's get her to the office," Jane said, and Mr. Lowell lifted Abigail into his arms as if she were made of cobwebs. Jane stripped off her bloody apron, then followed them across the hall and into the office. Augustine had made a bed out of two armchairs and the upholstered footstool, and it proved to be just long enough to settle Abigail into, like a nest.

Augustine appeared a moment later with a blanket. Jane helped him tuck it around her still body.

The careful blankness of his face told her everything she needed to know; he thought Abigail looked worse. He thought she was fading.

He was already anticipating this new spirit, come to haunt him.

"Mr. Lowell, once you've cleaned the theater, take a walk to clear your head," Augustine said. "Maybe get yourself a drink."

"Sad, nasty business," Mr. Lowell muttered, then disappeared back into the hall.

Jane settled onto the arm of the chair that held Abigail's head and stroked her brow. Augustine hovered nearby, watching the both of them. He'd shed his apron and scrubbed his hands and face mostly clean, but his sleeves were still wet, and he stank of butchery.

She existed half in the present and half in the day Mr. Renton had died. She had sat in the chair that now cradled Abigail Yew's head, and she had overheard talk of superstitions in the hallway. But now she knew what they meant. Chalk and salt, and why Augustine had summoned Dr. Nizamiev when he saw the impossible twisting of Mr. Renton's flesh.

"Was this magic, Augustine?" Her voice came out thin, afraid. "Was there chalk upon her dress?"

"Jane—"

"This was unnatural." She looked up at him. "Like Mr. Aethridge. Like Mr. Renton. So like Mr. Renton. Another malformation, another thing growing out of place."

He considered. "I don't think so. Mr. Yew gave no indication, and such things as this are known. The word is *ectopic.*"

The thought settled ill upon her, that horrors could come as much from vagaries of the body as from magic. It hardly seemed fair.

"Shouldn't you be with Mr. Yew?" she asked, to push aside her dark thoughts.

"He left when I informed him we would need to operate," Augustine said.

The words refused to process, and Jane lifted her gaze to his, brow creased. *"Left?"*

"Yes. He left. He didn't say if he'd return."

"She needs him," she said. "She needs *somebody.*" One anchor, in all the world—was that so much to ask?

Augustine's expression turned helpless. He looked down at his feet, as if unsure how to answer.

"She will have me," Jane declared, and found Abigail's hand beneath the blankets. She took it in hers, twining their fingers together.

"It will take several days—maybe weeks—for her to recover," he said.

"So be it. I have nowhere else to go."

CHAPTER TWENTY-FIVE

ABIGAIL YEW SURVIVED the first three hours.

When Mr. Lowell returned, he made up warm broth with the left-over fish heads from the previous night's dinner. Jane fed it to the insensate woman drop by drop, focusing only on the spout of the bowl, on Abigail's pale lips, on the flutter of her throat as Jane coaxed her to swallow. Augustine entered the room every half hour to take the woman's pulse, but he said nothing to her each time, and Jane was thankful for his silence.

Sitting with Abigail's body felt something like a ritual, Jane's stronger breathing timed to Abigail's own as if their parallelism could keep the woman alive. It was tempting to think of Dr. Nizamiev's lectures, to *know* that Abigail would recover and truly believe that meant she would, but Jane held fast against it.

There was nothing good that could come of it. Better to focus on realities only, no matter how terrible.

Patients came and went. Augustine met them in the kitchen and left her and Abigail to rest. She heard his unsteady gait in the hall. She heard his groan once his patients left and his door closed. The day wore on, and her charge rallied even as her husband began to fail. His hands trembled as he helped her change Abigail's bandages, as he checked the incision sites and declared them well, as he took her pulse and conceded that it had not faded any further.

She left Abigail's side only to change the hastily rigged bedpan and to relieve herself; she met Augustine by chance in the hallway on her way back from the latter. They regarded each other in silence.

He looked ill. He looked more than ill.

"Go back to Lindridge Hall tonight," Jane said.

Augustine grimaced. "Mrs. Yew—"

"I have accepted responsibility for her," Jane said. "You need rest. There will be more patients tomorrow." What would happen if he retched in the operating theater? If he collapsed in the compounding room? He was no good to anybody like this. Larrenton needed its surgeon.

Augustine looked as if he were about to argue.

"Are you afraid, then?" Jane asked.

He frowned. "Afraid?"

"Of the spirits. Of seeing Elodie."

By the way he paled, he hadn't imagined the possibility yet. Or, perhaps, a fever was come upon him.

"No," he said. "But leaving you alone seems . . ." He trailed off, uncertain, hand fisted at his side. He didn't meet her eyes.

"Our arrangement," she said, "is that I will sleep here, and you there. Right?"

Augustine nodded, and Jane left him to gather his things for his journey.

He departed without saying farewell, and Jane was glad of it. Mr. Lowell brought her dinner and more broth for Abigail, then shut up the surgery for the night. Jane drew the curtains on the office windows and made herself a bed of cushions stolen from other rooms. She ate slowly, then read aloud. The empty surgery folded its arms around them, Abigail's steadied breathing soothing and even.

She was alone, and it was good. It was safe, and simple, and real. She slept deeply despite herself, and when she awoke with the dawn, Abigail still lived.

Jane bathed and dressed once Mr. Lowell arrived to open up the surgery, and she was settled once more on the arm of the chair that supported Abigail's head when Augustine arrived from Lindridge Hall. She looked up as he entered the office, and he searched her face a moment before coming to the makeshift bedside.

She watched him as he took Abigail's pulse, checked her bandages, her incisions, the pallor below her fingernails, searching for signs that *he* was healthier today, as well. His color seemed better. Below them, Abigail stirred, murmuring in her sleep, whimpering with the first signs of pain she had given in a day.

"You have worked magic," Augustine said.

She nearly laughed, but stilled as she saw Augustine's expression. It was not an ill-chosen turn of phrase, a simple expression of thanks. No; he looked horrified. Awed.

He meant *magic*.

"No," she said.

"She could not have survived the night otherwise," Augustine said. "You have worked magic, magic surgeons would die for, magic I tried to teach myself and failed."

"Augustine—"

"She has been drawn back from the very edge of death," he said, abandoning their patient and taking her hand. "How did you learn it? The books in my study?"

She looked to the text she had left on the table by the window, the one she had read from the night before. It was only a novel. "I learned nothing," she said, turning back to him. "Do you see chalk and salt? I only gave her attention and company. I only believed that she deserved to live."

She had not even willed it strongly.

Had she?

Or was the intensity of the willing not the point, but the pervasiveness of it? She had not let herself falter in her belief the night before. Perhaps . . .

But no.

"What of your dire warnings?" she hissed, drawing close to him, nearly looming. "Of the risks of magic, of why Lindridge Hall should forestall me, forestall *you*? You seemed very clear the other night."

He stepped back, eyes going wide. "No," he said, hands lifting. "No, I didn't mean . . ."

"Hypocrite," Jane said.

"You cannot fault me for hoping that the world I used to dream of, the *potential* of magic, was real," Augustine returned.

Oh, but she could.

Abigail gave another whimper of pain, her head lolling. It was one of the first movements she had made besides breath. "She needs laudanum," Jane said, desperate to change the subject, to clear the sickroom air of their clashing anger.

"Not laudanum; it is a sedative, and might harm her already delicate breathing," Augustine said. The correction steadied him; he was once again his surgeon self. "An infusion of willow bark in her broth may help, though."

Jane nodded and, with reluctance, left Abigail's side and went to the compounding room.

Augustine followed.

She scanned the bottles of medicine lining the shelves, then pulled down the crock that contained willow bark. At her side, Augustine selected one of several bottles filled with fine white powder. When he set it on the counter, the glass clattered from the shaking of his hands.

Still ill, then.

"In addition to that, I will need your help," he said, tone strident to cover embarrassment. "I can't see patients as I am. Please compound a quarter measure with water."

"Cocaine?" she asked, drawing up close enough to see the label.

"It will steady me." He regarded her evenly.

"Did you not return to Lindridge Hall last night?"

"I did, though your intrusion seems to have riled the spirits," he said.

Jane stepped back, eyes wide. "What?"

"They would not leave me alone," Augustine said, glaring at her a moment before scrubbing at his eyes. "Before, I could sleep, after a fashion. They would come to me, torment me, and then leave, and I could sleep a few hours, then rest in the carriage on the way to town. But last night, they came to me in an unceasing parade."

"Do not blame me," Jane whispered, drawing in upon herself.

"But what else has changed, except your involvement? If I am lucky," he continued, "then with time, they will settle, like birds stirred from their roost. But you *will* stay far away from Lindridge Hall, for my sake as well as yours. And you will help me tend to my patients."

She eyed the jar of fine white powder, pictured the prick of the needle as he injected it into his veins. It was only medicine. It was a solution, a necessary one.

"You saw me, during Mrs. Yew's surgery," Augustine pressed. "I am just as much a danger exhausted as I was sick."

He was right. Damn the spirits of Lindridge Hall for responding to her so, for making her not just the betrayed victim, but a cause of harm to others. *Go back,* she wanted to tell him. *Go back and fix the root of this. You must fix this.*

But he didn't know enough, and was too afraid to try. And it was far too dangerous for her to touch.

And yet as she mixed his suspension, as she watched him inject it, as she fed bitter broth to Abigail, who should not have survived the night, she wondered if there was still some way for her to help.

THAT NIGHT, AGAINST her better instincts, she penned a letter to Dr. Nizamiev. She asked for guidance and help for Augustine. Anything she knew about how to avoid ending up floating in the air, how to touch magic without being seized by its impossibility. She'd seen the hunger in Augustine's eyes that morning when he thought she had worked magic. What else did he hunger for, what else did he wish were different? Just the smallest offer of help might be enough to push Augustine toward attempting to set things right, if it was specific, if it was actionable.

The letter went out at first light, shortly before Augustine returned from

Lindridge Hall, looking just as haggard, just as drawn. He took his dose of cocaine once more and tended his patients with less than his full focus, his full brilliance. His hands trembled. He dropped tools, forgot patients were waiting for him back in the kitchen, talked rapidly to himself about theories and frustrations. It was only by dint of his inherent need to heal and his long training that he managed at all.

Jane watched, and she helped, and she waited, hoping that a response from Camhurst would arrive with the evening post.

It didn't. Augustine did, however, ask her to measure out laudanum for him, that he might sleep through the night. She hoped it would help.

His carriage left as the sun set, and Jane took thickened broth up to Augustine's room, where Abigail now rested. She had woken up that morning, addled and in pain, but able to recognize her name. Her color was improving, her limbs warming on their own. Halfway through the day, Jane and Mr. Lowell had moved her at Augustine's suggestion.

Abigail stirred only enough to swallow her broth without aid, then fell into a light sleep, brow furrowed but cheeks pink. Jane left the bedroom door open and paced the hallway, scrubbing her face. Augustine's salvation was not her responsibility. She repeated that to herself over and over, but she couldn't shift the weight that had settled onto her shoulders when she saw him with his patients. Should she tell him to quit the surgery entirely? Let Larrenton find a new doctor, retreat to Lindridge Hall to live out the rest of his life, tormented until the last? Then, at least, the sick and injured and dying of Larrenton would be sent a new, more reliable steward. But what a monstrous choice to make, and how terrible that he might agree to it.

Her pacing took her to the door of the study. Inside, hoarded curiosities lined the shelves; how many were silent eulogies to dead magicians? Did they all serve as a constant reminder of the punishment he had earned?

Her hand was halfway to the knob when frantic knocking filled the surgery.

She pulled away as if singed and flew down to the foyer. "Mr. Lowell!" she called out. "Mr. Lowell, come quick!"

But she heard no other footsteps. She was alone; Mr. Lowell was out visiting his family. He wouldn't be back for another hour at least, perhaps many more.

It was only her.

She hauled open the front door, expecting carnage, a crushed limb, a pock-skinned child, but it was only a man and a woman, frantic but whole. "It's her son," the man said. "Illness. Wretched illness. She wanted to wait until morning, but he can't be moved, and he can't see. He's vomiting something horrible. Please, is the doctor in?"

Jane straightened up as much as she could. "He is out," she said. The woman wailed, and the man swore. Jane hesitated only a moment before saying, "But I can fetch him. Where is the patient, please?"

They gave her directions to their farm as she dragged on her traveling cloak and hat. "Stay here an hour more, if you can," she told them, mind racing. "Rest, eat something. The doctor's other assistant will be back, and he can accompany you to the farm, to see what he can do."

They nodded, and she bundled them into the kitchen, setting the kettle on for them. Her nerves were on fire, alive and roaring, and she rushed up the stairs to check on Abigail as well. She slept soundly now, deeply, and Jane felt almost confident as she raced from the surgery and fetched the neighbor who took Augustine to and from Lindridge Hall and paid him extra to drive out once more.

She had vowed to never again step foot in Lindridge Hall, for a hundred different reasons, but there was no other option. A life hung in the balance, and what was her fear to that?

The road was dry, and they made good time out of town and up into the hills. Even in the warmth of the box, she clutched her cloak tight to her, wondering what she would find. Would Augustine be conscious still, or in a drugged stupor? Would the spirits be at work? Would they leap upon her the moment she crossed the threshold?

The carriage slowed, then stopped, and she alighted, paying the man an extra sum to wait outside for half an hour. His eyes on her, or at least the knowledge that they could be, spurred her to a performance of confidence. She strode across the deadened garden as if she weren't quaking with terror inside. Her heart grew tight and cold as she came closer and closer to the door, but she made herself press forward, never slowing.

The door came open at her touch, as it had the night of the storm.

The lights were on, brilliant and high, gas flames leaping against their shades. But there was no movement, no sign of Augustine. She thought to call out, but her voice died in her throat. She was too afraid of what might answer.

Instead, she crept up the stairs and made for Augustine's study. She took each step with care, peering into shadows for any sign of movement, an elongated head, the hem of a nightgown. But everything was as she had left it, and she pressed her hand against the rapid beating of her heart. They had only come to her past midnight or in the cellar; she still had time, even with the heavy night pressing in on every window. The wind had picked up, and the glass groaned in its frames.

The study door was closed, as it had been on their wedding night. Now, though, she did not hesitate. She did not call out, or knock, before she entered.

Augustine did not stir from where he lay, sprawled on the low couch.

Laudanum. His exhaustion and his dread must have led him to dose himself possibly as soon as he got into the carriage, or through the front door.

She went to his side and took his shoulders, shaking him firmly. He groaned, his eyelids fluttering, but he did not wake. "Augustine," she hissed. "Augustine, wake up."

"Leave," he mumbled, barely loud enough for her to hear.

"A patient needs you!" she cried. Around her, Augustine's bookshelves seemed to prowl and watch. She could picture too clearly Elodie climbing the stairs, blood leaving a trail behind her, blood filling the hallways, blood drowning her—

The front door banged shut below.

Jane leapt away from Augustine, biting down her shriek. That stirred Augustine, at last, and he sat upright, bleary-eyed and bewildered. His gaze fixed on her. "No," he said. "No, no, you're not real. You can't be here. You knew not to come."

"It's one of the boys at the Thorndell farm," she said, coming back to him, seizing his hands and drawing him up from the couch. He staggered after her, pale. "He's vomiting—he's gone blind. We must go, quickly." Outside, the carriage sat, the driver unknowing. Time was passing, and if neither of them emerged, he would leave, and the boy would be without a doctor until the morning.

"That's right next to Maerbeck's farm," Augustine said, frowning. He swayed on his feet. "I was just there."

"Augustine, you must come. How much laudanum did you take?"

"I'll be fine," he said. He did not sound fine. "If it's the same sickness, he needs help immediately." He turned to her with fervent solemnity. But his eyes were having trouble focusing. "Where is Mr. Lowell?"

It was enough, that he was upright and talking. She led him into the hallway, down the stairs. Above them, the light wavered. Flickered. Threatened to extinguish.

"Out with family, I gave him the evening. He's to be back soon, and the boy's mother is waiting for him, but we will need you."

Shadows moved across the walls at the third-floor landing. Twisting, she saw more behind them, on the stairs. No figures yet, but they would come soon.

The door. They had to get to the door. Augustine might sicken in the carriage, to be drawn away from them so abruptly and in such a state, but she could still get him to the Thorndell farm in time. She could be his hands, if only she had his mind.

But the front door was locked, and the lock refused to budge, not for her, not for Augustine.

"It was open when I arrived," Jane said.

"I don't know—it's never done this—"

A shadow fell over them, its root stretching in the direction of the cellar, and Jane fell back half a step with a whimper of fear, her bravery faltering at last.

It was Augustine who steadied her.

"We must reach the kitchen," he said, urgent and low. His hand shifted in her grip, and then it was him leading her, through the door under the stairs that led to the sitting room, the dining room. "I will—I will work a protective circle, give us time to think. Come quickly."

"Magic? You would work magic?"

"What other option do I have to keep you safe? I can endure their taunts, but if they fall upon you again . . . Please, Jane."

They ran together.

The kitchen was dark and empty and the shadows of it were unfamiliar, drying herbs hanging from the ceiling reaching for her head. "Chalk and salt," Augustine muttered. "Chalk and salt." He let go of her to pull open drawers, searching frantically. Jane retreated farther into the kitchen, then froze.

Sitting on the central table was a black doctor's bag, cracked from heat.

"Where is the damned salt!" cried Augustine, slamming another drawer. They were running out of time; out in the hall, the lights began to blink out, one by one. Augustine hauled open another drawer, then stopped, going very still.

"Jane," he whispered, turning to face the door. "Jane, do you hear that?"

Jane heard nothing at all.

"Mr. Renton," Augustine whispered, taking a step back. "Can't you hear him? I hear his screams, his begging. Jane. *Jane*."

She took hold of Augustine's hand, pulling him close to her, back toward the center of the room. She heard nothing from the hallway, but she gasped as the first figure appeared, a solid silhouette, an unnatural shape. Its carved crescent head filled the doorway.

Augustine let out a low moan, and though he tried to stand strong in the face of the creature, she could feel him trembling.

Two more figures appeared in the threshold, all inhumanly tall with distorted proportions and malformed heads, featureless faces. They approached no closer, simply watching. Waiting.

"Mr. Renton," Augustine whispered. "Mr. Renton, and the Maerbeck boy, and Mr. Aethridge. All of them, here. Please, please, I'm so sorry—"

Jane kept hold of his wrist, keeping him upright when he tried to sink to the floor. "No, Augustine," she whispered. "It isn't them."

"Look!"

"Augustine, this is not what you think. Those aren't your patients. They're something else, something else entirely."

He turned to look at her, frantic, and then he froze.

The light in his eyes changed. He swore and took her head in both his hands. She jerked back, but he held fast, peering into her eyes.

"Jane, look at me," he said.

She strained against his grasp. "One of us needs to keep an eye on them."

He moved one of his hands to her throat, pressing his thumb against her pulse point and counting, numbers whispering over his lips. She began to feel light-headed from the pressure, and she tried to jerk away. Elodie had held her that way. And then, as suddenly as he had grabbed her, he pulled away. He left her, reaching for the table behind her. She heard the click of something opening.

The medical bag.

She spun around, eyes widening. The burned medical bag that Mrs. Luthbright had surely disposed of. But now, open beneath his hands, the insides gleamed, clean and new and whole. Or was it Vingh's bag, lost to the house just two days before? Either way, Augustine now wore the look he had when he performed surgeries: focused, cold, analytical. He held a polished lancet in his hand.

"Put that down," she said, taking a step back and glancing toward the creatures. "Augustine?"

"Why didn't you tell me? About the headaches? The fatigue and nausea? I know I haven't given you reason to trust me in most things, but this—you should have told me, Jane." He had something else in his hands, but in the gloom, she couldn't make it out. The lancet and the statue-like figures took all of her attention that wasn't focused on his face.

"Augustine, I am quite well." She'd had headaches, yes, but they came from stress, not illness. "We don't have time for this. You must focus!"

"That is how the fever works," he said. His voice softened, gentled, as if he were speaking to a spooked horse. "You feel as if you are on the mend. You think you will recover entirely. But you don't." There his voice cracked. "A few days of seeming relief, and then the end comes on swiftly."

He was describing the fever that had taken Elodie, and with a sickening lurch she remembered the bite of the scalpel into her fingertip. The cut had healed but was still visible, a faint pink line. Vingh had said the whole bag was fouled. Vingh had said—

"Augustine, I am *well*," she said, forcing the wild panic aside, gaze darting between him and the figures. "I will submit to an examination in the morning, but Augustine, the creatures!"

"I can prioritize the health of my wife over magic," Augustine said, refusing to so much as glance at them. His gaze was fixed entirely on her.

"Then Thorndell farm," Jane said. "We must get out. All the rest can come after."

Slowly, he set the lancet back in his case. Slowly, he closed it.

Jane turned back to the creatures, still motionless. Their impassivity made her deeply uncomfortable. It made her want to look away. She fought the impulse with all her focus, and so she didn't move when Augustine stepped up behind her.

The noxious cloth he clapped over her nose and mouth broke that concentration. She jerked forward, but his other arm was already around her, pinning her to his chest. She might have had a few inches on him in height, but he was far stronger. She tossed her head, desperate for a gasp of fresh air, but the ether was already in her mouth, cloyingly sweet on her tongue and against the back of her throat.

Her head began to spin.

The taste of the ether brought memories roaring back, not of Augustine covered in blood, but of sitting tucked in her mother's lap, waiting for the shelling to stop. The fumes—not ether, much worse, but so similar in how it had burned—had reached her first, crawling along the floor, winding up her mother's legs. She'd wrinkled her nose, not knowing what it was.

But her mother had. She'd shouted for Jane's father and stood up abruptly, despite the heavy vibrations rocking the foundation of the cellar. She'd pulled up the fabric of her overskirt, covering Jane's head with it.

Shallow breaths, darling, shallow breaths, she'd repeated, over and over.

But Jane couldn't take shallow breaths. She could feel the panic of that night as if the very floor was shaking beneath them from the impact of the mortars. She sucked in deep, desperate gasps of air, but they were all tainted, all soaked in that burning sweetness.

The creatures. She had to focus. She kicked backward at Augustine's legs, heel connecting with his shin, but her shoes were soft. He grunted and held fast.

"I'm sorry," he whispered in her ear, "but I cannot lose you, too."

CHAPTER TWENTY-SIX

A s Jane's vision swam and her lungs burned, she tried to shout. These spirits took joy in playing horrid tricks on Augustine. This was just the newest. If she could only remind him, he would see. He would let her go.

But everything felt distant, far away and teased apart into strands of nothingness. Her vision was going dark.

She felt herself sag against Augustine, felt him lift her in his arms.

"I'm quite well," she mumbled. Her lips hurt. Had the ether burned her?

"Your eyes have begun to yellow," Augustine replied. He eased her against the table just long enough to settle the burned case on her stomach, and she could smell it then, the fire, the smoke. Burned. It was burned. It couldn't have contained the bottle of ether. Then he lifted her again. Her head rolled back. She tried to stop it, and managed to get her cheek pressed to his shoulder. "The bleeding from your nose has already begun," he said, but all she could feel was mucus against her lip, courtesy of the gas. "If it progresses much further, you will begin vomiting up great masses of blackness, and you will be beyond my reach."

"No," she whispered. "No, I'm not Elodie. Augustine, the spirits. This is the work of the spirits."

"What spirits?" he asked.

Moaning, she closed her eyes, pressing her head against him as he began to move. His steps were heavy and staggering, but even with her vision obscured, she could tell they were leaving the kitchen. Full darkness enveloped them. He moved without hesitation.

"I was well a week ago, and I'm well now. Augustine, they are twisting your mind," she said, some strength returning to her voice as the ether passed off.

"Jane, I've been given another chance. I will not lose you the way I lost Elodie."

They reached a pool of light, a welcome reprieve from the suffocating darkness. It led toward the foyer, and Augustine turned to it without hesitation. Jane's initial relief from being able to see quickly soured as she saw more lights spring to life to guide their path.

To the crypt.

"Augustine, stop," she said. "Please. Please, don't take me there."

"It's the fever talking," he murmured. He sounded like a man possessed.

The crypt door hung unlocked and open. Candles had been placed along the stairwell wall, lighting their way down into the blinding white of the stone. She struggled, but Augustine held her fast as he descended into the crypt and through the first doorway. He laid her out, gently, on the white stone table.

It was cold and solid beneath her, and it seemed to sap every ounce of strength and warmth from her. Still she pushed and thrashed, trying to sit up. Just as she straightened, her head spinning, he fitted the ether cloth over her face again. She arched against him in struggle, but he held her down until, once more, the sweet gas slackened her limbs.

It was a small mercy, or a sickening curse, that the ether now removed the edge from her panic. Her head lolled upon the stone, and she saw no figures waiting for her at the margins. Elodie was absent, and Jane was stretched out in her place.

Had it always been destined to come to this?

Augustine set his bag on Elodie's chair, and she watched, blearily, as he withdrew the bleeding kit and its scarificator. He took hold of her arm, pulling it out over the floor.

"Stop. Augustine, stop," she begged.

She tried to wiggle her toes. They responded only sluggishly as Augustine pushed up her sleeve. He was gentle but firm, a perfect physician as always. His fear and worry had been overtaken by his training, and he looked at peace as he pressed the scarificator into the vein that pulsed at the inside of her elbow. Its springs jumped to action and she let out a weak whimper as it sliced three perfect lines into her skin. Blood, hot and thick, dripped with a stomach-twisting patter against the stone below her.

Her blood.

She could smell it. She could feel blood beneath her, covering the plinth, covering Augustine. Elodie, stretched out where Jane was now, chest split in two.

"It would be easier if you were upright," Augustine murmured, "but I cannot trust you to stay still without the ether, and the ether might lead you to fall."

"Augustine, please," she whispered. Her toes moved with slightly more force this time. "There's a carriage—outside, if we can get the door open—we can go to the surgery—"

Augustine set the device aside and circled around to her head to place his fingers against her pulse. "No time, Jane, and the cold of the crypt is best. The surest treatment for this fever is to weaken you. You are the host, and it thrives inside of you when you are strong. That is why it takes the best of us. It takes the hearty dockworkers, the soldiers, the athletes, and it took Elodie. Jane, you are so strong. It's no wonder that the fever chose you for its host."

"I am not ill," she said, staring up into his face.

He stroked a lock of her hair, pain rising in his eyes. "Men will return to work, thinking themselves entirely recovered. Then the vomiting begins, and they drop dead before noon." He hesitated, then bowed down, placing his forehead against hers. "Please understand. Before I left for the hunting lodge, Elodie had small symptoms. She was dead within the week."

His shame was like a physical weight, pressing down into both of them. *Shame.* It dripped from Augustine's pores, coloring everything he did.

She clung to the thought. It felt important. It felt so, so important, but as the blood continued to flow from her veins, it grew harder and harder to think.

From his bag, he pulled tools she did not remember cleaning. Clamps, saws, things to break a body open. "Just in case," he said, when he caught her staring. "I must be ready."

Ready to take her heart in his hand, so that she could die screaming.

"No," she said. "No, no, I am not ill. I—I—Do not hurt me, please—"

"We have caught it early, my love. I am only being thorough. Though the next step will be even less pleasant, I'm afraid," he said. "Calomel, to purge your body."

No. Any more, and she would succumb. She focused on the doorway. No figures lurked there, blocking her exit. She needed to get up, to flee. She had to get upstairs and put the crypt door between them.

She pressed her uninjured arm to the table and pushed with all her might, tightening her legs at the same time. Slowly, she sat up. Augustine was searching in his case, the glass of various vials clinking loudly against one another. The noise must have muffled her ragged breathing as she pressed her free hand against the oozing wounds in her arm, swung her legs over the table, and staggered to her feet.

She had nearly made it to the stairs when Augustine found the bottle of calomel and turned back toward her. He froze, staring at her, then swore and put the bottle down, rushing her. Jane screamed and threw herself up the stairs, staggering through the doorway above. She grabbed onto the heavy door and slammed it shut, leaning against it as she fumbled with the locks. *Keys, keys.* She had no keys. The bracket the padlock hung from was broken.

"Jane! Jane, open this door!" His body slammed into it, and it jumped against her. Her feet slipped against the floor, but she dug her fingers into the doorframe, hanging on with all her remaining strength.

"I'm sorry, Augustine," she said, then coughed, bending double. Her lungs burned from the prolonged etherization. She gagged, then took several deep, sucking breaths. The door jumped against her again.

"Jane, please!"

"I am well," she whispered. Her strength was failing. Her vision was swimming, black around the edges, and it was harder and harder to remain upright. She slid down the door, shivering, blood pulsing weakly from her arm. If only she had the chatelaine. If only force of will alone could turn the locks. She sobbed and felt one more great leap of the door—and then nothing.

Her world was fading, but she thought she heard Augustine repeat her name, a question in his voice.

And then his footsteps retreated, back down the stairs, and he called her name again, and cried out.

She lost consciousness.

CHAPTER TWENTY-SEVEN

THUNDER WOKE HER in the early hours of the morning, alone. She jolted upright, then hissed at the resounding spike of pain in her head, her arm following a moment later.

But as the pain cleared and she looked around herself, she realized she was still in the hallway outside the crypt. Augustine had not reached her, had not dragged her back down to the stone slab, and had not cut her one inch further.

She staggered up to her feet, leaning against the doorframe, until she realized there was no frame at all.

Where once there had been the heavy door, the many locks, the broken padlock, there was now only a stretch of pure white stone, the same stone as in the cellar below. Jane retreated, looking up and down the hall. Every other door was unchanged. The wall was undamaged. It was simply . . . different.

A vanished door, and inside of it, the plinth, the doctor, and Elodie. Slowly, trembling, she approached the stone and laid her hands against it. Pressed her cheek to it.

"Augustine?" she whispered.

A sobbing, wracking cry echoed to her through stone upon stone upon stone.

Her fingers clawed against the rock. "Augustine! Augustine, it's me!"

The door remained transformed. Once more, she heard Augustine's voice, pained and horrible, and so, so far away.

You're safe, a traitorous voice insider her whispered. *He can't get to you now.* But she had not wanted this. He had only been bewitched; horribly bewitched. She had wanted only to get him out of the house, so that he could realize how in danger they both were.

And instead, this impossible transmutation. Another trick of the spirits? Or Elodie, retaliating now that Augustine was in her crypt?

Shaking, she retreated from the unnatural not-door, her mind refusing to comprehend it and what it might mean.

She could not stay here. She must fetch help.

Outside Lindridge Hall, a storm raged. Wind bellowed against stone, and windows creaked in their casements. The foyer seemed to breathe, a living thing itself, as she crossed its grand space to the front door. Shaking, she tried the latch.

It turned. The door opened. The wind fought to seize it from her, but she held fast. The carriage was long gone, not even a wagon rut to mark where it had stood. How long would it take for Mr. Lowell to send a carriage up to find her? And who could she even go to? Dr. Nizamiev? It would take at least a day to reach her in Camhurst, and she might have no further answers.

Except she couldn't go to Camhurst. Guilt clamped shut her lungs. *Thorndell farm.* Even now, that boy was dying, frightened and alone. He needed Augustine. He needed a doctor. But there would be no doctor, and no way to explain it. And it would be her fault. That boy would die because she had returned to Lindridge Hall.

She was sobbing, tears streaking her swollen face, when she saw two figures struggling up the hill, sheltered by a snapping oilcloth they held above them. Mrs. Purl and Mrs. Luthbright. Jane fled back into the house. She raced up the stairs and into the bedroom, and she shut herself inside, chest heaving in panic. Why couldn't the storm have kept them away? Why couldn't she have been spared, granted time to solve the horrible, impossible problem of the crypt door? Her hands shook as she washed away the crusted blood along her inner arm, as she shoved her sleeve back down over the three parallel wounds. What would she tell them? How could she explain her presence, and his absence?

How could she open a door that impossible spirits had sealed?

She sank to the floor at the foot of the bed, drawing her knees to her chest, and moaned, low and pained. An echoing moan rattled from the pipes in the bathroom, Augustine, devoured by the house. Augustine, afraid and lost and consumed.

But he might have killed you, if you hadn't fled, if the door had not vanished.

And yet she could not find it in herself to be relieved. She could not help but fear for him.

She crawled on her belly into the bathroom, and she pressed her ear to the bathtub's piping. "Augustine," she whispered. "Augustine, speak to me. Where are you? How can I reach you?"

The metal trembled wordlessly, and then it shrieked. Below, she heard a woman's scream. Jane stumbled back to her feet, out into the hallway, to the balcony in the foyer.

"The main, the main!" shouted Mrs. Luthbright. "Turn it off at the main!"

The front door hung open, the wind howling through it, rain sheeting inside along the horizontal. Jane saw a flash of skirt, and then heard Mrs. Purl shout, "It won't budge!"

"Harder! Turn harder!"

Jane hesitated only a moment before she dashed out into the squall, finding Mrs. Purl just around the entrance, hauling on a great metal wheel. Jane joined her, and together they dragged it closed. Inside, Mrs. Luthbright called out encouragement. They staggered together, drenched, back into Lindridge Hall, and into the kitchen, where Mrs. Luthbright was standing ankle-deep in water from a burst pipe in the sink.

"Mercy," Mrs. Purl gasped, as Mrs. Luthbright made an old warding sign. "Do you think it was the storm?"

Jane thought of Augustine, his voice screaming in the pipes, and shivered.

"Must be," Mrs. Luthbright said, then turned to Jane. "Mrs. Lawrence! The doctor didn't say to expect you."

"There was an emergency," she said, before she could stop herself.

"Of course, of course. You do him proud." Mrs. Purl smiled, but Mrs. Luthbright sloshed out of the water with a scowl on her face.

"Well, and now we have our own emergency. No running water until we can fetch somebody to fix it from town."

"Of course. Can I help?"

"Stay out of the way and watch for the storm to lighten."

Cowed, Jane retreated up to Augustine's study. She could see the road more clearly from there. She stared out at the storm and the road, willing herself to wake up. This was a nightmare. This had to be a nightmare. There was no other logic for it, beyond the impossible.

A door could not become stone. A voice could not be imprisoned in the plumbing. And yet . . .

She was still standing there, two hours later, when a horse appeared in the sheeting rain. Atop it, a broad man in a cap.

The walls closed in around her.

Mr. Lowell.

She was back down the stairs in what felt like an instant, pressed up against the blank stone that had been the crypt door. Her fingers scrabbled at the margins, where the stone met the wood paneling of the hall without the slightest gap, and she whispered pleas to the rock over and over. It did not budge. She wished it open with all her heart, thinking glancing thoughts of magic, but the stone remained, unmoving. Even as she heard the squeaking hinges of the main door, the rain spilling into the foyer, she tried to pry it open.

"Augustine, they need you. I can't do this. I can't—"

"Mrs. Lawrence! Come quick!"

She was out of time.

Shivering, Jane stepped away from the door. She marshaled all her poise and tried to drag on a shroud of cool remove, like she'd felt when seeing Mr. Renton for the first time. It came in tatters, but it came, and she emerged into the foyer to meet her fate.

Mr. Lowell's cheeks were as flushed as if he had galloped the whole way himself, instead of the horse that panted out in the yard, unshielded from the weather. Mrs. Luthbright had gone to offer food to the animal, but it ignored her, stamping impatiently. Mr. Lowell looked much the same, gaze fixed on Jane from the moment she entered the space, ignoring Mrs. Purl at his side.

"The doctor," Mr. Lowell said. "He is needed. Where is he?"

"Out at an emergency," Mrs. Purl said, echoing Jane's earlier excuse, and Jane found herself only able to nod, voice seizing in her throat.

"He is not at Thorndell," Mr. Lowell snapped, looking away from Jane for just a moment to cast his ire on the older woman. She retreated, scowling. "Mrs. Lawrence, please, the boy is turning more poorly by the minute."

Jane's jaw trembled. What could she tell him? How could she give an excuse that would mean this child's death? "He's not here," she said weakly.

The house gave an echoing groan.

"Not here," Mr. Lowell repeated. *"Not here?"*

"He rode out last night," she said, fisting her quaking hands in her skirts. "I don't—I don't know where—"

Mr. Lowell cursed. "Then it must be you, ma'am."

"What?" She paled.

"I cannot handle this myself, and you are the next thing to a doctor Larrenton has."

"I'm hardly a doctor," she said, looking to Mrs. Purl, hoping for help. But Mrs. Purl was nodding with Mr. Lowell.

"You can handle yourself," Mr. Lowell said.

"You know far more than I—"

"I carry bodies," Mr. Lowell said sharply. "I clean up the mess."

"I do the books!"

"A child is dying, Mrs. Lawrence. We must try. We *must.*"

Her protests all seemed weak, pointless, and she crumpled, covering her face with her hands. She tried to breathe. She tried to think of Mr. Renton, of her steadiness then. But she could only see his death the next morning.

But Abigail. Abigail, she had saved. She had known that Abigail would live, and so the woman had. If it was necessary—if there was no other option—

Jane grabbed her hat from where it had been placed by the door, no doubt retrieved from where it had fallen the night before. Discovered, likely, incongruously, in the kitchen. Jane shuddered but donned it all the same, ignoring the faint whiff of ether that still clung to it. Mrs. Purl supplied her with one of Augustine's oiled overcoats, and then she was out of Lindridge Hall, following after Mr. Lowell, hoisting herself onto the horse just behind him. The two of them barely fit together, and the horse danced to the side in irritation.

But Jane was outside of Lindridge Hall. A sudden wash of relief flooded her, followed by peace, and she fought the urge to lean forward against Mr. Lowell's broad back. The horse began picking its way down the muddy road, and she rocked with each step, her nerves subsiding.

She was not a doctor, not a nurse, either, but she would find something that could be done. Abigail was proof of that.

THE BOY, NO more than ten, was curled by the fire on a hastily made nest of blankets. He had sweated through them already, though, and his cheeks were flushed red. The ceramic basin beside him was filled with an oily, thin vomit, and his mother hurried to clean it out when she saw Mr. Lowell and Jane appear in the doorway.

"Dr. Lawrence is here," she murmured to her son, touching his sweat-slicked forehead. "You'll be all right now, you just sit tight."

Jane's heart constricted.

Mr. Lowell doffed his hat, worrying at it in his hands. "I'm afraid the doctor is not here, ma'am," he said, eyes downcast. "The storm must have forced him off the road last night. We don't know where he is."

Mr. Lowell had embroidered the story for her as they rode, it seemed. She should have been grateful, but all she felt was a yawning pit of guilt.

"Can't find him!" the woman cried.

Jane flinched and ducked her head, looking again at the child. "I've come to help, instead," she said. "I have—I have some training."

Not enough, her logical mind whispered.

She approached the child. His thin shoulders appeared from within his nest of blankets, pink and studded with bumps. She reached out to brush the back of her knuckles against him. The rash felt like sandpaper against her skin, and he was burning up, far too hot. He didn't so much as flinch at her touch. "We should move him away from the fire," she said.

The mother shook her head. "He's shivering."

"He's feverish," Jane said. "He's too hot."

"Sweating out a fever is the fastest way I know."

Jane hadn't read enough, hadn't learned enough, to argue. She bit her lip. "How—how has he been eating? Drinking?"

"Naught of either," the woman said. She was hovering in the doorway, needing to go outside to toss the refuse from the basin, but unwilling to leave her son in the hands of an untested stranger. She was saved from the decision by Mr. Lowell, who took the crock gently from her white-knuckled hands and carried it outside for her.

"Please, tell me everything you know," Jane said.

"Scarlet fever," the woman replied. "Scarlet fever, that's what the doctor said Ben Maerbeck had. Is that what my Orren has?"

Ben Maerbeck. Oh, if only Jane had been back at the surgery, where she could have consulted Augustine's notes and seen what he had prescribed last. Fighting to hide the tremor in her hands, Jane pulled away from the boy and went to the door. Mr. Lowell had left a satchel there, full of supplies gathered at the surgery before he'd ridden to find her. Had he brought the notes? She crouched down, skirts spilling across the rammed earth floor, pulling the leather bag open. Bottle after bottle, labeled in Augustine's careful script, rolled over one another. She grabbed each and set them out in a careful line. Papers, she needed papers. And there, at the bottom of the bag, a whole sheaf of them! She grabbed them, poring over Augustine's less-careful handwriting, the scrawl he used only for himself.

Her heart gave an unwelcome, agonizing pang. *His handwriting.*

But behind her, the boy was whimpering. His mother was at his side, and she gathered him up in her arms, rocking him back and forth. Jane must act, not ache.

Jane became aware, then, of eyes on her. Many eyes. She looked up, and from the second room in the small farmhouse peered three small faces— the other children. Orren's father was likely close at hand, too.

Mr. Lowell returned, pushing past her and giving the bowl back to Orren's mother, just in time for her to catch the next stream of putrid vomit.

Jane forced her attention back to the notes. They seemed to be just what had littered the top of Augustine's desk, grabbed in desperation. *Maerbeck, Maerbeck,* she chanted to herself, wondering how it might be spelled, searching for anything that might match it in the tangle of letters on the crumpled pages. She found nothing, and changed tactics, looking for *vomit.* Nothing there, either, but then her gaze caught on one of the longer words on the fourth page in the satchel: *hyperemesis.* It seemed to throb upon the paper, and she frowned, reading the paragraph containing it. She knew that word.

There. *Maerbeck.* She'd found it.

If Vingh had not used that word . . .

There was no time to consider it. Sagging in relief, she scanned through the page from top to bottom, thankful for her time untangling Augustine's personal account ledger, thankful even for her discovery of Elodie, if it meant, now, she stood half a chance of helping.

Jane found the list of symptoms. Fever, vomiting, a red rash on the skin. But Jane had to be sure, because the list of treatments frightened her even to consider. To inflict them on the boy, she had to be certain that this matched what Augustine had seen before. Jane approached mother and son, paper clutched in her hands, and crouched down.

"Orren," she said softly. "Can you open your mouth for me?"

The boy stared past her, eyes glazed, barely blinking.

"He can't hear you," his mother said, then choked back a sob. She reached out and stroked her son's red cheeks, then gently took his chin in hand, and with her thumb pressed to his lips, pulled his jaw down.

Jane leaned forward, but the light from outside was dim with the storm, and the hearth's glow flickered. It was hard to see. She shifted, changing the angle, wishing there was gaslight. But this was a farm, and the farms had not yet been run with gas.

She tilted her head slightly and saw at last what she was looking for. The back of the boy's throat was streaked white and red. "Do you see?" she asked, paper crinkling in her first as she clutched it. "The pattern on the back of his throat, that means scarlet fever."

Orren's mother peered in, then eased her son's mouth closed once more. "That's what I was telling you!" she whispered fervently. Jane winced, but listened through the pain to the real question. *Does that mean you can fix it?*

Jane spread the paper out on her lap again. "For scarlet fever, Dr. Lawrence"— her voice caught—"recommends bleeding, first and foremost."

Her elbow ached where Augustine had sliced her open, and she wanted to take it back. She couldn't do that to the boy, already struggling to survive. But that was the difference: she had been healthy, and he was ill. Mr. Cunningham had been bled before, as had Mrs. Cunningham. Even she must have been in actual times of sickness, though she could not remember it happening.

And Orren's mother was nodding, accepting it as simple truth. Mr. Lowell pulled a case out of the satchel. He held it out to her.

She stared up at him. Couldn't he do the deed . . . ?

But she couldn't look weak, not in front of Orren's mother. Fear had to be answered with confidence, with strength. Jane took the case and opened it, revealing the same tool that Augustine had used on her the night before. Her hand shook as she lifted it from the molded interior, seeing her own reflection in the polished metal. It was simple enough to operate. A few presses of her thumb wound the spring, the blades drawing up inside the housing. She gently pulled one of Orren's arms from within the blankets, feeling again how hot it was, how much he shivered, how little he responded.

She placed the metal box against the inside of his arm, mirroring where Augustine had placed it on hers, and pressed the button.

Orren didn't cry out as the blades bit into him, or as blood began to run down his arm. Orren's mother held him cradled against her chest, tucked into her lap, with the basin out to the side to catch the flow. They sat, very quiet, until the bleeding slowed. Orren's family gathered around them, watching, waiting, hoping. Jane repeated the procedure on the other arm.

Augustine's notes were very clear. *Bleed until the cheeks become pale and the lips lose color.* Her heart seized at every leap of the scarificator, and she could not stand the smell of blood, but she repeated the procedure again, and again. Orren's mother whispered that she could feel his fever cooling. His vomiting slowed.

But Orren didn't rally as the storm outside the farmhouse calmed.

He died in his mother's arms.

CHAPTER TWENTY-EIGHT

J ANE WAS NUMB as Mr. Lowell saddled their horse. She was numb as
they made for the main road, and numb when he twisted in his seat to
ask her, "Will you be going to Lindridge Hall or the surgery tonight,
ma'am?"

She wanted to say the surgery, but Augustine needed her. And, more-
over, she knew she did not deserve to sleep under that roof and proclaim to
those who might come in the night that she could help. Who had she been
fooling? There was no help coming, not from her. If only Augustine had
been able to leave the house the night before—if only she hadn't lost him to
Lindridge Hall, to the inexplicable and impossible. A little boy might still
be alive. She might not have his blood on her hands.

There could be no others. She would get Augustine back. This was not
the death of her parents; she was not a helpless child. She would find her
husband and pull him from the bowels of the house, and she would restore
him. She wouldn't stop until he was back, safe.

And she could hope that she would not see those things again, those things her husband had sworn were the figures of his departed patients, but to her had only been monstrous. Without her husband in residence, she had never seen more than a flash in a window, as long as she was outside the cellar; perhaps she was in some way protected, able to be hurt only through her proximity to him.

"Lindridge Hall," she said, heart steeled against the fear. "In case . . . in case my husband returns."

Mr. Lowell made a concerned noise low in his throat. "I plan to canvass the farms for him tonight and tomorrow, ma'am. I worry that his horse may have thrown a shoe, or worse, in the dark."

She flinched.

"Pardon me, ma'am. Not meaning to frighten you. Just . . . I can't let him be, if he's in trouble somewhere. You understand."

"I do. Thank you."

They rode in silence. When she closed her eyes, she saw Orren's face, blank and helpless. She felt beneath her hands not Mr. Lowell's waist but the metal of the scarificator. She tried to conjure up Augustine's words the day of Mr. Renton's death, how he had entreated her not to blame herself, but here she could find no one else.

She hadn't followed Augustine's treatments to the letter. She hadn't had the training to find and apply leeches, hadn't had the purgatives, hadn't had the time to implement a diet of bland, soft foods and tonics. She could have shaved the boy's head, and perhaps should have. She should have blistered the tonsils themselves.

But she was not a doctor. She could not be blamed for her lack of skill.

She *could* be blamed for losing Augustine, right when he was most needed.

What would happen when the next child fell ill, and the next? Because surely it would spread. Surely it would move like wildfire, like gas in the streets. And now Larrenton was without its doctor.

The only choice left to her now was to fix this. To go to where the crypt door had been and strike down the stone with a hammer. She would find him. She would free him.

They reached the hall as the last of the sun disappeared behind the next hill. She waved off Mr. Lowell's distracted offers of assistance, and watched him gallop away, back into the dark. There was just enough light to find her way to the front door, and to open it, stepping into the warm glow of the well-lit foyer.

Mrs. Purl and Mrs. Luthbright were already gone, but they had left the gas lamps burning, and, following them with hesitant steps, she found a cold plate waiting for her in the dining room, beneath a tarnished but clean silver cloche. The gesture brought tears to her eyes, and she stared at it for a long moment, immobile. She had not eaten all day, and yet her stomach was filled with ash at the sight of food, turned sour by the care shown for her in such a small gesture.

And then she processed that there was only *one* plate.

This one was meant for Augustine.

She slammed the metal cloche back down, leaving the dining room behind. She could eat later, although her hands trembled already, and her head felt light upon her shoulders. First she must attend to the cellar door, white stone set into the wooden paneling, incongruous and cold. She placed her hands upon it, fingers spread wide, the same way she had that morning.

There were no spectators to shock, no one to hide from. She squared her shoulders and called out, "Augustine?"

The door was silent.

The pipes of Lindridge Hall did not groan. No weeping echoed from the rock. Had she heard such, truly, just that morning? But she knew that here had once stood a heavy door, and inside it a staircase, and a cellar, and a table.

"Augustine, I am coming," she whispered.

There—a weakened sob, an aimless prayer, addressed to no god that had ever existed, or that had ever listened to the cries of man. *Augustine.*

She placed her hand against the stone slab. "Wait, please wait," she whispered, then went in search of a sledgehammer.

She found it in an outbuilding, a dilapidated shed with a roof that threatened to collapse at every gust of wind. She wrenched the hammer free from the tangle of abandoned rakes and shears and axes. She could barely lift its great weight, struggling back across the brackish yard and into the house, stopping every few minutes. Her arms burned.

A small price, this discomfort.

Her first blow rang out shrill and shockingly loud in the empty hallway, reverberating up her arms and into her shoulders with a sharp ache. The head of the hammer struck the wall at an angle, then glanced away, pulling her off balance. She staggered, catching herself on the handle and crouching there, gasping.

There was no mark upon the wall.

Her next blow struck true, and her bones screamed in agony at the impact. But again, there was no scuff or dent, and none appeared after the third blow, the fourth, the fifth. At the sixth, she screamed in frustration and threw the sledgehammer away from her. It clattered down the hallway and took with it splinters of polished wood.

Jane stood there, panting, staring, *wishing*. But nothing changed.

Nothing changed, because this was not just stone. The slab was not impossible only in its appearance, but in its very makeup. She pressed her hands against it once more, and *shoved*, but only hissed at the pain it sent through her abused shoulders.

"Augustine?" she asked. There was no answer, not even a sob. The crack of the hammer against stone must have driven him away.

Defeated, Jane retreated to the sitting room, rubbing at her arms. She sank into a seat, trembling convulsively, unable to tell if she was cold from her journey to the shed, or too distraught to remain still. She thought of Orren, of his tiny body shivering by the fire, and dropped her head into her hands.

It was a good thing, she decided, that the Cunninghams were gone. They would not see how much harm she had caused. But word would reach them eventually. What would they think of her?

When she lifted her head, she half expected to see Elodie watching her from the darkened glass before her, the outside world obliterated in the gas lamp glare. Judging, perhaps, or even pleased at what Jane had done.

But the gas lamp was not on.

The room was not dark; light spilled from behind her, curling around her bloodstained skirts, but it did not come from any of the sconces on the wall, or the fixtures in the hallway beyond that had burned so brightly when she had arrived. Slowly, she turned to face the hearth that crackled with a roaring fire that had not been there ten minutes ago.

Jane gripped the arms of the chair, knuckles white and bulging.

She had not kindled the fire; she knew she had not, though perhaps she should have when she first entered. She also knew she had not turned the lights out. But that was the first sign, always, the darkening of the hallway lights. She had missed it in her preoccupation. And where were they, Lindridge Hall's ghosts? Were they closing in even now?

Outside, lightning arced across the sky, followed half a heartbeat later by the crash of thunder.

Jolted from her frozen dread, Jane ran, out into the hallway, into the blackness. She ran for the front door. She had walked all the way to Larrenton once; she could do it again. She could not remain here without daylight, not with these wretched spirits. But outside, the storm that had burst once more over Lindridge Hall brought with it pounding rain. It sheeted down the glass, and it fought her as she hauled at the door, desperate to be free despite the danger.

Finally, the door gave, and she looked out on sheeting water, on brilliant lightning. The drive had had no time to dry from that morning's storm; it was awash in mud, as silty-slick as it had been on her wedding night. She heard again the screaming of the horse as her carriage threatened to wash out over the ridge, and she retreated back inside, slamming the door shut behind her and breathing hard.

The house was quiet compared to the maelstrom outside. Summoning up what was left of her courage, she made her way to the nearest light switch and turned it on, praying that the pilots would rise into full flame once more, that they hadn't been extinguished entirely, to let creeping gas fill the hallways and choke the life from her.

The lamps lit.

Orren stood before her, tow-headed, blank-eyed.

Blood poured from his mouth.

CHAPTER TWENTY-NINE

JANE'S SHRIEK ECHOED off the high ceiling of the foyer. She was fleeing before she could think. Halfway to the stairs, though, she stumbled, fell to her knees.

She was shaking too hard to stand up again.

"You always want to run," Orren said behind her. His sweet boy's voice
was cracked from fever, muddied by blood, and brutal in its gentleness.
"You would have left me to die, but you were too afraid of what they would
think."

Augustine had begged her to see the ghosts of Mr. Renton, Mr. Aethridge,
the Maerbeck boy she had never met, and she had not seen them at all. Only
faceless statues. She had thought him mad, or bewitched by the spirits. And
yet here, now, it was Orren, little Orren, Orren who would have lived, perhaps, if Augustine had come to his sickbed instead of her. Not a statue; not
something as inhuman, or as distant, as Elodie was to her.

She had killed Orren, and here he was, come to punish her.

She had to get away.

Holding up her skirts and praying that the rug would not trip her, she finally stood again. She ran. She heard nothing behind her, but she could feel the boy at her back, staggering to the stairs, dragging himself along the banister. The study—she would take refuge in the study. She had found Augustine thrice there in the dead of night; she had to hope it would keep her safe now.

Her lungs burned, but she felt it only dully through her panic. Jane rounded the corner at a sprint and threw herself against the study door, forcing it open with a loud crack. She fumbled it closed as swiftly as she could and shoved one of the armchairs against it, then backed away, shaking.

The skulls gazed down at her, shadowed and indistinct. The weight of all of Augustine's assembled curiosities pressed in. She could hear Orren outside. She could hear faint sobbing, childish cries of pain. Her heart twisted with shame, with panic, with horror.

Was this what Augustine had suffered through, every night for months?

She forced herself to turn from the door, to go to the light switch. She cranked the gas lamps up as bright as they would go. Light, light would make her feel safer. More in control. The light meant Orren was not here.

The lights flickered.

The doorknob turned.

What if the study door did not hold? What if it could not stop a spirit? Jane staggered to the hearth, grabbing for the iron poker; she would fight, if she had to, if Orren tried to seize her as Elodie had. But he was just a child, and she had seen him die, and she did not know if she could strike him. Not even to protect herself.

She bit back a sob, looking around for any other option.

Elodie looked back at her from the window.

Jane fell two steps back, poker dropping from her stunned grasp. "No, not you as well," she whispered. "Leave. Please leave. I know his secret now, and what he did to you, and I am sorry, but you must leave."

Elodie did not respond.

She did not move, did not gesture, did not look pleased or contrite. In fact, Jane could not make out her expression at all; her face wavered and shifted, features arranging themselves differently every time Jane blinked.

One moment, she was just a skull with red eyes; another, and she could have been Jane's own sister.

"Are you happy, having him to yourself?" Jane asked, trembling. "A child is dead because Augustine is trapped in your crypt, and I . . . I . . ."

Footsteps shuffled in the hall, soft and rhythmless. Elodie, in the window, pointed down.

A book sat upon the blotter.

She crept closer, eyes darting between Elodie and the desk, afraid of another attack. Her ledgers and her mathematical treatise were all in Larrenton. The desk had been bare a moment before. But now there was a thick, old tome, lying open. A carefully inscribed circle took up the left-hand leaf, and close-printed text filled the right. Instructions; the text was instructions, step by step, in the casting of a protective circle made of chalk and salt.

"Why?" she whispered.

Elodie gave no response.

The door's latch gave way. The wood pressed against the chair blocking it, pushing with a child's strength.

Orren would soon be upon her. Last night, Augustine had not pulled her to the kitchen for a knife; he had gone in search of chalk and salt. The workings of magic. The workings, perhaps, of this very book.

Was she meant to do the same?

No. It made no sense that Elodie would offer help. She must turn and fight. And even if an iron poker was no use against a spirit, she had no chalk or salt.

But the book's front cover was propped up, just a little, just enough that she hadn't noticed in her earlier horror. With shaking fingers, she lifted the cover, and found beneath it a piece of chalk.

Impossible.

She looked up at Elodie once more.

"Why are you helping me?" she asked.

Elodie shivered, then disappeared. The chair blocking the door scraped an inch across the floor.

This was madness; Dr. Nizamiev's warnings echoed in her mind. But Orren was close, and magic was merely a matter of following the steps of a proof. She skimmed the instructions as quickly as she could, and found them clear. They were within her grasp.

What would happen to her if she did not at least try?

Jane didn't have time to wonder, to plead for Elodie to return. Trick or not, gift or not, she had what she needed, and when she turned back to the room, the darkness of the hallway slashed through the gap of the open door like a wound. She took the book and shoved the couch out of the way, pulled up the rug. Then she hurried to the hearth and crouched, making a bowl out of her skirts, filling them with several scoops of soft, silken ashes. Not salt, but maybe enough, maybe. She clutched the bundle close to her chest as she returned to the book, knelt, and began to draw.

She imagined a great stone wall, assembled piece by piece by skilled hands, as she inscribed the floorboards with chalk, then followed it up with carefully sprinkled ash. She recited the nonsense syllables from the instructions. She wished, and she hoped, and then she fought to know that she was already safe.

But her breath was coming too shallowly; her head swam and her vision narrowed. The chair screeched against the floorboards, and was at last moved out of the way. The door was open. The hallway yawned.

The lights in the study went out.

Something welled beneath her breast, but it was an eel between her fingers as she tried to grasp it. She felt like a child playing at games. A desperate girl wishing that her love alone could keep her mother safe.

There—a movement in the doorway, low, a young boy's head. She heard a wracking cough. A whispered plea.

Ignore him.

Jane's lips were moving, but no sound escaped them. She grasped again for the eel and thought of the circle. *A wall. Safety. Three hundred and sixty degrees, and also zero; everything and nothing. The infinite line in the finite space.*

The movement inside of her caught on the familiar logic and grew along the scaffolding of the chalk. She felt it click into place, saw the numbers resolve themselves into orderly columns.

The boy stopped just beyond the threshold.

In the flashes of light from the storm, he regarded her with bloody tears in his eyes. If he spoke, she could not hear him. The whole world was growing distant, far away and muffled. She stared across the boundary she had created.

She felt a flare of curious pride, beating out her shame and guilt for just long enough that she could breathe.

The dead boy studied her at length, and her knees screamed from how still she held, moving only to take the text in her arms and cradle it in her lap. The book sang to her, and she wanted nothing more than to dive into its instructions, its proven logic. But she didn't dare look down until, at last, the ghost retreated, gliding backward without turning, out the door and away.

She had solved the equation.

She sat vigil into the depths of the night. She might have dozed, but she never moved from her seat within the circle. At length, the storm lifted, and the gas lamps crept to half glow once more. She turned the pages slowly, wishing for her reading glasses, then stopped as she came across Augustine's dense, frantic hand, notes scribbled in the margins, filling them. Beneath them, inside them, a description of a resurrection.

Instructions for the impossible.

AUGUSTINE HAD SUMMONED up the dead by desecrating Elodie Lawrence's body.

He had made seven incisions into her cooling flesh: between the brows, on the tips of her longest fingers, on the heels of her feet, at her throat, and above her belly. He had driven a cold metal pin through her heart, and he must have been so relieved that he had already exposed it in his desperate attempts to revive her. He had burned candles and incense made of herbs Jane did not recognize the names of, from sunset to sunup, and he had sat with her for each hour of darkness, whispering prescribed chants detailing the world of the dead.

The world of the dead; the description in Augustine's notes was unfamiliar. It was not the old platitudes of Breltainian faith, nor anything else she had ever encountered. Now, people spoke of cold graves and the hard stop of the light of the soul, a limited existence but one made more precious due to its brevity, and more believable by its cruelty. But this text described a glass orb a thousand times the size of the world that the essence of every soul who had ever lived was thrust into, where they could make fecund worlds of their own.

The first act of the ritual had been to isolate Elodie among all the other boundless souls. Augustine had set about finding the world that Elodie had built, drawing on her life lived before, inflected by how she had died: in pain and afraid, her innards displayed in horrific tableau. There were no notes to what Augustine had envisioned, but Jane expected his assumptions had been filled with shame and apologies, crafted to punish himself more than to channel the soul of his beloved. He reached for an understanding of the world of the dead only available by casting off the sensibilities of life. There were terse notes from Augustine about purgings, visions, spasms. He had endured them, focused on how he believed he had made her suffer, marinating in his own guilt.

No wonder, then, that what had come through were the souls of his patients, every one that he feared he had failed. They were drawn to him in all his horrid vulnerability, his sacrificial offering.

With whatever sense was left to him, Augustine had gone through a pageantish sequence of rites, and he had begged Elodie to return to her body. He had placed incense in each of the wounds he had created, then sewn up the flesh. Jane could envision his precise stitching.

And then—

And then, sometime between the closing of the circle and when Augustine had written his final notes, Elodie's parents had found him, defiling her body, wild-eyed and incoherent, draped in magic that had already failed. His own parents had found him weeping on the floor in filth.

He should have known not to try. He should have left her there, at peace, without him.

"*Why?*" she asked the empty house. He'd been in love. He'd been convinced he'd failed her. But *why* go to such lengths, why do it alone, why fail again to save her? He was a doctor. He had seen death, had been its close companion as surely as the undertakers. Jane rose to her feet in the early dawn light, turning slowly in a circle, looking at the monument all around her to his knowledge, his learning, his brilliance.

It was just as she'd told him that night at the surgery. He was selfish. He was so *selfish*.

What could he have been, if he'd hadn't confused self-loathing with humility?

"How could you do this to me?" she asked the shelves. "To her? To yourself? You, with your doctor's arrogance, your loving arrogance! Come back!" Her voice rose until she was shouting, voice booming and strange in her ears. "Come back to me, and make this right!"

The house groaned in response, and for just a moment, she thought she saw Augustine's face in the wallpaper of the hallway, through the door Orren's ghost had left open the night before. Tears streaked down her cheeks. "I can't do this alone," she whispered. "I killed a boy last night. I killed a boy, and I am just like you. All I could think about was how I failed."

The wall was blank. The house was still.

She was alone in Lindridge Hall as the sun crested the horizon, the storm clouds cleared away, and light streamed in through the windows.

From below, she heard the front door open and the sound of chattering drift up from the foyer. Mrs. Purl and Mrs. Luthbright. They could not find her like this, and what if they had heard her screaming? Shuddering, she grabbed the book and stepped out of the circle.

She felt nothing as she crossed it. No popping, no membrane, no sign of the wall that she had been so certain she had built around herself. Jane turned back to the line of chalk and ash, frowning. She lifted a hand and felt for the barrier, but there was only air.

Had any of it been real?

Head spinning, Jane went to the bedroom. She made herself crawl beneath the covers of the bed—his bed, the bed she had not been able to look at before—and hugged herself tight, shutting her eyes against the bloody memories of Elodie and Orren. Dr. Nizamiev had called magic a focused kind of madness, but now, as she watched through lowered lashes as Mrs. Purl came in with a basin of hot water, then left again without a word, she wondered if she was simply mad.

She snatched a few fragmented moments of sleep but roused herself before an hour was up; staying abed would only lead to more questions. Jane rose and washed, changed her clothing and reset her hair.

There was breakfast waiting for her in the dining room, soft-boiled eggs and grilled river fish. She ate it despite the solid block where her hunger had once resided. Sleep, she needed sleep before she undertook any more investigations of the door, but how could she explain that to the servants?

She was contemplating asking Mrs. Purl to please build up a fire in the library, then leave her to some unspecified work, so that she might snatch a few hours of rest, when a rider made his way up the road to Lindridge Hall.

She went out to meet him, anticipating Mr. Lowell and fearing what new case she would be called to, but it was only a courier. He brought no word from Mr. Lowell, either, only the post. She retreated to the study, unsure if she should be relieved or distressed. She could offer no help to other patients, but for Mr. Lowell to have already given up, and to have sent no word of his search for Augustine . . .

The courier's package contained several brief letters, mostly from last week's houseguests, studiously avoiding any mention of the ritual or their hasty departure, and extending thin-sounding invitations to dine with them when next the Lawrences found themselves in Camhurst.

One envelope, however, bore the emblem of the Crown University Royal Teaching Hospital, and was tied to a small journal.

Jane's breath caught in her throat, and she seized the envelope, tearing it open with her fingers instead of the small cutter. She held the page at an arm's length so that she could make out the careful hand it was written in.

Mrs. Lawrence,

I hope this letter finds you well, and your problems already solved. If it does not:

I have enclosed a copy of a rite which several magicians that are known to me have sought to employ. It guides a magician to an awakening in exchange for deprivation. It claims to focus magical abilities, and to aid the practitioner in progressing along a path of attainment. It is not easy, and I do not recommend it. However, you have asked for help, and this is the help that I can provide.

If you can, charge Augustine with its performance. He is better used to deprivation in the pursuit of the impossible. But if his practice prevents him from taking a leave of absence, or if you have now grown curious about what you might achieve were you to dip your toe into the ineffable, embark on this journey with a clear purpose.

I will continue to search for an answer to your particular question about banishing the spirits of the dead, and will send word on any discoveries, but please know that what I send may not be true. It is hard to untangle fanciful ramblings from real knowledge.

Be careful, Mrs. Lawrence.

Your friend,
Dr. Avdotya Semyonovna Nizamiev

She stared at the page for a long time, disbelieving. What had Hunt and Vingh called it? Synchronicity? Basic chance, but chance that had deep meaning. Yes, she had sought out Dr. Nizamiev's help, but here was her response, actionable and useful, right as Jane needed it.

She had cast a circle. She had learned what Augustine had done. And now she had a way to move forward. The promise of salvation, for herself, for the town.

For Augustine.

The thought of him conjured anger in her, but not a sensible anger. Not anger at what he had done to her, at the lies and how he had attacked her in delirious hope of saving her. No; it was more complex than that, an anger that he was not there with her, that she could not point to what had happened and say, *See? See why you must fight?*

And anger, too, at herself.

And panic.

She was not ready to lose him, not so soon after finding him. For all his faults, he was hers; and while she could not have saved her mother, perhaps she could save him. Her enemy was not as great as a war; it was only the impossible. And perhaps all the horrors between them were their own blessing, because Augustine would never have taken heed of what Dr. Nizamiev had sent them. Perhaps this was her chance.

She could fix this, and damn his arguments against it in favor of his suffering.

Jane opened the journal where Dr. Nizamiev had copied out passages from a longer text referenced as *The Doctrine of Seven*, by Magistrate Symon Ginette of Lurania, first published two hundred and seven years ago. The page where the details of the ritual were described was marked with a ribbon, as well as a note from the doctor to still read the surrounding work for context. She knew Jane's mind well already; Jane tried not to shudder.

The rite required sequestration for seven days. The practitioner had to remain within the boundaries of a building. No size was specified, so she supposed the surgery would have qualified as well as Lindridge Hall, if only the surgery were private. The practitioner had to consume a minimal, ritualized diet of medicinal herbs and purgatives, and had to eschew physical intimacy and sleep for the whole duration. The former would be easily done, but the latter . . .

Was she really considering this? Starvation, isolation, sleep deprivation? But before she could hesitate, her mind was already racing through solutions. It was tempting to send Mrs. Purl and Mrs. Luthbright away. Privacy would let her work without fear of discovery or interruption. But the rites required supplies, and elaborately prepared meals, and Jane knew she would need help if she were to do it all with no sleep, no way to leave the house. The thought, too, of being entirely alone with the ghosts for that length of time nearly brought her to tears. No; she would keep them on, and do her best to hide the extent of her chosen madness.

They already thought her eccentric. She could last another week.

CHAPTER THIRTY

SILENCE BLANKETED THE surgery as Jane eased the door open. If Mr. Lowell was there, she could not hear him. She sagged against the wood, taking a moment to breathe.

Outside, it was the middle of the afternoon, and Mrs. Purl would soon be finished with the shopping Jane had tasked her with. The roads were soft but passable, as long as they returned to Lindridge Hall before the next inevitable storm came. There was much Jane needed to gather before she could lock herself away. She had sent Mrs. Purl by excuse and authority to fetch candles and attar of rose and lavender oil from the shops crowding the center of Larrenton, as well as fresh eggs and other, particular food stores, placing every purchase under Augustine's name to be paid for at a later date. The cart that had brought them from Lindridge Hall had left hours ago, and Jane would need to hire their return carriage soon. She had stressed to Mrs. Purl that she should take her time, visit with friends, but that would not occupy her forever. Jane had to make quick work of this last stop.

But as she looked around the quiet surgery, she felt a curdling in her breast. How many patients had she missed over the last day and a half?

How many had Mr. Lowell turned away, begging forgiveness? Even one was too many.

Focus. She had memorized the instructions from Dr. Nizamiev's text and had more to do here before she could return to Lindridge Hall. She slipped into the ground-floor office and penned a quick letter requesting a locum, then crept upstairs. She gathered books on magic from Augustine's study and avoided looking at the couch where they had shared so much. She took, too, her mathematical treatise, the one talisman of her life she allowed for herself. She packed all the texts away with fresh clothing and her spectacles.

There remained only the last few supplies on her list, the easiest of them all to acquire. As she descended to the storeroom, Jane's skirt hem and shoes left a trail of bog muck. They were still damp from a few hours ago, when she'd gone out to the western edge of Larrenton, where the ground had shivered and sagged. Two handbreadths of moss from the great stands that floated above old, still waters were tucked into her bag. Beside it, a packet of soil. She had wandered the winding, confusing paths of Larrenton's graveyard for too long that morning, too embarrassed to take what she needed, until her eyes fell on a fresh grave marker that read:

NICHOLAS RENTON

His death had been her initiation into magic, though she had not known it at the time, and that, more than any guilt she felt at disturbing such a fresh grave, let her act. As she had gathered fresh-turned loam from three inches below the surface, she'd tried not to dwell on the nature of luck, or on synchronicity. No groundskeeper had seen her, though they surely were near.

Now, this last theft, too, seemed fated to be unsettlingly easy. She hurried to the storeroom and began scanning the shelves for tincture of benzoin.

Benzoin, she had learned at Augustine's side, was a wonderful fixative for bandages. From Dr. Nizamiev's notes, she had discovered that it was also a fixative of the spirit, something to steady a magician when she reached for the impossible. Were the two concepts related? And was it chance, or something more, that a magician from over two centuries ago called for a substance Augustine stocked at his surgery?

There, a dark bottle of compounded benzoin that she had filled the fourth day of their courtship, as Mr. Renton was laid to rest. She plucked it from the shelf and placed it in her valise, alongside the bog moss and grave dirt. She turned to go, then stopped, her gaze alighting on the jar of cocaine.

Seven days without sleep awaited her.

The front door opened. Mr. Lowell's heavy footsteps echoed in the hall. She snatched down the jar, and a syringe kit besides, along with everything she would need to compound the powder into a serum. She stuffed it all into her case just as Mr. Lowell appeared in the doorway.

"Mrs. Lawrence," he said, frowning. "Have you news, then?"

She turned to face him, trying for a brittle smile, unsure if she succeeded at looking anything but stricken. "No," she said. "No, nothing."

"Then are you come to stay?"

His tone made it clear that any other choice would make little sense to him. He had been kind to her over that first week of courtship. He had been overjoyed at the marriage. And now, here she was, a presumptive widow, about to shirk her duty.

She took refuge in emotionality. "I cannot. What if he returns to Lindridge Hall? What if—" There she let her throat close up, thinking about the missing cellar door, the way the hammer had made no dent. There was no harm in him assuming it was merely at the disappearance.

He did not respond, and Jane noticed he had not taken off his hat, or his coat. His jaw jutted forward as he ground his teeth in thought. "Lindridge Hall is not a fit place for you, ma'am," he said after a moment. "You *should* stay here. Let the magistrate handle this."

"The magistrate?"

"I let him know last night that the doctor had gone missing. We've been searching the hillside all morning for him."

She felt herself grow pale. "And there was no trace?"

"No. No trace at all. Are you—are you sure you don't know anything else?"

"He rode out into the storm," she said.

"On whose horse?"

"I . . . I don't . . . I stayed at Lindridge Hall, he went out alone—"

"Ma'am," he said, sharply, and she fell silent. His nostrils flared as he drew his temper back in. "I know the doctor cannot be dissuaded from acts of heroism—I've tried more than any man. But I also know you two have been, pardon me, in an adjustment period. Getting to know what you intend, and all. If something happened between you two . . ."

An adjustment period. He knew she had stayed at Lindridge Hall longer than Augustine had wanted her to. He knew she had then returned and worked beside her husband with a coolness that did not follow from the flare of attraction between them during their courtship. What did he think had happened? Why exactly had he called the magistrate?

Her blood iced in her veins. She clutched her satchel more tightly.

Had something about her convinced Mr. Lowell that she would have harmed Augustine intentionally? Had he seen a monstrousness in her that even she had not known?

"I am frightened for my husband," Jane said, fisting a hand in her skirts to keep her balance. "I have no idea what has happened to him, and I blame myself for his loss, because if I had not gone to him that night, he might still be tending to his patients. What more do you want of me? Do you wish me to weep? I am not the kind to weep. Do you wish me to conjure him from the ether? I can no more do that than change the color of the sky. I *must* be at Lindridge Hall, in case he returns there. The servants do not spend the night. If he comes to the door at midnight, who will be there to feed him? To wash his feet? *Me.* I will be there. I will tend to him, because I sent him out into the dark, not knowing a storm would take him." The words poured out of her, a torrent that left her breathless and choking.

Mr. Lowell was quiet for a long time. Then he murmured, "I want to find him, too."

It nearly broke her, the momentary thought that she might not have to do this alone. But she stopped short of confessing her plans, too aware that they would sound mad.

"There is a letter," she said instead, clearing her throat. "In the office. Asking for a locum. Please send it. Larrenton needs *somebody*, if they cannot have *him*."

"Of course, ma'am." And he left her there.

She fled the surgery as soon as his footsteps faded. Mrs. Purl stood across the way, speaking with another woman, smiling in the late afternoon sun. Jane ducked down an alleyway and walked herself in circles until she was at last calm enough to hire their ride back to Lindridge Hall.

As she climbed up into the carriage and took her seat across from Mrs. Purl, Jane realized she had not asked Mr. Lowell how Abigail Yew fared, or even checked if the woman was still in Augustine's bed.

Her cheeks flushed and she felt sweat stand out upon her brow at the thought. But surely, if Abigail's recovery had stalled, Mr. Lowell would have told her. He would have blamed her, or begged her to remain and try to help. Anything but his coldness, his remove. No, that cold *must* have meant that Abigail was better—no thanks to her, not anymore.

"Mrs. Lawrence?"

Jane dragged herself back together. Mrs. Purl had been audience to the whole dance of emotions that must have possessed her face. "Yes, Mrs. Purl?"

"Was there word, at the surgery? Have you heard at all from the doctor?"

Jane shook her head. "Mr. Lowell is still searching. We have sent for a locum."

Aren't you afraid, ma'am? Jane expected her to ask, but instead she chewed at her chapped lower lip and said, "Only, it's coming up on the end of the month, and there's salaries to be handled."

Jane almost laughed. *Salaries!* Of course. And of course she, the accountant, should have already been primed to handle them. She should have drawn up the cheques while she was at the surgery. But she'd forgotten.

The first tears took her by surprise. *She'd forgotten.*

She pressed a hand over her lips and nose, blinking rapidly in a desperate attempt to clear them before Mrs. Purl could see. It was futile. The older woman grimaced, one hand lifting as if to offer comfort, then dropping back to her side. Jane waved her off and turned back to the carriage window, staring out at the trundling landscape.

The tears cleared, but left her trembling in their wake. "I'm sorry," she whispered, not sure if she was apologizing for her preoccupation or her weakness.

"I understand, ma'am. It's very disturbing, the doctor's disappearance. Everybody is worried."

She thought of Mr. Lowell and the magistrate, walking the countryside. What would they think, if they saw her bog moss and grave loam, and the strange assemblage of ingredients in Mrs. Purl's baskets?

"The food," Jane mumbled, then wiped away her tears and tilted back her head, inhaling deep and slow. "The food, I'm sure Mrs. Luthbright will ask about it." River grass, rabbit stewed in blood, an unchanging cycle of disgusting, ritual meals. Better now to get ahead of it, than to be caught flat-footed. "It's—it's a superstition I learned from my parents, to bring him back safely."

The lie came more easily to her lips than she wanted it to. But it was almost truth, and so she almost began crying anew.

She resisted.

"I've worked a love charm or two before," Mrs. Purl said, half confession and half balm. Wonderful it was, that superstitions provided a familiar excuse. "I would wager so has Mrs. Luthbright," the maid continued, "though she wouldn't admit to it. I'll let her know, if you like."

Jane almost said yes, then hesitated. "Will she make the food regardless?" she asked.

"Of course, ma'am."

She wetted her lips, her heart beating double-time in her chest. "Don't tell her, then," Jane said, voice throaty with nerves. "I feel—weak. I'd rather she not know, if she doesn't have to."

"Yes, ma'am." Mrs. Purl worked her mouth a moment, then asked, "And would you like one of us to stay the night, keep you company?"

She did not sound enthusiastic. It was an offer of formality, not desire, and so Jane didn't feel guilty when she responded with, "No, I'd prefer to be alone."

THEY REACHED LINDRIDGE Hall with only an hour left before sunset. Jane retreated to the study with her materials and shut herself up. Following the text, she cut into the wax of candles, braided thread, and felt herself grow drunk on the heady gasses of the oils she worked into it all.

The servants locked up and left without coming to fetch her, by her direction. Dinner would wait for her downstairs, beneath a cloche; it was to be taken after the dusk working, cold and wretched, a mass of river grass and sprouted grain.

When the sun was bedded down along the horizon, Jane took her supplies up to the library. She hesitated at the threshold, shivering, wondering. Dr. Nizamiev's photographs danced in the shadows of her mind, and Aethridge's ring felt heavy upon her finger.

But then she thought of Orren, and the safety of the circle, and Augustine's screaming from the walls.

If nothing else, her guilt would drive her forward. She dripped with it. She was pickled in it.

She stepped inside the room.

She pulled all the rugs aside and laid out her accoutrements: chalk and salt, candles, dark glass bottles filled with oils, a dish, bog moss, cold ash from the third-floor bedchambers, and Renton's grave loam.

Jane skimmed the instructions once more, then took up her chalk. She tied it to a length of string, fixed the other end to the floor with a heavy pin. Pulled taut, the string would keep an equal distance between chalk and center. She inscribed a perfect circle, then followed over it with salt, picturing the wall, building it up as she had before. For a moment, there was nothing—and then it came, its eel skin still slippery, but familiar and warm.

The wall went up steadily, stone by stone. She felt the world fade away, and where the night before she'd felt stunned relief, now she felt a strange wonder kindling in her soul. The rush and reassurance of magic's reality was intoxicating, frighteningly so.

She worked the pin free from the floor and coiled the string around it, then set it, the chalk, and the salt aside. She knelt before the rest of her tools. Cool evening air chilled the glass vault above her, and it fogged from the warmth within, the glowing coals in the hearth that Mrs. Purl had built up and banked for the evening.

It was time.

Taking a deep breath, she struck one long match and lit the thick votive in front of her, saying, "Let this candle be the light that guides me to knowledge." Her voice sounded ridiculous and thin. "Let this flame dance for the small eternity that my soul will sing inside of as I do the Work. Let the power in its incandescence enchant the circle that circumscribes the realm that I inhabit, so that I may do the Work safely and in total focus."

The wick caught slowly, and the resulting flame was weak, but it held. Jane set the used match aside. Her hands trembled.

Next, she took up the oils. The first, attar of rose, she dabbed on her right wrist as she read from her notes:

"The senses of the human body bring light into darkness, scent into blankness, sound into emptiness, taste into nothingness, touch into the cold of the unmade. Through our senses, we know the world and we are alive."

The next oil, strong lavender, she placed on her left wrist. "Through the manipulation of the senses, we see the world as a stage upon which the Work can be done." On her chest she pressed a dab of the essence of lilies. "As the senses are aligned with the unseen, so too, shall we be aligned."

Had Mrs. Purl thought Jane meant to use those oils as perfume? Had she judged Jane for her frivolity as she spent her husband's money while he was missing? And now, now that she knew Jane was trying *something*, did she reinterpret?

Later. Those were thoughts for later.

Jane opened the final bottle, made of familiar dark glass. She pressed a finger of the sticky benzoin compound to her forehead, just between her eyes. The odor was pungent, wrapping itself around her in a spicy, cloying haze.

"By the application of these oils, I align myself by scent to the Work."

Her head spun. Each note thrummed with potential, stirring in endless depths. She was on the verge of something, something vast, something beckoning.

She could do this. She could build a wall, and more.

In one hand she took up ash, and in her other fist grave dirt, pouring a measure of each into a small bowl she'd taken from the kitchen. She mixed them with a finger, stirring counterclockwise seven times, then pulled her hands away.

Her skin hummed as she watched the ashes darkening fast to black, the water leaching from soil to drier ground. Then she reached in with both hands simultaneously, scooping up just a bit of the loam on each finger, and brought them together, pressing the dirt into every ridge of her finger-prints. "By application of the ash from a long-cold fire and the soil covering a newly dead soul, I align myself by touch to the Work," she murmured.

The dark of the room pressed in upon her, a living thing. There was some-thing in the room with her, though she could see no ghostly figures, no watching statues. "By the lighting of the candles within the circle, I align my-self by sight to the Work. By my words, I align myself by sound to the Work."

She parted her hands and reached for a pad of moss. She tore it down to size, then held it before her lips. Staring out into the blackness, she said, "By the application of this bog moss to my tongue, I align myself by taste to the Work."

It was green and fetid against her tongue. Its curling branches pressed against her palate and her teeth, but instead of gagging, she felt her jaw go slack. She could taste individual pockets of bog water and rot, and those soon mixed with her saliva and coated the whole of her mouth.

She did not retch.

There must have been some mind-addling ingredient clinging to the moss. The candle flames grew brighter, her thoughts more expansive. Or, perhaps, it was magic. It was the pageantry, the power, and she felt herself begin to slip, the way she had at Dr. Hunt's feet.

Either way, drugged or touching the ineffable, she must continue the working. She took a deep breath through her nose and tilted her head back.

I walk the path of the student. I open myself to the fullness of the Work, and commit myself to its challenges. I will neither sleep nor take my pleasures in the lands of the flesh. I will fix my mind only upon the Work, and I will not give in to the temptations of the world beyond. The division between this place and the world outside are the divisions between myself and the world outside. I walk the path of the student.

She focused so hard on the words that they seemed to burn in the air above her. The iron girding creaked. A cool wind tickled her fingers. She spread them, trying to catch the movement, but it was gone.

I surrender control to the Work. I will go whither the Work leads, and only there. I commit myself to the Work. The sigil written below me is the map by which I will reach awakening. I have inscribed the path in true black ink, indelible and thick so that the path cannot be lost.

Before her was a page she had filled with carefully plotted angles, regular polygons inscribed one within the other, meeting perfectly. Dr. Nizamiev's instructions had called for a sigil, an anchor, but had given only haphazard explanations as to what that meant. It referenced alchemical equations that did not balance and letters of Old Breltainian that she was half certain were drawn upside down, and no order or logic to any of it. But this? This was elegant, and powerful, and it was the strongest anchor she knew of between herself and the seemingly impossible.

As she traced its lines with her fingertips, her spine arched. She felt something moving inside of her, beneath her rib cage, just below her lungs. It squirmed and writhed and tried to force itself upward.

I walk the path of the student, she thought again, bowing low and pressing her forehead to the inked paper, crushing down the slithering inside her. *I walk the path of the student.*

CHAPTER THIRTY-ONE

THE RIVER GRASS and sprouted grain was as horrid as she'd anticipated, but no more than that, slick and flavorless but gone fast enough.
It did nothing to shadow the glow inside of her. She had *felt* the working's
power, just as she had felt the circle's. It was all real, and it would work. She
wanted to rush upstairs and read through Augustine's text one more time,
pick out spells to test and try, set herself against the door.

But she restrained herself. She made herself look at the picture of the
hanging magician, and felt the throbbing in her veins lessen, her skin lose
its hot flush. She recalled Dr. Nizamiev's instructions, her admonition to
keep a clear focus in mind.

Augustine. She must never lose sight of him. It was for his salvation that
she pursued the impossible, not for herself. This house was his prison; she
would break down the walls.

Would it really take all seven days to free him, though?

She had raised circles. She had repelled ghosts. She could feel the power
within her breast. What else could she do? What else could she shatter?

She made herself clean up the dishes. It was safer, she lectured herself, to follow the instructions. Seven days. But the seven days were not to free a man, they were to reach an awakening.

Jane gathered the chilling photographs and locked them away in the sitting room desk. Then she went to the hallway.

Settling her hands upon the impossible stone slab, Jane fixed the image of a door in her mind. The wood—what had it felt like? She remembered it jerking against her shoulder, but nothing of the texture. What shade of gray had the padlock been? What shape the escutcheon? She struggled to recall the details, and felt a burgeoning press within her, below her diaphragm, heaving, shuddering. If she could only conjure them up, they might be real once more.

Or . . .

Did it matter what the details had been, if she could conjure new ones in vibrant reality?

She remembered a door in the magistrate's building, the one she had stared at, waiting for the wedding to begin. It had been made of old, old oak, with rose head nails and wrought-iron hinges, and it had been beautiful, and ancient, and possessed of an almost mystical quality. But she could not recall how it felt beneath her hands. She wasn't sure she had even touched it. She cast the image aside and thought instead of the door to her bedroom at the Cunninghams'. She had felt it so recently, and the details came to her in crystal clarity, down to the beveling and the odd joints where the pieces had not quite fit together. The oak had been worn smooth where people had pushed it open for generations, before fashions changed and the doorknob had been installed.

She missed that door with a feverish pain. She knew every inch of it in a fullness of detail that surprised her. It was as if she could feel it there, as if all she had to do was turn the knob.

But when she opened her eyes, the stone slab stood as before. Her heart fell, her eager confidence punctured, deflated.

It was not as simple as willing the world to be different from what it was. Dr. Nizamiev had been quite clear; the ritual was the thing, the rails upon which the magician's mind ran. The steps of the proof, to be followed conjecture by conjecture until a final logic was arrived at. This door would not move for her.

"Jane?"

She went still as a sighted mouse at Augustine's voice. It came from the other side of the wall, soft and weak. She was *certain* it was his.

"Augustine, I am here." She waited for the bursting of pipes or the rocking of the foundation that had accompanied his thundering cries of anguish a day before.

Neither came. Instead, Augustine let out a broken, muffled, distant sob. "Jane, where am I?"

Oh, Augustine. She could almost see him, huddled on the stairs. Confused. Afraid.

She sank to her knees, pressing herself against the rock, every inch of bare skin that she had. Her throat was thick.

"Jane?" Augustine called, and he sounded weak, so weak.

"You're in the cellar of Lindridge Hall," Jane said, unsure if her voice would carry far enough. "I am working to get you out."

"It is dark," Augustine said. "Jane, it's so dark."

No gas lighting down there, and all the candles that had been lit before must have burned down to nothing now, puddles of cooled and cracking wax.

But darkness and spirits were not the only dangers, she realized with a sick jolt, her dinner cold and heavy in her belly. He had been down there two days already. Two days without water, without meals. "Augustine, do you have food?" Jane asked, and held her breath.

Augustine did not respond.

If she were in that crypt, if she had been locked away for days in the darkness, she would have screamed. She would have begged, and pounded on the door, and torn at her flesh. She knew well what havoc a night of silent waiting in the dark could do after weeks of it as a child, but she had been able to go up into the light during the day. She'd had her mother with her, had food, had water.

If Augustine was silent . . .

Then all it meant was that he was not her.

"I need seven days," she said, louder this time. "Do I have seven days? Will you be all right for seven days?" There were rooms down there she hadn't explored. There might yet be supplies. Food stores, old but perhaps still viable. Perhaps he'd found them. Perhaps he was not dying.

The silence stretched, and Jane curled in upon herself, shivering. Night had come in full. Perhaps . . . perhaps this was not Augustine at all.

"I think so," Augustine said at last. "But it is so dark."

She closed her eyes, measuring each word. Were they his? Were they vital, alive, proof she had not already failed?

"Jane, what are you doing?"

"Magic," Jane whispered. She took a deep breath, then said, louder, "I'm getting you out. Just a little longer, Augustine. Wait for me."

He didn't respond.

JANE WALKED THE halls into the darkest part of the night.

She must not sleep. The dictate consumed her, her head already foggy after the vigil she'd sat the night before. The longer she went without the house creaking, without the sound of ghosts or the moaning of her husband, the more unreal her world became. There were instructions she was meant to follow this first night, small workings, small sacrifices: blood upon the hearth stone, inhaling the smoke of three rooster feathers, walking in circles while reciting chants, and all of them felt like games. None felt powerful. None felt *useful*.

Magic was real. Of that, she had no doubt now. But her intoxication had been tempered, adulterated with a child's first failures. She had not removed the stone. She had not fed her starving husband.

A few hours before dawn, she found herself in the bedroom she had shared with Augustine. She stared at the mattress, its indentations. For most of its existence, it had held only one body, but she could already see a faint blurring of the edges where two had lain, tangled and sweaty, both desperate to believe a fiction.

"A clear purpose," she murmured to herself, and turned away. Dr. Nizamiev's instructions had been specific: she must fix herself upon the work, the work that she *wanted* to do. Her willpower was great. She could do it, if only she began.

Something moved in her bed.

Confused hope swelled in her, and she froze, unable to turn around and look. Was it Augustine, somehow returned? From behind her came wheezing, rattling breaths. The sheets rustled in the soft sounds of suffering. Weak legs pushed at the sheets, a heavy head tossed and turned upon the pillow.

Jane knew those sounds.

Jane did not want to know those sounds.

Abigail Yew.

A thousand warring impulses leapt to life inside her and left her paralyzed: drop to her knees and cower, or flee, or scream in rage, or ignore the impossible, or take up her chalk and draw a circle. But all she could do was clutch at the wardrobe and whisper, "No, no, no."

Not Abigail. Not here. She was not dead. Jane remembered the weight of Abigail's chin as she guided broth to her lips. She remembered her strengthening pulse, and her eyes, gradually focusing on her nurse. But then Jane thought of the room she had not checked at the surgery. A scream built inside her.

These ghosts, these specters, came in the form of failed patients. Dead patients.

Abigail Yew was dead.

And if Abigail Yew was dead, if her ghost had come to Lindridge Hall, then Jane needed to guard herself, as she had against Orren. She needed . . .

What?

Why did she need to protect herself? Orren had not attacked her. He had only said what she knew to be true, what she did not want to face. And she had fled. She had abandoned him and failed him again. How selfish was she, that she would do it once more, and to the woman whom she had so faithfully tended to for days?

She forced herself away from the wardrobe and came to the bedside. Abigail Yew lay beneath sheets and coverlet, feverish and pale. Her chest rose and fell with a wheezing whisper. Her hair clung to her flesh, and her fingers curled atop the blanket.

Shame and guilt surged inside Jane.

"I am afraid," Abigail whispered, and remembering Augustine, Jane nearly retched.

A dark stain spread across the coverlet. Blood, and too much of it. The stench filled the air, and Jane jerked forward as if on strings, hauling back the blanket. Below, Abigail's body was hemorrhaging, great gouts of blood surging forth from her pale, limp body. Abigail's head lolled back, etherized, even as her fingers gouged into the incision in her belly.

"You missed something," Abigail whispered. "You always miss something. Get it out of me. Get it out!"

But Jane couldn't move, and so Abigail grabbed her wrists and dragged her close, forcing her hands into her abdomen. The flesh parted, revealing a skull festooned with rot, worms writhing in every crevice, every shadow. Slick ropes of intestines wound around her fingers while her thumbs pressed into the dark, impossible softness of the skull's eyes. It wasn't an unborn child, but the head of a full-grown person, erupting into reality and dying before it could be born.

Jane cried out and dug her fingertips into the crumbling bone, pulling and twisting, desperate to free Abigail of it. But it did not move, and Abigail screamed, tears streaking her cheeks. Her head rocked from side to side on the pillow, and Jane remembered herself, brought to ecstasy in that same bed by a surgeon's brilliant hands.

Please, she begged of herself. *Please, discover a way to save her. Be brilliant. Be mad.* She looked to the window, too, searching for Elodie.

The window was empty.

And when Jane looked back, the bed was empty, too. Only the blood remained.

CHAPTER THIRTY-TWO

MRS. PURL COULD not know what had happened.

Jane stared at the empty bed, at her bloodstained hands. The sun would rise soon. The servants would return. Strange dinners and chalk circles could be explained, but this? Here? There was no lie she could offer, no gentle misdirection. This bed looked and stank as if a woman had died in it, and Jane stood there, still alive, still hale.

Jane tore the sheets off the bed. The fabric clung to her, cold and wet. *Real.* As real as the ghost had felt. As real as Abigail had been.

The ticking of the mattress was stained scarlet as well. Jane stared at it helplessly, then cast aside the sheets and knelt, pressing her hands up through the bedsprings to feel at the mattress's bottom. Not cold. Not wet. She grabbed the cover and heaved, flipping the dense horsehair mattress.

Passable. She would have to find another solution before Mrs. Purl could turn it again, but she had time. She had time.

She dragged the bundle of sheets to the bathroom and dumped it into the tub. She grabbed the tap. Stagnant water burst forth from the pipes, stinking of mildew, and then sputtered out.

The main was still closed. The kitchen plumbing was still destroyed.

Another mistake. She should have had Mrs. Purl hire a plumber yesterday when they were in town. The old Jane, the sensible Jane, would have been sure to.

If she could not wash the sheets, she would need to conceal or destroy them. There was no room in all of Lindridge Hall that Jane could reach but Mrs. Purl could not access, but there were hearths she might not check immediately, giving Jane time to make sure no evidence survived. Clutching the sheets to her chest, Jane crept back into the bedroom, looking around for any sign of movement.

Nothing. No lurching patient or fresh spot of blood. Soft rain pattered against the window, and she could hear the croaking chorus of frog song faint in the distance. The hallway was as empty as the bedroom, and the lights burned brightly all the way up to the library.

The hearth there had not yet gone cold, and Jane stoked the fire, sitting close and hugging her knees to her chest. The red-gold light flashed starkly across the sheets, sparking crawling shadows in every fold and hollow. When the fire was so hot Jane could hardly stand to be near it another moment, she pushed the fabric into the flame.

It caught slowly, reluctantly, and where the blood had flowed too thickly, where the fabric had not yet dried, it smoked and sputtered and smelled of horrors. And yet even that burned, given long enough, given gentle tending and prodding. The light it cast illuminated the stains on her own clothing, and as the sheets became ash, Jane stripped out of her dress and fed it, too, to the fire.

When at last every scrap and stain had been consumed, Jane made her way down to the kitchen. There was water drawn into a bucket there, gray and used from washing, and Jane scrubbed her hands clean in its icy depths. Ignoring the murk of it, she splashed it on her face, shocking herself half senseless. The evidence was burned. The spirits were gone. The sun was rising, and she had work to do.

She shivered as she gathered what she needed for the dawn ritual. Salt and a hen's egg from the kitchen, chalk and benzoin and a fat taper candle from the study. She risked the bedroom to dress again, then returned to the library.

The stench of burned fabric still lingered, turning her stomach, but the room's remoteness might shield her from prying eyes if the servants arrived before she completed the working. She put down her basket of implements inside the circle she had drawn at dusk. She set the pin and pulled the string taut, and traced it out fresh.

She circumscribed herself with the utmost care, and settled down in the exact center, reaching for the eel inside her. But as she did, she saw again the rotted skull, felt again the writhing of worms. Abigail's flesh, hot and slick. The eel darted away. She tried again, and this time, it was a pop from the fire that distracted her. The next, it was the memory of Augustine's desperate voice behind the stone.

"Just get it over with," she whispered to herself, and abandoned the circle, reaching for the candle instead. It was decorated with lines and shapes that she had inscribed in its surface according to the text. She rubbed benzoin into the hollows, then set the wax before her and lit it. The perfume almost overwhelmed the stink of burned fabric and blood, but instead of feeling stronger, she felt ashamed.

"Let this candle be the light that guides me to knowledge," she said. Her voice trembled.

She felt nothing.

She wanted the certainty, the ecstasy that had come with the working before. Instead, she felt . . . normal. Foolish.

A soft thrumming came from the hallway. No—the wall itself. The empty water pipes?

Augustine. He was listening. He needed this as much as she did.

She fixed him in her mind's eye and reached once more for the eel. She smelled blood. She felt the worms. But her fingers closed over the writhing flesh, and the first bricks fell in place in the circle around her. Power flared in her breast, and she could have cried from the relief.

Jane started the incantation over, reading line after line, her voice tremulous but constant. She anointed herself, invoking her senses.

She whispered her intentions to the ether: the attainment of knowledge, entry to the greater world beyond the limitations of man, and the salvation of Augustine. She bowed low to the candle, so close she could feel the heat on her chin, as she had felt the heat that burned away the sheets. And then she sat back on her heels and reached for the egg.

"The thin shell protects the potential within from harm; it cannot survive unaided, in the way that the grown mind protects the unprepared soul from the expansion of the universe without. But the shell must finally give way; the mind must blossom and allow that which lives within to breathe in its birthright."

She cracked the egg into a dish with faded flowers painted around the chipped rim. The yolk was vibrant orange, leaking into the clear albumen in a plume on one edge.

On the other was a spot of brilliant crimson.

Jane pressed the fingertips of both her hands into the bowl. The yolk came apart into an undifferentiated mass of gold and she stirred it, each hand going in a different direction.

"The mind is not yet ready to give way," Jane whispered, lifting her hands from the bowl and painting lines of sticky egg across her forehead, her cheeks, the hollow of her throat. "But through the resonance of the pantomime, I prepare the mind and the soul. I prepare myself for the first glimpses of the unknown."

She forced herself to lift the bowl and bring it to her lips. The crimson spot was still there. Her exhausted mind conjured up images of baby birds, fledgling feathers, thin bones that would crack at the slightest pressure.

Just a spot. Just a spot of blood. She had eaten such before, she must have. But the more she looked at the crimson spot, the more she was able to make out the branching of veins, and a murky center that might be the beginnings of a chick. *Synchronicity,* she told herself. The coincidence had to mean the spell was working. Didn't it?

She fixed her eyes on the door, on Lindridge Hall beyond, on its ghosts and the man lost in its bowels.

And she drank.

The egg slid down her throat, fast and heavy, rich and wrong. Her stomach heaved, but she kept it down. The bowl nearly slipped from her fingers. In a blinding rush, she felt power course up her spine, filling her to her fingertips, to her toes. Something hurt in her belly, but it was a beautiful kind of pain, sharpening all her senses. *Awake.* She felt awake. She felt disgusting. She felt glorious. She felt—

She put the bowl down and retched, clawing her fingers into the wood as she made herself swallow, swallow, swallow. She felt sick. Yolk and spit stuck to her jaw.

"I walk the path of the student," she gasped.

By the time she dragged the rug back over the circle and stashed the basket out of the way, she could hear movement downstairs, Mrs. Purl's voice distant but unmistakable. Jane looked her reflection over in one of the murky panes of glass and scrubbed at her face with the inside hem of her gown. Her hair was frightful, and she looked hollow-eyed, worse than Augustine had after a night of torment.

Was she going to be able to keep this up for six more nights? How soon before Mrs. Purl was not so understanding anymore?

She made her way downstairs, creeping through the halls. She could at least reset her hair. That, by itself, would do much to disguise her privations. She was halfway to the bedroom door when Mrs. Purl rounded the corner.

They both stopped, regarding each other in silence.

"Breakfast is waiting for you," Mrs. Purl said at last. "The one you requested, the hare." Her tone was perfectly polite, but Jane recognized the look in her eyes from the carriage ride the day before. She had questions.

Ah. Salaries. "Of course, thank you. I'll be sending over a letter to the bank today, too, for your pay."

More silence. Then, "Pardon, ma'am, but would you not prefer that I send for a carriage? It would be faster."

"I . . ." She could think of no real excuse; Mrs. Purl was right, except for the ritual prohibitions that Jane could not bring herself to speak of. "If

Dr. Lawrence returns while I'm out—and I had wanted to spend the day improving the master bedroom. There is much to be done. A letter—a letter should work—" It sounded feeble, even to her.

And what would Mrs. Purl think? That Jane's excuses hid that there was no money? Or that Jane did not respect her the way Augustine had?

This was only the first day. She must get better at this. Plan better. Control everything.

"Of course, ma'am," Mrs. Purl said. "Please let me know how I can be of assistance."

Don't let me sleep. Forgive me everything. Send for a plumber. But she could not risk workmen at the house, not where they might see her madness or hear Augustine's cries, not until this was done—just as she could not go to town, just as she could not seek support.

Mrs. Purl didn't move, and Jane smiled. She smiled until her jaw ached. And then, giving in, she passed Mrs. Purl in the hall and left the second floor without redoing her hair.

After all, she was dressed, wasn't she? She must be ready to face her day. She crossed the foyer and didn't look toward the cellar. She sat down and didn't acknowledge the place set across from her by a hopeful—or superstitious—Mrs. Luthbright.

She ate her hare stewed with blood and a riot of disparate herbs. It was bitter but warm, nourishing. She thought of Augustine starving in the cellars beneath the house and set her fork down.

She fled back up to the third floor.

Mrs. Purl was already hard at work in the master bedroom, no doubt because of Jane's comment. Jane joined her, but was almost immediately at a loss for what to do. She looked at the empty wardrobes, the wood in need of polishing, the curtains caked in dust. She looked at the empty hearth, where Mrs. Purl had found the impossible bag.

Mrs. Purl made as if to speak several times, then left without a word.

Jane tried to see the room as it must once have been, when the Lawrences were in residence, when Lindridge Hall had not yet been spoiled. But the air was stale. The plaster was crumbling and water-spotted.

She could see no trace of Augustine.

She sank onto the musty couch pushed up against one wall. Her hip pressed into something hard along the side of one cushion. Frowning, she slipped her hand into the crevice. Her fingers brushed over a rigid, rough surface several inches long and only half an inch wide, entirely out of place, and she drew it out with trembling fingers.

It was a small, thin volume. Opening it, she saw the unlined pages were covered in clear, precise script, the handwriting completely different from Augustine's. Possibly feminine. His mother's? But as she leafed through it, she caught sight of a name. *Be serious, Elodie!* started one page. Jane's throat tightened, and she sat up, placing the diary in her lap.

Elodie Lawrence, the next page said. *What a handsome name! But to tell the truth, it still doesn't sound like me, and I suspect Augustine will always feel more like a brother than my husband. Is that wrong? I always knew we would marry, but the daily reality of playing in creeks together, of growing up by our parents' hearths—it outweighs that sort of indistinct certainty. Elodie Lawrence. I shall have to get used to it.*

Her heart ached, her head pounded. She did not have room in her soul for Elodie the woman, not on top of Elodie the tragedy and Elodie the monster. She barely had room for Augustine, crushed in beside her own racing thoughts, her own desperate heart.

She slipped the journal back into the couch and fled.

She took refuge in Augustine's study, taking up her old seat at the desk and putting on her spectacles, reaching not for magic but for her mundane work. She had not brought the ledgers back with her, but she would do her figuring, write a letter to the bank to send for the servants wages; all simple, all steadying.

But exhaustion clawed at her, worse than before. She dropped her pen more than once, botched a simple subtraction. She found herself looking at odd corners of the room, no longer remembering what she had meant to do. She thought of the cocaine and syringe stashed nearby, then recoiled from the thought.

Jane was no doctor. She could not imagine piercing her flesh, and feared drawing the wrong dosage. No, she would wait until she could stand it no more before reaching for the syringe.

In the meantime, she would find other solutions. She would cinch her stays more tightly, reset her hair with sticking pins, fill her shoes with grain to dig into her still-aching feet as she paced. And she would give herself over to work. Work would keep her awake.

But inevitably, the work ran out. The figuring was finished, the letter written and delivered to Mrs. Purl to be sent off. Magic, then, was all that was left. She selected a tome from Augustine's collection—*The Unveiling of the Panoply*—along with the mathematical treatise and a half-empty journal, and brought them with her to the library. She also took a chair from the dining room, when she was certain Mrs. Purl was upstairs and Mrs. Luthbright was occupied. It would be a small enough thing to explain, but she didn't want to speak.

She placed the stolen chair in the far corner of the library, faced away from the door. She removed its cushion and then, clutching a candlestick, she sat. The chair had no arms and was desperately uncomfortable, just as she had hoped for. The candlestick wasn't too heavy in her hand, but it took focus not to drop it, and when she did, it clattered loudly against the floorboards, sharp enough to wake her from the edge of sleep. She settled Augustine's text in her lap and set to reading.

The hours crawled by. Down the hall, Mrs. Purl dragged furniture in the master bedroom, muttered to herself, went up and down the stairs. Outside, the road was still. Jane drifted in and out of full wakefulness, and each time she came too close to sleep, she dropped the candlestick and lurched forward, heart pounding.

Noon came. She ate again, bread baked with goat's milk. She continued her studies. She felt stronger now, surer, with the lowering arc of the sun. She dropped the candlestick less often. She read of other worlds—fanciful stories, but stories the author claimed were true, or at least full of truth. Worlds where humans were as dust motes, worlds governed by will alone, worlds under five suns and seven moons. Nonsense. All nonsense. And where it wasn't, she could pick out the threads of stolen stories, tales from

Ruzka and farther abroad. She'd heard some from Ekaterina, read others during the course of her schooling, and here it all was, jumbled together, removed from any meaningful context.

How many hours remained until sunset? Until privacy, and the flare of power inside of her? She wanted to set aside the theoretical. Reach for the real.

Heat grew at her back. A fire in the hearth? But Jane hadn't heard Mrs. Purl enter, and if she'd seen any scrap of fabric in the grate, surely . . .

But this had happened once before. She twisted in her seat, breathless.

All the shelves were now full of books.

Heavy tomes and slim treatises, leather bound and barely bound at all. A crackling fire danced in the hearth, illuminating everything. The library was beautiful, resplendent and enticing. Plush armchairs stood by the fire, so much more comfortable than her own seat. The floor below was polished to a mirror finish, and the air was no longer still and dusty, but fragrant with wood smoke and furniture polish and a faint floral perfume. An unfamiliar woman stood in the library doorway. She was dressed in robes not dissimilar to Dr. Hunt's, her dark hair loose around her shoulders. She clasped a branch in one hand, a candelabra in the other.

"Augustine?" the woman called.

Jane's fingers tightened around her own candelabra, for Augustine was sitting by the fire.

He was younger and better rested than she had ever seen him. His hair was trimmed fashionably short. His clothing looked expensive. "Is it time, then?" he asked. His voice was light and affable, easy, unaffected.

Content.

"Just about, yes. Why aren't you dressed?"

"Georgiana's latest theory," he said, waggling his book in the air. "On possible transmission vectors for swamp illnesses, now that miasma theory has been firmly put to bed."

The woman—older than Augustine, but similar in bearing and the lines of her cheeks, perhaps his mother?—looked distantly amused. "It will be there when we are through. Elodie is waiting."

Augustine conceded with a smile, one Jane knew well, and rose from his chair.

I am dreaming. Panic shot through her, and she rose to her feet, staggering forward. Nobody looked up at the noise or movement. Augustine left the room, and she followed him down the stairs, candlestick clutched tightly in her hand.

Lindridge Hall in all its splendor was breathtaking. Every window was gleamingly polished, every rug washed and beaten and just so, every piece of furniture lavishly upholstered and bedecked in finery. The house pulsed with vibrancy, and every odd angle in the walls, every strange geometry was now beautiful to her. In context, around this cheerful family, it sang in a distant but recognizable harmony.

Augustine disappeared into his bedroom and Jane followed, slipping in just before he closed the door.

He was already tugging off his waistcoat.

"Augustine," she said, rushing to his side. If this was a dream, if she had ruined the ritual, she would have this, at least. Some little contact, some kindness. "Augustine, it is Jane."

Her husband did not respond.

She tried to take his hands and found she could not. She did not pass through him, or feel any resistance, but still she could not reach him. It was as if she were looking through a mirror, and her idea of where things might be was not quite right.

A mirror.

She could see Elodie in the mirrored windows of Lindridge Hall. Might dream logic allow the reverse? She followed him to his dressing table as he shucked his shirt, his trousers.

She had no reflection.

"Augustine!" she cried. "I must speak to you. I have so much to tell you, so much you need to understand. Please—"

He stepped into the washroom and closed the door.

Numb, Jane stared after him, then retreated from the bedroom.

In the foyer, Augustine's mother waited alongside three others: two men and a woman, one in Augustine's image and the other two fair and copper-haired. Augustine's father, and the Pinkcombes.

And beside them . . .

Nothing.

Not just the empty foyer, but blankness. Jane's eyes refused to focus on it. Her gaze slid away. She watched instead as Augustine's mother approached it, holding out her hands.

"He was caught up in his work, of course," she said. "But he will be down soon, my dear."

The blankness encircled her hands. Jane's throat grew tight.

Augustine's mother canted her head, as if listening, then laughed. "You must learn not to forgive him so easily," she said to the blankness, "or he will govern your future."

The blankness was Elodie.

Augustine descended the stairs, dressed in dark blue robes picked out with shining green thread. They were cinched at the waist, with a mantle about the shoulders. They were finely made and well kept, but they, like the robes the rest of them wore, looked old. Very old.

She watched, frozen, as Augustine drew close to the blankness and pressed his face against it, a gentle kiss to the top of the lacuna. He murmured something she could not make out. The families laughed, then processed together down the hallway toward the cellar.

The door was closed but had no shining padlock on top of it. Augustine's father was the one to open it as the rest of the group came to a halt. "Elodie, dear," he said, his voice lower than his son's, more resonant. "Can you recite the order in which we are to enter the ritual space?"

Silence. And not just silence, but an absence of all sound, so deafening it made Jane cry out. But the Lawrences and the Pinkcombes did not notice, and they smiled, then schooled their expressions to firm solemnity. They were like Hunt and the others, but unlike them as well—possessed of a careful grace, a seriousness that the doctors had not had. Jane followed them beneath Lindridge Hall, ghostlike at their heels.

They did not go to the funeral chamber, with its carven chairs and long table, but instead to another room, the stone floor worked in concentric circles and fine patterns. Jane watched them place anointed candles at each spoke of an inscribed polygon, then take up carefully chosen positions within.

For now, for this moment, Augustine did not have blood on his hands. No horrors had been enacted. Her husband had only powdered pigment that he pressed to every person's forehead. He had only poetry, recited until his words vibrated into meaninglessness. She felt power on the air, on her tongue, and she leaned forward, desperate to reach it. To feel it, to *know* it. But as the circle raised around them, firm and real, their voices became distant, their outlines blurred.

Except for the gaping wound in the world that knelt on the other side.

Why was Elodie gone? It was too early for Augustine to have done his working. She lived. She was happy, and loved, and hale.

And if Elodie was not here, if there was only this blankness in her place, where had she gone?

The nothingness rose up to full height and stepped forward, crossing the boundary. It slid into the pattern on the floor, and set the whole thing pitching, rocking. Nothingness reached out and grasped a blade that was offered to it.

Nothingness dripped down like blood, eating away the floor.

And then there was only the sound of afternoon crickets, the glow of sunlight, the swirl of dust around her. Distant footsteps in the hall. She was still in the library, surrounded by empty shelves. She lurched forward, heart pounding, and cast aside the book in her lap. A nightmare. It had been a nightmare. Had she slept? Had she ruined the ritual, set herself back an entire day?

But no, in her left hand, she still clutched the candlestick.

What, then, had she seen?

CHAPTER THIRTY-THREE

A s SOON AS the servants were gone, Jane went in search of Elodie.

She looked in every darkening window, every mirror. She shouted Elodie's name. She retrieved Elodie's journal, still where she had left it tucked in the couch, and read every page aloud, hoping, hoping. Elodie had written of the day Jane had witnessed, her "initiation into the mysteries" at the hands of her families. She had been nervous, delighted, bewitched. There had been no magic, none that Elodie could say for certain had been real, but she had been ready to hope. She had *believed*.

Jane looked as well for any sign of blankness, but Elodie's name remained in the journal. It remained in Augustine's notes on the resurrection ritual. She suspected that if she had them at hand, his ledger would also still contain her name. There was no gaping hole where Elodie should have been, beyond the normal absence that death left in its wake. When Jane looked in empty windows, she saw herself, or darkness outside, or the reflection of gas sconces. Her eyes didn't slide away. She didn't feel a writhing wrongness.

And yet she was certain that the blankness had meant something.

Why had Elodie been gone in *that* vision, but there in full, horrific agony in the vision Hunt's games had bestowed on Jane? There with her red eyes in the window before? There with her blood-soaked gown in the cellar?

"She's trapped," Jane whispered to herself, staring at her smudged circle in the library.

But Augustine had said he'd never seen her. It all connected, but Jane was missing some crucial variable, some indispensable operation.

She made herself breathe and draw the circle anew. She knelt in the center of the library. This progression, this ritual deprivation, it offered knowledge. This vision might not be the last. There might be more to come, more context, more explanation.

"Elodie," she said to the creaking darkness of Lindridge Hall at night, "I will find you. I will solve this. I will fix this."

In answer, the dusk working ran smoothly. At its conclusion, she rocked back onto her heels, feeling drunk and dazed. She reached for the magical texts. Even in her addled mind, the illogic of the haphazard scholarship refused to coalesce, but certain phrases burned bright to her. She found a half-used journal in Augustine's library and set to writing down her observations, her experiences, her theories.

The circle is the thing.

She had observed that the presence of an invoked circle could stop a ghost's approach and make it leave her. It could not cross the boundary, and it did not linger as a hungry wolf circling wounded prey. It was the purest form of magic she had yet discovered. She must press its mysteries.

She had paper and ink up in the library, but not much, and she quickly exhausted it by drawing circles and laying out every geometric theorem she remembered. She spent long hours following deep trails of logic, wishing for more than her book on fringe mathematical theories, wishing for a blackboard. But what she had was ink-filled paper and the floor beneath. She grabbed her stick of chalk and continued to draw. When that wore down to almost nothing, she took her pen to the wood itself. Her eyes ached and burned behind her glasses.

She felt so close to something, so close to a solution. She sketched out equations, including childish attempts at using zero in strange new ways. Zero, which could also be written as a circle. Was there a connection there?

A scream pierced the silence of the house.

It came from the lower floors, both muffled by the distance and amplified by its echoing in the cavernous foyer.

The cellar.

She sprinted from the nest of circles and was halfway down the stairs when the next scream came. It was a man's voice, a man in agony. *Augustine.* The pipes began to creak, to thrum in time to his pain.

But when she rounded the last turn of the stairs and stepped down into the foyer, the man in the center of the room was not Augustine. He stood inside a circle of chalk, and he was silent, arms spread, looking up at the ceiling.

It was Mr. Renton.

His skin was purpled with rot, his abdomen split open and gaping where he had injured himself, where Augustine had sliced through deeper, where Jane had spread the gash apart. His open shirt and trousers were stained with grave dirt, and Jane could feel it under her own nails, could remember the warm damp of the putrefying loam when she had dug below the graveyard lawn.

He screamed again, though he did not move except to let his jaw fall open. For all the pain in his voice, he looked like a photograph, a statue.

A statue.

She had spent the long night drawing circles, but now she was frozen. A little chalk, a little salt, and Renton could not get to her. But she would still be able to hear him, screaming, screaming.

Except he wasn't screaming now. He was looking at her. He did not blink. His eyes bulged in their sockets.

"Jane Shoringfield Lawrence," Mr. Renton said.

"How do you know my name?" she whispered. Augustine had only ever called her *Miss Shoringfield* during the surgery, and Renton had been far gone by then.

"Where is the missing part of me?"

In a jar, on display, in the surgery of a man who can no longer be reached.
She stammered out, "Gone."

"No," he said. His lips sagged from his face, revealing teeth, worn and yellowed. "I would know if it were gone, but I feel it still. We are connected, me and it. The magician and the Work. If it were gone, I would know."

The magician and the Work. Chalk and salt found around his body. Augustine's fears. Here it was, confirmed: Renton had been a magician, and he had paid the price for it. A hysterical laugh threatened to bubble from her throat. What stood before her was an unnatural ghost, but more than that, perhaps. What happened when a magician died? What happened when he came back?

"It isn't here." How could she have known he would want it back? How could she have known they could *give* it back?

But they could have buried him with it at the first, or disposed of it like they had Abigail's pregnancy.

Abigail. The memory brought with it the feeling of worms beneath her fingers. What had the skull meant? Had Augustine been wrong, that the cause of her affliction had been mundane?

She hugged herself tightly, swaying on her feet.

"You will put me back together," Renton said. "You will fix this."

"I—I can't—"

"Something must be given for what has been taken."

Her hands dropped to her stomach, which, as if on cue, gave an answering ache, called by the still corpse before her. "I don't understand."

"Something that grew out of place."

A tangled bowel. A dead infant. A magician's bones, growing wildly after a spell miscast. What might be growing inside of *her*? "And will you leave me, if I give it to you?" she whispered. "Leave this house, be laid to rest?"

"Make me whole," Mr. Renton said.

She had no offal to give to him, but she had Augustine's collection of strange growths, of other things out of place. They were the same. They were all the same.

"I can do this," she said, though she wanted nothing more than to flee.

Augustine's medical equipment was sealed away with him, but there was needle and thread in the kitchen, for stitching up roasts, and elsewhere, for doing mending.

"The grave loam," he said. "That as well."

How did he know she had it? Did he also require the moss? The benzoin? Was this some wicked trick, to drain her supplies?

Or was this the next step of the awakening promised by the ritual?

"Can you move?" she asked, making herself meet his eyes.

He took one step, and then another, a jerking, stiff-legged puppet. But he moved.

Jane recoiled, bile in her throat. "Up to the second floor," she gasped. "I will meet you on the landing."

He stepped out of his circle and began to climb.

She retrieved the needle and thread from the kitchen, and tried to breathe, now that she could not see Renton. But she could smell the rot of him, and paused a moment before she returned to the stairs. When he reached the landing ahead of her, he tipped his head back and screamed again. His face remained impassive as she passed him, racing up to retrieve the loam, and, in an abundance of caution, the moss. He watched as she set her things down outside the bedroom, nodded at her selection. Jane ducked her head and slipped into the study.

She stared up at the rows of misshapen skulls, at tight-packed coils of hair, calcified tumors, and other strange things she did not know the name of. What was best? What would fit? The skull in Abigail had not been right, had been out of place. And for Renton, the hair made no sense. But there—a burl of wood, a knot of root that had grown inside some vessel, that had curled back upon itself. *That.* It looked almost the same as Renton's bowel.

He waited for her on the landing. The stench of him hit her again in a fresh wave, then faded, transmuted to something heady. Enticing. She smelled benzoin, antiseptic, attar of rose. The scents of a magician, of a surgical patient.

Jane held out the knot of wood in offering. Renton reached out one arm and touched it, a silent blessing.

She led him into her bedroom, then the washroom. The tub was just long enough for him to lay down inside. Jane had only one set of hands, and no retractors to help bare his viscera. The work was messy. But it focused her, shut out the panic and steadied her hands. His abdomen was filled with a wet, dark slurry. His flesh seemed to fade in and out of reality as she worked, heavy and clinging one minute, a doll made of ephemeral silk the next.

She had no water to rinse the wound, so she used brandy left by Hunt, filling her tub with fumes and filth. She placed the knot of wood where the twisted section of bowel had been, then filled the rest of Renton's abdomen with bog moss and grave loam, saving only a small fraction for herself.

He did not speak until she had taken the needle and begun to stitch him up.

"You are monstrous," he said.

She flinched and pulled thread through the ragged edge of the torn hole with more force than she intended. It split the delicate flesh. "How so?"

"You do not weep or scream. You did not weep or scream when Augustine Lawrence split me open, either."

"You are not real," she said.

"Am I not?"

She looked up at him then, hands still holding his flesh together. "You are not a man." She hesitated. "Not anymore, at least. Where are you, when you aren't here?"

He considered, or waited, silent and still. Jane set a few more stitches. Her work was unsteady, childlike. Her hands shook.

"There is a world beyond this one," he said at last. "Very different, and very far away."

"The world of the dead?" she asked.

"Of many things," Renton said. "Of things long gone from this world."

A shiver went through her. "And when you died? What was there?"

"Pain," Renton said. "Pain, and knowledge. I played at magic, and I died. I died, and I knew magic."

"Can you teach me?" she asked, voice barely a whisper.

Renton did not smile. He also did not frown, or laugh, or say no. "Finish your work," he said.

She placed the last few stitches. She cinched the thread tight. Standing, she helped him from the tub. His stomach shifted as he climbed out, but her stitches held. He looked down at himself, filthy but whole.

"It is almost dawn," he said. "Show me your ritual."

She bound him up in her old nightgown, so that he would not drip along the floor. She left him standing at the top of the stairs as she went to retrieve the next hen's egg and a fresh candle. As she drew out her original circle in chalk and cemented it in salt, she looked up at him, willing him to say something. To correct her. To enlighten her.

He was still as death.

Shame began to creep in at the edges. Renton did not look away. He watched as she muttered to herself, as she painted herself with oils, as she playacted something she did not understand. Power tingled in her finger-tips, coursed through her veins, but it felt sour. *Can you see it?* she thought, gaze boring into Renton's. *It's real. It's real, isn't it?*

He did not respond.

She did not want him to see this, she realized. She did not want *anybody* to see this. This ritual, this magic, was wrong. It led to a man tearing open his abdomen because he had perverted his own body. It led to ghosts walk-ing the halls.

She wanted to shout, to scream, to throw him out of the room. But if she spoke any but the prescribed words, would it break the ritual? She could not ask, could not risk it, and though the circle stood firm between her and Renton, she felt exposed. Vulnerable. Naked. Flayed.

Renton stood by, unmoving, watchful.

Her voice trembled and cracked as she said, "The thin shell protects the potential within from harm; it cannot survive unaided, in the way that the grown mind protects the unprepared soul from the expansion of the universe without." Philosophical poetry. Wishful wanderings. Not science, not logic. She swallowed, cheeks burning, eyes burning. "But the shell must finally give way; the mind must blossom and allow that which lives within to breathe in its birthright." The words blurred. The power in her was distant now. All she felt was shame.

And then, outside the circle, Renton at last began to move. He mouthed the words along with her with his lipless maw. The stiffness of death sloughed away, and he was fluid again, slumping and shifting, emotions passing over his face.

He was expectant, fascinated. He looked *hungry*, for what she had achieved already, for what she might still achieve.

She reached for the egg and the dish. The shell gave way under her thumb where she gripped it too firmly. Quickly, she cracked it open, searching for another flash of crimson. The words began to make sense anew. The egg— might it develop a little more each time, just like her understanding of the world? A synchronicity, or a sign of the magic?

She could see a small pink form inside the mass of gold and red, with two dark pebbles for eyes. She thought of the malformed infant that Augustine had pulled from Abigail Yew's body. Nausea rose in her and her stomach gave another pang. Renton would see her eat this. He would see her swallow down this abomination, and then wouldn't she truly be the monster he had named her?

Her thumbs touched the embryo. She broke the yolk around it, painted her face with its leavings. And then she gripped the bowl and raised it to her mouth, letting the egg—it was still only a hen's egg, it was still small—slide between her lips. She swallowed.

She looked to her ghost for guidance.

As she watched, as sunrise filled the room, Renton disappeared. He left nothing behind him, not one scrap of knowledge, and Jane yelled, throwing the bowl across the room. It shattered into sticky fragments.

CHAPTER THIRTY-FOUR

DID HE TALK to you of magic?"

Jane sat in front of the stone wall, face streaked with egg yolk, fingers caked with filth. The sun was rising. The servants would be there soon. She didn't care.

"Did Aethridge tell you what he'd learned, in all his years of study, all his mistakes?" she asked the stone. Cold roiled from the impassive surface. "Did you never think to ask?" She ran her hands over it, feeling for imperfections. There were none. "Speak to me, Augustine," she begged.

He did not respond.

Scowling, she sketched a hasty chalk circle on the floor with the stick she had tucked into her sleeve, alongside a pouch of salt. She didn't want to be without these tools, now; to be separated from them was like a physical pain. She cast the circle and built it up, then focused on the door. Abigail's miscarriage; Renton's twisted bowel; Aethridge's bones. Things growing out of place. This wall, grown out of place.

Open. Open!

The wall did not move.

She slammed her fists against the stone, then pulled back, hissing. The servants would be here soon; she was running out of time to make herself presentable. But she would not leave this, could not leave this, until it was solved. The answer was so close, and if Renton had just remained—

But there was another option, wasn't there? Her nails dug into her palms, and she leaned forward until her lips were barely separated from the stone.

"Was he *lying* to me?" she whispered. "Was he haunting me in the way most calculated to destroy me?" For why should she trust a ghost? And if she could not trust what he had said, what else was in question? "I wanted what he knew. I *believed* in what he knew. Was he lying? Is *it* a lie? When I call a circle, what am I doing, Augustine? Augustine! *Tell me!*"

The last words were a roar, and the house roared back, creaking, groaning, its whole monumental edifice threatening to come down upon her head in answer. Augustine, trying to communicate? Or just an ill-maintained house built on ridiculous occult principles? It had to be the former, *had* to, and yet—and yet—

"Why?" she whispered. "Why can *I* do this? You studied for years. Dr. Hunt studied for years. Renton, Aethridge—you all *wanted* this, and yet I can call the circle? I can work rituals and feel *real power*?" She shook her head. "I'm—I'm deluding myself, aren't I? I'm just so desperate for something, anything . . ."

She trailed off into silence, staring hard at the white stone. It did not change. It did not ripple, did not shiver. It was only stone.

Stone. Surely Mrs. Purl had noticed it by now. Hadn't she?

And there was the test of her reality. When Mrs. Purl arrived, Jane would ask about the hallway. Casually. Calmly. And if Mrs. Purl saw the stone, Jane would know this was real. If she said, what about that door? then Jane would recommend they go down in search of Augustine, because the passages below Lindridge Hall were *dangerous,* he had told her they were dangerous . . .

Beneath her cheek, the stone whined.

She jerked back, staring, looking for some other sign. There was none. But as her heart calmed once more, she realized how close to sleep she had been. *Sleep.* She could not sleep. The painful exhaustion of the day before had gone, but now her fatigue was insidiously gentle, waiting quietly.

She stood up, unsteady as a fresh foal, and leaned her shoulder against the stone. She didn't dare close her eyes, but she whispered, "Thank you," in case it had been Augustine who had woken her. Then she pushed herself away and staggered upstairs to the bedroom.

Her pins and tight stays weren't enough anymore. She would have to turn to Augustine's means.

She'd stashed the cocaine and syringe kit in the wardrobe, and she drew it out now, shaking. She laid it out on the bed; Mrs. Purl had remade it the day before without comment. Jane opened the polished box. The syringe gleamed up at her alongside a small, empty bottle to compound in and a collapsible brass scale. By the light of the rising sun, she measured out the powder into the bottle, and combined it with cold, still water left in her basin by Mrs. Purl the previous day. It was thankfully clear of yesterday's old egg yolk, and once she had measured out the appropriate proportion, she washed her face.

The cocaine compounded and loaded into the syringe, she attempted to roll up her sleeve, but it was too tight. So she undid her bodice and dragged it down, then undid her stays and pulled the laces from them, tying them around her upper arm the way she had seen Augustine do in the surgery.

Her bared stomach bowed out.

Jane paused, frowning, and set down the needle. She touched the distended flesh, a little to the left of center, just above her hip. It hurt. Faintly, but it hurt, and her hand shook. Abigail's miscarriage. Renton's bowel. Augustine's voice: *He'd discovered certain books, and had played at spellcraft until he felt something quicken inside of him.*

How quickly would it grow in *her?*

She snatched her hand away and took up the syringe once more. *No.* She had to focus instead of fear. She did not feel ill; and so long as she did not prod the growth, she did not feel *pain,* either, though she understood now what had surged within her at the first dusk working, and last night when she had tended to Renton.

It meant only that she needed to be efficient. She could not afford to fail, to begin again.

She found the vein, as Augustine had, and steadied herself. Her vision tried to swim, but she stilled it with careful breaths. She focused, the way she focused when building the circle.

She pressed the needle into her vein.

The cocaine felt like molten metal, filling her body in a filigree cast. She bit down on an agonized cry, and panted as it faded, breath by breath. But in its wake, it left a gentle wash of alertness, and with it, the confidence she had lost in the past night.

Then, from the door: "Good morning, ma'am. There's a letter for—oh, my—"

Jane looked up.

The letter was in Mrs. Purl's hands, clutched tight. Jane hurried to drag her dress back on. With her stays unlaced, it fit ill.

"What is that *smell*?" Mrs. Purl gasped, then covered her nose and retreated into the hall.

Smell? But then Jane realized the stench of death and filth was still all around her, emanating from the bathroom. She cast the syringe onto the bed and rushed to look. The tub was still filled with brandy and rot, and Jane fought down bile.

"Ma'am, pardon, but you must go into town to see Mr. Lowell, to see the locum," Mrs. Purl said, her words twisted by nausea. Jane turned back to face her, flushed. Mrs. Purl held out the envelope, gesturing wildly. "This—whatever this is, it is not healthy. You are not well."

"I am *well*," Jane said. She listed to one side, and Mrs. Purl moved, reflexively, as if to catch her—and then stopped, just one step inside the room. "Give me the letter," Jane demanded, stepping forward.

Mrs. Purl retreated.

Jane squinted and made out the handwriting on the envelope. *Nizamiev.* "It is—it is from a doctor. A woman who works with the shell-shocked. Please give me the letter, Mrs. Purl."

She held it out, but only grudgingly. "It would be better if she sent a nurse, I think, than a letter."

"Was Augustine never like this with you?" Jane snapped, remembering the dark circles under his eyes, the odd lies he'd told her from the first. "Withdrawn and bewitched and confusing?" Jane tore the letter from Mrs. Purl's hands. The older woman flinched, then drew herself up to her full height, scowling.

"No, Mrs. Lawrence," Mrs. Purl said, steel in her voice now.

"Your salaries must have arrived with this letter."

"They did," Mrs. Purl allowed, "though you have shorted us."

Jane had a finger beneath the envelope's seal. Slowly, she withdrew it. "Impossible."

"Mrs. Luthbright and I compared. It is true."

Jane turned away, pressing the stiff paper against the bulge in her flesh. "I am sorry," she muttered. "I made a mistake. I will fix it. Forgive me, please—my mind is not my own."

Mrs. Purl relaxed a fraction. "Let me send for a carriage," she said. "The surgery is better for you."

Anger rose up over her momentary shame. "No. This is where I belong. My husband was allowed to remain here alone every night. Why do you hold me to a different standard?"

"He never made this house smell of *death*," Mrs. Purl cried, then mastered herself again. "Mrs. Lawrence, please. Return to town."

No. He had never brought filth into this home, only guilt and shame. But she was not worse than Augustine for it. He had not been seeking enlightenment; he had given up. He had only endured. She was trying for so much more.

Wasn't she?

Her resolve faltered.

She made a quick bargain between the obsession inside of her and the reasonable, responsible Jane who had come before her. If Dr. Nizamiev called her mad in her letter, she would heed it. She must heed it.

She tore open the envelope and scanned the words inside.

Dr. Nizamiev said nothing of the sort. She wrote only that she had heard of Augustine's disappearance, and followed it up with one bare line of encouragement.

I know that you will keep your wits about you; you are uniquely suited to your task.

"My husband will need me when he returns," Jane said, lifting her head. "Until then, I will remain here. Does that satisfy?"

"No, Mrs. Lawrence," Mrs. Purl said. "Come downstairs. We will remain here day and night until he returns, but you must go to the surgery. You must rest. You look as if you haven't slept in days."

"And who are you to care if I sleep or not?" Jane snapped.

Mrs. Purl's mouth dropped open, so much like Mr. Renton's.

What benefit did Mrs. Purl serve for her? Mrs. Luthbright cooked, but Jane did not require *sustenance,* only ritual. Jane could tend a fire. She could do it all. She *would* do it all.

"I am not a fit mistress—you are right," she said. Mrs. Purl's shoulders sagged in relief. "I will have the balance of your salary and additional severance pay sent to your homes. Leave your chatelaine in the study."

"Mrs. Lawrence—"

"Your services are no longer required. Thank you for your loyalty. Goodbye."

CHAPTER THIRTY-FIVE

MRS. PURL AND Mrs. Luthbright left immediately.

Jane watched them from the bedroom window, shivering with relief and pride. She felt euphoric, freed. Without them hovering, she would achieve more. She would learn faster, test herself more, take advantage of the daylight hours when the ghosts left her alone.

Yes, this was for the best. Why hadn't she done this sooner?

Fear. Self-consciousness. Shame. But shame was what had kept Augustine bound to Lindridge Hall. She should never have indulged her own, never let it get even a toehold. She was better than him, in this; that was her strength.

With the servants gone, there was more work to be done. She must take stock of what she had, measure out her remaining moss and grave loam, plan out her ritual meals. Had they already made today's stewed hare? Had they left her enough hens' eggs? If they had not, she would need to find a way to send for more.

She redid her stays and gown properly. Her stomach ached at the added pressure, and she curled in on herself, touching one hand to the caged bulge. It already felt larger. It did not kick or move as if she were with child; it was hard and unyielding. But she felt a thrumming in it, far apart from her pulse but just as insistent. A living vibration, responding to her will.

She could not name it.

Jane descended to the kitchen. There were more than enough eggs, and fresh milk and a new loaf of bread besides. And sitting on the dining table was her stewed hare. But there was only the one plate; the icebox held sea grass and nothing else.

Very well. She would eat a small portion now and save the rest. She wasn't hungry anyway.

That only left the question of magic.

The ghosts that had visited her these past two nights were real beyond dispute; her mattress was still stained, and Mrs. Purl had smelled Renton's filth. Now she must test herself beyond simply drawing circles and building walls and swallowing eggs. She needed to influence the world around her, make something that was impossible, that proved she had real power. Since she could not remove the stone slab yet, she must try something else, and mark her progress.

She retreated upstairs once more.

The study was filled with small stacks of books she'd considered and discarded in her research. On the desk, in the corners, by the circle drawn on the floor. She planted herself in the center of that circle and turned slowly, surveying the mess.

A test. Could she work her will upon the environment? Building the circle was second nature now. She stopped at the height of it, poised like Renton, arms spread, body rigid.

She focused on the nearest book. Nonmagical, useless, but the title, *History of Breltainian Thought*, had seemed promising, and so she'd paged through it before casting it aside. It needed to be put away. She brought her hands before her and willed it to rise from the floor.

It did not move.

And why should it? Dr. Nizamiev's explanations echoed through her mind, winding together with scraps and fragments of countless texts, snippets and phrases that never spoke of easily comprehensible feats. Everything was internal. Everything was *instant*. Knowing, knowing that the world was other than it had been a moment before.

The book was on the shelf.

No, it's not. She was looking straight at it, and it had not moved. It was on the floor, because where else could it be? She had not touched it. She had not moved it, and how could a book move on its own?

Jane turned away from it, until it sat only in the corner of her eye, barely visible.

The book was on the shelf. She must believe it. No; she must *know* it.

The book was on the shelf.

The book was on the shelf, where its gray cloth binding barely caught the lamplight enough for her to see the snag at the base of the spine. A thread had pulled loose. The book was on the shelf.

The book was on the shelf.

Jane stared.

Where there had been an empty slot on the shelf across from her, there was now a gray, clothbound text of the size and shape of the one on the floor. And when she looked, the one on the floor was gone.

She clasped her hands over her mouth, giddy, laughing. Shaking, she left the circle. A grin split her face, and she felt as if she would come apart. Filled with wonder, she pulled *History of Breltainian Thought* down. It was real. It had weight, and it was as she remembered it. It was a book, and she had moved it with a thought. *She* had done that.

She had changed the world around her. With five nights left of the ritual, she had influenced the world.

The book fell open in her hands. Idly, she read the page.

She *tried* to read the page.

She could not.

The printed ink looked like words, but they were nonsense, jumbled and meaningless. She turned the page. The next was just the same, and the next, and the next. She closed it, heart pounding, and inspected the cover. *That was sensible, History of Breltainian Thought,* but the author's name—was that the same as it had been before? Was it even a name?

She dropped the book and grabbed another, one she had not moved. It was filled with intelligible text, word after word, sentence after sentence. The next book was the same, and the next. They were all as they had been, except for the one she had moved.

She had known it was on the shelf. What had it done to the book?

Known.

Perhaps *knowing* was too simple a term. What was it Dr. Nizamiev had said? Jane remembered balancing equations, the flow of logic in a proof. Every variable needed to be defined. Every element known. *To truly bring somebody back from death, the changes to the world that would be necessary to make that happen would require knowledge too complex for the mind of man to comprehend.*

She had not moved that book. She had known it to be somewhere else. But she hadn't known its contents, back to front. And so the book she knew was not the book that had been.

Knowing she was safe inside a circle was different from knowing a book. One was simple, the other far too complex for realistic interaction. And by *knowing* something that was not fully described, she had changed it. Irrevocably.

What would happen when she freed Augustine?

The thought paralyzed her. She did not cry or make a sound, and her heart did not even beat quickly. She was as stone, because to be anything else was too momentous, too all-encompassing.

A door. A door was simpler than a book. Wasn't it? A door only had to open. But did she need to know what lay *beyond* the door? Did she need to know the whole layout of the crypt, and where Augustine was, and what state he was in? What happened if she changed too much? What assumptions would she make without realizing it, and what would she alter?

She moaned.

When Augustine had tried to call back Elodie, he had not fully understood what he was doing. He had done something other than he had intended, because his assumptions, his knowledge, had not been enough. Elodie—Elodie was *gone*, in that vision of the past, and in her place, a blankness. He had torn her from her life, and fixed her in the moment of her death, suffering, down in that cellar. He had known only that the dead could come back.

And so they had.

They had come back to Lindridge Hall, regardless of how or where they died, their only connection that Augustine had felt responsible for their deaths. And by the same rules, Orren and Abigail and Renton had come to her. Who else was waiting in the wings? She had led a quiet life, a small life, insulated from death by sheer dint of having few connections. The Cunninghams and their children all lived. Her only other connections were the servants.

And Augustine himself.

If she took too long, if she failed, would he come to her? Would she hold his weakened body in her arms, feel how cold he was, how hungry? Would he beg her for food, only to disappear with the sun?

All the magic in the world was worthless if she failed. She could not bring him back from the dead. She could not even move a book.

Weeping now, she curled up at the base of the shelf, the wood pressing against her spine. It would be best to give it all up; how much time did she even have left? Below her left ribs, a mass pressed against her flesh; with more magic, it might grow. And without Augustine, what would be left of her? A broken madwoman, her body growing out of order, knowing of the impossible and knowing she could not grasp it. Another failure for Dr. Nizamiev to add to her collection, to study endlessly. And perhaps that was what the doctor had hoped for all along; new data, a new experiment, a new subject.

Perhaps she'd never intended to help.

Jane was alone. More alone than she had been when she had fled Lindridge Hall, more alone than she had been the day she realized she would have to change her life, either by going back to dreaded Camhurst or marrying to stay behind. More alone than when she was a little girl, staring at the ceiling in her room in Larrenton, wondering if the bombs were still falling. Wondering if her mother was alive. Her sobs turned to gasping breaths, and she turned herself toward the shelves, pressing her forehead against all the books. Their dusty scent should have been grounding, but instead she smelled the stench of spreading gas, felt the shudder of buildings barely holding up to assault.

But . . . if she let that memory wash over her, she could still remember her mother's touch. What it had been to sleep near her, protected, and to hear a familiar, soothing voice, murmuring in her ear, as the whole world came apart around her. And by comparison, even the pain of Camhurst was familiar; it was terrible, but in the way that old wounds were terrible. She knew its shape, its texture. It offered the comfort of an old friend, rather than a new agony.

She *wanted* that comfort. And suddenly, selfishly, she was thankful her mother was dead.

Because with her mother dead, couldn't she appear at Lindridge Hall?

If Jane squinted, the leather bag set atop the bookshelf looked like her mother's gas mask. If Jane *knew* her mother's boots were over by the doorway, they would appear; she still remembered their sulfurous reek, the way her mother had stuffed the toes because the boots were not made for a woman's feet, the cracking and burns on the leather itself from incendiaries. With every detail, her world narrowed focus, her heartbeat slowed.

She might still call her mother's spirit, if she learned to blame herself again. And she had shame enough to drown an army.

It would be easy; she'd blamed herself for her mother's death from the day the notice came, years ago. She had wished she were better: more compliant, more loveable, so that her mother wouldn't have sent Jane away to safety. She had wished that she were worse, crying and screaming and objecting so loudly, so strenuously that her mother would have had to take her to Larrenton herself, and then be enticed to stay.

Her breathing regained some semblance of rhythm. Yes—she could peel up the scab and feel all her old terrors once more, if it would bring her mother to her. It was something actionable, her will worked upon the world.

Because Jane was alive. She lacked control, perhaps, but not power. As long as she could still think, still know, she could take another step, and another.

She did not even have to conjure her mother; if there truly was no other way to save Augustine, then she could conjure his ghost, for it would be her failure that condemned him. The torment would be worth it, to speak to him, to compare notes, to have him in some capacity.

The thought hurt, but with the hurt came certainty. Logic. Her chest no longer felt so tight, her head so heavy.

She had told Augustine that death always won. But now she was not so sure; now she knew that, in at least some spectral way, the impossible could be made real. Death could not be defeated, but it could be amended.

And there were still five nights left in the ritual. Augustine had not yet appeared to her, and so she could assume he still lived.

She pushed herself upright.

She had her proof, now, that magic was real. All that was left was to make it cohere.

CHAPTER THIRTY-SIX

S HE WOULD PICK up where she had left off the night before. The rituals, the mathematics, the circles—all necessary steps that she must take with thorough care. And when night fell, Renton might return to her. Or Elodie might appear again, ready to divulge wisdom once more. Even if they came in opposition, Jane might still glean some new meaning, some new fragment.

All she had to do was work and keep from sleeping.

She set herself up in the library, sitting against the far glass wall, the chill there keeping her alert as she dove once more into her mathematical treatise. What could she learn there, with her new, more worldly context?

She read through philosophical musings, poetic flourishes that the Jane of a week ago had been irritated by, had skimmed over except where she failed to understand the next proof, and had to go back and untangle the logic. Now, those same esoteric passages held special meaning, seeming to vibrate on the page. The author paired zero with an empty nothingness, but a nothingness that went on forever, for nothing could have no bounds. The infinite and zero were one. Except that the infinite was the greatest thing in the world, and zero was nothing at all. They were opposite.

They were the same.

Surely there was meaning in that?

She watched as the values of equations, plotted as curves, approached zero, and watched, too, as their component parts shot off into infinity. Another curve, complex and oscillating, seemed to go mad as it approached zero, swinging through every value on the chart on its way. She followed along as the mathematician inscribed triangles beneath an arc, until there was no empty space left. The answer, of course, was that it would take an endless number of triangles to reach zero, even though the space beneath the curve was fixed.

Impossible. *Impossible.*

And yet, there it was. She could find no flaw in the logic.

Far too soon she felt the sharp edge the cocaine had given her begin to ebb. She tried to wait it out, doing small geometric proofs on paper to produce new ideas and test her awareness, but her vision blurred. Her head drooped. She dropped her pen on more than one occasion.

The second injection was easier than the first, though she had to use a different spot along her vein; the original hurt too much to try. When it was done, Jane wrote *Augustine* in ink beside the pinprick hole, the better to keep him always in the forefront of her mind, keep herself fixed upon her purpose and her goal. Her mind was apt to wander now, and her field of study was too deep. The lack of sleep would only make it worse.

She returned to the library, alert once more. Her mind full to bursting with mathematical contortions, Jane took up her pen and returned to the previous night's testing.

She soon ran out of floor space in the library, drawing out circles and testing variations. She began drawing her circles down the hallways. She inscribed one on the wall, carving through the wallpaper when the pen blurred and skipped. Her back pressed against the plaster behind her, she visualized the circle growing out and away from her, a tube that stretched to the opposite wall. It took and held steady, but felt no different from the other circles she had built.

More tests: she measured them carefully so that when she stretched out all her limbs, her fingertips and toes touched the inside of the line exactly—and then again so that she was curled up tight, and again where the diameter of the circle was three times the length of herself. She varied her method of visualizing the wall, digging moats instead, or wrapping herself in sheets of metal. She walked the inner perimeter and sat stock-still in the exact center. She lit candles and burned herbs and screamed and threw her notebook across the second-floor hallway.

Nothing she did produced any difference, inside her or around her. But she held on to hope. The circles—perhaps they were static. But there had been other figures in the ring inscribed in her vision, in the floor of the crypt beneath Lindridge Hall. What of those?

Dusk came. She laid a three-fold circle in concentric rings and raised the walls, and they came in a heady rush. Something new, something different! She could have danced if she hadn't been so exhausted. She used the remaining moss and loam as sparingly as she could, fearing some dulling potency, but the flow of power within her was familiar, strong. Stronger than before.

Progress. She was making progress.

She stepped away from her work only to eat the ritual meal, pulling the sea grass from the icebox. It tangled around her fingers. She swallowed down each bite even though every motion of her throat produced pain.

The Doctrine of Seven had given only half-formed reasons for the ritual's structure, but it was working; of that much Jane was certain. The changing of the egg each dawn was proof enough of that. But as she chewed, she wondered if all the details were exactly right. After all, the concepts she'd read in Augustine's texts had seemed haphazard, cobbled together from a thousand disparate threads. Perhaps the rules were not actual rules, not in any immutable sense. The ritual, after all, only guided the magician's force of will. Perhaps there were acceptable deviations. Some were obvious, and she had already taken advantage of them; there were no specified portions of the ritual meals, or the bog moss, or the grave dirt, and she had adjusted to use less and less of each. And she had crafted her own sigil, when she could not make sense of the moth-eaten, senseless instructions provided her. Could she push at others? Accelerate the timeline, so that Augustine would not be trapped for quite so long without food, without water, without warmth?

By midnight, she was back in the kitchen, counting out the remaining eggs. She had more than enough to finish out the rest of the mornings.

She could afford to experiment.

Intention and knowledge were everything. She had to be careful. She had to keep in mind, at all times, the truest depiction of what she was doing, why, and how it would happen. So Jane held Augustine (healthy and whole and waiting for her, with that light in his eyes when he wanted to kiss her, with that sureness in his hands when he saved his patients) foremost in her mind as she gathered her supplies.

His study, more than any other room, provided specific details and vibrant memories upon which to anchor herself. Her warning, too, was writ large across the shelves. It was the perfect place to work. The rug she'd pulled aside when she cowered from Orren was still heaped against the couch. Her first faint lines of chalk still stood out against the wood. She redrew her circle and knelt there, inhaling the scent of him, the resonance. She lit the candle and placed one hand over where she had scrawled his name upon her arm. She remembered his hands holding hers beneath the surgery faucet as she spoke the dawn invocations. She pictured him standing just outside the study door, flushed from kissing her, as she cracked the egg.

When the shell gave way, it revealed a half-formed chick, eyes bulbous and skin fuzzy with the beginnings of feathers. The yolk was smaller than before, and spidered full over with red.

"Yes, yes!" she cried, falling back onto her heels and clasping her hands over her mouth. Another component moved into place. She could work the rituals in sequence without caring for the time of day, and she could get to him soon. Soon! She looked to the clock that sat upon the desk. It had been less than five hours since she worked the dusk ritual. In another five, she would put the moss into her mouth again, and sequentially reduce the time between until either they ceased to progress, or she completed the sequence. At most, it would take forty hours.

Just two days. *Less* than two days until she reached the end of the path and saw where it had taken her. Even her earlier failings had been but lessons; every new step was new knowledge, blossoming inside of her.

Nascent feet pressed against her esophagus as she swallowed down the chick. She choked it down, the sharp, small barbs of early feathers scratching at her throat. Her eyes watered, her lips twisted.

Just a little longer. Just a little—

"Jane."

It was not the sound of the pipes creaking, or of muffled pleas through unbreakable stone; Augustine's voice was clear, and gentle, and tired, coming from just outside the study.

He stood in the doorway, correct in every feature as he sagged against the frame. His clothing was rumpled from long days and nights sleeping in stone hallways. He watched her, pale and worn, relieved.

How?

She had swallowed down a half-formed chick, yes, but there were still four more iterations to go. She had not left the study. She had not stood before the crypt wall and willed it down. So how was he standing here, now, looking at her with such joyous desperation?

He needed food. He needed water. And yet she could not make herself leave the safety of the circle. She had already imagined this once, knew what it meant.

If he was here, and the door below still stood, then there was only one way: She was already too late.

"Stay back," Jane whispered. Her stomach soured and lurched. She trembled. All her haste and experimentation, for what? He was dead. It no longer mattered.

He lifted his hands and did as she said. "Jane," he repeated. "You're still here."

"Stay back, and be silent," she hissed.

He winced but nodded.

He didn't move as she tested the integrity of the wall around her. She built it up higher still, even though her heart was breaking, even though she was filled with rage. She felt dizzy from the effort. Her latest dose of cocaine was wearing off.

Augustine watched the whole while, patient, pained, and far too real. He didn't plead with her, didn't argue that there was no need to cast a spell, or that magic was impossible, and when she felt the wall go up, he seemed to feel it, too. His lips curved into the faintest, proudest smile.

"There," she said, rising to her feet. "If you are a spirit, you can no longer reach me."

And if he were a man, if he had somehow freed himself without her help, if she was wrong and he still lived, he could walk across and hold her.

There was an old thought experiment, proof of the impossibility of the infinite. A soldier ran at twice the speed of the prisoner he pursued, but the prisoner had a head start of one hundred yards. By the time the soldier crossed that first one hundred yards, the prisoner had run another fifty. The soldier plunged ahead, but when he'd covered those fifty yards, the prisoner was twenty-five ahead. And so on, and on, and the numbers alone would never allow the soldier to reach the prisoner.

But the world did not function on such mathematics; the soldier would eventually be close enough to the prisoner to reach out and seize his quarry. The prisoner would flag, too, exhausted by privation to continue fleeing. Reality proved mathematics wrong, and proved infinity impossible, because eventually a step became too small, a space too narrow, for anybody to move and not collide.

Augustine approached, slowly, as if afraid to startle her. He came to the edge of the circle. She could feel his breath on her face. She could see the smallest pore on his cheek.

He lifted his foot.

He stepped across the line.

He was real. He was *alive*. All her resolve, all the armor she had carefully cultivated over a lifetime, dissolved the instant he reached out and touched her elbow. It was the lightest touch, but the first gentle one she had felt in what seemed like years. Her exhaustion and desperation and loneliness came crashing down upon her, and she threw her arms around him, hiding her face against his shoulder.

"I'm sorry," she whispered. "I'm sorry."

Beneath her hands, Augustine was solid, and he was breathing, and he clasped her tight against him. Her knees weakened, gave out, and she was so heavy, so tired, aching for relief.

"I should never have brought you here," he murmured, taking her weight in his arms. His voice thrummed through her, a plucked note on a harp's string.

It was over.

She had won.

She could sleep, and in the morning, her life would make sense again. A whole world rolled out before her, and she realized, trembling, that until that moment it had all fallen away. She'd been floating on her little island of stone and iron and glass, Lindridge Hall set apart from all the rest. But now she could leave. They could leave, together.

And yet . . .

And yet she did not want to.

Augustine lifted a hand and cupped her cheek, turning her face to his, seeing her exhaustion and sickness. "The surgery," he said. "You need the surgery, and I as well."

Jane shook her head. "We have no carriage. It is late."

"How long since you slept? You're growing thin." It wasn't so different from how he'd looked for signs of yellow fever in her, and yet it felt far more like the night he had bandaged her feet. He was solicitous, apologetic, wholly focused on her. Not distracted, not bewitched. He was not strong yet, and he had not proven his safety again, but it was a start. A perfect start.

She did not want to go back into the world with him, not yet.

"You should not leave, not tonight," she argued. "I'll prepare dinner. We can rest here. And I can find a way to fix it, Augustine. I have learned the impossible, and I know I can free you. Magic is real, and I can work it."

"They will come for us tonight," he murmured. His breath ghosted over her lips. Her heart fluttered, her belly twisted. "I fear what I will do. What they will do. Let us leave this place."

Again she shook her head. "The magistrate, Mr. Lowell, they think I am responsible for your disappearance."

"Then we will prove them wrong with my return. Jane, why won't you leave with me?"

Magic. Intoxication. She did not want to break the ritual, did not want to give up what four more days might teach her. Or even just two, if she followed her accelerated schedule!

But she did not want to tell him that. She did not want to argue. Instead, she slid her hands along his waist and tipped her head down. She kissed him, stilling further protest. She had learned from him.

She felt him give in.

Elodie and the echoes of the dead had set them against each other, but she was stronger than he was. She could reorder their world and keep him safe. They did not need to build a new fiction together, for she could make reality.

She sank to her knees, and Augustine followed her. This was a man who could cut her open, who had nearly killed her in the cellar, and yet she felt a surge of desire despite it. No, *because* of it, because she could feel him growing helpless at her touch. She had mastered him from the first, had overwhelmed his objections, had brought his world crashing down around them, because in his heart he was hers.

Her hands went to his high-collared vest and worked free the buttons one by one. He gasped against her mouth, his hands on her hips, her thighs, then sliding up beneath her skirt. His surgeon's calluses trailed along her calf and she shuddered, answering him with matched desire.

He was solid, real in a way that a ghost of him could never have been, real in a way that *he* had never been. Magic had created an impossible, infinitely minuscule gap between them, breaking trust and poisoning her desire, and now he had crossed it. He had come to her. She should have feared that he would turn on her again, and he should have hated her for sealing him into the crypt, but there was no pain in the way their breaths mingled, in the weight of his body as he bore her down to the study's floor, in the tension in hers as she wrapped her legs around his hips.

They coupled like wild things despite their exhaustion, their hunger for food replaced with hunger for every inch of each other's flesh. This was not the sweet yet fumbling first time in Augustine's bed, but something else, something purer, something perfect. Jane never looked toward the door, or the window, focusing only on the scent of Augustine's skin, the rasp of the starched collar of his shirt against her jawline when he leaned down to kiss her. She marked him with bruises and love bites.

She gave herself over to a focused kind of madness.

IN THE MORNING, Augustine was gone. The wall remained. The crypt was sealed.

Jane screamed until her throat began to bleed.

CHAPTER THIRTY-SEVEN

O UTSIDE LINDRIDGE HALL, the sun had risen.

Jane sat, her dress poorly fastened around the bulging of her belly, shivering in the middle of a circle. She had drawn it with desperate, shaking fingers, but it had come to life despite its wavering perimeter. She had repeated familiar invocations, and had cracked open a fresh hen's egg, hoping against hope.

The yolk had been yellow and unbroken.

She didn't know if that was because she had already worked the dawn ritual once already that day, or if it was because she had violated the dictums of chastity and sleep. It hardly mattered. She was fixed, instead, on the memory of how she had drawn the circle in the study, how she had built it up. How Augustine had stepped across it without issue, though Orren had not dared to try. Augustine had not flinched. He had not dissolved. He had come to her, and held her, and felt just as real as she did.

But Renton had felt real. So had Abigail. And she had challenged none but the first to cross a circle, taking it on faith that she had been right, that Elodie had helped her, that Orren had left her because she'd triumphed.

Augustine had crossed the circle. The crypt was sealed. An equation at its simplest, its solution plain:

A ghost could cross a circle. She had been wrong.

Augustine was dead.

She had failed.

What now?

Did she leave? Did she go to the magistrate and confess? But the crypt was sealed; there was no body. She was a poor liar, but she could play the grieving widow. The pain in her breast had fangs and claws, tearing at her lungs, her heart. She could go to Camhurst, go to the Cunninghams, find some way to earn her keep. Start over, keep her world small, the way she had lived her life before Augustine.

She didn't want to leave.

She could start over. There wasn't enough food to keep her for seven days, or enough wood to heat the house, or running water, or a hundred other things she would need, but she could leave now, could gather new supplies. Did she owe it to him, to keep going, to carry his body out? Or was she only being selfish, filled with desire for the impossible, drowning in shame and longing to fix her mistake?

A mistake. She'd made a mistake. Somewhere along the way, she had erred. Could she follow her path back to where it had all gone wrong, and find some way to change it, some variable to tweak? What if it had been not her assumptions that had failed her, but her own weakness? Her desire to touch him might have allowed him to reach her. She should have feared him, should have mistrusted him, should have believed with all her heart that he had been sent to torment her, and instead—instead—

She turned away from the pain.

Jane stared at the boundary around her, with its haphazard salt grains, its skipping lines. This. This was what was true. This was her constant, her starting point, and all her derivations should arise from it. She reached out, searching for the eel, and found it gliding along the walls she had built. She urged it higher, stacked brick upon brick.

Her power grew. It gave her some relief. She had destroyed the ritual, might have already lost Augustine, but she had not lost *this*. She built a little higher. A little more.

Peace spread across her, and she stretched out on the floor in the middle of the circle. The aching of her heart grew distant, eclipsed by the surge of power in her.

She built, higher and higher, and the world around her faded in color. The room was still filled with early morning light, but it grew thinner. The edges of the furniture became indistinct, the joining of the walls and ceiling extending out endlessly away from her, like faint pencil lines measured out along a straightedge.

It was soothing. It was calming. She could feel tears upon her cheeks.

The world fell away, and she fell away with it. Had this been here all this time, this gentle succor, this sweet emptiness? Her lungs expanded and contracted as normal, and she knew that she was getting air, but it felt distant. It felt immaterial. Ecstasy danced across her nerves, a sweet delight, perfect in its tenor, blotting out all else.

No—not all else. The mass was moving, shifting inside of her, the way infants were said to kick within the womb. It hurt. She pushed away from the feeling, weaving her walls higher, reaching for more delight, more gracious bliss.

Instead came agony.

The mass pulsed, sharp and angry, the pain more horrible than anything she had ever felt. It throbbed and arced and wracked her down to her soul, and she clutched at her belly, gasping for breath. She lost her hold upon the eel.

The pain quieted as the wall around her lowered a few feet, the ecstasy leaching from her brain.

That mass was magic. That knot, when all else was gone, thrummed and sang within her. What did it mean, that it hurt as the wall grew higher, as the world grew more distant? Another clue. Another variable.

A loud crack startled her.

There—harsh footsteps in the hall. And now she heard voices, heard the footsteps slow, and then—

Mrs. Luthbright and Mrs. Purl appeared in the doorway.

Their features were abstracted, splashes of pigment and emotion that Jane could feel more than she could see. Mrs. Purl recoiled at the sight of Jane, and whispered something she could not make out, but Mrs. Luthbright stormed forward, shouting, "I will not let this continue any longer, Mrs. Lawrence!"

She reached the chalk line, and not seeing it, stepped over. It did not stop her, did not bow and flex like an infant's caul. She stepped across it like it was only chalk.

The world crashed back into Jane.

She retched.

Mrs. Luthbright sidestepped the mess and seized one of her arms, hauling her up. "Come, we have brought a carriage," Mrs. Luthbright said. She was rough as she dragged Jane to the hall. Mrs. Purl stared, hands outstretched but not quite touching.

"Genevieve!" Mrs. Luthbright snapped.

"What if the madness is catching?" Mrs. Purl returned.

Jane reeled, barely tracking the conversation. Everything was noise and emotion and pain. She curled in on herself and wailed. Mrs. Luthbright flinched but did not let go.

"Mrs. Lawrence, *stop.* We must get you outside; the carriage is waiting."

"Let me go!" she begged. "Let me go!" The thought of being taken from the house sparked panic in her, and she jerked back, trying to break Mrs. Luthbright's grip. But she was weak. She had not realized until that moment how her muscles cramped, how they refused to work in concert with one another. She turned to Mrs. Purl, desperate. "Please, let me go! I am trying to bring him back. I have to fix this, I *can* fix this. I must get him out, I must—I must—"

Mrs. Purl approached with cautious steps. Hope grew in Jane, then fell dead as Mrs. Purl seized her as well. They dragged her toward the front door.

"He is *in the house,*" Jane cried.

They stopped.

"Mercy," Mrs. Purl said, looking at Jane, then up to Mrs. Luthbright. "We need to get the magistrate. He's dead in the house?"

"Please, he's trapped, did you not see the cellar door? It's gone. It's *gone*. The house has taken him!"

"You need rest, and food, and quiet," Mrs. Purl said, though she kept casting worried looks at Mrs. Luthbright. "You are seeing things."

"I am *not*!" Jane yelled, and wrenched herself free with an eruption of rageful strength. She fell to the floor, crawling backward. "I know exactly what I see! This house crawls with spirits, and I let Augustine lie to me once about that; no more. This house is *infested*. They have taken him, and killed him, and I will set him free again." Her fingers swept in an arc around her, their ridges coated with chalk and salt from her days of drawing. "I will fix this! You will not remove me!"

"Mrs. Lawrence—" Mrs. Purl began, and then was gone.

The foyer was smaller than it had been before. There was no door.

Jane was alone.

CHAPTER THIRTY-EIGHT

THE WALL THAT split the foyer of Lindridge Hall spanned neatly from floor to vaulted ceiling and was made of pristine, unbroken, familiar stone. It was white and cool to the touch.

And Jane had conjured it.

She had not meant to. She had not *intended* to, not like she had intended to move the book, not like she built her circles. But she had done it. She had, in one terrified, overwhelmed, desperate moment, gone from *wanting* to be left alone to living in a world where she simply was.

She sat for a long time in front of the wall, listening for the sounds of voices beyond it. But if Mrs. Purl and Mrs. Luthbright remained, they were silent. She hoped they had left. She hoped they had fled. She hoped that she had not unmade them with a thoughtless working.

And what of the world outside of Lindridge Hall? What would she see if she looked through the windows? Would the hills still roll in their gentle way? Would farms dot the landscape, would the dead tree still stand out in the front garden, would Larrenton and Camhurst and, beyond them, cities she had never been to or heard of—would they all still exist?

She was too afraid to look.

Instead, she stared at the wall, and felt a different kind of dread, spreading through her limbs and making them heavy. Choking her. The wall was familiar, terrible in how it matched, exactly, the featureless stone that had replaced the crypt door. It led to only one conclusion:

She had sealed the crypt.

She had locked Augustine away from her in a moment of terror. There had been no circle around her, and yet, perhaps helped along by the magic that had soaked into the cellar over generations, Jane had sealed the crypt. Just as she had panicked as the servants had tried to drag her to salvation, she had, exhausted and terrified, given over to desperate dreams of safety.

And the wall had come.

Augustine was dead, and he was dead because of her.

She wanted to be angry. To blame *him,* because he had hurt her, terrified her, looked at her with a bewitched light in his eyes that he refused to fight. His physician's godhood, stoked by the ghosts of his failures all around him, had stopped his ears. And even before that, he had made her love him, had pulled down the walls around her with his generous spirit, his aching tenderness. It had all been his fault, because he had loved her and so made himself vulnerable, desperate to save her.

But he hadn't deserved to die. She hadn't wanted to kill him.

If she had this power inside of her, the power to make a wall exist where none had before simply because she was afraid, why couldn't she unmake it now that the fear had passed? Why had she been forced to forgo sleep, to learn secrets she had not strictly *needed*?

A thousand answers presented themselves: because she had not felt as strongly when she tried to return the door as she had when she created the wall; because it was easier for her to want to be alone than it was to form connection; because she had felt guilty for her own actions, and not desperate for his safety, not really.

She remembered how happy she had been in the arms of his ghost, and she hated herself.

Eventually, Jane rose, her knees screaming with pain, her head swimming.

She had slept only a few hours in Augustine's arms, not enough by far to undo the damage she had wrought upon her mind, but rest was a thousand miles away. Instead, she made her way to where the crypt door had stood, and stared again at featureless white stone.

"Should I try to open it, Augustine?" she asked, voice so quiet that the stillness of the hall absorbed it. "Is there any point? Nobody will mourn you. Nobody will mourn me. We are together in that, at least."

There was no answer. The house did not roar. The pipes did not groan. She did not hear his voice, his breaths, his sobs. Lindridge Hall was silent.

She was too much of a coward to try to pull the wall down. Instead, she went into the sitting room and, head bowed, pulled the curtains tight over the windows, dropping the room into darkness. She went back to her circle and sat within it, and built it up, brick by brick, then tore it down again. Mindless motion, mindless experimentation.

She was so tired, and yet she didn't think she would ever sleep again.

She kept the walls at a manageable height, not tall or thick enough to cause more than a twinge of pain in her gut. The pain was too sharp, too distracting, too liable to make her panic and do something else. Instead, she built just high enough to see, in the angles and lines of the joinery of the house, a subtle structure. Perfect solids inscribed one within the other, transections of angles, a sequence of numbers processing in orderly fashion and adding up toward infinity. She could reorganize it, change the rules upon which the sequence grew. All she need do was reach out and grasp it, and her fingers itched to do it.

But she didn't, because she did not know enough to reset the bones of the world without causing unintended harm. The walls lowered, and Lindridge Hall was once more just a house.

A familiar cough from behind her roused her from her reverie sometime later; Mr. Cunningham, smoking his cigars. The room glowed with the light of a well-built fire in the hearth, a fire she had not lit.

She covered her face with her hands, unwilling to look.

No. No, please no. She could take no more of this. She was heartsore and exhausted. *Dreaming. You are dreaming. Waking dreams, can they not come to the sleepless?*

"Come, now, Jane," Mrs. Cunningham said. "Have a brandy with us."

Jane thought that she would surely cry, but her tears had dried days ago. Her mouth had dried, too, and her bones and sinews. She felt made of dust. If the Cunninghams were here, it was because they were dead. Augustine's impact upon the world, his reordering of the patterns of death, had drawn their spirits here. That had clearly not unraveled at his passing.

But she was sure she would have known. If they were dead, she would have been sent a letter, by . . . by . . . someone. *By nobody,* her thoughts whispered. *Nobody else connects you to them. You left, and now they are gone.* They had been her world, but she had been only a small part of theirs. Fifteen years of guardianship where she had never demanded their attention, compared to four decades of the Cunninghams raising their own children and building Mr. Cunningham's career—it wasn't enough. She had squandered so many chances.

Why did that hurt so much? Why had standing in their empty house hurt so much? She had *chosen* to relate as she had to them. She had decided to spare them her expense in Camhurst. She had been a good child, an easy child. She could understand pain from grief, but not from the distance between them.

"Jane," Mr. Cunningham said, pulling her back to the present so firmly she swayed where she sat. "Come sit with us."

Jane turned. They were real in every detail, down to every age spot, every wrinkle. Jane knew the bobbin lace on the collar of Mrs. Cunningham's gown. She knew the smell of the cedar blocks Mr. Cunningham's jacket had been packed with during the summer months.

Mrs. Cunningham came to the very edge of Jane's circle, frowning down at her. "Why are you on the floor, dear? Come, get up, let me have a look at you. Tell me what has happened."

"He's dead," Jane whispered, and then began to laugh, helplessly, hysterically. "*You're* dead."

But that, too, seemed wrong. This all seemed wrong. What could have killed the Cunninghams, so soon after they had left for Camhurst? Even illness rarely moved so quickly. A carriage accident? A robbery gone wrong?

"Jane!" Mrs. Cunningham chided. "You're being foolish. Are you ill? Are you feverish? You should be in bed."

"You cannot be here." She recited the facts she knew. "You went away, to Camhurst—"

"Can we not visit you? Come, at least sit with me a moment." She reached out a hand. Jane stared at it.

Yesterday, in the study, she had dreamed of this. Oh, not the Cunninghams; she'd thought to summon her mother, indistinct and lovely. But the Cunninghams would do just as well, now that they were just as deceased. Jane could reject their comfort and feel her shame, or lie down in the warm sunlight of their regard until she, too, starved.

It was an easy choice.

Jane reached across the chalk line and took Mrs. Cunningham's hand. The walls she had built up came crashing down in a shiver inside her skull.

Mrs. Cunningham smiled and drew her to the couch. Her skin was cool, as if she'd been walking in the autumn air, and her cheeks were pink to match. She felt solid.

"You look well," Mrs. Cunningham said once they were seated, heedless of Jane's turmoil. She settled a hand onto Jane's belly, where the seams of her dress strained, unable now to contain the knotted swelling. "To be with child so soon after your marriage is a lucky thing."

"No," Jane said, heart aching. "No, you misunderstand."

Augustine hadn't said a word about it, she realized. She should have known then that something was wrong. He would have seen it, would have tended to her, fussed over her, whether he had been a ghost or living. So what, then, had he been? She felt sick.

"Really, Jane? You'd reject this blessing?" Mr. Cunningham said from where he stood beside the fireplace.

She shook her head, confused. "That's not—"

"You marry a man, and expect him to never ask children of you? Do you think yourself so far above all of us, that you can reject our kindness in favor of marriage, and reject your marital duties in favor of self-satisfaction?"

"What do you mean?" Her brow tightened, confusion deepening. He had never been cruel to her, not even when, as a child, she'd lashed out, still heartsore and shell-shocked. The Cunninghams had been firm, kind, and distantly warm. Even in her childish imaginings, inventing reasons to hate them before she learned to cherish them, she had never imagined Mr. Cunningham being cruel. These words, they didn't sound like his at all.

But these were their souls. Orren and Abigail had accused her only of what she knew herself to be guilty of, what they themselves had seen, somewhere across the boundary of death.

And yet something was wrong. She was sure of it. Why were they *here*?

"Why did you stay in Larrenton, if this is not what you wanted?" Mrs. Cunningham asked, voice softer, gentler. "We know it would have been hard for you, to go back to Camhurst, but if you had been with us, you could have gone to university. Created something new for yourself. Used your brilliance, instead of bartering it for a quiet life you didn't fully understand."

Her head ached. They spoke of things Jane had kept from them, and things she had thought after they had gone, wishes inspired by the derision of Augustine's colleagues. It made no sense, that they had suspected it all.

"I thought you'd at least pretend to be sociable." Mr. Cunningham sighed. "I thought we taught you better than this."

And Jane went very still, a field mouse who had seen the shadow of a hawk.

The Cunninghams had never known the deepest interior of her mind, where she had taught herself to make eye contact and to handle small talk, and to smooth over how indelibly odd she was. Everything they said was an accusation she had leveled at herself at her most unkind. They could not know that. They were pulling it from her thoughts, *buried* thoughts, digging deep into her skull.

"You cannot control everything," Mrs. Cunningham added, more quietly now.

"I just wanted to keep things simple," Jane whispered, hunching in on herself.

"And look at what it's brought on," Mr. Cunningham said, tapping his cigar ash onto the floor. "You forced a man to marry you so that you could remain small and unremarkable, and now you have killed him because he would not bow to your wishes. Worse, you are bringing all of Larrenton down around you. We should never have taken you in."

"I never said—I never said I killed him—"

Mr. Cunningham harrumphed. "How else could it have gone? You have always been selfish. I imagine it is because you learned at a young age that *you* deserved to live when others stayed behind to die. Ruined from the first."

"Why are you *doing* this?" Jane begged.

Mrs. Cunningham touched her shoulder, drawing her attention. She smiled. She was kind.

"Because," she said, "we are starving, my dear. Our hunger is endless compared to yours." Her features smoothed out, becoming featureless stone from the cheeks up. Below was carved into an emaciated jaw and exposed teeth.

And then Mrs. Cunningham was herself again.

CHAPTER THIRTY-NINE

J ANE STARTED FORWARD, focusing her eyes so hard that her vision blurred, but it was only Mrs. Cunningham before her. Panicked, Jane rose, but Mrs. Cunningham seized Jane's wrist.

"Jane, do settle yourself. We did not adequately prepare you for the world—that is our failing." Her voice was sweet and light, a mockery of the woman who had raised Jane.

"Let me go, fiend," Jane whispered.

Mrs. Cunningham let go, eyes wide and soft tears welling up inside of them. "Fiend? Oh, Jane—"

"Stop." She glanced at Mr. Cunningham, but there was no trace of stone to him, either, no more cruelty in the set of his mouth. Her resolve faltered. Had she really seen that, really heard it? *Hungry*—Mrs. Cunningham had said she was hungry. And what should a ghost hunger for?

She was exhausted. She was falling to pieces. Her guardians were dead, dead and gone, and so was Augustine, and . . .

And Mrs. Cunningham had not crossed the circle, had she?

"Leave," she mumbled, thickly. She needed space. She needed air. "You must leave. I do not want to see you." She struggled to remember. She had knelt *there,* and Mrs. Cunningham had come to the very edge of the circle. She had reached out a hand, and Jane had taken it, but had her hand crossed the boundary?

"Sit down, darling," Mrs. Cunningham crooned.

Her hand had not crossed the boundary. Jane was sure of it; *she* had been the one to reach out. Mrs. Cunningham had not crossed the circle.

Orren had not crossed the circle.

Whatever Augustine had been, then, he was not the same as the Cunninghams.

She tore at her hair, falling back one step, another. Her head pounded.

"You're overwhelmed. You're seeing things. We will send for the doctor."

"No!" Thoughts of these creatures wearing Dr. Nizamiev's face drove her to her feet. She threw her aching, wrung-out body toward the hall.

They followed behind her, hunting dogs that had scented prey.

She broke into a run, through the bisected foyer and up the stairs, staggering into the banisters and hauling herself up, step after step. "Cease your childish flight, Jane!" Mrs. Cunningham called from behind her, voice echoing in the vaulted space. "It does not become a young lady! It does not become a new wife!"

"You are not her!" Jane cried, crashing onto the second-floor landing. "You may have died as her, but you are not her now. Something has happened to you!"

"The girl's gone mad," Mr. Cunningham said. "I will send for Dr. Nizamiev."

"And how do you know her?" Jane hissed, then tore herself away. She could not get drawn into this. She had to get to a safe place. But where was safe? She could not afford to build a circle so high as to obliterate the sound of their voices.

She climbed to the third floor. They followed, but they did not run. They proceeded, arm in arm, as if out for a stroll by the river. They fell away below her, but Jane's flight bought her only a few minutes, a brief reprieve.

She had to find a way to banish them.

Whatever these starving creatures were, however the spirits of the dead had been twisted, they came from what had been done to Elodie. Hadn't they? Everything began with Elodie; the ritual had been worked with Elodie's flesh. Jane needed to find her, to demand answers, demand solutions. But Jane had not seen Elodie in days. Since the blankness had replaced Elodie in her hallucination, there had been no trace of the fair-haired, red-eyed ghost in any window. *Why?*

Was it connected? It had to be.

Jane ran for the third-floor bedroom, slowing only to turn the gaslights up to full brightness. She had found Elodie's journal here, the only trace of her left in the whole house. If Jane was to find Elodie anywhere beyond the crypt, it would be here.

But the rooms were empty, and Jane could not bring herself to look at the windows, too afraid of seeing something other than fields and farms beyond. Even with every light turned up to full brightness, there were only walls and ceilings and floors, ghost-empty furniture with no trace of character, of inhabitance. Jane found herself standing in what had been the bedroom, staring at a tarnished, floor-length mirror, helpless, wishing Elodie would appear.

"Elodie," she said, addressing her own reflection. "Elodie, come!"

Her own eyes stared back.

Of course; Elodie had never come when called, appearing only when Elodie herself willed it. Where did she go, when she was not there? Jane tried to sort through her harried thoughts, organize them into sets and work through each with logical precision.

First: Elodie had died, and from her body Augustine had worked a spell that pulled the ghosts of the dead back into the world of the living.

Second: Magicians changed the workings of their bodies. Things grew out of place. Natural occurrences were not merely natural in the hands of a magician.

Third: When Jane had seen Elodie's life, she saw a hole where Elodie should have been. But when Jane had seen Elodie's death, Elodie had been present, and since her death she had appeared to Jane, out of place, out of time.

From these points, she could construct a chain that linked Elodie's presence directly to magic, and from there, a solution: Magic should be able to call her back, and Jane could work magic.

There was no way to make chalk and salt stick to the slick surface of the mirror, so Jane pulled out her hairpin and began to scratch at the glass. The metal squealed, loud enough that her ears hurt. She was careful to make it as perfect a circle as she could manage, holding the radius steady by way of a strip torn from her dress and the straining of her thumb upon the mirror.

Her reflection, as she worked, was wild. Unhinged. Her eyes had grown as red as Elodie's, blood vessels burst from constant wakefulness and her injections. Her hair fell around her face in knotted tangles, matted with oil and dust. Her lips were colorless and cracked, her fingers ink-stained and swollen.

But it felt good, to see the violence of the house written upon her flesh. It meant she was real. It meant *this* was real.

The circle inscribed, she used the pin to cut her thumb. She pressed her blood into the grooves, and it caught in the channel and spread, wicking halfway around before she had to add new drops. Then she crawled back, until her whole reflection was encompassed by the circle, until her image was centered. She hugged her knees to her chest and reached for the eel.

It leapt to her, eager for blood. She built the wall, doubled, around her image and through the other side of the mirror. It made a tunnel, and in it she heard a roaring, rushing sound. Her blood within her ears? A storm building outside?

Power. Power, flowing.

Jane stared into her own reddened eyes, her tangled hair. Her reflection was almost Elodie's already. All she had to do was know it to be Elodie in truth. But she hesitated. When Jane cast the spell, Elodie might appear, but might know only as much as Jane herself did. Or Elodie might take the place of Jane's own reflection and, from there, Jane's entire self. The dangers that had kept her from looking out the windows of Lindridge Hall, fearing what she would learn to be true, stilled her hand. They were the same dangers that had kept her from pulling down the crypt door when she might still have had a chance to save Augustine, afraid of what she might create when she conjured the open stairs.

But she had no choices left. She could hear footsteps again, the Cunninghams' slow processional reaching the third floor.

Sharply delineate and define the bounds of your knowledge. She did not know Elodie's mind. She knew that Elodie and she were not the same. She knew that Elodie had come to her before, with her own mind, her own intentions. She did not know what those intentions were.

Jane looked at her own reflection, and knew only that Elodie had come to her, and nothing more.

Elodie looked back at her, face shifting, features distorting.

She wore her bloody visage, her gown split, her flesh moving as she breathed. Behind her, darkness and the palest stone of the crypt floor where Jane's gaslight fell upon it.

Jane's breath caught in her lungs, pushed down beneath her heart.

The crypt.

"Is Augustine alive?" Jane whispered, the only question she could form.

Elodie said nothing. Jane crumbled, sagging, fisting her hands in her hair. She struggled to breathe at all, then to breathe evenly. She had thought him dead for sure until just a few minutes ago. To know it again was not so bad.

But she had let herself hope, and that tremulous hope was crushed with every second that passed.

"Were you with him, when he died?" she asked, fingers twisting at the torn edge of her skirts. "Was that what kept you away?"

Elodie twitched. It was almost a nod. Jane cried out, but Elodie made no more motion, and, as always, made no sound.

Another variable described. Elodie was not like the creatures down below. Her very silence, and her confinement to reflections when not inside the crypt, set her apart. Whatever Augustine had done to bring the ghosts, he had done something altogether different to her. She did not *seem* hungry, after all.

Jane licked her cracked lips with her papery tongue and ventured, "Is there something I can do to fix this? To save him?" Elodie hadn't nodded, after all, when Jane had asked if Augustine was dead. Silence was not certainty. Jane clung to that thought, and held her breath, and waited.

After what felt like an endless stretch of time, Elodie nodded.

Yes.

Elation made her heart hammer painfully in her chest. "Can you tell me?" she asked, barely louder than a whisper. Again, Elodie nodded. "What? What must I do?"

Elodie opened her mouth, but no sound came out.

Without sound, Jane could ask her yes or no questions, but could not have more beyond that. Unless . . .

Elodie's journal lay discarded elsewhere, past the Cunninghams, but it was simple enough to know the journal had been there, and to know that the journal was now before her, a pen beside it. The contents no longer mattered, after all. She did not have to remember them in perfect detail.

She needed only to offer it to Elodie, to write down something new.

"What must I know," she asked, sliding the journal and pen toward her knees, toward her reflection's knees, "to fix everything?"

Elodie looked at the pen, then lifted it up in the reflection. On Jane's side it did not move. She stared as Elodie took up the journal as well and opened to a clean, fresh page. The world around her fell away, and there was only the young woman, bloodied and alone. Elodie was still, save for the trembling in her fingers.

Jane felt so very like her that she wanted to weep. She wished they could have met some other way, in some other life. She wished she understood what had made the woman attack her, what had made them set themselves against each other. Elodie had helped her, the night that Orren came. Elodie had never appeared to Augustine. Something connected her to Jane, something unknown. Perhaps unknowable.

Elodie began to write.

She did not write much. A few words that Jane could not make out. She blew upon the ink, then carefully closed the notebook, pen inside the pages to mark the sheet. She set it down where Jane had placed it, and Jane was careful not to look beside her. She had not looked at her own notebook since the moment Elodie had touched it, in the reflection.

Elodie nodded.

Jane mastered her breathing, then closed her eyes and picked up the notebook by touch alone. She slid her thumb along the shaft of the pen. Not daring to hope, because to hope was not to know, she opened the journal and her eyes. Elodie had written only four words:

Ghosts are not real.

Jane stared, then looked sharply up at the mirror. But the mirror held only her own reflection, even as she stood, even as she rushed forward and grasped the molded edges. "I don't understand!" she cried, shaking it as if she held Elodie herself by the shoulders. "Come back, I need more! I can't understand this!"

Ghosts are not real. The words echoed inside her head. They collided with the stone she had seen beneath Mrs. Cunningham's skin, and the glide of statues in the hallway, Dr. Nizamiev's explanation of death and resurrection, and her own theories about how much Augustine might have changed the world. The Cunninghams appearing, even though the chance that they had both died was so low, even though she felt no responsibility for their unknown deaths.

If ghosts were not real, what were the things wearing the faces of the Cunninghams, tormenting her, pulling thoughts straight from her mind?

If ghosts were not real, what had she lain with, if not Augustine?

If ghosts were not real, how could she be certain Augustine was dead?

The creatures down below followed certain rules. They came after dark. They disappeared at sunrise. They could not cross her circle. Whatever had come to her in Augustine's form had not been them, and had not been his spirit.

Augustine might yet live.

"Come back!" she cried, falling to her knees before the mirror. Her fingers pressed so hard against the glass that spidering cracks began to spread across its surface, but Elodie was gone. "Tell me he is alive. Tell me he is suffering, if only so that I know he still breathes." If he was alive, if she hadn't failed—if she knew now how to call a wall, and how to summon the visage of an impossible dead woman—

She could bring the crypt wall down. She could save him.

CHAPTER FORTY

THE CUNNINGHAMS WERE mere feet from the bedroom when Jane emerged to face them. They stood together, with the dour-faced concern they usually only showed for the matters of Mr. Cunningham's worse-off clients. Jane's heart pounded in her throat, and she tried to see a way past them.

There was none. They filled the hallway.

Jane fell back a step, and then another.

"Jane, please," Mrs. Cunningham said. "Come here, darling." She held out her age-spotted hands, her knuckles thickened, her wrists plump.

Jane retreated.

The anger in her breast, the righteous fury and the fear—she kept it all tempered, banked inside her, though it made her hands tremble until she fisted them in her skirts. She had to be calm, and clever, and focused. She had to be everything Augustine was in the throes of surgery. A life depended on her.

But she was exhausted, and as she backpedaled, her ankle twisted. She stumbled, nearly falling—and then she looked down and saw them: all the circles she had drawn, all her experiments, covering almost every inch of the floor.

She could use this.

Drawing up to her full height, Jane made herself reach out and take Mrs. Cunningham's hands. Her stomach twisted in revulsion at how solid and comforting they felt. *Ghosts are not real,* she told herself, and then buried the thought, because she could not let herself feel horror. Not now, not yet.

"It's always been easier to run," she made herself say.

Mrs. Cunningham—the thing that wore her face—smiled at that, and gave Jane's hand a squeeze. "Come, let us begin again," she said. She glanced at Mr. Cunningham.

He nodded solemnly.

"I want an apology," Jane said as she took one step forward. The Cunninghams stepped back, as if in a dance. They were just outside an unbroken circle, one drawn with ink and metal rather than chalk.

"An apology?" Mr. Cunningham said. "It is the role of a parent, of a guardian, to tell a child when she has grown wayward. I am only helping you."

"You were cruel," Jane said.

"Cruelty has a way of cutting through to the heart of things," Mr. Cunningham said. "Surely you have learned that by now." They both smiled at her, and their smiles could have been loving, from a desperate angle. But Jane saw only hunger.

She clasped both by the shoulder.

"You're right," she said. "I have."

She shoved the Cunninghams over the bounds of the circle, and Jane drew up the wall.

She didn't know what to expect—if they would howl, or shout abuse, or throw themselves against it—and so she built it high and fast, reckless with her conceptualizing. The bricks she envisioned teetered and threatened to fall. Her stomach gave a raging pang. Inside, the Cunninghams only stared, no rage in their faces, only stillness.

And then their flesh began to crack.

It gave way in flakes and peelings, not like skin or muscle or organ, but like burning wood, craquelure spreading in fine-webbed networks across their faces, their hands, their clothing. It sloughed away in curls and fragments, and beneath her guardians' familiar shapes, their mortal bumps and curves, there was only impassive stone. They grew tall and attenuated, their heads stretching out in downward-arcing crescents, and Jane made herself watch it all.

These were not the Cunninghams. Ghosts were not real. Jane could not know if her guardians lived or died; the masks these creatures wore were no proof at all.

If they spoke, she could not hear it. The wall obliterated all sound. But they moved, heads tilting, bodies beginning to glide. Jane built higher still, shoring up the misplaced blocks, building floors and ceilings.

The creatures contorted. They lifted from the ground, limbs twisting in upon themselves, until they were only strange sculpture, barely recognizable. They hung, motionless, in the mirror image of Dr. Nizamiev's photographs, imprisoned as magicians had been before them.

Jane realized with a lurch that she had almost joined those photographed magicians. If the servants had not come back for her that morning, she might have built her walls this high, despite the pain in her belly, and she would have been only another collection piece for Dr. Nizamiev's asylum. Mad or frozen; the doctor would have accepted her either way.

She stared up at them, her unreal tormentors, and slowly began to back away. She let go of the wall, expecting it to tumble. But it stayed erect, no brick sliding out of place, no flexing of the structure.

They could not pursue her.

And yet, though they were immobilized and fixed in amber, she could not leave that hallway without a surge of fear. Gathering her supplies—fresh chalk, fresh salt, a candelabra with fresh candles, and every other tool of ritual she had amassed, all bundled into a bag made out of Mrs. Luthbright's abandoned apron—was the work of frantic, harried minutes, each one a panicked opportunity to glance again at the stairs to the third floor.

She did not hear their footsteps or their voices.

At last, Jane went to where the cellar door had been transformed. There, she built up her own walls, and sat in contemplation.

Everything in her urged her to barrel on ahead, to know the wall was gone and simply walk into the crypt. But she knew now that to rush was to falter. She might bring the whole house down upon her head if she erred, or erase the crypt from existence entirely. Could she bound her knowledge enough, by focus of will alone, to know she was not changing the reality below?

When she had built her circle high around the creatures, she had seen their true form. If only she could have worked a circle around the expanse of stone, she could have investigated it, flayed it down to component parts, drawn up some equation, some geometry, to reorganize it.

But perhaps the circle did not need to be around the stone. When she had built her circle too high around herself, she'd seen the world fade, revealing hidden details, inner truths. She had seen the angles of the house's joinery, and some meaning in them. Reality could be delineated. The wall was as much a lens as a fortification. Looking in or looking out—did it matter which direction?

She drew up the walls around her, overhead, thick enough that she could see the lines of truth sketched out upon reality. Her stomach gave more angry protests, but she blocked them out, searching for the borders of the slab before her. Its corners were an inhumanly perfect ninety degrees, traced out in blinding light. Its sheer unreality, its divorce from any earthly manipulation of pen and paper, leapt into her fingers.

She peeled.

The stone came away.

It buckled under its own weight, its impossible existence, and crumbled into nothing. She fell back against the metaphysical bricks she had built up around her and felt them give way as well. The circle settled out. The world regained its color and solidity.

The opening yawned, dark and ominous, as she struggled back up to her feet. Her stomach was a seething molten mass beneath her lungs, and her head spun. She clutched the revealed doorframe, panting, until she was still enough to light the tapers of the candelabra.

And then she plunged down into the crypt.

The candelabra's light flickered and guttered from her harsh pace. The cool, dank air of the tunnels closed in around her, but Jane pressed forward, heedless of the spirits that might gather. She felt eyes on her, heavy and pressing, closing in as she reached the room with the table and chairs, but no looming shadows waited for her in the doorways. She slowed only long enough to look at Elodie's name engraved upon a seat, and then she pressed onward.

"Augustine!" Her voice rang out, amplified and echoing down the hall she found herself in. "Augustine, I am here!" For half a second, she was terrified to let the sound die out, too afraid of what she wouldn't hear when it was gone, but she stilled her lungs. She looked from side to side, scanning every inch of the hallway for a figure, a shoe print, a smudge.

There was nothing, nothing but white stone.

The hallway seemed impossibly long, studded with branches and broken once or twice by turns that did not double back but instead pressed outward to new dimensions. The cellar was a maze. How had it been built? How had nobody questioned it when they laid the huge stone slabs, joined almost imperceptibly? Had it been built so long ago that the builders had understood, implicitly, the promise that its geometry made, or had it been built piecemeal so that no one person but its designer could see the final sequence?

It went beyond the surface boundaries of Lindridge Hall. Whatever magic of Dr. Nizamiev's ritual still remained failed in that moment. She felt the rupture throughout her body as she crossed the threshold.

She kept walking.

But not three minutes later, the hallway she staggered down ended in a blank wall, carved with faint shapes, shapes she traced with her fingertips but could find no meaning in. More esoterica, more fervent beliefs held by generations that had gone before, beliefs she could not access, let alone know with such certainty. She stared at it, wavering on her feet. Her legs ached. Her feet screamed. Her stomach . . . it did not help, to think about the pain in her stomach, the pain that called when the magic came thickest in her veins.

Stopping did not help, either. The longer she was still, the harder it would be to move again. She knew that. She had learned it on the long road back to Larrenton and in the emptiness of the Cunninghams' home. She made herself turn around, even as her candles burned lower, even as the cold bit into her, ticking down the clock of her endurance.

She was not alone.

Just far enough from her that her candle's light limned the outline but not the substance, somebody waited. Jane surged forward, then stopped again as she made out the slightness of the frame, the curve of the throat, the line of the clothing. It was not Augustine. It was not Elodie.

It was her mother.

CHAPTER FORTY-ONE

HER MOTHER STOOD turned away from her, dressed in her auxiliary uniform. Even before Jane was sent away, her mother had joined Jane's father out in the streets, part of the corps of volunteers who helped people who were trapped in wreckage and cordoned off unsafe areas after each round of shelling. A stitched leather gas mask hung loose around her neck, as grotesque as Jane remembered it, and her hair was cropped close to her head.

This was not the mother she had dreamed of conjuring. This was plucked impossibly from her memories. Dreams of her parents had long ago faded to bare suggestions, and when Jane *had* thought of her mother, her vague form always had long hair. Her vague features were always happy and loving. But this . . . this was her mother as her mother had been, the last time Jane had seen her.

Until that moment, Jane had believed she'd forgotten her face.

But Jane knew the lines that were just beginning to form at the corners of her eyes, the sweep of her pale lashes, the upturned angle of her nose.

All the details a child had memorized in happier times, fixed fast upon her mind by the bright panic of calamity, as sure as any photographic plate.

"Do not do this," Jane said. Her voice trembled.

Her mother made no response, as if she hadn't heard. And even though Jane knew that it was not her mother, that it was only one of the creatures wearing her face, that quiet disregard broke her.

Jane sank to her knees, undone.

"I forgot you," she breathed. "I wanted to forget you."

Still her mother did not respond. It would have been easier if she had; Jane could more readily argue away a kind and loving apparition, or a cruel one, the way she had with the Cunninghams. She could have walked past, or locked the apparition in another infinite circle.

But this, this disinterest? Jane reached out for her, before recoiling.

Did it matter that ghosts were not real and this was not her mother? Or was it only the beating of her own heart that mattered, the longing there, the loneliness?

To walk past her was abominable, when Jane had no other trace of her left.

"Please, please look at me," Jane whispered.

Her mother shifted then, and Jane's heart leapt, but it was to take a step away, leaving once more. Jane surged forward, then, desperate to see recognition in her eyes. She seized her mother by the shoulders, turning her around. Her mother's body was warm, and her features were so detailed, so specific. It could have been her mother, if she had wanted. If she could have known it to be true.

Surely magic could transform the creatures it had given life to.

The temptation consumed her, and she whispered, "It's your daughter," as if it were only aging that caused this distance. "Your daughter, Jane. I am here. I am here."

Her mother's expression flickered with faint annoyance, and her eyes focused briefly on Jane's face. It stole Jane's breath. And then her mother's attention moved on again to somewhere beyond her. How fitting that Jane could not see recognition in her eyes, or interest, or awareness. Jane had shut herself off from the memory of her mother long ago. But now the old scar inside her was torn open afresh, and she was bleeding, hemorrhaging a pain she hadn't touched in near on two decades. She had forgotten how to stanch the flow.

Crying, Jane let go of her mother's shoulders to touch her cheeks, her fingers light over the warm, real flesh. She brushed her thumbs along her mother's hairline, and sought out every element of herself in her mother's face.

She found the smallest buckle along the line of her jaw.

At first, her eyes slid off it, her mind unwilling to accept the fracture in the illusion. But beneath that buckle was dark granite. Its weight anchored her when everything else threatened to fade away, and she dug her fingertips beneath it. It was tempting, so tempting, the idea of giving herself over to the melancholic, aching dream of her mother the way she had planned to so many days ago, but she forced herself to fight instead, tearing at the false flesh, unveiling more and more of the truth beneath.

She had forgone sleep for this. She had subsisted only on bits of hare, tangled sea grass, raw eggs. She had made herself half mad, following a set of rituals designed to open her mind to the workings of the world, and she *saw* them now.

The flesh sloughed off like a drumhead cut from its frame.

The statue rose above her, looking down with the same dispassion as her mother's eyes had held. It had always been that. Always, always.

why will you not feed us? the creature said, its words unlike anything she had ever heard. They were more than sounds. They snaked over her chilled flesh, her tired bones. **feed us, and we will carry you out of here.**

The same hunger that Mrs. Cunningham had voiced. These things grew desperate when denied, she realized, and that knowledge gave her strength.

"And what would feed you?" she asked, stepping back and regarding it with her chin lifted.

your shame.

She remembered Augustine in the kitchen, bewitched, staring at her and seeing blood in her eyes, sickness under her skin. Shame was overwhelming in its paradoxical comfort. When Jane saw her mother, she felt the desperate need to fix things. When Augustine saw his patients, he saw the chance to heal what he had failed to repair.

Simple. It was so simple. These were not the ghosts of the dead, but hungry things that wore their forms, extracted from memory, bound to cause the maximum amount of pain because they drew only the details that hurt from their victim's minds.

Jane bared her teeth. "I will not be ashamed," she said.

you will die down here without our help. It was barely a threat. It sounded like truth, and Jane had to claw her way past it, like spiderwebs tangling between her teeth and nails.

"I will fight," Jane spat.

There was no circle she could force the creature into. Could she draw a ring before her, and drag it there? The thought seemed ludicrous, seeing the heavy base of the statue before her. But she could still draw one around herself.

When she crouched, her legs gave out beneath her. She fell, exhausted, to her knees. She forced herself to reach, to scribble, to think of eels and walls.

you are so much greater than he, the statue murmured, words sliding across the folds of her brain. **so much more resilient. he had so much shame. so much regret. but yours is harder given and sweeter for it.**

She reached behind herself with shaking hands and completed the circle.

you tried to live a small life, jane shoringfield lawrence. you tried to have no regrets. you tried to control everything. and now you are here, filled with guilt. how many have died because of your actions? because you married a man who did not want to marry, because you made him care enough to lie to you, because you forced him to confront those lies?

The creature spoke the truth, and the truth was so heavy that it bore her down to the ground. She curled around the pulsing mass within her belly.

what have you lost, it asked, gliding an inch closer, **in pursuing the impossible? you have frightened many. forced your care upon**

them. made them fear you. you have ruined lives, more than you have killed.

"No," Jane whispered. "I will not regret that. I will not regret any of it, not until I am through. Not until I have saved him." She glared up at the thing.

It stopped.

It regarded her. Its crescent head did not move. Its carved robes did not shift.

then think back to before. think of when the bombs fell. remember the fear. the guilt, when others around you died but you lived. there is meat enough in that for me. think of it, and i will let you live.

It was close: the hiss of gas, the heat of the flames, cowering in a basement and breathing through the filter of her mother's skirts. Emerging each morning into the blasted-out streets of Camhurst. All the memories became real around her. She felt again the terror, the deprivation, so many days with so many dead.

Before her, the statue's lower half became fabric, familiar, the very wool her mother had pulled across Jane's nose and mouth to save her from the gas.

Beneath her, the stone hallway shook, as if with the impact of shelling.

She stared at it. It wasn't hard-packed soil. It wasn't dirty stone. It was white, and chill, and so very different from the buildings in Camhurst. Camhurst was far away, and Larrenton far inland. This was where she had been *safe*. The war had never reached here.

She must fix the truth in her mind. If she knew she was in the cellar of Camhurst, she would be there again.

And she wanted to be at Lindridge Hall.

She lifted her head, seeing the statue before her in granite only, and built her walls so high that the dim hallway was lit, as if it were all only lines upon a page. Her abdomen exploded with pain. She grasped the outline of the statue, and she tugged, and pulled, and knotted, until there was nothing left but a dense, dark scribble. Beyond her, something smooth and hard dropped from the air, clattering upon the stone. Jane sobbed with relief, then with pain, and dragged herself through the flexing caul of the circle, back into the real world.

Jane stood. Jane thought of Augustine. Jane pitched forward, once more, into the dark.

No more statues appeared before her. There was only empty hall after empty hall, with no sign of Augustine, or of death, or even of herself.

She turned down another pathway, staggering, close to exhaustion. Her vigor drained with her flagging candlelight. The cool air pressed in around her, on the little that was left of Jane Shoringfield Lawrence.

And then, finally, there was a change.

There was the faintest of shapes ahead of her, cloaked in shadow, a pile of dirt or the form of a slumped body. *Augustine.* The possibility flooded her mind, overtook every inch of her, and she fell to her knees, trying to claw closer to it. But her stomach screamed and her candle guttered. The light went out. She cast aside the candelabra and dragged herself forward, hand over hand along the cold stone, until the pain grew so great that she could not move, until exhaustion made the last of her willpower buckle.

And then she felt warmth, hands against her shoulders, her back, hands that shook with hunger and fear and worry, hands that carried with them the stink of a man trapped in the dark for six days, and beneath that, the faint smell of antiseptic.

CHAPTER FORTY-TWO

S HE WAS COLD.

It was the first thought to swim into her consciousness, followed swiftly by *It hurts.* Her stomach was flooded with liquid agony, and even wiggling her toes made the pain spike. She groaned and pressed back against the surface below her, but it did not yield. Around her was darkness.

And then: a light. A candle flame, burning where there was no wax left, above an iron candelabra that she recognized. And there, beside the flame, was a face that she recognized, a face that she had come to know so well she could have conjured it in her dreams. Augustine sat beside her, elbows braced upon his knees, hands tangled in his hair, clawing at his scalp.

He was alive.

Do not be so hasty, she thought, but it was so hard not to believe, and she had no way left to test him. He had crossed her circle before, and beyond that she did not know how to verify his reality, his breath, his life. Her only hope was that he could see her suffering, that he could worry over her as he had not that night in the study, and by the pain writ upon his face, he knew. He knew, and he was frightened for her.

And with that thought, *she* was afraid, because the last time she had truly seen him, he would have killed her to save her.

He was sitting in a high-backed white stone chair. She was lying on something cold and hard. She knew this room. She knew this plinth. Elodie had died here, her husband's hands inside her chest, and Jane had nearly followed.

She did not feel the press of an ether sponge against her lips, but still she wanted to run. To hide. To close the door on him again and—

She tried to lift a hand and moaned in pain, so softly that he did not stir, so softly that she did not know if she'd truly made a sound. Her eyes rolled skyward, houseward. Just one staircase between them and freedom. Why had he brought her here, instead of their bedroom? Instead of the surgery?

But he made no move to threaten her. He was still as stone, head in his hands, as if already mourning her.

"Augustine," she whispered through heavy force of will.

At that, Augustine looked up at last, eyes widening, lips twisting into a smile for just a moment before he registered the pain creasing her brow and came to her side. "Slow breaths, Jane, slow breaths," he said, stroking her hair, brushing the backs of his knuckles against her cheek.

He held no scalpel in his hand. No purgatives lined the plinth beside her. She remembered the desperate light in his eyes that would have led him to kill her, those many days ago, and she did not see it here.

This was the Augustine she had first met, not the one she had feared so much that she had sealed him in this tomb. This was the Augustine she had come to save. He was both doctor and husband in that moment, and he stared at her as if he did not dare hope *she* was real, though he could surely feel her pounding pulse beneath his fingertips.

"Jane," he murmured. "Jane, you have come back for me."

Come back for him. She laughed, bitterly, and the laugh sent a new wave of agony through her. Come back for him, but what could she do now, immobilized and in so much pain? She had used the last of her strength destroying the memory of her mother, and she had nothing left to give him.

"I'm sorry," she whispered. "I trapped you here. The wall—I conjured the wall."

He frowned, then looked toward the entry room, the stairs beyond. "No," he said.

"I didn't mean to, but it was my will worked upon the world." Her voice caught. "I've taken the wall down now, though. We can leave."

Augustine bowed his head, and she glimpsed how stricken his expression was, how desolate. She had seen that before, after Abigail Yew's surgery, when he was convinced Abigail would die.

She was very cold.

"This growth," Augustine said, ignoring her apologies and directions, his hand dropping to hover just above her belly. "When did you first notice it?" He slipped so easily into his doctor's cadence. It wrapped around her, familiar and calming. She pushed that comfort aside.

"I have worked magic, Augustine," she said. "Like Renton. Like Aethridge. I have worked magic, I have changed the makeup of the world, and I . . . I have changed something inside me as well."

He did not thrill to hear that she was a magician now, that she understood him in a way she had once refused to. Instead, he shook his head and said, "It is killing you."

No. She would not die. She did not want to die, and would not settle for it. She shuddered with dry tears.

"You thought I was dying before," Jane whispered. "But I was well. You saw only what you feared, what the spirits of this house *knew* you feared. They preyed upon you. They preyed upon us both, Augustine. But I have learned how to repel them, how to stop them. I am not dying, Augustine."

He didn't argue. He only stroked the hair from her face, grief in his eyes.

Perhaps he was right. Perhaps it was too late, grown too large; she could hardly move for it, and she was so cold.

It had been so easy to borrow time against her future.

"Jane," Augustine said. He took her hand, settled it on the mass. The pain lanced again. This was real. This was not spirit-led madness. This was going to be the death of her. "It is pressing too hard upon your organs. It grew too swiftly. I can't move you, not safely."

"Then send for help," Jane said. But the words were hollow, light as ash, dissolving as she spoke them. She did not know if Larrenton still existed beyond Lindridge Hall, did not know if he could bring the larger wall down himself, did not know if he could escape. *I have doomed us both.* "Mr. Lowell. And there is a locum. They can assist in surgery—"

"Jane." He cupped her cheeks, gently, and held her frantic gaze. "I do not want to hurt you. I am not sure I could, not even to save you."

"Why not?" she cried.

"The last time I tried, I was wrong, and I might have killed you. And for that injury, I have been trapped down here for days." He bowed his head, his brow pressed to hers. "You were right. Death always wins. It is arrogance to think that when I fail, it is always due to error. Sometimes . . . sometimes there is nothing left."

"I am asking you to save me," Jane whispered.

He flinched, pulled away, and said nothing more.

She had bent the world to one single purpose: to rescue him. She had driven herself mad with lack of sleep, had swallowed half-formed birds, had sat with ghosts and screamed and cried, and now, here, she was so close to her goal that she didn't know what came next. She had never thought beyond opening the stone blocking the cellar. She had never thought she might not follow him out. She had never thought she might die.

She pressed her hand to the aching pain in her gut, forcing her fogged thoughts over what she knew, desperate for a solution. Here she was, a magician newly trained in ritual, disciplined, used to suffering, and at her side was a surgeon who similarly knew the rules of magic. They had, together, seen how an unpracticed magician could create something in his body that grew out of place, and now something grew out of place in her. Beneath her was the stone plinth where a woman had died. Elodie's death had bound the house in such a way that Jane would one day come and be forced to learn how mathematics could be used to organize the impossible, how zero could lead to provably true answers by impossible means, and how geometry could be used to divine the easiest way to protect herself, or to provide a lens to see the bones of the world.

They were all together here, now, and they had all come to this place soaked in blood, in one way or another.

Synchronicity.

"Do you have your doctor's bag?" Jane asked. She could smell the blood already, Abigail's blood, Mr. Renton's. Her own, pattering against the floor. The ether, the blade, both filled her with horror—but they were necessary.

"I have it," Augustine said, "right where I left it the last night I saw you."

"Cut this thing out of me," she said.

He recoiled in horror. "Jane, I can't. Not without an assistant, better lighting, antiseptic. I can't—"

"We don't have a choice," Jane said. She forced herself to move, a little twitching of her hand; it drew him to her side, close enough that she could touch his wrist. He felt warm and solid. Alive. "Do you want to leave me down here, then remain to suffer in this house where I have died? Do you want to add to your sins, your regrets, your shames?

"Do you want to lose me?"

"No! No, but . . ."

"If you tell me this is your deserved punishment, I will scream," Jane said.

He ducked his head. His breath shivered in his throat, close to tears.

"You are a better physician than that," she murmured gently. "You are a better *magician* than that. I understand the surgery is dangerous, that you might fail. But this is not *just* surgery. This is ritual. You wanted magic that could save your patients—I have found it for you. You wanted a chance to atone for your failures, you wanted freedom, you wanted to know there was more left for you. We can do it here, now. A surgery and a working both."

She scanned his face, searching for understanding, acceptance. It had to be there. It had to come now as she laid out everything he had wanted but not dared to hope for, in service of her salvation.

But he shook his head. He clasped her hand tenderly. "This talk of magic," he said. "This is my fault. I have filled your head with nonsense. Jane, there is no magic that can save you. There is no magic at all."

"But you yourself have—"

"Imaginings. Wishful thinking."

She stared in horror. How could he not believe it anymore? How could he so easily cast aside what had sundered his entire adult life? Something had happened. Something had happened down here in the crypt, and she did not know what it was. She did not know how to undo it.

"I've been down here—so long," he said, brow furrowed. "I've had time. Time to think. My obsession with the impossible cost me the dignity of Elodie's death. It has almost cost me you. And none of it is real."

"But you've seen them. The spirits. And you thought me ill when I was not."

His forehead creased more deeply. He twitched. "I . . . I . . ."

"You saw them; they tormented you."

"Guilt. Only guilt. Jane, there are other explanations. We can send for Dr. Nizamiev. She can help."

"If magic is not real," Jane gasped out, her last desperate volley, "then where did the door go? Why haven't you died from thirst? It has been six days, Augustine."

His entire body shuddered, his flesh rippling, and Jane cried out, sobbed, expecting him to fall into nothing, another apparition, another spell. But he remained. He shook his head violently. "Jane, Jane," he mumbled.

"You must do this working for me, or else we have no chance at all. Look at me, please."

He met her eyes. His were filled with tears and panic, deep panic, and beneath that a layer of paralytic confusion.

How to go on? How to settle him? Dr. Nizamiev would have known what to do.

And then it clicked.

"You must promise me one thing," she said to Augustine, repeating Dr. Nizamiev's words. Her words, which Jane now recognized as an incantation. An establishment.

"Anything," Augustine said.

She smiled, trembling. "That you will accept as true everything I am about to tell you. It will not be easy, but it must become a part of your understanding of the world, or else I will have wasted my time."

A beat of silence. A held breath.

"I promise," he said.

"Magic," she said slowly, with all the weight of ritual, "is real."

And with that, the panic left his eyes. Simple. Simple, and terrible, and she did not have time now to think of what must have happened to her those weeks ago in the sitting room, facing down a specialist of madness.

"This is it," she said instead, exultant. "It is the unspooling of everything that has gone before—down to the moment when you held Elodie on this plinth and could not save her life. Save yourself instead. This mass is magic itself. We can remove it, make it the centerpiece of a spell, do a working so that you, at least, are freed. The spirits that feed on you, gone. The tether to this house, the sickness—all gone, and you free to help others, to save lives."

"And you?"

"You have told me I will die either way," she said. "But maybe, maybe there is a chance. *Knowing* is the thing. Do the surgery, and I will know that I will survive, and we will see what happens. Undo the magic that is killing me."

Augustine stared back at her for a long moment, then nodded. "I will do the working."

THERE WERE CANDLES in sconces along the stairwell wall. Augustine collected them and lit them from the impossible flame clinging to the candelabra. Illumination spread, dancing across the banquet hall, the burial room, the esoteric mausoleum that the Lawrences had built.

They were not alone.

Shadows gathered in the hallways that branched off the room, shadows with misshapen heads and still bodies. Augustine watched them warily as he scraped caked chalk and egg yolk from Jane's fingertips and used it to draw out the thinnest of circles around the table. Jane called the base of the wall up when it was done, building until she cried out in pain.

Augustine stepped in to build the wall the rest of the way. It took the pressure off her, and the pain subsided.

Her husband stripped off her soiled, torn dress and pushed her chemise up above her stomach. She kept her gaze fixed on him, not on the figures that glided closer, coming to the very edge of the circle. When he looked at them, he did not flinch; he, too, must have seen the truth at last.

"Do you see their gowns?" he asked.

She did. All the gathered statues were in full surgical gowns, pristine white to better show the blood on them at the end of the day.

"They are dressed as nurses and surgeons," he said wonderingly. "They have come to watch the operation. This is to be theater for them."

"They wish to see us work."

"They wish to see us fail."

Jane grimaced but could not argue. "If you fail," she said instead, "you must promise me you will not feel ashamed. You will not feel guilty. It only feeds them, Augustine."

He nodded, pulling himself away from his audience to tend to his patient. He settled a hand against her belly, palpating the margins of the mass. "Ovarian, I think," he said. "Over the intestines. Better than it could have been. With ether—"

"No ether," Jane said.

"Without ether, the shock might kill you."

"With ether, I cannot help you work the spell."

"It will hurt," he said, stroking her cheek. "It will be the worst pain you have ever felt. Are you sure?"

Augustine had taken the wall she had started and built it strong. He was a magician, or had been, or believed himself to be now. He might be able to do the working alone.

But she knew herself; the ether would bring up the old panic, no matter how much she trusted him, how much she focused. That panic lived in her bones, emerging smoothly when it thought it might protect her. It could not be reasoned with.

"I am sure," she said.

Augustine nodded, pressed a quick kiss to her forehead, and went to his bag.

He set out his tools: straps of leather, carefully coiled; scalpels; curved needles and catgut thread; benzoin; laudanum. He left the ether and its sponge inside.

"I will bind you now," Augustine murmured. His eyes kept darting to their ghostly audience, but he worked quickly, drawing a strap along the underside of the table and buckling it around her wrists. He did the same for her ankles, then across the tops of her thighs.

She reached for her belief, her unerring faith that this was her Augustine, that this would work.

He tightened the final strap holding her shoulders in place and reached for his scalpel.

Steady, Augustine. Steady, Jane.

"I incise the flesh," Augustine said, words methodical and melodic, the expert tenor of a teacher explaining his next cut. "The flesh is the boundary between the internal world and the external reality."

The blade cut into her.

She jerked against the leather. She screamed. The pain was blinding, unimaginable. Distantly she could feel his hand steadying her abdomen. It burned where he touched.

Had this been what Renton felt, when he had torn into himself? This pain, all-consuming, all-encompassing? She was ruptured. She was torn asunder. She felt one layer of flesh parting, then the next, and she howled, shutting her eyes against the pain.

Augustine did not stop, though she could hear herself begging, pleading.

Fear suffused her, fear that was not instinct, but something else. Something darker, older, unfamiliar. A fear that was not hers. Elodie, half dead, borne down to the cellar so that her limbs would cool, so that Augustine would have more time to save her, but not comprehending what he was attempting. Elodie, struggling, confused, because she trusted Augustine, but she was afraid.

"The internal world of the body is shaped by the external reality," he said.

She could barely hear his voice over the pain, but she felt the incantation, the words throbbing inside her head. "The correction of a rupture in the workings of the internal world may be used as a map whereupon we fix an aberration in the external world."

That she could feel Elodie's fear was evidence that the spell was working, that she had been right. She bore down upon herself, pulling on all her discipline. It lay in her marrow as surely as Elodie's fear did, as surely as the pain did. His knife was no different from her tightened stays and pricking hairpins in kind, only in intensity.

"I am awake to the Work," Jane mumbled. "While the world closes its eyes, I remain alert." She fought to keep her eyes open, to stare at the vault of stone above her and see its architecture, its geometry. It fitted together so smoothly, as if even that had been planned by a magician's hand.

Her stomach heaved as she felt his fingers slip beneath her skin, into her viscera, searching, pushing, pulling. She pressed down against the stone beneath her, trying to retreat, trying to flee. And then she spasmed against her bonds, as if to fight, the motion drawing another scream from her. The muscles of her belly had been cut, and her tensing had torn them further.

This was impossible. She could not endure this. She heard Augustine curse, felt his hand withdraw. There was no relief, no easing of the pain, not even as he pressed his bloodied hand against her temple as if to soothe her, then fumbled for another tool. He did not have his surgery here, or Mr. Lowell, or her to attend without flinching.

How could he succeed?

Jane's head lolled back on the stone. The pain never ceased, but it grew faint, distant, along with all the world. *Feel it,* she demanded of herself. *Feel all of it.* She could not give in, would not give in. She had to fix this. She had to fix this for all of them. For Elodie, on this table, confused and staggering toward death, only to be hauled back just long enough for horror. For Augustine, his hands inside both his wives, soaked in his own failure. For her, forcing her way upon the world and struggling to pick up the pieces when the world rejected her.

The darkness closed in around her.

CHAPTER ZERO

Jane stands at the head of the banquet table, looking out across the cellar of Lindridge Hall. There is no pain left in her. Where her stomach was is a gaping wound of blood and absence that does not match the form of her corpse on the slab in front of her. She wonders about that, but only distantly.

All around her, Lindridge Hall spreads out in a scaffolding of half-sketched lines, atrophying ligaments that flex and contract. Echoes of the dead ring her, wearing a hundred faces, layered one atop the other, none and all at the forefront. Augustine stands before her, too, hands inside her corpse, still and silent.

She leans forward, looking at her face. Agony. Is that what she feels? No; she feels nothing but a deep placidness, a calm, a level of detachment she has longed for all her life.

But even in the moment of her death there is more, multitudes upon multitudes, condensed until she cannot breathe, condensed until it is nothing at all. She dissolves, spreads, coalesces, shifts.

Time is only onionskins marked with similar drawings of place and actor, arranged in different scenes. Unexcavated earth presses in around her, all worms and soil and water. Men and women move within a warren of chambers, draw out circles, perform faded incantations. Initiations, desperate workings, children's games. Workers lay down white stone in heavy slabs. Spells pull at the bones of the world, failing and changing reality, ripple after ripple.

She lies unconscious in the passage where she meets her mother. She touches the cellar door for the first time, and all her body is ice and pain. She watches flames consume her bloodstained sheets, and kisses her husband, and works at sums.

She sits in a chair in the dining room, happy, newly wed, still deep in dreaming of the possibilities before her, unknowing of what will come. But in her mind coils the first stirrings of confusion and distrust. She does not yet know Elodie's name, but she knows her face: red-eyed Elodie, quiet in the windows.

But the windows are empty.

Is this that night? Or is it another? There are many nights during which Jane sits in that chair, the window frames holding only night-black glass. But there is no sea grass or sprouted grain tangling down her throat. Her clothing is not torn, her body not shivering with exhaustion. She can still do her figures, would not short the servants, is in control of herself and does not seek to control more beyond.

For an eternity, a lifetime, the blink of an eye, Jane is happy, even knowing what comes next if Elodie appears. But Elodie is absent and if she does not come—there is only a void, a yawning white expanse that Jane cannot cross. There is something on the other side. She does not experience *hope* when she looks at it, because to hope is to imagine, to conceive of new worlds, but she lies curled in her mother's arms, in Augustine's arms, as if the past is the future, as if time is mirrored, and she feels safe and loved and whole. Perhaps this is what exists, on the other side.

But the white void remains. It spreads. Jane sits in the dining room at Lindridge Hall and does not see Elodie. The world beyond the windows disappears. She sees Augustine and the Lawrences and the Pinkcombes in a stone-hewn room, and sees the nothing that is Elodie. It spreads. It is everywhere. Jane can no longer tell where it ends and where the white expanse of her own paradox begins.

She is afraid.

She takes the measure of herself, of her boundaries, and she unplies the skein of her existence into its component strands, one following the other. It warps, bows, threatens to snap. Without Elodie in the glass at Lindridge Hall, she does not have the information needed to understand her circumstances. Two impossibilities rise, fall, struggle to resolve.

She steps into the windowpane herself.

She looks close enough. Her eyes are bloodshot from days of sleeplessness, her hair tangled, her dress bloodstained. Jane, living, looks up from the dining room table, sees herself, then quickly turns away. She tells herself it is nothing.

Jane, dead, goes in search of Elodie.

Statues stand motionless in the halls. They have no faces; there is nothing human about them except for their vague form, their uprightness. Augustine steels himself for the suffering to come, and she sits in the library with her tome of the impossible.

Elodie is absent.

The white spreads.

Jane steps in for her again, feeling worry now, feeling dread. Her death unravels. She must remember time if she is to fix this. She must sort the onionskins, lay them out in order, find the mistakes.

She follows statues that march motionlessly down the stairs into the study. Augustine carries her to bed, tucks her in with loving care, goes to meet the ghosts in what he thinks is bravery but is only cowardice.

And where is Elodie?

She is not in the darkness of the crypt. Jane does not see her as she staggers through the impossible maze of passages and does not see her as she lies on the slab. Where is she? She is meant to be trapped, but she is as absent now as she was in the windows up above.

This is a problem. This is a problem not because Jane wants Elodie there to suffer, or even to be freed, but because without Elodie's spirit, there is no death, or life, or Jane. Without Elodie, Jane is lost a hundred times over, and time, incomprehensible and tangled, falls apart to dust.

What has happened? What has gone wrong?

Jane's initiation. Her vision. She must resurrect it into bloody, screaming life, study it for clues. Jane peels herself from the flow of time, the ply of her life twisting back on itself. She sees Elodie split open on the plinth, her heart in Augustine's hands, and then—

Nothing.

Elodie is gone.

Forward and backward, she is gone. In the past, the great nothingness of where she was still grows. There is wrongness. There is rupture. Jane touches the margins of Elodie and feels cold, feels her fingertips fragment away. Shame coalesces in their place. She draws back, stunned, then turns once more to herself. The white has slowed its advance, held back by her redefinitions. The variable of Elodie must be replaced, the fragmentary rupture of the past papered over with Jane's will, until Elodie can be restored.

So she exists in those moments Elodie comes to her, searching for that yawning nothing. Does it climb out from Jane's vision and jump from moment to moment, obliterating as it goes?

But there is no blankness in the windows. Elodie is simply not there.

She continues to search. She hides in the study, pursued by a hungry thing wearing the face of a boy dead before his time. She gives herself Augustine's text. She builds the circle, learns magic, begins stumbling down the path again.

So many moments threaten to fracture, even moments when Elodie never was. The doctor's bag that will almost be her undoing is not in the third-floor bedroom hearth. She sees Vingh leave his unattended, and does not know if they are the same, or different, or both. She takes it anyway. She burns it. The scalpel cuts into her finger. The ether burns her nose and mouth. Her mother's skirts wrap around her.

Jane flees, blood streaking from her arm, and Augustine chases just behind. Augustine is slow, but not slow enough. He will reach her. He will catch her, and drag her back down here, and she can see the shame in him, a living, twisting thing that curls around his heart and gnaws at his spine.

This is not how this moment goes. She must change it. She must recalculate.

Must she? The whiteness is held at bay, steady and distant. Perhaps she has done enough. Perhaps, here, she can fix what comes next, truly fix it. If she lets herself be caught and dragged back down, she will never conjure the stone that will doom Augustine.

But she might die. The light in Augustine's eyes is not sane. The creatures that feed upon his shame have stoked him to a fever pitch, because what would be more shameful than to think he is about to save his new wife, only to be the indisputable cause of her death? In the morning, when the clouding clears, he will hate himself. It is genius. It is horrible. She must stop it, for her own sake, for his.

She shouts his name.

He falters.

Jane reaches the door and slams it shut. Augustine looks back once over his shoulder, searching for the cry that staggered him, but continues his climb. He beats himself against the wood, howling, "Jane! Jane, open this door!" On the other side, Jane is slipping, weakened, whispering.

"Jane, please!" Augustine begs.

I am well. Jane mouths the words in the crypt and says them in the hall. This is when she falls. This is when she is too weak to keep fighting.

The stone wall does not appear.

She does not know enough to will a wall into existing. She can't even draw a circle.

Is that true?

Yes. And no.

She does know enough. She can draw a circle. She knows what will happen if she does not summon the wall, if she does not lock Augustine away.

Jane reaches out and conjures the stone herself. The white expanse of an unknown future begins to crumble.

She condemns Augustine to suffering.

Augustine falls back. He stares at the unyielding stone for one long moment, then turns away. He sees her, standing at the base of the stairs, and his whole face falls. He is confused. He is despairing. He knows something is very wrong.

He comes to her. "Jane? Jane, I saw you, I saw you leave." He collapses at her feet, staring up at her. "I don't understand."

Jane, fading fast toward oblivion, hears him speak to her from upstairs in the hall. His voice is distant. It is close. He is reaching for her. She cannot see him. She watches everything.

She flees, unwilling to see Augustine alone, afraid, because of her.

The maze of the crypt folds around her. She steps past frozen statues, peers at their faces, and tries not to hear Augustine behind her.

He collapses without a sound and curls up, weak and drawn. She does not face him, but still sees his hunger, fierce and gnawing, tangled in his abdomen and pulsing with bright fury in the lines of the world. He has tried to work magic. Tried to feed himself with wishing, tried to conjure water, conjure warmth. He cannot do it, because he does not know the ritual forms, and the forms control him, though they are man-made, and magic, Jane knows, is not.

He is weak, and Jane is, too. She holds him in her arms, and he curls into her, whispering her name. She strokes his hair. She cradles him as he shivers, but she is not alive; she can provide no warmth, no help.

He dies.

He dies afraid. His body grows cold. He did not last long at all. She smells the smoke of blood-soaked sheets burning in the library fireplace.

So soon.

She never had a chance of saving him. He was dead as soon as Jane conjured the stone door, desperate to save her earlier self, heedless of the consequences. Just now? A lifetime ago? She looks at the body in her arms. And yet he comes to her, in the study. She feels him move inside her. His hands are deep within her body. His lips are hot against her cheek. But no; it is not him.

She looks at this form that is shaped from him, shares the lines of him. In some places, like his hands, his face, there is intricate, exacting detail, fine-sketched shapes against a chalkboard. But in his chest, his legs, there are gaps. Great, gaping holes where magic cannot describe him, because Jane does not know him well enough.

She stares. She frowns. She touches the chest of the Augustine who operates on her, and the chest of Augustine, nervous on their wedding night, and feels both, warm and solid beneath her fingertips. And yet they are not the same.

What is her surgeon? What is it that has killed her at her demand? Is he free to leave, or will he, too, evaporate with the dawn?

She does not want him to. She wants him to be real. She wants to have had some chance at success.

Augustine dies. Augustine lives.

Both are true, here in death. She wishes that could be true elsewhere. But in life, time is linear. One thing happens, and then the other. There is no changing that.

And then there is Renton.

He exists two feet off the ground, his limbs knotted back on themselves the way his bowel had twisted and killed him. He stinks of filth, the scent pungent and real in a way the burning sheets are not. His head is bent back, tucked beneath one arm, and he looks at her calmly.

He is not a statue. There is no blankness clinging to him, or the white expanse of Jane's paradox, or shame, or anything she has come to associate with the wreckage of Augustine's working.

Jane frowns.

I KNOW YOU. Her voice is not speech, not sound, but it ripples through the extended, compressed space around them, the space that is and is not Lindridge Hall. They are deep inside unhewn earth. They are inside a brilliantly lit ritual space. They are nowhere at all.

GHOSTS ARE NOT REAL, she says.

He does not disappear, despite her logic. No, he replies. THEY ARE NOT. WHAT ARE YOU?

AN ECHO. SOMEWHERE BETWEEN MY MAGIC AND AUGUSTINE'S AND YOURS, I AM
TRAPPED.

IS IT BAD, TO BE TRAPPED?

NOT WHEN GIVEN FORM.

She takes him at his word. What else is there?

MY MAGIC? she asks.

IT MAKES ME REAL.

AND THE REST?

MY MAGIC MADE ME OTHER THAN HUMAN. AUGUSTINE'S MAGIC DREW THE MEMORY
OF ME TO THIS HOUSE, BETWEEN YOUR GUILT AND HIS. AND YOUR MAGIC MADE ME MORE
THAN HUNGRY, MORE THAN ENDLESS.

YOU MEAN YOU ARE NOT LIKE THE STATUES?

He nods. It is unsettling.

She considers him. Her magic made him real. She looks at Augustine,
half sketched, half real.

Renton sees where she is looking. He shrugs. That is worse than unsettling. WE ARE MORE OR LESS THE SAME. YOU ARE VERY GOOD AT KNOWING THINGS TO BE
AS THEY ARE. I WAS NOT AS GOOD. I KNEW WRONG THINGS.

AND THIS IS NOT WRONG? she asks, and they gaze together at Augustine
cutting out the mass from her belly. It has hair. It has teeth. It has one green
eye.

That is worst of all.

IT IS INTENTIONAL, Renton replies.

Jane frowns and thinks to ask a question, but is interrupted. (Interrupted.
Interrupted how? There is time now, imposed upon no time at all, and
Jane's confusion grows.)

"Elodie, come!"

The voice is her own, but from a different time. Jane lifts her head. A
mirror sits on the far side of the banquet hall that was not there before, and
in it is Jane. Jane, ringed in blood.

Jane knows this moment.

If Elodie does not appear, Jane does not open the crypt. The white expanse of paradoxical future will grow again, will become unbounded. The

nothingness it hides within it, Augustine's working and Elodie's absence, will metastasize. What comes next Jane cannot know, because Jane only exists within a precarious sequence of events, a knot that she cannot untangle. If Elodie does not appear . . .

In the mirror, Jane focuses. She knows that her reflection is Elodie. Jane, dead, looks at the space before the mirror, and hopes. She hopes that this is where Elodie returns, that she conjured Elodie from nothingness, and that, perhaps, Elodie did as Jane did, working backward, filling in where she was needed.

But Elodie does not appear. It is Jane that feels a calling. A pulling.

She looks at Renton, twisted in upon himself, impossible flesh in an impossible space. WHAT DOES THIS MEAN? she asks him.

He does not speak.

She wants to beg him for answers, but he offers none, and so she leaves him. She approaches the mirror. She sits.

She looks at herself.

Jane sags and sways with exhaustion and terror as she focuses. Jane remembers going through her precepts, limiting her knowledge. Did it matter? She still willed Elodie to appear, and Jane is not Elodie.

She searches herself. Is she changing? Will she now become Elodie? Is that how all this falls into place, becomes true, becomes what Jane knew?

Nothing shifts inside of her.

"Is Augustine alive?" Jane whispers to herself.

She fights to control her expression, but she knows she looks pained. She still holds Augustine in her arms.

"Were you with him, when he died?" Yes, a hundred times. He had known her, when he died. She does not like to think of it, or else she will be drawn to that moment, and not here at all.

"Is there something I can do, to fix this? To save him?"

No.

Jane looks at the plinth where the wrong Augustine works upon her. You will think there is, she almost says. You will believe you've saved him. But you have not.

And yet . . .

And yet, who is Jane to make that choice for her living self? This moment was what allowed Jane to continue on. To surmount the challenges before her, to feel as if she had atoned. She brought down the wall. She found Augustine.

That he is dead does not matter, because Jane is dead, too.

Finally, Jane nods.

"Can you tell me?" Jane nods again. "What? What must I do? What must I know to fix everything?"

There is no way to fix everything. There is only the way to this moment, now, but Jane is glad that she has it. She is glad that Elodie is gone; she is glad Elodie has not been here to suffer for so many years, to torment, to wait, to long for. She is glad ghosts are not real.

And that is when she realizes: she has always been Elodie.

No. Not always. She is the woman who married Augustine, who died upon the plinth, but she is not the first woman to do so. There was Elodie, and then Elodie died. Augustine ripped her from her time, fixed her at the moment of her death, at least in echo—but she has not existed since. It was not Elodie who came to Jane. Elodie is gone.

It has always been herself.

She has not been Elodie's replacement. There was a mistake, a rupture, but it was long ago.

Ghosts are not real.

She needs only to write the words. Those four words change everything, and they are easy enough to spell out. They mean that Elodie is not Elodie. They mean that Abigail, with her rotted skull in her belly, did not suffer so. They mean that the Cunninghams have not died, and that the creatures wearing their faces have no power. They mean so much, and they free Jane, free her to triumph, to press onward, to reach this moment of understanding.

And if ghosts are not real, then Augustine is not a ghost. He is something else. Perhaps he is alive. She wants to know he is alive.

She takes up the journal. She writes the words. She sets the journal down, carefully, to mirror where it is in living Jane's reflection. She watches herself grow calm, grow still, then pick up the journal. She watches herself read.

It is almost enough.

Jane leaves the mirror. Renton is gone. She stands among the statues ringing the operating table, and she looks at the redness of her blood, the orderly disorder of her viscera. It does not look as painful as it felt. It looks, in the candlelight, like ink in water. Like a painting. Like something delicate and rageful. It looks like she felt, all those days alone in Lindridge Hall. It looks like the forming of the chick within the egg.

Ghosts are not real. The thing that operates upon her as she dies is not a ghost. The thing that pulls a tangled mass of the impossible from her belly is not a ghost. It is intentional. She first felt the mass quicken inside of her when Elodie grabbed her in the crypt, and that is the only moment she has not visited, has not repaired.

She looks again at the Augustine-who-is and follows back the threads of him. The first shards of bone are laid down while Augustine-who-was still lives, while he wanders, lost, far from Jane's voice. When Jane, alive and beyond the crypt, calls out for him, it is this new creation who responds, because she needs him to. It is this new creation who asks Jane where he is, and quickens when she tells him, "You are in the cellar." Even as the real Augustine fades, unable to move, lying in her arms and waiting to die, another Augustine is built, piece by piece, in answer to queries Jane doesn't realize she is posing, that he is asking, that she is answering. He is kind. He is gentle. He is the greatest surgeon the world has ever seen, and he does not believe in magic, because if only he had not, none of this would ever have happened.

She does not need to build him, because she already has. Her living self knows beneath thought, knows in place of wants, and so this new Augustine comes to her, and crosses her circle, because ghosts are not real, and he is not a ghost, not exactly.

He is something where magic converges.

She can undo him. She does not need him to exist, not if she is dead. But she looks at him, in the fullness that she has sketched him. He draws not only from her, but from the house, from his own memories that fill every crack and crevice of it. His magic still exists, and she can see it working its way into him, making him not just her creature, but his own.

In her longing, she has taken the man she married and rebuilt him the way she dreamed he could have been. Subtle variations on the original pattern; he is himself but better—or not better, but better suited to her tastes. Possibly he would have approved. Possibly he would have rather been made confident and proud and easy, the Augustine who has nothing to hide, who does not stand upon a shifting foundation of shame and obsession. She has not made him flawless—she does not know what he would look like, flawless—but she has made his weakness conquerable.

Or has that been his doing?

Whoever has made him has made something wondrous and terrible, but they have made a man, and to unmake him would be to kill him. He lacks certain finer points of existence, but he is a living thing. To unmake him would be horrible.

No, she cannot unmake him.

But she can finish him. She can kindle in him true life.

She can hope he never learns what she has done.

The day the magicians leave, and Jane goes down to the cellar, she finds herself. She begs Elodie, not knowing, not understanding, to explain it all. And instead, Jane seizes herself. Terrifies herself. Breaks herself down, knowing where it will lead, the pain that will come, the anger, the hatred. But it is necessary.

She plants the seed, a quickening of an egg outside its time, and gives it meaning, a sequential ordering. She takes from the Augustine who lies dead in her arms and gives to the mass the truth of him. It grows his hair, his teeth, his eyes. She watches as it grows with her obsession, with each forward step she takes to knowledge, and as Jane begins to know, the mass begins to know, too. When Augustine at last removes it from her body and burns it in ritual offering, it will banish his ghosts, replace the nothingness he has left in his wake, and complete the absent parts of him. The paradox will be resolved. The white brilliance of a life Jane could not have lived will shrink to a mere point buried in his heart, because, at last, all their actions will lead here.

He is her great working.

And then Jane Shoringfield Lawrence closes her eyes and for the first time in many weeks accepts what life has given her.

She dies.

CHAPTER FORTY-THREE

A GASP.

A name.

"Jane?"

Jane. *Jane.* Jane, with a body, a body that had weight, that felt pain, that breathed, that was no longer bound to cold stone. She gasped, air filling her lungs in a fiery cold rush, and then she was falling, falling, into Augustine's arms. The world was faded around her, blurry, but she saw black statues with crescent heads all dressed in blood-spattered white stepping back, beginning to crumble. She heard rock upon rock, pebbles falling, then greater stones. The statues' crescent heads broke apart, unmade, banished from the world.

Shame followed with them, and then nothing except the roar around her and Augustine's arms beneath her.

"Augustine," she murmured, but was too weak to move.

"Hold tight," he said, and began to run.

Her world expanded. They were in the crypt, and she was very cold. The room smelled of blood and burning hair. She clutched Augustine, craning her head, trying to see behind them, see the table where she had died, see the table where she *hadn't died*. She saw a bowl, and in it a mass with dying flames around it. Her wedding ring was no longer on her finger. It, too, smoldered in the dish, another thing grown out of place sacrificed for their freedom.

Dust rained down from the vaulted ceiling. The house was coming down, as surely as its ghostly inhabitants had fallen to pieces.

Augustine surged up the stairs and down the hallway and Jane held her breath, remembering the great barrier bisecting the foyer, but it was gone. From above them came a great groan of collapsing metal and the shriek of shattering glass as the library fell in upon itself, but ahead of them was the door.

Its frame was already distorting from the great weight upon it, the stone entryway beginning to buckle, but with a great shove Augustine heaved the door open. They spilled down the front steps, onto the mud drive.

Behind them, Lindridge Hall collapsed upon itself.

A huge cloud of dust and force slammed into her, rolling her farther through the muck. Her stitched-up belly burned, but it was outmatched by the cacophony of wreckage falling to the ground. In the distance, she could hear the crackle of flames. She blinked, stunned, trying to see, but found nothing. Then a hand touched hers. She grabbed it with all her fading might.

The noise died to the hiss of fire and the last shifting of metal and stone. The dust settled enough for her to see. Augustine crouched beside her and gathered her up into his arms.

"Is it done?" she asked him. "I saw the statues crumble—I saw something burning on the plinth—"

"It's done," he whispered. "The spell worked. But Jane, you died. I felt you die. I saw it."

I saw you die as well.

She had meant to die. She had accepted death. That she hadn't died meant—what? That Augustine had worked a spell of his own?

"I died," Jane agreed.

He kissed her brow. "We need to get down to the road. A carriage. Some-body will find us, they'll have heard the house collapse."

The house was gone. She wanted to laugh. She wanted to cry. Of course the house would come down, when the spell that had all but consumed it was untangled at last, and when its original master was dead. The house was gone, and with it, every white wall she had conjured, every scrap of magic that she had added to its teetering edifice.

"The magistrate will come," Jane said. "He will have me taken away."

"I will not let him."

"I told the servants I had killed you."

"And yet here I am. Come on, we must go—the gas lines will feed the fire. It's too dangerous to stay." He staggered upright, favoring one leg, and tried to take her with him. She couldn't stand, though, not with the stitches in her gut, and she closed her eyes and wept from pain, and confusion, and relief.

They were alive, in one fashion or another.

Then, voices, rising up through the fine shower of mist chilling them both. The sound of horses. More hands, words exchanged, and Mr. Lowell covering her with his cloak before he and Augustine lifted her into the back of a carriage. She heard them arguing, swearing, begging, and then the carriage was off, and Augustine sat across from her, the same way he had the day they were married, before everything went wrong.

She traced a faint circle on the seat of the carriage, willing the wall to grow.

When it didn't, she smiled and slept.

CHAPTER FORTY-FOUR

S HE SPENT MUCH of the next four days unconscious or barely otherwise, attended to by her husband when she woke. His leg had been
injured in the collapse of Lindridge Hall, but it didn't stop him from
curling up beside her, holding her in his arms. The splint on his leg pressed
awkwardly into hers, but it was bearable, and she found the feeling of his
breathing, *their* breathing, to be almost as much a balm as the laudanum
she took to ease the aching burn of her gut.

The magistrate came, and the servants, and even Abigail Yew, alive and
almost well again, asking what had become of the woman who had stayed
by her side during her early recovery. Jane hid up in her bedroom from all
of them, not ready to sort out her emotions, not ready to perform rational-
ity for an audience. Mr. Lowell, however, was unavoidable, and though all
was restored, he did not trust her. She heard him often in the hall outside
her room, hesitating, wondering. He did not talk to her when he brought
her food. Augustine offered to replace him with somebody less judgmental,
but Jane stilled his hand. She had earned his doubt, after all.

Augustine stayed every night at the surgery, and did not sicken. It was more a relief to her than to him; he barely seemed to remember what had gone before, though he could talk endlessly of his days at university. He skimmed over the memories of his games with Hunt's eating club of magicians, but told her all about Elodie, about his family, about his joys and losses before everything had come undone.

She could only track perhaps half of what he said at first, but with every day, she grew stronger. Her wound did not become infected. In fact, it healed faster than it should have, though it promised to scar in the process.

Nearly a week after she had died, Jane sat propped up in bed, reading a text on pharmaceuticals, their origins and compounding formulae. Below, Augustine met with patients. Outside the sun drew low, though there was still at least an hour left before dark. With each dusk and dawn, the memory of half-formed talons scraping down her throat retreated a little more.

From the road came the sound of carriage wheels, closer than usual. She tensed, reading forgotten, anticipating some disaster, but there was no screaming when the door below opened.

And then Dr. Avdotya Semyonovna Nizamiev appeared in her doorway.

She was much the same as Jane had last seen her: slight, dark-haired, sharp-featured, and entirely focused on Jane. She did not wait to be invited in, but came to Jane's bedside without introduction.

"Where is my husband?" Jane asked. She was not ready for this meeting.

"With a patient, downstairs," Dr. Nizamiev replied, settling into the chair Augustine had placed at her bedside.

"Did he send for you?"

"No. Your housekeeper wrote to me after you threw her out of Lindridge Hall. She said she found you naked, covered in filth, at which point you fired her. And that when she came to fetch you to a doctor, you screamed about having killed your husband."

Jane flinched with embarrassment. She glanced at the doorway, half expecting to see orderlies waiting to swoop down upon her, but to all appearances, Dr. Nizamiev was alone.

"Not exactly," Jane said. "But I understand why she was distressed. It was a trying time."

She expected Dr. Nizamiev to understand, to cite the ritual steps she had sent to Jane, to ask how things had gone.

The woman withdrew a small notebook instead.

"And why was that?" She was the solicitous doctor, searching for symptoms, arranging a diagnosis.

"I was grieving," Jane said, confused. "And ill. Dr. Lawrence has explained that such a growth as I had places an inordinate amount of stress on one's faculties." Along with the lack of sleep, the lack of food, the constant focus required of the working. Surely Dr. Nizamiev understood that.

"Grief can certainly perturb the mind." She scrawled a few lines, and Jane realized, with creeping discomfort, that she spoke in a different tone from the one she had the last time they met. Then, Dr. Nizamiev had been sharp, engaged, didactic.

Now she sounded like she was only humoring Jane. She made no mention of her own contributions, of the excerpt from *The Doctrine of Seven*, of her warnings and guidance.

"That night at Lindridge Hall," Jane ventured warily. "You made me promise to accept everything you told me." And when she had repeated it to her husband, he had remembered to believe in magic. It had unlocked something in him.

It was intentional, echoed Renton's voice.

Dr. Nizamiev gazed back, placid. "Did I?"

Jane's heart gave a sideways lurch. She remembered that conversation with piercing clarity, more than all that came after.

She weighed her words carefully. It would be better not to press, not when everything behind her now felt like shifting sand. But she could not bear not to know, not after everything that had happened.

"You're not just a doctor, are you?" Jane whispered.

"I am many things besides my profession. You will have to be more specific, Mrs. Lawrence."

"You told me you were not a sorceress."

"And I am not."

Her throat was dry. Her belly clenched with frustration and fear.

"Is it a matter of semantics? Do I only have to guess the right word? Are you—" She cut herself off, clutching at the counterpane. She must not show distress or agitation. One deep breath steadied her, and then she asked, "You do not play games with Dr. Hunt and the others, but do you—do you believe that magic is possible?"

"If it were, it would hardly be a matter of belief," Dr. Nizamiev responded.

True, but in what direction?

"Do you claim to be able to do magic, Mrs. Lawrence?"

Nizamiev was a rational doctor. And Jane knew what answer to give her, the answer that was simplest. The answer of a rational woman.

"No," Jane said. "Of course not. Magic is impossible." She met Dr. Nizamiev's gaze and refused to flinch, refused to back down.

Magic was real, but they were not magicians. Of course they were not. If Jane began to believe otherwise, she might be lost again. But if Jane could know there had been no magic at Lindridge Hall, it could all be over. She could no longer raise a circle, there were no spirits, and her husband was as whole as any man—so what was there tying her to that fiction?

A useful fiction, yes. A fiction wherein a sort of *truth* lay. But there were other truths.

"And your husband?"

"He no longer plays such games."

"I'm sorry, I will clarify—your husband, does he know what happened to him?"

Jane's breath caught.

In the long, blurred days of her recovery, it had been easy enough to forget what she had seen in that indistinct, unreal place at the edge of death. The holes in Augustine, the yawning gaps that proved he was not the same man who had married her. When those memories came, as if from dreams, they came, too, with a vision of the final piece of the working, the mass of hair and eye and flesh, grown from the both of them and destroyed to set them free. It was easy to believe she had succeeded, or that there had been no trial to best at all. Because to bring a man back from the dead was impossible, and he was there, and present, and warm, and did that not mean that he was as he seemed?

But there had been moments. Glimpses in the mirror. Gaps in his memory. Inescapable evidence that he was not a man at all, but something else.

Had Dr. Nizamiev seen it, too, in what could only have been a glance in the hallway?

"I don't know what you're talking about," Jane said at last, though her voice trembled.

"His long absence. Where was he?"

Another leading question, another balancing upon the precipice. Jane wanted to scream, hurl insults, drive Dr. Nizamiev away. But it was only for an instant; she and Augustine had already rehearsed this answer.

"The cellar," she said. "The tunnels are unstable. He was trapped for a time. Their total collapse after he escaped is what destroyed the house. Or hadn't you heard?"

"He went down below instead of attending a patient? My understanding," Dr. Nizamiev said, making another note, "was that you saw him go out. Mr. Lowell mentioned searching the hills with the magistrate's men."

"I was wrong," she said. "Overwrought. Exhausted. He left me to sleep, and I assumed he'd gone, but apparently he had stored books down there. Medical texts. It was dangerous, but less damp than the house proper."

Dr. Nizamiev had not seen Augustine's study in the house. The lie came easily, and Jane saw no flicker of distrust in her.

Or of faith.

"I'm sorry," Jane added, before Dr. Nizamiev had a chance to probe further, "but I fear I must ask that you leave me to rest. You understand, the surgical intervention I required, it has left me quite worn down."

"Of course," Dr. Nizamiev said, rising from her seat, her dark skirts undulating. She closed her notebook, tucked it away in a pocket. "You have gone through a harrowing trial, and I am glad you have made it out the other side."

"Thank you. I'm glad, as well; more glad that Augustine has come with me."

Dr. Nizamiev inclined her head, bid Jane farewell, moved toward the door. But she hesitated at the frame, turned back to Jane. "Do not be a stranger, Mrs. Lawrence. It may be that in the weeks and months to come, you find you are not as much yourself as you would hope; please do not hesitate to call on me, should you need my services."

And then she was gone in truth, her boots light on the stairs. Jane listened until the front door opened and closed, and only then began to sob.

Relief. It was relief only, that Dr. Nizamiev had not lingered to see Augustine, though it was the final confirmation that Dr. Nizamiev had been here to evaluate *her*.

"Jane."

She lifted her head to see her husband waiting just outside the room, his brow furrowed in worry.

"Are you well?"

The question stilled her tears. It brought with it a moment of panic, but it passed off quick enough. Her nightmares would not fade for some time, but this man who came to her, sat on her bedside, stroked her hair—she trusted him. She trusted him in a way she couldn't have two weeks ago.

She no longer needed the impossible. It was time to put away the reaching, grasping, arrogant part of herself, the part that had hungered for *more* than her husband's salvation. She knew where that led. Dr. Nizamiev had done her a favor.

Whether it was *intentional* or not.

"I am well," she said. She turned her head, kissed his palm.

He smiled, and did not mention their visitor. He might not even have seen her pass. Jane did not bother to ask as he toed off his shoes.

"Don't you have patients?"

"I've asked Mr. Lowell to close up the surgery for a few hours," he said. "I need rest." He levered himself into bed next to her. "I've been doing far too much thinking today."

"Thinking? About what?"

"What do you think of moving to Camhurst?" he asked.

"Camhurst? Why?"

"You could attend university, study mathematics. And Vingh has sent me word of a surgical posting. We could leave Larrenton, Lindridge Hall, all of it behind. Start over."

Jane hesitated, thinking of bombs and basements, but her old fears felt smaller now, a marble bumping across the floorboards until stopping, silent, in a dark corner. She thought, too, of cells and floating magicians. Of being so close to Dr. Nizamiev. But she was not a magician anymore. She would keep her silence. There was no danger.

"That sounds wonderful," she said.

Augustine kissed her forehead and drew her closer, mindful of her injury. She nestled in against him and closed her eyes, and knew that she was happy.

The lights guttered out.

ACKNOWLEDGMENTS

I STARTED WRITING *The Death of Jane Lawrence* almost five years ago, and it has gone through several iterations, getting weirder, bloodier, and more personal each time. While some parts remain recognizable, others have changed astronomically between then and now. Five years is a long time to work on a single book (at least for me), and while I never gave up, I also know I likely wouldn't have gotten this book into your hands without a lot of help over that time.

So first, I need to thank my early readers. Ellis Bray and Kiki Nguyen, you were both invaluable for helping me diagnose the major fault in the first version of this project. Augustine will never be the same, thanks to you two. Emma Mieko "Screaming T-Pose Renton" Candon and Shyela Sanders, you both have read through multiple iterations and sat up late with me while I ranted and theorized and finally made my way to this final result. Thank you for being my rubber ducks and therapists.

To everybody who has cheered me on from the sidelines, I needed that ongoing support more than you can know. Neme, Thea, El, Casey, Val, Seth, and Caitlin—without you being absolutely feral in your support, this would have been a much harder and lonelier road.

I learned to write largely through text-based role-playing, so I owe a huge thank-you to all of my role-play partners over the years. In particular, I want to thank Krystal Loh and Dan Rodgers: through our games, I created and refined the character who would become Dr. Avdotya Semyonovna Nizamiev. She's very grateful to you for her existence.

To my agent, Caitlin McDonald: you pushed and pushed at me to make this book as good as I could make it, and then found it the best home it could have had. Thank you for listening to me cry and rip my hair out every time I hit a wall, and for the blood, sweat, and tears you poured into helping me bring it these last few miles to the finish line.

Thank you to my editor, Sylvan Creekmore, for seeing exactly what I loved so much about this book and loving it, too. You've made this book the most true and thorough version of itself. Thank you, also, to the art and production team for supporting the text with absolutely gorgeous design and art, and to the rest of the SMP team for bringing the book out into the world.

Thank you also to my aunt, Dr. Kristin Cowperthwaite—you took my out-of-the-blue question about how a Victorian-era abdominal surgery would go, and my vague ideas of just what might have gone wrong with the patient to begin with, and not only sent back a thorough answer regarding techniques and risks but also coined the phrase "the location of the magical insult," which I have delighted in and cherished ever since. You rock, thank you so much. I hope I didn't get too many things wrong in surgeries I didn't have you consult on!

Elsa Sjunneson, you are both an incredibly skilled sensitivity editor and a fantastic friend. I'm so glad we got to work together on this project.

I owe much of my understanding of *why* gothic horror is so effective and enticing to Jeanette Ng, who reminded me that the power is in letting the protagonist desire, in every sense of the word.

(Thank you, too, to Donald Maass, who, over the course of one coffee and without having read a single page of the book, cracked open the entire problem with my original third act.)

To my husband, David Hohl—thank you for not only supporting me through this book and the whole whirlwind that has been publishing but also not running away screaming after what I did to Jane's husband in this book. Jane and I share a lot in common, but I promise you, I have no intention of making a "better" magical copy of you. Maybe let's avoid houses with basements, though. Just in case.

Thanks also to my parents, David and Stacey Starling, for bragging about me to everybody you know and always being ready to cheer on each new milestone of mine. To my great-aunt Lynn Narasimhan, who is always ready with a willing ear and a glass of celebratory scotch, and who also has housed us during the upheaval of both graduate studies *and* a pandemic, I owe undying gratitude. Thank you, too, to my in-laws, Dave and Sukey Hohl, and the rest of my family, on all sides, for your constant support of and delight in what I do next. I hope this book hasn't been too traumatizing to read.

And to all my readers who have trusted me enough to follow me from high-tech suits in far-off caves to a haunted house in faux-English hills—I hope you've enjoyed and that you're just as excited to see where we go together next.

Beth Olson Creative

CAITLIN STARLING writes horror-tinged speculative fiction of all flavors. Her first novel, *The Luminous Dead*, was nominated for both the Bram Stoker and Locus Awards. She is also the author of the gothic horror tales *Yellow Jessamine* and *The Death of Jane Lawrence*, and her nonfiction has appeared in *Nightmare* and *Uncanny*. Starling has been paid to invent body parts and is always on the lookout for new ways to inflict insomnia.